DEAD IN THE SHADOW OF DOUBT

To Barbara,

With love, good memories and thanks for your friendship!

Sandy Barnett

Sandy Slaughter

ISBN: 1984033395
ISBN 13: 9781984033390
Library of Congress Control Number: 2018901712
CreateSpace Independent Publishing Platform
North Charleston, South Carolina

The law, in its majestic equality, forbids the rich as well as the poor to sleep under bridges, to beg in the streets, and to steal bread.

—Anatole France

SATURDAY
DECEMBER 14

She was bent from the waist in an awkward angle, but the body was recognizable even though the men approaching the Dumpster could only see layers of skirts covering a wide rump. She was a familiar figure to the people of Riversbend. The old woman had walked the town's alleys, streets, and train tracks for years, pushing a grocery cart, scavenging their trash bins, selectively collecting bits of their lives. The town called her Raggedy Ann.

Always queasy in the presence of death, Detective Lieutenant Tilman O'Connor Quinn knew the woman couldn't hear him, yet he whispered to her as though he wished otherwise.

"Raggedy?" Skirts hiked up, bare legs—except for a pair of mismatched socks—dropped from her haunches like hindquarters in a slaughterhouse.

"Hang on, Pauley; don't touch her. We're waiting for the coroner and the crime-scene guys to get here before she can be moved. We need pictures."

A shorted street lamp flickering at the edge of the parking lot gave Tick light enough to see that the woman's legs were pooling. Not wanting to draw attention to his and Pauley's activity from the occasional passing car, he used his flashlight discretely. He imagined her face had pooled too, head down as it was. His stomach churned.

"Heart, you think?" Pauley McCrary, the newest recruit slipped a handkerchief out of his hip pocket to mop his face, even though it was the middle of December and the temperature only a few degrees above freezing.

"Prob'ly. Get some air, pal. And just so you know, it won't be any easier next time." With that avuncular advice, Tick walked under the street lamp and pulled a small notebook from his inside pocket.

"What're you writing?" Pauley stepped up behind the lieutenant.

"Move it, son. You're in my light." Tick rolled his shoulders as if shrugging off a burden. "You scared of the dark? Go see if there're any killers 'round here, and quit crowding me." He moistened the end of his pencil. "I can hardly think with you hovering over my shoulder like a damn moth. Go look around."

"Right—what am I looking for?"

"Answers."

"What's the question?"

"You don't get questions first."

"That's not right."

"It is right. It's like one of our answers is we found her in the Dumpster. The question then that follows is, who put her there, or how'd she get in there? Get it?"

"Gotcha." Throwing the beam of his flashlight in broad sweeps around the service area of the store, Pauley peered into matted leaves bunched in wet clumps on the asphalt. With the toe of his boot, he pushed at bits of winter debris: brush, twigs, and a scrap of wet cellophane that held evidence of the evening's rain. He examined the cellophane wrapper with the concentration one might give to a cipher; he made a note to tell Tick he thought the answer for *"What is it off of?"* would be *"It's off a cigarette package."* So the next question logically would be, *"What brand?"* He didn't know the answer to this yet. Remembering not to move anything, he carefully returned the wrapper to the ground where he'd found it.

"She's got nice shoes," Pauley said more to himself than to Tick as he approached the Dumpster. He spoke to dispel his nervousness, his discomfort at seeing the disarray of clothing and exposed body parts before him. He could see the back of her knees, vulnerable and streaked. "They're fairly new. A little worn, maybe. Scuffed heel. The label is barely hanging on."

"Who sells 'em? Write it down."

"How would I know who sells it?"

"The torn label. Who sells this brand? Then maybe we can find out who they belonged to before they belonged to Raggedy.

"It's a popular brand."

"Write it down."

The clean, silvery mesh of athletic shoe was incongruous with the ragged layers of the dead woman's clothing. "They're untied. Should I write that down?"

"You think her untied laces are important? Write it down." Tick's tone was edgy.

"That's how kids wear 'em nowadays is all I'm saying. Maybe she took them off some kid." Pauley shrugged. "That's what I'm saying. She could've."

"She could've. So go find us a barefoot boy."

Pauley groaned, moving away from Tick, who was always snarky but tonight seemed snarkier than usual. *Lord, don't let this lady be dead from natural causes.* The odd prayer swept through Pauley's mind as he jotted down his notes. But he was sure natural causes would be the coroner's ruling. He wasn't lucky enough to be investigating a murder this early in his career. He glanced at the landing. She could have jumped, he guessed. Who could say what some crazy old bag lady might decide to do?

Eyeing the Dumpster Pauley paced backward to the far edge of the parking lot for a different perspective, for the big picture, as Tick was fond of saying. Seeing nothing that struck him as different, after a few minutes, he circled back toward the lieutenant. He moved slowly, noting what lay about: the minutiae, the out of place, the overlooked. He wished he could find a crumpled cigarette butt to go with the cellophane. Back at the Dumpster, he dropped to his knees to peer under it. There was something midway under, something looped, ropy, hard to exactly identify in the dark. He flopped down on his belly. The beam from his flashlight identified the curled strip to be plastic packing tape. The evidence kit was in the patrol car.

"How'd she get herself up there, you think?" Pauley hopped to his feet.

"Must've stood on something?" Tick Quinn glanced around the base of the Dumpster, hoping for the something to suggest itself.

"You see anything? I don't see anything," Pauley said. "That Dumpster's what, six or seven feet from ground to rim. Over my head." Pauley stuck his hand above his head in a gesture of measurement. "It'd take a gorilla to toss her in."

"A g'rilla, huh."

"I don't see how she got up there by herself, that's all. Someone had to have helped her. Killed her; dumped her."

Tick cocked his head. "You're speculatin'. Go look for some evidence. Where's her stuff?"

"Someone could have killed her and dumped her. What stuff?"

"Pauley, if we knew that, I wouldn't be out here in the cold yakety-yakking with some boy who don't know his ass from straight up," Tick harrumphed. "If I knew, I'd be head of the FBI and I'd be sitting home in my easy chair, watching *Frosty the Snowman.* But I *don't* know anything at this point except that Raggedy Ann is dead in that Dumpster. All I know is dead weight's heavier than live weight, and I doubt even a g'rilla could've throwed her in there."

"Do we even know she's dead? We haven't touched her—haven't really looked at her. We don't even know for sure it is her."

"It's her," Tick snapped. "Maybe she fell off that landing up there." Tick pointed to an upstairs walkway.

The platform a few feet above them, running parallel to the Dumpster, was almost invisible. Pauley squinted into the darkness, willing, if he must, to agree with the possibility.

"Naw, the angle don't seem right."

The landing was a good five feet above and five or six back from the gaping mouth of the Dumpster. Raggedy Ann's body was caught on the corner opposite. "She could have been thrown off, I guess," Pauley conceded, "but she didn't jump."

"Pauley, you see anything that would make you suspect a second party is involved here? 'Cause until you do, drop it with the idea that this is a murder investigation. She's a Dumpster queen, a bag lady. Maybe she had a friend, a helper, and he helped her up and then left, and she had a stroke, hanging over the edge like that."

"Yessir," Pauley said brightly enough. "You just told me a few minutes ago to go look for killers. And you're always sayin' we have to consider everything."

"Well, we ain't there yet."

"A helper would be a second party, wouldn't he?" Pauley shrugged.

"Dammit, Pauley!"

"Well, if you can introduce a helper, why can't I introduce a murderer?"

"Because jumping to conclusions is a bad habit for a cop. If there's any jumping, she's the one who did it, off the landing there."

"Why would she do that?"

"To get inside it. Hell, Pauley, this thang's bound to be full of stuff the old woman would have give her eyeteeth for."

"May be. But you come stand d'rectly under the landing with me. It's too far back, and the angle's skewed." Pauley was emphatic. "And she's fat, and she's old."

"Skewed is it. Well, what if she thought she could, but she miscalculated?"

"Lieutenant, her body is on the wrong side of the Dumpster. Besides, old people don't gener'ly go leaping off landings. My grandmother wouldn't have jumped no matter how much she might want whatever was in that trash thing."

"Just how old you think Raggedy Ann is?"

"I don't know. It's hard to tell how old you white people are. You all look old to me." Pauley twirled around to hide his grin. "Not enough lanolin's the problem. Makes you wrinkle up."

"What you talkin' about? Sheep? What you talkin' about sheep for?"

"Uh-huh. That's what I'm sayin'." When Pauley turned back, his face was straight. "She could have come off those steps there, though. Not the landing, but the steps going up to it." He nodded toward a steep of wooden steps that approached the Dumpster on the far side before they bent away in the opposite direction.

"Maybe she could have if the steps weren't running the wrong way. As is, she would've had to climb over the rail and try to balance herself on an edge too narrow for anybody's feet and then jump."

The stairway in question led to the second level, which accommodated an entrance to what at one time had been an apartment but now served as extra storage for Adler's antique business. It was a peculiar design. Tick wondered why anyone would build a set of steps that appeared to wing up off the loading dock and then lose its direction. The Adler family always had been a strange lot, he concluded. More money than sense, he remembered people saying.

Tick pocketed his notebook and joined Pauley, who was staring at the body. "She could have hoisted herself. Look at those calves," he said.

"She would have had to chin herself first. Like I say, she's no spring chicken, man."

"First, it's sheep; now it's chickens." Tick snorted, looking down at Pauley's shiny boots. "I bet you've never even been on a real farm. You wouldn't know a Leghorn from a guinea hen. You better stick to shoes, city boy."

"What you talking about? My grandmother's got chickens in her backyard, right now. I just mentioned those shoe laces being untied 'cause what I was tryin' to tell you about teenagers. My cousin's boy—"

"All you blacks are cousins, ain't you?"

"Ah, no, sir—not us. It's you people who go knocking up your cousins. We generally don't mess with 'em if they're kin to us." Pauley stuck his thumb in the air for trumping his superior officer twice in one day.

Tick chuckled lightly. "You better quit smarting off, and see if you can get yourself more than three feet from my warm side. I'm going up on the loading dock and take a look around. When you finish looking where you're at, go clear on up to the second story, and see if your angle problem gets itself straightened out."

Pauley, taking the steps to the landing two at a time, disappeared. Tick could hear boards creaking above his head as his young partner walked around.

Below, the loading dock was a play of shadow and light. A chiaroscuro made even more surreal by the Escher-like patterns thrown against the sandstone from the stairs. A light wind suddenly swept up off the bayou. Tick tugged at the collar of his jacket. He could smell more rain in the air. Not good, not what a thorough investigation needed. Not what he needed; he wanted to go home. After a couple of hikes up and down the dock, he retreated to the partial cover of Adler's back entrance. Hunkering down, he protected the timid flame of a match with his palm until the glowing tip of his cigarette had become a dot in the darkness.

As he smoked, he listened to Pauley work. Tick liked him. He wished he could work with him longer; he wished he could know how things would play out for him. In three short weeks, Tick would be officially retired. If the investigation ran smoothly, Pauley could have a nice boot-up in his career if Price Latimer, their new sheriff, played fair and square. If the investigation didn't go well, it would be a helluva three weeks for all of them.

Ordinarily with an unexplained death of a vagrant, like Raggedy, with no family, the coroner would rule death from natural causes. On the other hand, should anyone bother to question how she got herself in the Dumpster, well, that could produce another kettle of fish.

Tick inhaled deeply and blew the smoke out of his lungs in an explosion of air. He stood up, dropped the butt, and tapped out the fire with the toe of his shoe. Habit taking over, he picked up the stub and stuck it in his jacket pocket.

"Find anything good?" he asked, hearing Pauley come down from the upper levels.

"Don't think so. There's a piece of strapping tape under the Dumpster and, up against the building, some cellophane probably from a new pack of smokes. Should we bag them?"

"We'll wait for the photographer. I guess we'd better quit mucking around and report this. I'll go radio the station."

"Want me to do it?" Pauley asked eagerly.

"Why not? It's Christmas."

Pauley smiled.

"Don't make it bigger than it is, Pauley."

Pauley started for the patrol car.

"Call Latimer before you call headquarters," Tick hollered after him.

"Shouldn't we call the first-on-sight people first?"

"We should, but this way it'll give our sheriff time to come down and strut around like Kojak."

"What's a Kojak?"

Tick groaned.

"You think this is big then?"

"I think I can't answer right off how she got herself in the Dumpster without her having anything to stand on. Like I said, just don't go making this death bigger than it is."

"Gotcha." Pauley trotted toward the patrol car. He glanced at his watch. It was a few minutes after midnight. They'd been at the scene less than half an hour.

"Sheriff? Detective McCrary, sir. I'm calling to—yes sir, I know it's going on one o'clock, but—Pauley McCrary, sir. You know me—sort of new, I guess—I've been with the metro division for several months. Been training with Detective Lieutenant Quinn for several weeks now." There was a pause. "Yes, sir, black."

SUNDAY MORNING DECEMBER 15

The telephone rang. Rhys Adler, slender arm snaking out from under the eiderdown, assumed it was her first cousin, nothing removed, Richard Fordyce. Richard had appointed himself alarm clock to his younger cousin in 1982, the year she graduated from the university and returned home. Daily he awakens her to action, to aggravation, or to gossip.

"Morning, Dickey." Rhys yawned into the receiver.

"Iz diz Rise Adder?"

"Pardon me?" She opened her eyes.

"Iz pronounce Rise? How you say? Rise like de sun? Adder like de snake dat puffs up?" a female voice in a fake foreign accent asked.

"Rhys, as in Peanut Butter Cup. And it's A*d-ler* with an *L*. Are you conversant in English?"

Rhys pushed herself further up in bed, reaching for her new bifocals before glancing at the dainty cloisonné clock on her bedside table. It was five o'clock, early by an hour for Richard's ring. The voice was vaguely familiar.

"Is this a joke?" she asked sharply. "Because if so, I'm not laughing."

The voice giggled. "I think you have not a *bery* good sense of humor, no?" The accent was wasting away rapidly.

"I have an excellent sense of humor. I just don't like being teased when I'm still in my nightgown."

"Oh, dat's not what I hear."

Fortunately, the caller couldn't see that the tips of Rhys's ears reddened.

Rhys Adler didn't have an excellent sense of humor, especially when it was still dark outside. Moreover, this particular morning she had no patience for silly people. To be profoundly truthful, some days she didn't care for people at all, silly or otherwise. On those days, and this was starting off to be one of them, she preferred dogs. Darlings like her two long-haired dachshunds, Jolly and Old Bay. Dogs—though they might pee occasionally on one's Tabriz, they never annoyed one with prank calls before daybreak.

On the heels of fifty and sure she was thoroughly acquainted with the foibles of human nature, of late Rhys was finding most people too diluted for her interests. Their lives dulled to gray by a steady wash of trifling matters, hers included, but how to alleviate these little droughts and locusts, Rhys hadn't a clue.

As Riversbend expanded, Rhys's world shrank. Once she knew most people in town, by name and where they lived, but now, there were days she rarely ran into anyone she knew.

People might move from one house to another, but Rhys always envisioned them as living where she first knew them. Consequently, she sometimes turned up at the wrong house for a party, sometimes no one would be there, or sometimes the guests would be people she didn't know well or run with, leaving her to wonder why she'd been invited, or if she'd been invited only because she was an Adler. People ought to stay put, she thought. And as for new people, she didn't know why anyone would move to Riversbend in the first place, and she didn't see much point in having them come. They added little and threatened a lot, to her way of thinking.

She usually did have an uncanny ear for voices. "Look, whoever you are, tell me what you want, or I shall hang up."

"I'll give you a clue. I'm—"

Rhys recradled the receiver, daring it to ring again. It did.

"Rhys." It was Richard.

"Why are you whispering, Richard?"

"The police are here. Can you come over?"

"What have you done?"

"There's been an accident, I—"

"Are you hurt?"

"Quit talking and listen. Francie Butter is dead."

"Do I know her?"

"Raggedy Ann. Of course, you know her. The bag lady, the Dumpster queen." Richard cleared his throat much like his father used to do before delivering an ultimatum. "Francie Butter is her real name."

"Did you kill her?"

"Dear God in heaven, Rhys, someone might think you're serious. They found her in our Dumpster. I'm very upset, and you need to get your tiny ass over here."

"I'm not dressed."

Richard's clamp-jawed silence, initially stony, turned staticky. She took the receiver from her ear and peered at it. She knew what he was doing. His eyes would be closed, and he would be holding his breath in concentration. She had seen him try to mastermind people over the telephone before.

"Okay," she said. "Here's what you do. Tell Beau to brew a giant pot of coffee. Then, if you still have some of those good English muffins, ask him to toast them up." Rhys paused. "Lots of butter. I'll be there in half an hour to eat breakfast with all of you. Don't forget the guava jelly. Who's there? Is Mr. Tick there?"

"Rhys, they're not here for breakfast. I hope by the time you get here, they'll be gone."

"I know, darling. But if you're guilty, it won't hurt you to be nice. You'll have to learn to make concessions."

"Guilty!"

"Shh. They might hear you. Do we need an attorney, Richard, since they found her in your Dumpster?"

"My Dumpster! *My* Dumpster!"

It was moving on toward nine o'clock when Kate Wesley of the earlier foreign accent called back. "Are you still angry with me?"

"I was never angry with you. I knew it was you," Rhys said.

"Of course, you didn't."

"I wasn't very polite, was I?"

Kate grunted. "Downright hateful is more like it."

"I agree. I was. But don't expect an apology," Rhys said.

There was a slight pause. "I'll accept your apology, but not until you admit you didn't know it was me. Admit it."

"I recognized your fake, whatever it was, accent," Rhys said.

"Liar, liar, pants on fire."

"Okay, I admit it."

"My God, that's amazing! I've never heard you admit to anything."

"And you may never again."

"I have a surprise for you."

"I don't like surprises."

"I'm coming to see you. That's why I called, to ask if you are going to be in town for a couple of days?"

"I just saw you. Ten days ago. At the Brindlewick Museum—remember? We had a delicious salad plate in that tiny bistro off Market Street, and you got deaf on one glass of sherry? Why don't you come after Christmas, when we haven't seen one another for a while, and you have some expensive little antique to palm off on Adler's Antiques?"

"You're about to get rude again. Anyway, I can't wait. I'm coming on family business. Mother had a piece of property I need to either sell or pay back-taxes on before they put it on the block. If they haven't shipped your boxes from the estate sale, I'll stick them in my trunk. Save you shipping."

"Are you driving a grown-up vehicle? I doubt you could get half my crates in your fancy-schmancy Cooper Mini."

"Mini Cooper."

"Mini Cooper, Minnie Pearl, whatever. Anyway, this conversation is ludicrous. The crates were trucked days ago, Kate. You know that. You called to tell me there would be crates and some smaller boxes."

"I forgot. So, did everything arrive safely? Nothing broken, no surprises?"

"Richard hasn't called in with that particular alarm, although he is rather panicked about the police finding a woman in our trash."

"Richard? No kiddin'? Nude?"

"Better than that! Dead!"

"Wow, given a choice. But dead doesn't preclude nude, does it? Did Richard know her?"

"Everyone knew her. She was our resident bag lady, and despite what you might think, Richard and I are a little upset over this. For one thing, she was in *our* Dumpster, and for another, this is Riversbend we're talking about, not some huge, heartless city. We take our derelicts and disadvantaged seriously."

"So, what was she doing in your Dumpster?"

"Going through our trash would be my guess."

"What a gold mine. Imagine what you could find in Adler's trash. Wonderful old things, barely chipped treasures that a dab of glue or bits of fringe could mend." Kate hesitated. "Does Richard know antiques, Rhys? When he sees a piece, does he know if it's valuable or not?"

"Not really. Not Always. What about it?"

"Just wondering if he could have thrown away something valuable, and the bag woman found it and got herself killed for it."

"Your imagination seems to be in free fall this morning. The old lady probably had a heart attack. I can tell you more when you get here. When are you getting here? I'll ask Matte to bake you a pie."

"Oh, please, rhubarb. And Rhys, tell Richard if he hasn't finished unpacking the boxes, I'd love to help him."

"Kate"—Rhys paused—"nothing has changed. Richard may not want to see you. Hearts, unlike chipped plates, can't be mended with a dab of glue and a bit of fringe."

"Well, you tell him, anyway."

In memory's imperfect eye, Rhys held a vivid picture of Kate as she first knew her, skipping up the driveway toward the farmhouse, waiting at the breakfast table for Dora Adler, Rhys's mother, to exit the kitchen so Katy could finish Rhys's egg, runny yellow and all. Great conspiracies had always been Rhys's and Kate's MO. Rhys sighed—Kate inspired memories of Dora that no one else on earth could. And when Kate and Richard had become friends, then sweethearts, she had to admit to being a bit jealous, two of her favorite people leaving her standing to the side.

"Are you still there?"

"You still haven't told me when you're arriving."

"Tonight."

"Holy mackerel, Kate, where are you? You may have to wait for the rhubarb pie. Matte's a dust-mite maniac. She won't even think pie until she has changed the sheets and beaten the curtains in the guest room."

"Be calm. I'll see you tonight."

"I am calm." Rhys was not calm. As they disconnected, half-formed thoughts floated through her mind like dust particles in a sunbeam. If Kate was arriving tonight, she would have had to have been at least part way to Riversbend when she called. So, what was all the bull about bringing Adler's boxes in the back of her car? She had left Delaware hours ago. Kate was up to something.

"Hey! You! McCarthy!"

Pauley McCrary cringed. He was the only man scrambling to prove himself as a homicide detective in the metro division of the Quick County Sheriff's Department, but his name was the only one in the entire division who the sheriff could never remember. When Pauley had been assigned his recent duty with Tick Quinn, the department's best detective and old war-horse, Pauley thought he'd found the golden egg. But the way Sheriff Latimer had been stomping all over Tick this morning made Pauley wonder if his golden egg was about to be scrambled.

"I've got a question for you, McCracken. I want to know how, when you couldn't see her face at all, you still knew who she was?"

Still in his office, Latimer's question came rolling like thunder into the hall as Pauley tried to sneak past the door, but then he heard Latimer's chair scraped back from his desk. "Hey boy! Are you deaf? Get in here."

"You talking to me?" Pauley jabbed a thumb at his chest. "It's hard to tell. McCrary's my name, sir. Not McCarthy or McCracken. I was heading over to Pat's for a cup of coffee. Want a cup?"

"No. What I want is for you to answer me. How did you know the woman in the Dumpster was that Raggedy woman?"

"Funny you should ask that, boss. I wondered the same thing. But it was her, all right. Anybody who knew Raggedy would have known."

"Y'all never saw her face until the coroner pulled her out of the trash? How'd you even know she was dead?"

"Yessir, but Tick said—"

"Si' down." The sheriff nodded at a chair in front of his desk. "Procedure. Dat's what we follow round here!" Latimer often slipped into his Cajun mother tongue when he was emotional.

"Tick told me not to disturb the body until the coroner and the—"

"Quit wiggling. You're making me nervous." Pauley put his hands on his bobbing knees. "I wanna get your side of dis fairy tale from the time you found the woman until I was called to the crime scene. First off, s'plain to me why y'all were down on Bayou Street?"

"We were coming back from the college. There's been a flurry of off-campus kids breaking into cars. But last night seemed quiet, so we were headed out to the Morrissey place to check on an old boy out there who's pretty bad to get drunk and start shooting phantom squirrels. You know what I mean?" Pauley raised a knowing eyebrow. "Hallucinations, his wife says. Tick said she calls us about every other weekend. The wife does."

"Why would you go to the Morrissey place by way of Bayou Street? Dat isn't the regular route. Who saw her first?"

Every action, every detail of Saturday night, was burned into Pauley's brain. "Raggedy? Tick saw her first. I was driving."

He told Latimer that after discovering the body, the lieutenant had warned him not to touch or move anything but to start looking around and take notes.

"Which I did do. I made a mental grid of the crime scene and paced around in circles like Tick taught me." Pauley wondered briefly if he'd remembered to tell Tick about the wet cellophane or the yellow packing tape. He remembered them talking about her shoe laces being untied and about sheep and chickens. Pauley smiled. He remembered telling Tick that white people didn't have enough lanolin and that was why they looked so wrinkled.

"What you smilin' at?"

"Sorry, sir. I'm just a natural smiler, I guess."

Pauley tipped back in his chair. Latimer did the same. Pauley wasn't about to tell the sheriff everything. He wasn't going to tell him how he hoped the death would be a homicide. He hadn't told him how Tick thought Latimer was a little too much of a hot-dog to be a good sheriff, but aside from needed to show off, he wasn't a bad law man. To hide another grin creeping up, Pauley turned to look out the window. He watched a couple of attorneys heading toward Coffee Cupp.

Latimer drummed his thumbs on his desk and stared at Pauley. When it was clear Pauley wasn't going to say anything, Latimer said, "Who did you contact first?"

"You. Why isn't Tick here?"

"Because I don't want him here. I'm askin' you."

"Tick asked me to contact you first."

"Why? Why me before the dispatcher, the on-site people, or the coroner?" Latimer leaned toward Pauley, his palms flat on the desk and his elbows at right angles to it. "That's out of order. Why did he want you to notify me at one o'clock in the morning before notifying the on-site people? That is not how it's written in the book."

Pauley looked perplexed. "You're the sheriff. Tick felt you'd want to be there. It didn't seem wrong to me." Of course, it had. He'd even asked Tick if they should contact the team first. Seeing Latimer was making an allowance for the rightness of Tick's wrong action, Pauley added, "After radioing you, we contacted the on-site people and old Castro."

"Who?"

"The coroner. The one they call Castro. He smokes a cigar when he's examining a body, and the guys nicknamed him Castro. May not be a Cuban cigar. All I know is the body gets a pretty good dustin' of ash." Pauley wrinkled his nose. "It's a kind of smoke screen, don't you see. Warm blood and all."

"And Quinn does nothing to stop him contaminating the scene?"

"Nobody wants to stop him. We hope he will smoke. I guess it's been a while since you been close to a fresh dead body. Death stinks, sir."

Price Latimer stood up. "Don't you tell me about death. I've been in law enforcement for more years than you are old, McCloud. I've seen plenty of dead bodies, and I don't need a lecture from you about the nature of it either."

"No, sir." Pauley was on his feet. "Want that coffee now?" He was backing toward the door.

"I want you and Quinn to get this case off the books by noon."

"But..." Pauley was speechless. "But..."

"Cream, no sugar, and quit buttin'. Go on; get outta my office before I throw you out."

In all fairness, the initial investigation had not been a textbook example of sound police procedure. On the night of Raggedy's death, neither Tick nor Pauley had found her grocery cart, nor the diary that would take on significance in the case. Just as later, Castro, assuming too much too quickly, dislodged his stethoscope from the chaos of his medical bag and, pressing it to the woman's chest, pronounced her dead. The coroner, finding insignificant soft-tissue damage around her head and face and no ligature marks around her neck, checked to see if the hyoid bone in the neck was broken, which it was not. Believing this confirmed his pre-autopsy conclusion that this was a heart-attack victim, still he checked the dead woman's eyes for petechial hemorrhage, and finding some, it was easy to affirm his erroneous conclusion that the woman in the Dumpster had died of natural causes.

"Probably a stroke," Castro'd said through a camouflage of smoke rising in a wreath around his head. "Since the old thing had no family, we may not even need an autopsy." He bagged her hands as a matter of course.

Mistakes were made. It was easy to do. Just as later the forensic people in Little Rock would jump to conclusions that she'd probably stolen the tiny bottle they found in the woman's palm.

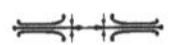

When Price's feet had hit the floor that morning, he had known it was going to be a bad day. He hadn't slept his required eight hours, and his back bones cracked like knuckles as he stretched. Nude except for the socks he slept in, he ambled into the bathroom, dressed, then headed for the kitchen in hopes Janine had brought in the Sunday paper.

As a boy growing up on a dirt farm with a mother who would never let him go barefoot for fear of hookworm, he never knew the pleasure of walking with bare feet on cool grass in the summer or on warm sand or splashing in a Louisiana mud puddle after a rain. In fact, he never learned to abide the feel of any surface on the soles of his bare feet.

"Coffee ready, Boo?"

"How late did you get in?" Janine still wore her housedress in the early mornings.

"One o'clock—two."

"I take it you won't be going to mass."

"Cain't. I gotta a dead woman to deal with."

"We're singing carols this morning and having cookies and punch after."

"Don't count on me, Cher."

"Depend on it, Romeo."

Price Latimer wasn't listening. He'd mentally moved on. The coroner had suggested natural causes, and that should tie up the unusual circumstances of old woman's death fairly quickly.

Not long after kissing Janine good-bye, he rushed through the back entrance at headquarters with one aim. *I'm gonna remove Tick Quinn from the case even if the bag woman is a throwaway. I don't care if he is 'bout to retire. We don't get on good together, I don't trust him, and he makes me uneasy.* Comfortable with his decision, he swaggered down the hall to the kitchen for his glass of hot water with the teaspoon of vinegar. "Aaaaah." He acknowledged the sour elixir he tossed back every morning to cleanse his liver. He didn't acknowledge—maybe he didn't see—a trio of officers sprawled at a table in the corner over lackluster coffee and the morning gazette until he heard a callous remark about piss and vinegar, which was applauded with a rattle of newspapers. "I see y'all are hard at it this morning."

The men grunted in reply.

"Drake, I'm thinking about handing the bag woman over to you."

"No, thanks," Drake mumbled.

If the sheriff had actuated a system of rank and file in the department, Tom Drake, in Latimer's mind, would have been second rather than Tick Quinn. But rank was not driving Latimer's decision this morning.

"Tick's retirin'. I don't want unfinished business hanging around when the time comes. Understand what I'm saying?"

"She was old. It was natural causes. What's going to hang on?"

"If this isn't finished up pronto, I'm handing it to you," Latimer muttered to the soberingly depressing lichen-colored walls of the central hall as he headed toward his office. He was tired of seeing his men glance to Tick for guidance or throw looks between each other when he'd issue an order. Latimer had stopped to belch the vinegary water and to rearrange his balls when he spotted his nemesis at his desk bent over a stack of files.

"Quinn! Just thinking about you."

Tick continued reading.

In two steps Latimer was peering over the detective's shoulder.

"Working on the Dumpster dipper, are you? Wrap it up by noon, or I'm givin' it to Tom Drake. No point in you getting caught up in a dull case here at the end of your career, huh?

You need to be available if something big comes along." Latimer kicked Tick's chair lightly with the toe of his boot.

Quinn glanced up. "Morning, Price."

"Are you 'bout finished?" Latimer rocked back on his heels.

"Sure. But if it's not all sewed up by the time I leave, put Pauley McCrary on it. Let him wrap it up. He's a good cop. Don't screw him around."

"What you sayin'?" The sheriff hunkered down close to the detective's ear. "You saying I'm some kinda bigot? You got nothing on me, Quinn. I'm as fair as the next man, and I'm good at what I do."

Tick scooted his chair, forcing Latimer to step back. "I let a man's actions speak more than his words, Price." Both men were on their feet. "I'm not here to argue about your prejudices or anything else. I have a responsibility to this case, and I'm gonna keep things moving along in the right direction for as long as I can. But just so you'll know, I ain't the least bit interested in you nosing around in my business this morning or any morning. When I'm gone, you're shed of me, but until then stay out of my way. Understand?" Tick stuck out his hand. "I'll shake your hand, but whatever this little visit was about wasn't necessary."

The few minutes it took Latimer to traverse the minefield from the maze to his office gave him ample time to reach a full-blown rage. *You need not think you gonna go into retirement like a blazing comet with a long tail, you sorry sonabitch. Who you tink you are? Dick Tracy? Riversbend is not Bayou Bleu.*

It was at this precise moment that Pauley had tried to slip by his door on his way to Pat's Coffee Cupp.

"Hey! You! McCarthy!"

Following the less-than-satisfactory interview with Pauley, Latimer was contemplating a quick nap. Just as he propped his feet on his desk, the telephone rang.

"Sheriff speaking."

"Is this Price Latimer, the one who used to be sheriff in Bayou Bleu? What you been doin', sugar? Or should I say *whom* you been doin'?"

"Who…is this?" Latimer's voice faltered. He reached automatically into his desk drawer to find his pint of bourbon.

"An old friend you haven't seen in a while." There was a slight hesitation before she continued, "I thought we might have a drink together, old time's sake. You interested?"

"I don't know who you are. Why would I be interested?" Latimer's voice was flinty. He uncapped the bourbon and took a long mouthful, grimacing as it marked his throat.

"I'll buy. Aren't you up to seducing other men's wives anymore?"

"Who is this?"

The voice became harder. "Was the woman who died in that Dumpster another one of your accidents?" She laughed, and the next sound was the dial tone.

He didn't recognize it, but there was no doubt the accent was a Louisiana one. The veins in his neck were pulsing.

Latimer took another slug. The voice rang in his ears. The debacle in Bayou Bleu was not forgotten. His bête noire had followed him, and he knew exactly who led it here. Latimer shoved his chair back from his desk with such force that Gladys Gray at the front desk looked up, figuring he'd fallen out of his seat.

Richard Fordyce swept the loading dock behind Adler's in his Sunday suit, true navy, dark as a country sky at midnight. He wore a Christmas bow tie, red, imprinted with holly berries and leaves.

Outside the back door, a line of dead leaves blown up from the bayou clustered against the threshold as if for comfort. Seldom bothered by clutter, Richard Fordyce swept because he didn't know what else to do.

Richard watched as Pauley McCrary walked the Adler Antiques side of Bayou Street. His head bowed, holding his arms behind his back as might a contemplative. He guessed this fresh bustle of attention from the sheriff's department meant the impromptu breakfast he'd hosted at Cedars that morning was an indication of how intrusive a police investigation could become.

Richard wondered what Pauley sought. The young cop vanished momentarily as he dropped to his knee, having seen something, touched something, taking it or perhaps not. On rising he looked across the parking lot toward Richard.

"I'll be going to church shortly, Brother McCrary," Richard hollered. "It's Sunday. We devout Anglicans must dust the dirt off our knees on Sundays, or the week doesn't move smoothly." Richard leaned on his broom as Pauley approached.

"You're in a crime-scene area, Mr. Fordyce. You shouldn't be sweeping." Pauley had stepped across to the parking lot so they could talk without shouting.

"There, you see, I'm a novice. Don't have an inklin' how to behave in a crime scene. What you lookin' for, Sergeant?"

"Tell you the truth, I don't know yet. Hope I'll know it when I see it."

"Well, if you're through with me, I need to leave in ten minutes or so, or I'll be late for church." Richard reached for the stock-room door to return the broom.

"Are you devout, Mr. Fordyce?"

"As a church mouse. And you, Mr. McCrary? Do you go to church?"

"When I can, sir. My grandmother wanted me to go this morning for the carol singing." They both glanced at their watches as though God had, at that moment, synchronized with Greenwich Mean Time. "She's probably there by now."

"And how is Mrs. Robinette?"

"Doin' fine."

"You better hurry if you're going to join her."

Pauley nodded. "I don't reckon I'll get there this morning." He pointed toward Egner's Green, the bayou that stretched east and west through the middle of Riversbend. "I've got more poking around to do. Guess I better get moving." He crossed the street again and this time walked along the berm, the narrow strip of grass and gravel above the still water.

Before the police had insinuated themselves into his life at breakfast, Richard had planned to skip church. But the police finding Raggedy had unsettled him. He had come to the store only because Tick had asked him earlier to accompany Pauley. "Just in case," Tick had said.

Just in case what? Richard had wondered.

Had he not been asked to be available, he would be in his kitchen up to his elbows in cranberries and sugar, making brandied chutney about now. He had given brandied chutney to his closest friends at his Tipsy Eve suppers for years. This morning he'd hoped to sterilize the jars and lids and start peeling the oranges and cooking the chutney. Richard sighed. It took the flavors days to brew, seven at least—ten was better. The sugars had to ferment and clear into a sweet, witchy batch powerful enough to embellish any old tom or hen.

He watched Pauley start down the slope toward the bayou, his hat vanishing as he sank below the edge of the berm. Richard liked the young man. He wished he could help him. He jabbed aimlessly against the building with the straw of his broom. But there was nothing he could tell the police except he felt more troubled about Raggedy's death than he ever imagined he would.

Pauley felt like a cop this morning, leastways sort of like one. Would have felt more like one if Latimer hadn't put the whammy on him before he'd had a decent cup of coffee. He still wasn't sure what the man was out to prove.

Pauley inched toward the bayou. *Just another no-count, good-lookin' rookie lookin' around for whatever it was he was lookin' for* ran like a jingle in his ear as he searched the ground.

Growing up as a child of mixed parentage, Pauley had often wondered what he was supposed to be looking for. His birth had raised eyebrows. But more fascinating to the town than his biracial bloodlines was the fact that he was black but he was a McCrary, and the McCrarys were white, and prominent, but despite—or some might say because of—their affluence, the McCrarys were a troubled family. Reckless, overindulged, they often appeared in the newspaper, and the news was most often unfavorable. Adam, the younger son and Pauley's blood uncle, was mentioned regularly in the *Riversbend Profile* police reports for traffic violations or DWIs, usually both. Yet most of the people in Riversbend thought Pauley would be lucky if he ended up like Adam, rather than like his father, Adrian, who was a petty thief and junkie.

It never occurred to any of the community to consider Pauley white. Not that he wanted to be white. He didn't think of himself as such; he didn't think of himself as either. As a teenager, when he began to realize that his world seemed to insist on his being black, he started cracking jokes:

What do you get if you cross an elephant with an ant? A dead ant.

What do you get if you cross a rich white boy with a pretty, black girl? A nigger. Or an abortion, he sometimes would answer. The jokes and his answers changed according to his frame of mind.

Had it not been for his mother's mother, Opal Robinette, Pauley, like his worthless father, he probably would have spent the best part of his adult life in and out of prisons. Now that he was in his early twenties and turning out better than anyone could have hoped, most of the credit was given to Opal Robinette, who had taken the baby when her daughter, little more than a child herself, had left him along with the impediments of an impossible marriage. Riversbend gave another piece of the credit to Tick Quinn.

It was not that the McCrarys ignored Pauley. It was that their lives simply didn't have room for him. Adrian had married her; the child carried the McCrary name. Most of them saw no reason to draw further attention to the unfortunate alliance. The exception was at Christmas, when old Mrs. McCrary, Adrian's mother, invited her grandson to her fine house overlooking Riversbend and gave him a cup of no-nog eggnog, a piece of fruitcake, and a crisp one-hundred-dollar bill. She handed the money to him in a Christmas card signed Sarah McCrary.

One foot in the car and ready to go, Richard caught a glimpse of Pauley climbing backward up the embankment from the bayou. He was tugging something. "I could have told you what you were looking for!" Richard waved and jumped out of the car. "That's it! I knew something was missing, just couldn't remember what." That grocery basket was as much a part of Raggedy's persona as her skirts of many colors. "Had it rolled into the bayou?"

"On the edge of. It was lodged in a pile of brush." Pauley parked the basket at the base of the loading dock, success lighting up his face.

"It must've rolled down the parking lot, crossed the street, and gone over the edge," Richard added.

"Guess so. Speculation's a bad habit for a cop."

Richard hardly heard him. "Her rolling stock, so to speak. The cart was kind of a moveable feast. It contained most of her belongings and went wherever she went. I know she had a big piece of cardboard in there she could use for shelter. She had her bedding, a small pillow, an army blanket, usually a stack of newspapers. Can't beat newspaper for insulation, did you know that,

Officer McCrary? You should find a few utensils in there too: tin plate, plastic flatware, and a ground cover, a tarp."

"I thought she lived in the homeless shelter at the Searcy Hotel," Pauley said.

"She did, most of the time. She slept up there sometimes too." Richard pointed to the screened door above the loading dock on the catwalk.

"Had she broken in?"

"We never locked it. They say people can break simple locks with a credit card. Anyway, I didn't care. Glad for her to use it. There's nothing of importance up there. Storage, family junk mostly. She wasn't a thief, you know. It's a place our family uses to put all the stuff we've accumulated over the years and don't know what to do with but can't bring ourselves to throw away. Sentimental clutter, I call it."

"So if she had a room at the Searcy and one over your business there, why would she want to haul this mess around all the time?"

"Security maybe. Distrust." Richard shrugged. "Also, the grocery cart would hold whatever treasures she found in a day's work. She had a room all right, but she was nomadic in spirit. Her route was broader than just here in Riversbend. I saw her in Bridgeport once. Walking and pushing that grocery basket. Want to bring the cart up here on the loading dock? I might be able to tell you if anything's missing."

Pauley pulled a wad of latex from his pocket. Gloves, a single pair, he kept one for himself and gave the other to Richard. "Put that on, and don't touch anything with the other one." Pauley tugged at the tightness covering his hand. "Evidence, you know." He smiled big. "I'll get one of our mobile units to come pick this grocery cart up. If you'll grab hold of that end, there we'll park it up close to the stairs till the unit can get here."

Jockeying the shopping cart between them, they maneuvered it into place. Pauley pulled his cell phone off his belt. "I'm gonna see if I can get hold of Tick."

"How 'bout I come down to headquarters after church. I pretty well know what she carried in her cart. Something could have fallen out when it bounced down the hill. Or if something's in there that doesn't belong, well then..."

"Hello, Tick. Guess what!" Pauley turned his back to Richard and walked away.

"Was your lieutenant impressed?" Richard asked after a few minutes.

"You know Tick; he believes if he shows enthusiasm, someone might think he cares."

Richard chuckled. "Her flatware would be in that paper bag there. White plastic knife and fork but a stainless-steel spoon."

"You know a lot about her, Mr. Fordyce."

"She dined here on these steps more than once when she'd come calling on my Dumpster."

"Speaking of the Dumpster, mind if I take a quick look in that storage room you were telling me about? Last night it was pretty dark even with a flashlight." Permission given, Pauley started up the steps. He was on the landing before he saw that the screen door was slightly ajar. "I don't want to make you late for church. I'll be back down before a pig can twitch its tail. Just wanted a little look."

"No hurry. Probably heard today's sermon once or twice already. Father Burkett is a repeat performer."

Pauley, true to his word, came back from the catwalk a little faster than the hypothetical tail twitch. "This belong to you?" He handed Richard a small book.

Richard rolled it over in his hands. "I don't imagine it's one of Raggedy Ann's finds—could be, I guess. I'll ask Rhys. Our grandmother was a great collector. She had a whole collection of Victorian poets up there."

The book, dark leather and smaller than the palm of a man's hand, had fallen between the screen door and the door itself. Pauley frowned. He hated making mistakes. If he'd known the door wasn't locked, he should have looked better. It could be important—probably not, though. "Don't guess Miss Adler would have been up here this morning? Is she an early riser?"

"You had coffee and muffins with her early this morning, remember?" Richard stuck the book in his suit pocket. "If it's not a poetry book, it could be a diary." He tapped the lock. "I'll give it to Rhys. It could be her mother's, or one of our ancestor's. It's old enough. She wasn't born—Raggedy Ann, you know. Would you like to know her real name? Butter," Richard said before Pauley asked. "Francie Butter. Miss Butter, I believe, but I don't know that for fact."

"You knew her pretty well."

"Yes, pretty well. We all know Miss Butter was an accomplished bricoleur. We've seen her at work for years."

Pauley's face was blank.

"A bricoleur is someone who collects odds and ends and often puts them to good use. A recycler. The word is French—rooted in Latin, perhaps."

"You know a lot about a lot of things, Mr. Fordyce." Pauley was a little put off by Richard's easy pedantry. "Would you say you knew Raggedy better than most people knew her? I'm wondering how that is, Mr. Fordyce, how as you two come from different sides of the track?"

Pauley would have elaborated except a choir of chromatically tuned bells began to peal from the towers of the Episcopal, Methodist, and Presbyterian churches a few blocks away. The concert escalated into cacophony of competitions. He slapped his hat against his leg. "Well, looks like you're about to be late, Mr. Fordyce. I wouldn't want to keep a man from his church."

The words were light, but the small smile cornering his mouth warned Richard Fordyce that their conversation regarding Miss Francie Butter was not finished.

"One more thing, Mr. Fordyce, you might want to stay in town—in case we find some reason we want to talk about Miss Butter's grocery cart."

Like most small towns, Riversbend had what you could call a possessive interest in her people, even the anomalies. Take Doctor Poof, a wizened old man, who sat on the courthouse bench year-round, sucking his lips in and then puffing them out in billowy expulsions of air. Few could remember when Doctor Poof began doing this, or why Miss Radley, Riversbend's only octogenarian noted for riding a bicycle all over town, claimed to know why. "After the war," she'd say mysteriously. Doctor Poof on the courthouse bench and Miss Radley rattling by on her bicycle both looked so ancient that schoolchildren assumed she meant the Civil War, their parents thought Vietnam, and their grandparents, World War II. "After the war," she'd say and then quickly put her finger to her lips, as if she'd said too much.

Like other small places, Riversbend had its share of odd ducks, but they were Riversbend's odd ducks and harmless for the most part. They provided a lot of color to an otherwise-very-conventional tableau. Raggedy Ann had been one of the town's favorites. People knew her. They either spoke to her or shunned her, depending on the depth of their own neurotic behavior, but they mostly left her in peace to ravage their trash cans.

Awake in the middle of the night, Richard Fordyce sometimes wondered if he was an anomaly too. Aging bachelor, the words were almost oxymoronic to his ear. Where was the young man with a future that stretched ahead of him forever? What would his life be now had he fathered a son, or a daughter? Had he a wife?

A few months back, he'd taken to tinting on his hair, and everyone in Riversbend had an opinion concerning it. To some Richard was a bit of a dandy. The overeducated few might add "effete." To the new modern, he was a metrosexual, or so they said as they toyed with the meaning of the word. He was well turned out: never in public without a crisply laundered shirt, sharply creased trousers, and with a necktie or not, he always had a jacket either on or near at hand. And the prize, the single aspect he possessed that saved him from too harsh a jury, and which often offered him affection if not downright love, was the particularity that people most desired for themselves. Richard was rich.

Richard knew he was peculiar, but most of the time, he didn't give a fig; he was happy. He and Riversbend belonged together. He knew everyone, and everyone knew him, and the people knew him precisely because he kept an interested finger in everyone's pie. The cousins, he and Rhys, despite their individual demeanors—one salt, one sugar—for the most part, understood the world to be their bauble.

In August, Richard planned for Christmas, and after New Year's, he yearned for spring, when Riversbend's social season awakened to warm, caressing breezes and a surfeit of jonquils. In the spring, Richard would set aside his angst about aging and settle into the more comfortable role of Riversbend's most desired dinner guest.

His presence at table could seal the success of a fair-to-middling beef bourguignon, and his charm and wit complimented a rosy evening as much as a good bottle of wine, or recessed lighting. Friends might smile if, after a martini or two, he became a bit too gushy, a little too highborn, and he did possess a double handful of embarrassing affectations, but they did not laugh, because Richard was not only prosperous but also an amazing bridge player.

If in his social popularity a little excessive *avoirdupois* over-took him by summer, he bought larger suits.

Maryjane Petitjean, who ordinarily kept her head under two pil-lows past noon on Sundays, was awakened at quarter past five, or so her oversized, aggressively red and flashing digital clock informed her. She was awakened not by the clock but by a ring-ing from her bread box in the kitchen. Her telephone lived in the bread box for its preservation. Otherwise it would have been demolished regularly with brutal yanks from the wall or flights out the window or crashes down the metal stairs outside her apartment.

Maryjane's feet hit cold linoleum. In her birthday suit, she padded into the kitchenette, knowing that the call was from the morgue.

"Doc Rakhshani has been called back to Texas unexpectedly. Could you come in for the early shift?" Petitjean heard the undis-guised glee in the messenger's chirpy voice.

"Balls," had been Petitjean's response.

The night staffer who'd lost the coin toss on who would wake her giggled. "Sorry, Dr. Petitjean."

Despite the requisite Sunday-morning heavy head, dry mouth, puffy eyes, and overall intolerance for anything living, Maryjane Petitjean was a serious pathologist. She was intelligent, diligent, and skilled, traits that had bumped her to second-in-command at the state forensic lab two years before.

This morning was the second Sunday in a row the lab had called. If Dr. Rakhshani's father would go on and die instead of piddling around out in the tumbleweeds of west Texas, Maryjane Petitjean could be in Hawaii for Christmas. If the old fart could just gasp his last, she would have ten beautiful days of sunshine and half-naked men on a white sandy beach. That vista, as far as she was concerned, beat the hell out of a white Christmas. She would ring in the New Year with a lei of hibiscus around her neck and, if lucky, a good lay in her bed.

Dr. Petitjean stood at the metal sink in the inner room of the autopsy suite, washing her hands and complaining to the stream of warm water that splashed a fine rainbow mist onto her lab coat. She turned the tap and grabbed a towel from a neatly folded stack on a nearby cabinet. Dried, she dressed out in protective plastic, from the hair cover, similar to a shower cap, to shoe covers. All except for her face mask; that would go on last.

"And please," she prayed to the god of overworked women, "no homicides or suicides until I'm in the air, flying happily over water with a glass of champagne in each hand."

She shivered with pleasure at the thought until she heard a door slam down the hall.

"And while I have your most hallowed attention, whoever the corpse is who's responsible for waking me this morning, could you see to it that he or she roasts in hell for a day or two?" Maryjane tossed the towel in a hamper. The large light over the examination table flickered and dimmed. "Okay, maybe not roasts," she said, crossing herself, even though she was not Catholic and wasn't sure if the order was head, heart, left, right or right, left, head, heart.

She heard the gurney's squeaky wheels begin their journey down the short corridor from the receiving wing of the creepy, stinky old building toward the autopsy room.

Dockers, long, loose jointed, and smelling of chemicals, rolled the sheet-draped body, like a snow-covered mound, into the lab and parked the gurney under the bright lights. Securing the stretcher in place with wheel clamps, he stood up straight and grinned at Petitjean.

"Breakfast, m'lady?" He flipped a paper napkin from a cafeteria tray that sat on the edge of the gurney. Two cups of coffee and two egg sandwiches appeared. "A breach of rules, I know, but at five frigging fifty-six in the morning who gives a rat's ass, huh?"

"Uhhh. None for me. No taste for food just yet. Coffee, though. Black. Thanks, Dockers."

"What time did you turn in last night?" he asked as he settled into a metal folding chair and began neatly unwrapping the sandwich balanced on his knees.

"I don't have a clue. It was still dark, I think."

"Who brought you home?"

"Can't answer that one either. He wasn't there when you people woke me up a little while ago." Petitjean held her cup with both hands, enjoying the warmth.

"Hmm." Dockers bit into his breakfast. "Have you read the charts to see who our first guest is this morning?"

"No." Petitjean leaned against the cabinet, her eyes closed.

"Are you interested?"

"Should I be?"

"Aren't you from Riversbend?"

"From Pearl. About twenty minutes northwest of Riversbend as the crow flies."

Dockers picked up the chart that lay on top of the draped body. "Have you ever heard of a Raggedy Ann in Riversbend? No other name given."

Maryjane's cheeks rounded into a smile. "Everyone in Quick County knows Raggedy Ann. Fact is she probably knows more about the people in the county than we know about her. She's been going through our rubbish for a while now. She's even been seen down at Pearl."

"Well, she's our first customer of the day."

"Sorry to hear that. Raggedy Ann is destined to become a legend, I suspect. Anyway, I hope she's not in hell." Maryjane with lifted eyes piously petitioned the ceiling.

Dockers cocked an eyebrow.

"Ignore me. Just canceling a small intercession, I invoked earlier."

"Cool. So, you'll know her when you see her then?"

"Maybe. Never seen her naked, though."

Dockers's cheeks reddened. The idea of naked on a gurney set off his current favorite sexual fantasy of Petitjean naked on the gurney. Alive, warm, and writhing in an erotic frenzy under the ministrations of his practiced tongue.

"Dockers, you're rocking the gurney." Petitjean pointed to the foot of the padded table.

In two steps he was at the bottom of the gurney, nudging the deceased back to the security of the middle. Struck by how vulnerable bare feet were, he was very gentle as he repositioned the sheet.

"Go wash your hands, glove up, and don't forget your face shield." Dr. Petitjean picked up the admission document and began reading. "The medical examiner in Riversbend thinks it was natural causes. But who knows. Castro is Methuselah's uncle, and Raggedy may not have medical files. Toxicology results are not in I see. Okay." Dr. Petitjean continued reading, mumbling to herself. "Says here they found the old dear hanging over the edge of a Dumpster. Okay, Dockers, let's get her on the examining table. Ready? One for the money, two for the show..."

They lifted the body from the stretcher to the table. When Petitjean signaled, he pulled back the sheet to expose only the face and shoulders of the corpse for the beginning of the external examination. Dockers hated this part, the moment he came face-to-face with the newly dead, but this was Petitjean's way, this slow unveiling. She had been taught to de-sheet a corpse in sections so as not to rush to wrong conclusions.

"This is the first cadaver I've ever known personally." Petitjean's tone was thoughtful. "She looks different. The skirts, I guess. She wore layers of skirts. Without the layers she's thinner, stringier than you'd have thought." Drained of life, still the face held a flush of color. Eyes closed, stubby lashes resting on flattened cheeks, a mass of unkempt hair framed the familiar face.

"The face is flushed, and a thin smear of blood has dried on the right ear," Petitjean began documenting her findings into a small recording device pinned to her lab coat. She felt behind the older woman's ears for a wound. Finding none, she gently lifted the head to examine the back of the skull. "Some blood in the occipital area matted in the hair from a blow to the head, possibly from a fall. A hard surface, rough, grainy, or uneven surface, as the wound appears to be a scrape as well as a bump. From the grit, it looks like dirt or fine gravel maybe." Next, she peered intently at the woman's upper region for contusions, cuts, or abrasions. "There's a medium-sized bruise on the chin approximately one point five centimeters across." Petitjean frowned in concentration as she worked her fingers around the skull; as she ran her hand across the corpse's jaw, her frown deepened.

"Who brought her in?"

"It's on the chain-of-custody document. Want me to look?"

"Not this sec. Go on. Let's see the torso."

Dockers folded the sheet further down to expose the chest and upper abdominal area.

"Ribs don't appear to be broken." She glanced at him and continued to record. "A belt of bruising is below the stomach and about the waist and hips. Probably due to hanging on the Dumpster."

With practiced hands, the young pathologist pressed on the soft tissue of the corpse's stomach. She lifted the dead woman's left hand and removed the protective bag that had been guarding any evidence from the night of her death. The cold hand in her latexed one, she looked at the back of it, running her thumb over the shallow veins, the spots and wens that confirmed age and unprotected exposure to harsh sun, wind, and cold. She turned the hand over and studied the palm, the fingers, and last the nails. With small scissors, she snipped a section of nail and dropped it into a plastic bag. Then, taking a thin blade, she scraped under each nail. Massaging the muscles up the dead woman's arm, she looked for anything that might tell the story of what had happened to her.

"What's this?" Petitjean had removed the bag from Raggedy's right hand.

Dockers leaned forward as Maryjane Petitjean pried the stiff fingers into a fan. She handed Dockers a very small narrow-throated bottle.

"What is it?" he asked.

Maryjane shook her head. "If she was at the antique store when she died, it must be something she purloined from the Dumpster. Put it over there." She motioned to a metal tray. "Make a note of it when you get a chance." She looked at the lab clock on the wall—6:37 a.m. "I'll give it to the Riversbend police with the report when they come for the body. The old gal is still in rigor mortis. We'll keep her in storage until we can autopsy."

"Curious the old medical examiner didn't see it," Dockers said.

"Not really. Small towns do what they can and use whom they can, often with marginal staff and equipment. The ME up there is old but capable enough most of the time."

Petitjean leaned in toward the body. If Raggedy had been doubled over the edge of the Dumpster for several hours, they should see more discoloration.

"It wasn't a stroke. A hemorrhage, granted, could cause the blood around her ear but not the blood on the back of her head. I think she hit her head against something. She may have had a hard fall, although there aren't many bruises on her arms to indicate that. If she were concussed"—Dr. Petitjean moved back to the top of the gurney and lifted Raggedy's eyelids—"why was she holding that bottle? If she was hurt enough to bleed in her ear, what was so important she continued poking around in the Dumpster?"

"Maybe she wasn't. Maybe someone put her there," Dockers, back at the examining table after setting the glass bottle safely on a tray and scribbling a cryptic notation of sorts, suggested.

"Could be, I guess. We'll know more about what, when, where, and how after we do the autopsy. Okay, strip her down."

Dockers lifted the rest of the sheet from the body.

"Whoa!" Petitjean sang out. "Can you reach the custody document? Find out who brought the body in. I hope the principal investigating officer is my old bud, Tick. He enjoys a cadaverous surprise as much as the next fellow." She bent closer to the body. "This injury doesn't have anything to do with her death, though. I can tell you that."

"T. Quinn brought her in. Is that your friend?" Dockers said. "Do you want him down for the autopsy?"

"I want him before I do an autopsy. If I were a cop in charge of this case, I'd want to see for myself before someone started carving."

Most everyone in Riversbend knew of Tick's endeavors when young Pauley, like a weed growing wild on an unkempt lot, had his first encounter with the law. People who worked at the courthouse knew. The McCrarys knew, Mrs. Opal Robinette and the Lafferty AME Church knew, and Pat Cupp, proud owner and loquacious waitress of the Coffee Cupp, knew. In fact, most of the locals who soaked up the news on weekday mornings along with their coffee knew.

There was a revolving-door effect at the Cupp most mornings. The café, across the street from the courthouse, was inviting with its sparkling windows and welcoming Tinkerbelle bells. Pat Cupp had skillfully coalesced Riversbend's business and legal professionals along with her courthouse parolees and hangers-on with an innocent impartiality. Secure in their choices of regular or decaf, black or creamed, the customers exchanged gossip or bits of news or rehashed old stories with little fear of judgment. Memory had it that, a few years back, Tick had brought Pauley in for joyriding in a borrowed car one hot summer night.

Escorting the boy by the elbow into headquarters that fateful night, Tick had walked Pauley straight back to interrogation and closed the door. Sixteen, not yet having reached his full height but lanky as a sapling, Pauley was dressed in baggy shorts and a ragged Jimi Hendrix T-shirt, which hung on him like tired clothes on a sales rack. His hair, in tight cornrows over half his skull, fell loose behind his ears.

An arm flung across the back of a spindle-back chair, he periodically glanced from under lowered lashes at the fat, white man sitting on the edge of the table in front of him. He figured he could outrun him if push came to shove.

"I busted your dad the first time he broke the law," Tick said slowly, gazing at a map of the county tacked on the wall behind Pauley's head.

"So?"

"I thought I might do a better job with you than I did with him."

Pauley shrugged. "I'm not my dad. But since you know who I am, you know it was my uncle's Mustang. I didn't steal it. He let me borrow it."

"Let's give him a call." Tick bent back across the table to a drawer and pulled out a telephone book. "You know his number right off?"

"He's probably out."

"Maybe he's back."

"I mean like passed out."

"It won't take a minute to check and see if you're taking his car was okay with him." Tick thumbed through the *K*s, the *L*s, "Mas," "Mc." "Here we go. Adam McCrary."

"He said I could borrow it, but he won't remember." Pauley started to say something more but stopped. He grinned instead. "Okay." He sat up straighter. "I don't lie. That's something else you can know about me. I don't lie. That's my motto. Okay, it is my uncle's car. That's the truth. He didn't offer it to me, though. He probably doesn't know it's gone. It's Saturday night. Like I say, he's probably been pissed and passed out since noon."

"What you figure is the problem with the McCrary men, son? Your dad? Your uncle? Neither of 'em much count. Both born with more going for them than you or me. How you feel about that?"

Legs stretched out in an attitude of indifference, Pauley stared at the toes of his sneakers. He could no more answer the question of *why* the McCrary men were no count than the honkie who asked it. He wondered when this bullshit talk would stop so as they could toss him in a cell like usual. Uncrossing, recrossing his feet, he suddenly pulled his legs back, put his heels together, which caused his toes to point east and west like Gregory Hines might have done at a ballet barre.

Tick waited until Pauley looked up from this silent engagement with his shoes.

"Ever see your dad?"

"How long am I going to be here? You gonna book me? My grandmother will be worried if I'm out too late."

"Got a curfew, do you?" Tick flicked a thin smile that in time Pauley would come to recognize as his I've-about-had-it-with-you smile. The older man, who in truth was bushed and not much interested in wasting any more time with an uncooperative ego, began wrapping up the interview. Do you have a girlfriend? How's your grandmother? Is she home? What kinda grades you make, you an A and B smartass or a D and F dumbass?"

"You forgot C."

"You make Cs mostly then?"

"I can make any grade I set my mind to. I can make an A or an F, depending on how I feel."

"How you feel about a doughnut?" Tick stood up and moved behind the table to get an arrest report. If he had any sense, he would book the kid, lock him up for the night, and go home to a cold supper.

Pauley looked puzzled.

"You know, sweet, glazed, hole in the middle."

Pauley grinned. "You mean pussy?"

Tick blushed. "You better learn whom you're talking to, Mr. McCrary. The next cop you meet may not be as nice as I am."

"Yeh, well, I guess you don't like my humor. You got any milk?"

"You got any manners?"

"Do you have milk to go with that doughnut you're offerin' me?"

"You got an ulcer?"

"Wha' the hell you talkin' about?"

"Did you mean to say, 'No, sir'?"

The two stared at each other for an in determinant time until Pauley, once again, looked down, seeking the solace of his sneakers.

"Yes, sir, I meant to say no, sir. I don't have an ulcer."

"Lockhart," Tick hollered through the door, "would ya bring us a couple of milks?"

Pauley heard a chair scoot somewhere and then shoe taps click down the hall. He listened as the eurhythmic beat faded into silence only to return a minute or two later as the light-footed go-fetch-it came back up the hall. A rap on the door admitted a weaselly man into the room. He blinked at Pauley, grinned at Tick Quinn, and placed two half pints of milk on the edge of the desk.

"Now, if you would, would you go find us a dozen doughnuts and a cup of hot, fresh coffee," Tick growled and sank heavily onto the swivel chair opposite Pauley.

It was in the amazing twenty minutes or so it took Lockhart to return with the doughnuts that the relationship between Tick Quinn and Pauley McCrary changed. Unintended it began in an effort to kill time while they waited. Tick asked a question. The question he asked was innocent, simple, but apparently loaded, and Pauley tumbled to it.

"Do you want to get arrested so you can quit wonderin' who you are? So you can just get on with being a criminal like your no-good dad and uncle?"

Pauley reddened. He opened his mouth as if to speak but then a miracle happened: his face softened, and Tick glimpsed the child all teenager boys so desperately want to hide.

"I bought myself a baseball glove when I was thirteen," Pauley said.

Tick didn't move. He had been in police work long enough to know he was about to hear something important.

"I got a great knuckleball. Spitball too, but spitballs are illegal. I'm left-handed, you know. You ever see me play?"

Tick nodded. "Yeah, lots of times."

"Coach took my glove." Pauley searched Tick's face for sympathy. "Before All State. I can't pitch without my glove. It's my good luck. I would have gotten a scholarship if he'd let me use my glove."

"Why did he do that?"

"The scouts were there. College and university scouts from all over. Coach didn't want me to play because he didn't want them to see how good I was. If my game is off, if I'm in the dugout, Bronson Halliger pitches. I'm a better pitcher than Bronco. Coach knows it, Bronco knows it, and the team knows it."

"I know it too," Tick said.

Pauley lowered his head to hide a prickling of tears. "You know then that Bronson is coach's nephew."

"I know that too."

"So that's how it works, right? Being good at what you do doesn't count if you're a black kid with a no-count white dad. It's called a lose-lose situation."

"Yeah, I know," Tick said, hesitating. "Seems like that's how it works, but I'll tell you something, Pauley." Tick looked the boy in the eye. "Most people here in Riversbend don't care if you go to jail. They expect you to. You know why? Because that's your script. You didn't write it, but you bought it."

Pauley stood up. "Why are you saying this? I was telling you about my glove. You don't get it, do you?" His voice cracked. Tears welled into his eyes and would have rolled down his face except he wiped them away too quickly with his bare arm.

"I'm trying to help you. There's something important you need to understand."

"I don't need your help."

"Did you know your grandfather? One of the finest men I've ever known, black or white. Ever hear some of the stories about Lucien Robinette?" Tick reached into his pants' pocket. "Lucien gave me a silver dollar once." Tick smiled as a well-worn memory edged into the present. Sitting down, satisfied he was back on track with Pauley, he tilted his chair and then let it drop back to the floor. "Old Lucien believed there were two kinds of men in the world, chumps and bounders. 'Can't be both,' he told me. 'You have to choose, Tick,' he said. And that's what I was trying to tell you, Pauley. It's your choice, no one else's."

Pauley didn't say anything.

"Tendencies, you see. Neither chumps nor bounders seem to have the traits we say we admire. No man wants to be thought a fool, and no one, deep down, ever thinks he's a louse. But we have leanings, don't you see. It's in comparing one to the other that you begin to see the difference. And there's a world of difference, if you think about it. You ever see a two-headed silver dollar?"

Pauley shook his head enough to let Tick know he was listening.

"Your granddaddy flipped me a silver dollar once."

"Two-headed?"

"Your granddaddy said my old man, Jim Quinn, was as confounding as a two-headed silver dollar. That every time you thought you had him figured, he'd do something nice and come up heads. Truth is your granddaddy thought my daddy was a bounder, but he wasn't. One time I saw my dad make an old boy confess to a crime, and all Dad did was just stare him in the face. It was his eyes. Dad had the palest, bluest eyes that could look right down into a man's soul. Jesus eyes, I called them."

"Jesus had brown eyes," Pauley, not willing to concede, grumbled.

"Is that so. Well. I'm just trying to say we're neither one of us our dads."

"My grandmother has a picture hanging behind her kitchen table of him."

"Of Lucien?"

"No. Jesus. He was a Jew, and he had brown eyes."

"What you keep going on about Jesus for? What difference does it make if his eyes are blue or brown or red?"

"It doesn't matter to me. Only, if truth matters to you, they're brown."

"Okay, brown. I don't want to talk about Jesus. I'm trying to tell you about your granddaddy."

"Okay. Tell me."

In the quiet, the water cooler in the outer office gurgled comically. A door opened somewhere down the hall, and voices emerged, men's voices already in the middle of what seemed an indifferent conversation. Tick tried to piece together his story about the two-headed silver dollar and wondered why he'd brought it up and was trying to tell something so complicated to this boy.

At the same time, Pauley McCrary was wondering if, and if so *how*, two-headed silver dollars had anything to do with him.

"Old Lucien had the second sight, you know?" Tick continued. He knew stuff other people didn't. Or he at least knew it first. He knew I wasn't cut out to be a hero like my old man, and that being the case, I might oughter make a decision as to whom I was cut out to be. I could either be me or a poor imitation of someone else. 'Because, young man,' I remember him saying, 'Because, young man, if you *don't*, you'll end up trying to go two directions at once, and you're liable to get your feet tangled.'" Tick laughed. "He was right."

"So, you a chump or a bounder?"

"My dad wanted to be a policeman, but he never got to go to school. I guess I'm like him in that I never wanted to be anything other than a cop, and one right here in Riversbend. Your granddad saw it.

"My dad, Jimmy people called him, saved a boy's life once. Found him out in the woods during deer season. Dad patched him up and took him to the hospital. To me, Dad was a real, genuine all-American hero." Tick scrubbed his forehead with the heel of his hand. "That's a lot for a boy to live up to. And I don't know which is easier, son, living up to or living down to our fathers."

"What you tellin' me all this for?"

"Hell, I don't know. Like I said, I'm trying to help you."

"It ain't helping. You still got that silver dollar?" Pauley asked just as Lockhart bumped against the door with his knee.

"What silver dollar's that?" Tick winked. "Come on in." Lockhart set the sack of doughnuts in the middle of the table and a steaming coffee in front of Tick.

"Eat as many as you want, son." Tick walked over and put his hand on Pauley's hand, which was already opening the sack.

"And when you're finished, I'll escort you personally down the street to the jail."

"Aw man! I thought we was getting on."

"Getting on? If you're talking about being friendly, well, friendship is a slow-coming thing. We neither one of us knows yet if we want to be friends. Right now it don't seem likely."

"Well, I know I'm not all that interested if you're a son-of-a-bitchin' bounder!"

Tick laughed and reached into his trouser pocket, producing a coin. "I owe Lucien Robinette a favor." He flipped a silver-dollar toward Pauley.

The carjacking hadn't been Pauley's first offense, but without Tick's involvement, it could have been his first felony. Tick had little hope for the boy's turnaround. Nonetheless, the course Pauley set that night sitting in jail had the outcome Tick would have wanted for him, although it came with a price. In the process of staying out of jail, and in time becoming an officer of the law rather than a professional ball player or even a coach, Pauley learned to lie.

Addie Wagner loathed Richard Wagner more than most of the dead composers. She hated his music galloping up the hall into her bedroom while she dressed for church.

"Ride of the Valkyries," Addie purred to Sourpuss, the gray-and-white tabby perched on her dresser, grooming his claws. "What's a valkyrie? I wouldn't know one if it rang our door bell. What do you think about that, pussy puss? I'll tell you what I think. I think Logan doesn't give a fig about classical music. This is Monsieur Connoisseur's doings." She picked up the cat and buried her face in his fur and then dropped him lightly onto the floor. "Go catch a mouse. I've got to do something with my hair."

After years of listening to Logan poke fun at eggheads—as her husband called all people who pretended to the highbrow—Addie never expected him to become one. Not even a middlebrow. Until last year, he'd never shown enthusiasm for anything unless it related to balls—his, or those you pass, kick, or knock around with a stick. So why in the past month, particularly on Sunday mornings, he felt called upon to load his *Top 40 Classical Hits* in the portable CD player and then blast the neighbors, she couldn't guess. And if he did it to make an impression on some neighbor, Addie didn't know which one, or for what gain.

Addie briskly toweled her hair until it was nearly dry and then brushed it free of tangles. A couple of head tosses, and her dark, shiny mane fell effortlessly into place.

Her lingerie, arranged on the bed in a pattern suggestive of the body it would soon envelop, was silky to the touch. Addie stepped into the pair of panties. Braless, she let her camisole slide down over her shoulders. Her breasts were bare, small, firm, her nipples obedient to the light caress of the silk. A black dress, put on a hanger on the closet door, waited in shimmering liquidity.

She shouldn't complain about Monsieur Connoisseur or Mr. C. as she called Logan's most current persona. It was only last year that these fantasies began. Only a year—it seemed longer to Addie. They began one morning, unannounced, when Logan emerged from the bathroom sprouting the dark stubble of what would become his Jesus beard. Saint Logan, Addie teased him. His mission, this first time, was weird but okay; he wanted to put Christ back into Christmas out at the high school, old RHS. In contrast, the refined Monsieur Connoisseur was a relief. He was a totally egotistic, self-gratifying character, Addie thought, and far safer than the entrepreneurial alter ego who'd stood clean shaven at the foot of their bed a month or so earlier to announce he'd invested his 401(k) in Logan Wagner's Hog Spit-Barbeque Sauce. Addie could have named that venture Up in Smoke.

Logan wasn't crazy; he was always Logan. It was just that, for the past year or so, he kept slipping into new skins, hoping, she assumed, he would discover which one fit him best. Most of his roles didn't hang around too long. Saint Logan had disappeared much like Father Time at the end of the year. The trappings were sometimes expensive, like the barbeque-sauce debacle, but usually subtle. Most people wouldn't have noticed. Addie leaned toward the mirror. Still...

Seated on the edge of her kidney-shaped vanity chair, she applied a slick of moisturizing cream. With her ring finger, she smoothed it into the tight skin around her eyes.

Initially, she had attributed his strangeness to male menopause. At the health club, she'd laughed about it with her girlfriends. "Most men," she'd said, "have an affair or buy a convertible."

But it had become less funny. For one, Mr. C. had arrived rather more intact. Logan's clothing should have been a clue that someone new had moved into her husband's skin. Always a sweats or gym-clothes man, now Logan rarely was seen in anything other than creased slacks and a sports jacket. She suspected the monsieur was greedier than the others too. Unlike the crusader or the entrepreneur, she felt this alter ego left less room for the old Logan.

Addie wondered if Logan did have a lover, if this pretentious personality was another woman's dab of clay to mold. She mentally scanned the women in the neighborhood, wondering if one of those wives had stolen her husband's attention. She wouldn't have been totally surprised. Neither of them were innocents. She ran her hand slowly down her neck and up along the fine line of her jaw. Good bones.

If he did have another woman, it wouldn't last. Addie knew that. A little intrigue to add a dash of spice to their bed—well, how bad was that?

Addie pinched the tip off a capsule of expensive oil and began rubbing it in upward strokes under her chin. Her mouth stretched in a skeletal grin, she inspected the whiteness of her teeth, running her tongue over them.

But if living with Logan's imaginary friends wasn't taxing enough, he'd started misplacing things. First his glasses and then his nail clippers, which stayed in his pocket and practically had to be signed for to borrow. Poor Logan, she sighed. He left his hedge trimmer in the grass, and she found the nozzle to the water hose in the mailbox. She was more baffled than annoyed until her things started showing up in strange places. One Sunday she blamed him for losing the tiny gold cross that had belonged to his mother and that he'd so ceremoniously given to her on her last birthday. Later she found it in his coat pocket. It could have fallen off—the clasp was weak. He'd probably found it. But then her birth-control pills, which were never out of her vanity, disappeared.

"You've let yourself run out," he challenged when she cornered him.

"The packaging is even gone, Logan!"

"They'll show up."

"You took them! Is old age bothering you? Are you hoping we'll get pregnant now that you're old enough to be a grandfather?"

She didn't know how much longer she would hang in. She had little sticking power when life turned its ugly face. He would be fifty in January; she was thirty-six. When they'd married, the years that separated them hadn't seemed so important.

She did still love him, didn't she? The fluid black dress slipped down over her body. She had loved him passionately, and she had taken him hungrily from the first Mrs. Wagner without a qualm. He was a handsome man. The memory sent a flush of heat through her body.

She brushed her inky hair back into a low ponytail, then twisting it into a smooth bun that she expertly secured with three well-placed hairpins. She removed a smart, black, wide-brimmed hat from a milliner's stand and placed it on top of her head. Turning before the mirror, she inspected all her angles, with a final check of her shoulders for any stray hair or dust of powder. She finished by pinning a rhinestone-encrusted Christmas tree to her dress, and a splash of Vera Wang on her wrists and in the hollow at her neck. Collecting Sourpuss, who was back on her dresser, she whispered in his ear. "If I turn a few heads coming down the aisle at church this morning, it might be worth going."

As Addie crossed the foyer into the living room, she listened as her high heels clicked against the terra-cotta tile, quick and light; the staccato effect momentarily lifted her from her worries.

Logan rose from his chair, folded the thick Sunday paper into a precise rectangle, and dropped it onto the leather ottoman behind him.

"Ready?" He turned off the music.

"I'm ready."

"You'll knock 'em dead, Mrs. Wagner." He moved toward her, taking her fur coat from her and draping it around her shoulders. After fifteen years, he still could hardly keep his hands off her.

"Humm. No bra? Who are we seducing today?"

Her lips parted into an enigmatic smile; Addie Wagner was unaware that she flirted with her husband as naturally as she flirted with other men. "Only you, baby."

She hoped she was right. She'd done a pretty good job squelching her latest fancier. Fun was her game. She was rarely serious. But with the last one, the flame had flared a little too brightly. She didn't want to risk seeing her fancy for a while, not until they had both cooled off.

As she watched Logan negotiate their car between posts on either side of their drive, she spied the corner of a pink envelope in their mailbox. "I thought we brought in the mail yesterday?" he said, apparently seeing it too.

"Guess not."

As the car swung into forward, the envelope, now on Logan's side, seemed to glow. "I'm expecting a letter from Marilyn," Addie offered casually. "I've been thinking about going to Chicago to see her after Christmas."

"A sister trip?"

Addie placed her hand on his leg as they drove slowly down the cul-de-sac toward Crescent Moon Drive. "I think after lunch a nice nap might be in order," she said. "Do the coaches have a golf game lined up for this afternoon? Did Larry call, or young Buck now that he's back?"

Logan glanced at her. "Yes, we have a game, and yes, I've talked to Larry and Bronson. But this is not a game; I can't put off for half an hour." He grinned. "Would that be long enough?"

"Maybe. We'll see."

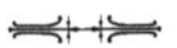

The news of Raggedy Ann's death buzzed in restrained whispers all around the sanctuary as St. James Episcopal filled for the ten-thirty service. The only one in the Adler pew this morning, Richard was attempting to pull the prie-dieu forward without too loud a thump when his cell phone rang. He pushed the prayer bench back, rose, and slipped out into the narthex. It was Rhys.

"Where are you?" she asked.

"About to be on my knees."

"Ohhh? Should I call at a better time?" Her tone was salty.

"Don't be a gutter rat. Why aren't you here?"

"I'm having a cup of coffee with Matte," Rhys said.

"Ohh-la. You're about to miss an entrance. Mrs. Wagner is walking up the steps as we speak. She appears to be peeping out from under a large, blackened pancake." He was whispering now.

"I thought you were making chutney today," Rhys said.

"Angel, the service is about to begin. I must get back on a higher plane. After church why don't you drop by for sherry and a bite of lunch?"

"What are you having?"

"That's rude. Grandmother would not have approved, but to answer your question, I don't know. Something good. Oh, and Rhys, would you lower yourself to helping me at the store in the morning? All this business with the police, you know. You can keep them entertained while they pry among our closeted skeletons. Speaking of prying, we found something that may interest you. I don't know whose, but we may have found a diary. Dah-dah!" Richard trumpeted more loudly than he'd intended. Sidling into a corner of the narthex to shield his next words, he whispered, "Sex scandals, embezzlements, circus performers, et cetera, et cetera; just think. We could be ruined."

"Whose is it? And who is the *we* who found it?" Rhys asked.

"Young McCrary found it this morning in the junk room off the catwalk. I left it in the stock room for you. Got to go, love; the choir is gaggling up to process. See you at lunch?" Richard had started back down the aisle to his pew.

"Morning, Logan, Addie."

"Merry Christmas, Fordyce. Long time no see." Logan reached for Richard's hand.

"You're right, buddy. Way too long. 'Tis the season as they say. Maybe we should try to remedy that. Maybe catch an eggnog or two somewhere between now and the big day. I haven't seen you out at Par Green lately. Are you and your pretty wife still members?"

"We golf mostly—dinner occasionally. Don't hang out at the bar very often," Logan said as the couple slid past Richard to take the middle of the pew.

It was known as the Adler pew, but anyone was welcome to sit there since the family presence had shrunk to him and occasionally Rhys, and his mother, Rachael Adler Fordyce, who would turn up in Riversbend ever so often. She usually was in transit either to or from one of the little time-shares she had dotted about the Western Hemisphere. She was currently in Aspen. She called this morning as she did every Sunday morning at six o'clock—her six o'clock, which meant when she was abroad, the telephone would awaken Richard in the wee hours.

"You still have your Christmas party?" Logan asked over a weak smile. Richard, cupping his ear as if he hadn't heard, bent to pull down the prie-dieu. All three knelt together.

Before the divorce, Logan and Marybeth, his first wife, had always been invited to his Tipsy Eve dinner. Richard had enjoyed them, and Rhys too. He actually missed them. But Addie Wagner hadn't gained acceptance in the group—at least the women's acceptance. They still pretended to wrinkle their noses at Addie's questionable past. Their complaint usually began with poor Marybeth. Not that many of the wives were lily white. They were more forgetful than chaste, Richard mused.

A few weeks back, broaching the subject of a Wagner invitation for this year's dinner, Richard teleconferenced with the two most broad-minded of their female friends in hopes of easing this pinprick to his conscience. At the end of a rather long and smug conversation, he cradled the phone in defeat and scratched a thin line through the Wagners' names. He accused himself of having no balls; Rhys had agreed.

"It's our party, Richard."

Rhys's solution, which was no solution, was to invite all three.

"Why not, Richard. Logan, Addie, and Marybeth. Just think how delicious. We'll have forced smiles and snide remarks and whispered asides for our early morning *tête-à-têtes* to carry us into next year."

Kneeling in the gray haze of guilt, and with Addie's perfume wafting about his head, Richard had little chance of keeping his mind on a higher plane for stretches long enough to satisfy one's weekly call to worship.

Off his knees and seated in the pew, he struggled to concentrate on the prayer book, but the evergreens banking the altar rail were fresh and fragrant, and he found himself wishing, not for the first time, that Episcopalians were not so ascetic in their liturgical tastes. Surely, they could allow a bit of red ribbon and maybe a sliver more silver on the altar. He couldn't think the Baby Jesus would mind. He sighed and pulled his attention back to the service. He managed to stay focused through all five verses of the processional hymn before devotion completely abandoned him.

If Rhys will come tomorrow, I can finish those ads, he mused during the collect. *Of course, I'll have to keep her busy, or she'll follow the police around, asking questions. So why do I want her?* He scratched his ear. *Ah, yes, she will be a nice counterforce to Miss Day.*

Viola Day was Richard's secretary-cum-bookkeeper, who scorned shoppers as interlopers whose only purpose was to interrupt her loud crunching of numbers. Viola Day could and often did offend the antique shop's best customers by closing her eyes, lizard fashion, when she saw them approaching her desk. If that didn't dissuade them, she would lift her tiny-hairy chin and growl. A frumpish powder puff of a woman, little more than five feet tall, Viola Day could cast gloom much like a vulture circling carrion. Richard considered firing her every week. But she was A-one with numbers. Never missed a decimal.

Rhys, on the other hand, was totally unpredictable. She would, on occasion, melt into the woodwork with an almost Victorian reticence. When she did go dormant, it was usually at times when people were gathered in large numbers. But in any case, with Raggedy Ann dying in their backyard, so to speak, Richard doubted not that Monday would bring customers into the store off the back forty. Riversbend had not had a mystery to solve of this magnitude since Beryl Hammer cut all the sleeves off her husband's suit coats in '83.

Churches gave Addie the heebie-jeebies. Every Sunday when she and Logan walked down the aisle, she imagined she could hear the congregational necks creak as faces turned to see what they could add to their list of grievances against her. Not that she cared. And not Richard Fordyce, perhaps. He was friendly with a nice bit of chitchat, but no sneaky little hands or fondness for accidentally passing her in tight places. He was a puzzle: attractive, attentive, but aloof too. She suspected if he could crack his upper crust, he would be as horny as the rest of them. She glanced, catching him unawares. His eyes, on slant as if studying the stained-glass window at the end of their pew, had been, in fact, assessing her hat. She tilted her head slightly and smiled from under the wide brim.

As soon as the organist hit the first chord of the postlude, Logan had dropped the prayer book and hymnal into the rack on the back of the pew. Was he an idiot to think that if Richard saw them, if they sat on *his* pew this Sunday before Christmas, it might jog his conscience, his memory, or his oh-so-arrogant sense of graciousness?

Fucking faggot. Logan knew Richard had heard him ask if he still had his big fancy-assed Christmas dinner. Logan had seethed throughout the church service. He had no intention of getting into some absurd conversation with him following the service. Richard Fordyce had skeletons. He wasn't perfect. He'd better watch out.

Logan grabbed Addie's coat, and taking her elbow, he guided her down the side aisle through the narthex and out the front door.

SUNDAY AFTERNOON DECEMBER 15

December gray with temperatures dropping, "Hark! the Herald Angels Sing" trumpeted the congregation out into the narthex on a swell of good wishes. In minutes, Richard zipped through the drive-through at Lotta Latte. He ordered hot chicken-salad sandwiches and chocolate scones and two grande-sized cappuccinos to go.

At Cedars, he transferred the coffee into a heated china pot and carried it into the library. He poured one cup and took it upstairs to Beau, who would be recuperating from the holy hysteria that followed the service at his Church of the St. Vitus Dance. This was Richard's preferred name for Beau's church. It was an apt name, and Richard thought it very funny, but he had to practice restraint in Beau's presence. Beau had accused him of being hateful. Such a painful word, "hateful."

Beau, back in pajamas, was stretched full length on his bed, covers up to his chin, but showing signs of recovery. After words of encouragement and a brief pillow fluffing, Richard descended the steps two at a time to wait for Rhys.

He lighted the neatly laid pine cones and kindling in the fireplace. When the crackling began, and a bright flame bloomed from behind a pair of Hessian-soldier andirons, he dropped in his easy chair and reached for the sherry decanter. Rather than cappuccino, he should push for a dram of spirits. He intended to plead once again for Rhys's assistance on Monday, and a tot of Harvey's Bristol Cream would surely smooth her resistance. He poured one for himself, splashing it in his coffee.

What a morning! He drew a measured breath. It had started like any other Sunday. Aspen had called at 5:00 a.m., which allowed him and his mother to wrangle for position in their usual guilt-driven conversation for twenty minutes or so. Then, bang, he was serving muffins to the Riversbend police force. Poor old Raggedy dying in his Dumpster had sent him to town, only to end up being interrogated by young McCrary. And then, if this weren't enough, he'd had the poor luck to run into Logan Wagner at St. Jimmy's.

The logs shifted lazily, creating a blaze of warmth. He wished Rhys would come on. He was hungry. He was not absolutely sure if she had agreed or not to drop by. His cousin could be a ridiculously irritating woman, independent, headstrong, bristling at the slightest whiff of a whole catalog of things she considered slights. Yet, if given a choice, Richard knew he'd rather be with Rhys than anyone. Autocratic, willful, maybe, but also fun. If you were lucky enough to know her deeply, it was easy to see that, under the layer of weirdness, she could be extraordinarily kind. She was his best friend. No doubt about that.

It had been a sad weekend. Young McCrary was right; he did know Raggedy pretty well. He knew she slept upstairs in the junk room from time to time. Why not? She had become a friend, of sorts. Frequently, bringing him the odd piece, some gaudy something or other from an unknown trash heap. "Something nice for you to sell," she would say. "Now, I've brought you a bit of luck in this one."

Richard heard a car spinning on his gravel drive. He grabbed the coffee carafe and his cup and hid them under the floor-length moiré cloth on the round table beside him and was flourishing his sherry glass when Rhys walked into the library.

After her chat with Richard before church, Rhys's curiosity was at peak. She couldn't wait until Monday to see the diary. As always when chasing after a potential clue that could shed light on Dora's disappearance, Rhys sought solitude. No distractions. It was 11:45 a.m. Richard was in church, so here was her chance. *If I can see the diary, hold it, I'll know if it was Mama's.*

She disinterred the keys from the bottom of her purse. As she drove into Riversbend, she braced herself against the exhilaration and the disappointment that usually followed one of these forays. Even so, she was never too busy to orchestrate a visit with a relative who wanted to reminisce, or one of Dora Adler's friends who suddenly remembered something Dora had said or done in the hours prior to the day she disappeared.

In the first months following the shock, Rhys had begged for facts that could quiet her imaginings, for answers that could end the endless questions. She had spent hours with her mother's lawyer, hours plowing through the vaults at Adler's Antiques, poring over dead receipts, old bills of sale, deeds, abstracts, and wills.

She had scoured her mother's massive desk to find deep drawers stuffed with bundles of correspondence tied in blue ribbon: birthday cards and Christmas cards with faces of children now grown and with children of their own. Rhys read stacks of letters long gone stale. But it was the grocery lists that had brought her to her knees, the simplicity of the ordinary, the marvelous everydayness of a grocery list.

In Riversbend one can get anywhere one wants to go in ten minutes. From the farm it ordinarily takes twenty. This morning in fifteen, Rhys was nosing her grandfather's 1955 vintage, red, paneled, small-block, 265-cubic-inch OHV8 truck onto the parking lot at Adler's. She parked adjacent to the yellow-crime-scene-belted Dumpster.

A section of packing paper blew across the empty lot and danced along the high side of the loading dock. But then she saw Raggedy's grocery cart. Unlike a standard basket, this one had baby-buggy wheels on the back. She recognized it instantly. Rhys shuddered at death; the way it took one's light and made mockery of one's possessions.

She glanced up and down Bayou Street. The buggy was too enticing to ignore—not to mention Riversbend's curiosity. Raggedy had died on their property. A crime, any crime of this magnitude, offered Riversbendians an unofficial, yet understood *right-to-know* license. Rhys knew her neighbors would believe it their obligation to poke into her, or Richard's, privacy, and in some instances to question their motives.

Assured she was not being watched, she touched a white sack in the grocery cart that made a disturbing squish. "Yuck." She quickly retracted her fingers. The cardboard around the cart, slightly damp from last night's rain, looked as if someone, not Richard, might have thought the grocery basket was for recycling. Richard was apolitical; he paid only a modicum of attention to anything unpleasant like holes in the ozone layer, or climate change, water shortages, or sorting one's trash. His civic duty, as he saw it, was to vote.

Eyeballing Bayou Street once again, she unlocked the door to the antique store and rolled the basket into the stock room.

Fingertips on point, she cautiously removed the top pieces of cardboard.

She easily recognized Raggedy's gray sweater with the moth-eaten elbows. She laid it aside. Shuffling the cardboard panels up and out from the sides of the basket, she saw a plastic tarp tucked tightly into a corner. From the opposite corner, she freed a brown-paper bag, and unrolling the nappy-soft top, she identified utensils, a tin plate, cup, and an assortment of plastic, some white, some clear, all cheap forks and spoons like homeroom mothers purchase for an elementary-school party. A family-sized bag of potato chips had been opened, but now it was rolled and securely clipped with a grocery-store chip clip.

There was a red vinyl purse, but no pieces of paper or little cards inside to help identify who Raggedy Ann was—really was—or what she did. No social-security card or insurance cards or membership cards to private clubs or gyms, not even one for a scheduled doctor's visit or hair appointment. On the very bottom of the cart was an olive-drab army blanket. Rhys left it in the cart and began piling the tarp and sweater, the paper bag of utensils, and the bedding on top. All the things representative of humankind's most basic needs.

She wondered why the police had not taken the cart. She didn't know that it had been discovered down by the bayou only a few minutes before or that it had been waiting in the shadow of the steps for Pauley to return with a larger police vehicle to rescue it.

Pushing the buggy-wheeled cart toward the large table where Richard mended and glued and wrapped and boxed, she spied what she thought was a square brown box, but on closer inspection, she realized it was the diary. Tears sprang into her eyes. With the cart and its mysteries, she'd forgotten for a moment why she had come to the store.

The diary was old enough to be Dora's, with an early twentieth-century marbled frontispiece. In the center was an ecru rectangular nameplate large enough for a name. And at one time, there had been one. Rhys peered closely in search of a trace, a mark that might identify the blur as Dora or Eudora or less likely Birdsong. At some time or other, the diary had been wet, and all that remained in the space where the name should be was a tantalizing smudge.

Turning the first few pages, which were prone to stick having dried tightly pressed together, Rhys saw there were entries in a light, precise hand, but it was not recognizable, nothing familiar. It was the hand of a female, probably a child's, maybe a teenager's. It could have been Dora's when she was a girl, before her mature hand was set. But not likely, and even so, her mother at this age would have been too young for the diary to reveal anything about her disappearance. Unless Rhys fanned through the pages, stopping once or twice to puzzle out an entry—unless she had come upon it in a trunk, perhaps, and reclaimed it later in her life.

Some of the entries were in ink, some in pencil. Sentences gone cold, and others faded with time. Jottings, numbers, clippings wedged between pages, tantalizing phrases as obscure as undeciphered hieroglyphs.

There were several entries in January and February of the diary's first winter, but as with most daily journal enthusiasts, the diarist's fervor gave way to monotony as the year advanced. Rhys did note with a frisson of excitement that the later entries appeared to be from multiple diarists, different inks, finer-point nibs, pretty scripts mixed among scribblings. But after a hurried perusal and finding nothing telling, she closed the book and put it back on top of the worktable.

Turning from the despair and disappointment that always accompanied her futile search for her mother, Rhys returned to Raggedy's grocery cart to stash it up against the wall next to a lopsided bureau. She started to leave for Richard's and the promised lunch, but midway to the stock room door she had a second thought. Hurrying back to the worktable, she hid the small diary in a drawer behind a pile of pencil stubs, dried ballpoints, partial rolls of packing tape, and X-Acto blades. She hid it. Not sure why. At least she'd know where it was should she want it.

⁂

Back home, a Sunday-afternoon nap in the back of her mind, Rhys retreated to the quiet of her library with a cup of tea. She curled in the well-sat relic of her favorite chair, warming in a slant of sunlight like a turtle on a rock. She should have felt dozy, but rather than sleepy, she felt uneasy. Her thoughts slipped back to the stock room and the diary and her strange conversation with Richard at lunch. Why hadn't she told him she had hidden the diary? If she wanted it, Richard would have understood. He would have been happy for her to have it. Why the subterfuge?

The diary might have been used by a dozen different women. Made from fine-grained leather in a rich chocolate color, the book, though scuffed, would have been eye-catching to many, to any antiques buyer. If it could speak, it could tell a hundred different stories. But aside from an historian interested in local history, Rhys knew it had little monetary value. Yet this small gem held secrets. Intriguing and disturbing secrets. Rhys frowned as she stared into her tea leaves.

The real question wasn't ownership. The question was, why were she and Richard being drawn into the mystery that surrounded Raggedy Ann's death? Was there something she knew, but didn't know she knew? Something they owned? Was it coincidence that the diary, which neither of them even knew existed until this morning, had suddenly appeared in their junk room, on the catwalk above where Raggedy Ann had died?

Rhys sat up. That explained her unwillingness to share the diary with Richard, didn't it? Until these questions of why were answered, the diary was her charge. She wanted it, and its intrigue and disturbing secrets, near her—for safe keeping, and perhaps for Richard's safety too.

Her tea having cooled, she took a sip before setting her cup on the small, round pie-crust table. Concretizing her odd behavior, thinking she felt more settled, Rhys lifted the idle Christmas catalog from her lap and began turning pages through perfumes, scarves, lingerie, and cashmere.

Unlike Richard, Rhys hadn't known Raggedy Ann well. She closed her eyes to draw the old woman's image to her mind. Physically Raggedy Ann had been stout and rather short. Her hair was orangey red, dime-store dyed, wiry and long enough to brush her shoulders. She was energetic, always talking, chattering to herself if she couldn't find someone nearby to collar. Always in motion, Raggedy was hard to picture dead. Had she known she was about to die? Had she been busy about life, and then, plonk, she was dead?

Plonk, no warning, no closure. Rhys had struggled in that airless limbo for months after her mother's disappearance. At least death was conclusive. Although, wasn't it said that ghosts were unresolved spirits, restless souls left to wander in a vaporous world until there was a resolution of some sort?

Rhys stood, arousing Jolly who slept beside her. She believed in ghosts, as do most people who grow up in old houses in which family possessions outnumber their own few pieces. As do people who live in houses rife with memories, and sometimes troubling values inherited from a plethora of dead relatives from a bygone era.

Taking the last sip, Rhys carried the cup to the kitchen. The dachshunds close on her heels. Rhys was a realist most days, but she was also intuitive. The realization that caused her cup to clatter as she placed it in the sink was that she no more believed Raggedy's death was from natural causes than she believed a man lived in the moon.

"Poppycock! We tend to see what we think we'll see. Look again, Rhysie, look again," her grandmother would say. "Look again."

At the sink Rhys stood very tall and very still to let this notion come into full consciousness. If Raggedy Ann's death was not natural, then didn't that prove there was another person involved? Whether deliberate or accidental, Rhys didn't know, but someone had killed her.

Unsure exactly how she was going to manage this, she walked to the nearest phone and began dialing Richard's number. Did she believe in miracles? No, but she did believe this diary had wanted to be found.

"Dicky"—she smiled—"I've changed my mind. I'll help you tomorrow, under one condition."

"And that would be?"

"I want to work in the stock room, and I'll distract the police, which will leave you free to ooze charm all over your customers, who you know will be flocking to Adler's, with that dead woman ending up in your Dumpster."

There was a hollow pause before he said, "I don't want you talking to the police, Rhys. I want you to come and anoint our customers with your cool, ladylike graciousness. Encourage them to buy or not, as you will, but do keep them from approaching Viola Day's chamber of horrors or from bugging me. Bad for business."

"*Au contraire.* Let the police nose all they want. I'll assist. I'll tell them things while I unpack. I'll even bring the Carlton goodies into the store from the stock room, and you can sell the stuff hot out of the box. Trust me; it will be the biggest day we've had since the fire sale in '72. Moreover, while you're striking your famous bargains, I'll chat up the police, and maybe we'll discover who wants us in the smack-dab middle of this mess."

"What a damn nuisance you are." She heard him sigh before he said, "You've seen the diary?"

Richard couldn't see Rhys cross her eyes, but he heard her hesitation. "Rhys?"

"I'm right here?"

"You have something up your sleeve. You can't deceive me."

"Only one arm in each sleeve. It's the style."

"You're hiding something. You're like a snake in long grass."

"Richard, I'm trying to be nice. I'm trying to free you from having police anxiety. Is anyone mad at us, Richard? Don't you think all this is strange, everything happening at our store?" She didn't give him much time for that to sink in before she added, "And yes—I have seen the diary."

Was confession good for the soul even if it was slant? "I don't know if it was mother's. Could have been. I'd like to have it. I'd like to ask the police a couple of questions. Is that snaky?"

"What kind of questions?"

"I haven't decided."

"You make me nervous."

"Don't worry. I'll come early, I'll use my own key." This was the danger zone. Richard was obsessive about the store. Rhys hurried on, "I can't stay all day, mind you. Company's coming!" With that, Rhys's plan smoothed out as though she had blocked the scene for a play. "Kate's coming." Obviously in matters of deceit, she was gifted.

"Wesley? Are you serious?"

"Afraid so. I'm trying to protect you."

"From what? From Kate Wesley? Good Lord, Rhys." His breathy resignation slid through the telephone. This was definitely the ultimate sigh, the last one. She even felt mildly sorry for him in his defeat.

Kate Wesley had been anathema to Richard since college. Rhys thought maybe she had jilted him. "Listen, I won't bring her with me—I won't harass the police—and at noon I'll leave. Is that unreasonable? I think not. Gotta go, *mwah, mwah.*" Her air kisses buffeted his ear with just the right touch of disregard. "Love you."

Rhys settled the telephone with a sense of triumph. Tomorrow she would comb the junk room, and she would assess the grocery cart before the police found it. And perhaps she would take the diary to the farm. She wanted to have it near her. How did Raggedy come to have it? Could there be some remote connection between the Raggedy and Dora Adler? Nah. Wishful thinking. But even if the diary could tell her nothing about her mother, it could shed light on Raggedy Ann and why her death was infringing on their innocent lives.

The Westminster chimes in the foyer announced an arrival: a person or a parcel, or best of all a Kate. She was humming a tune as she reached the door. The diary's mysterious presence, a woman's dying suspiciously in one's Dumpster—it was heady stuff, and having careless Kate around to help her plot would be a curl of icing on the cupcake.

She heard the door swing between the dining room and kitchen. She heard the dogs running in circles, their nails tapping on the tiles, at the prospect of visitors. "I'll get the door, Schreiber." She waved him back. "Keep the dogs in the kitchen if you can. Kate's here."

She gave the heavy oak door a tug. Swathed in her brightest smile and prepared to sing out her biggest welcome, Rhys's greeting froze. "Oh," she said, the tiny word drifting between her and her caller as dry and as light as a snowflake.

She had been about to kiss a stranger—a man, a noticeably dirty man. He sported what—had it been clean—would have been a burnished beard full to the collar. This afternoon it was dull with dust. Mesmerized by a small leaf caught in the thick of it, Rhys found herself staring longer than manners permitted. A moth-nibbled brown knit cap was pulled low on his forehead. All in all he looked quite the Neanderthal. She wondered if he had emerged mysteriously from some cave. Caves were common to Quick County. Spelunking was a local sport. Her first sensation on seeing him had been the color orange.

The man stared at the stone floor of the veranda, as though he were unable to raise his head. He made no move to enter the house, to explain his presence, or to acknowledge hers. He stood speechless, as if he had forgotten why he came.

"May I help you?"

When he didn't respond, she wondered if he was afflicted.

"Hello? Can you hear me?" she shouted.

This elicited an unexpected jolt. His arms shot up, and he stuck his hands straight out, splaying his fingers wide.

"I'm sorry. I didn't mean to frighten you. Are you looking for Schreiber? I'm Rhys Adler. I've seen you before, haven't I?" She couldn't think where.

His eyes darted to a bouquet of sugarcanes pressed into a Christmas wreath on the door and then to her face for a fraction of a second, but long enough for Rhys to see that he was younger than she'd first thought. And long enough for her to recognize he was agitated, and possibly dangerous. His eyes, very light in color, were accusing. He shoved his open hands toward her again, this time demanding by gesture that she give him whatever it was he thought she had.

"I don't know what you want. Please leave if you won't tell me." She started to slam the door, but he thrust his foot in the space availed him. It was a simple movement but abrupt movement that propelled his body against the doorframe, and he would have lost his balance, except Rhys gave him a slight shove that righted him.

"Either tell me why you are here, or remove your foot from my door at once!"

At that, with the jerkiness of a squirrel, he spun away from her and seemed to dart in several directions at once. Bypassing the steps, he leaped directly from the veranda, over the boxwood, and disappeared around the side of the house.

"Missy?" Schreiber had come up behind her.

"Did you know that man, Schreiber?"

"No, sir, don't believe so. I'll go check to see if he's hid hisself in the bushes?"

"Be sure he's not in the stable. The dachshunds had set up a howl in the kitchen. "Get Old Bay. She'll help sniff him out." Rhys edged over to the end of the porch, watching Schreiber investigate by poking a sturdy twig in the shrubbery around the house. "I think he would have barged right on in if you hadn't come to the door when you did," she said as Schreiber and the dogs came around the house.

"He was probably a runaway looking for a meal."

"Should we make sandwiches?"

"Hobos is a lot like stray cats. Feed one, and he's yours for keeps."

"He may not be a hobo. I think I've seen him fairly recently.

"No'm." Schreiber shook his head. "I'm not good at faces. Maybe I have; maybe I haven't."

Rhys had seen him. That morning he'd been standing on the grassy verge on the far side of Bayou Street when she pulled off the parking lot on her way to Richard's. She'd nodded to him.

"Schreiber? Have you ever felt you were caught up in some-one else's nightmare?" The bearded man's visit to the farmhouse convinced her she had right. She had been chosen for a role in a drama that was unraveling around her, and she didn't know why. Not yet, but she would.

"You oughter always let me answer the door, Missy." Schreiber interrupted her thoughts as he scraped the bottoms of his boots against the edge of the stone porch. "You, me, and my Matte are out here in the country by ourselves, no way of knowing who's gonna show up."

"Oh, Schreiber, I feel safer out here than anywhere on earth."

"Well, times aren't like they used to be." He didn't say it, but it had crossed his mind that Rhys Adler could disappear just like her mother. Stolen right off that porch, and who would know it. "Maybe I should install one of them little eye-telescope things in the door."

Rhys laughed. "Or better yet, maybe I should just look through these." She pointed to the glass panels on either side of the door.

"Yeah, that too," Schreiber allowed.

Rhys turned one ear to the road. "Listen." She held her finger to her lips. In the crisp, light winter air, sound traveled easily. "I hear a car." It was behind the hill and still some distance from the house. She could tell it was moving slowly by the way the gravel was being chewed a few pieces at a time. Whether it was moving toward them or away was hard to say.

"You remember my friend Kate Wesley, Schreiber?" Rhys was laughing.

"Sure I do, Missy."

"Well, prepare yourself, friend. I think we're about to be bothered by another intruder. And this one is far more dangerous." She laughed.

The bright feeling of orange faded as Rhys's thoughts left the whiskery man for Kate.

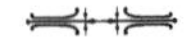

Rhys was a synesthete, a condition that gave credence to her sensation of *seeing or feeling orange* as up against the extraordinarily common sensation of *tasting an orange.* Had someone asked how one experiences orange, she would have been at a loss to say. Synesthesia suggests an explanation for this atypical condition, but it doesn't answer why a particular color or shape or sound interrupts one's otherwise normal palette of sensations. Why orange this time? Why not purple? Why triangles and not a double helix? As a child, Rhys thought everyone knew how orange felt and that the scent of machine oil brought a sensation of juggler's rings.

Waiting on the porch with Schreiber for the approaching car, Rhys remembered the first time she'd been enveloped in a sensation of color. She'd been a girl, young enough to be playing in the woods near the farmhouse. It was early spring, and on this particular day, it had started to sprinkle, causing Rhys to scurry for shelter in a tunnel of yellow blooming forsythia. It was her secret place. She had sculpted a room for herself beneath and inside a tangle of branches. Crawling inside to escape the unexpected rain shower, she came nose to nose with her grandfather's Irish setter, Bones. He was dead, bloodied, laid out under the bush as if someone was attempting to hide a terrible wrong.

Rhys had read that one's emotions didn't have a place in synesthesia. But her first experience at seeing death had been orange.

⁂

Rhys and Schreiber watched from the porch as the car crested Blue Creek Road and then turned onto the McGuire farm's private drive. It was still known as the McGuire farm even though a McGuire hadn't lived there since Rhys's grandmother had died a decade ago. The car approached through a double sentinel of white pines. Rhys could see the light bar across the top from the road. Now, as the car came nearer, she could see the distinctive blue and white on the side panels flashing through the trees. She assumed that the patrol car's arrival meant the law had nabbed their strange, bearded visitor.

Schreiber pulled up to his full height when the cop car rolled to the front steps and the passenger door flew open. Tick

Quinn, boots firmly planted on the ground, hoisted his large frame from the warm cab into the December chill. Making way for Richard in a full-length, sable-colored cashmere coat with a winter-white cashmere muffler neatly tucked around his handsome neck room enough to emerge from the back seat. From the veranda, Rhys bent down to see into the car. She expected the kid with the leaf in his beard to unload next, but no one else materialized. All passengers discharged, the patrol car eased off the pine-needled drive into the tall grass along the fence row. Parked to his satisfaction, Pauley McCrary pocketed the keys and caught up with the others.

Pauley had passed the McGuire farm many times, but seen from the road, the house in its tree-softened backdrop had seemed more impressive. From a distance the place appeared substantial and as rooted to the acreage as were the oaks. Up close, it looked like it could use a fresh coat of paint. It was a good house, large enough to be important but not arrogant. Built from wood hewn from trees off the land a hundred years before, the house still had its original sandstone chimneys, front and back. Worn steps, also stone, led to porches as deep as rooms. Four porches there were, a porch for each side of the rectangular farmhouse. The house was not fancy: two storied, but no imposing columns graced by prissy topiaries. Pauley glanced toward the softly rolling landscape around them. A small barn sat in the distance, but he could see no cows from where he stood, no chickens. He wondered why it was still called a farm.

"Miss Rhys." Tick removed his hat. "We oughter have called ahead instead of just popping in like this."

"Not at all. Our strange young visitor could be anywhere had you not come straightaway."

Ursine and awkward, Tick appeared to bob in his confusion. His smile ordered and quickly delivered, he stuck out his hand toward Schreiber. "Sammy."

"Tilman! Til!" Schreiber's hand was firm, and his response sang out on a note of relief.

Then for the next several minutes, Rhys and the collection of men crossed handshakes and exchanged neighborly greetings. All were saved from waning enthusiasm when Jolly and Old Bay bounded around the corner of the house.

"Quit licking, Bay." Rhys pulled the mother dog back from Pauley's pant legs. "Don't worry, they're half dachshund and half nuisance, but they won't attack unless you're bad."

Pauley, unsure how he would be judged, jiggled his legs enough to send Old Bay over to Tick for a quick sniff test. Tumbling over each other, the dachshunds led the assemblage through the front door.

"Psst," Richard, holding the heavy door open for all to enter, whispered to his cousin. "Don't say more than you have to."

Seasoned to his taunts, Rhys ignored him and turned to look for Schreiber.

"Schreiber, would you muster the dogs while I make our guests at home?" But Schreiber had already disappeared, leaving Rhys's request aloft and unheeded. Men were odd, she thought, especially around other men.

Offering Richard, the role of host, she followed Schreiber into the kitchen.

"Before you totally run away, old buddy, would you stoke up the fire in the living room?" She reached into her pocket. "And here"—she handed him a few dog treats—"see if you can entice the hounds to run away with you?" She smiled, taking the opportunity for a closer look. She couldn't explain the pink around his ears, or the look of—what was it, embarrassment? Or something else? It was as if Schreiber was somewhere other than their kitchen, somewhere very far away. "Schreiber, are you okay?"

"Just fine, Missy."

"Are you sure? I'll get Richard to grab the dogs, and I can stir the fire if you're busy."

"I'm fine, Missy. Better go take care of your company."

Her guests left to Richard's command continued to stand in an uncertain clump in the foyer. They watched the change in command switch as Rhys, hands and long arms flying about her as if she were conducting the Boston Pops said, "This way, gentlemen."

She pointed to the beautiful, old oak-paneled door ahead of them. "At the farm, we cherish our warm spots during the winter. The house is filled with drafts from all the ghosts flinging themselves around. It'll be cozy in here." She stepped aside as the police were escorted into the living room by the pair of dancing wiener dogs. Jolly led, his head held high, the silky auburn hair of his tail flying full show like a flag.

The living room was elegant yet obviously lived in with its old rugs and well-sat chairs. It was spacious yet cozy, and as Rhys had said, it was warm from the morning fireplace. Its scent was mostly of cedar and wood smoke. It was a long room, taking almost the entire length of the north side of the house, but it was a space, once he'd been allowed to enter, that Pauley felt he could live in comfortably for a while. A small stack of unshelved books on the floor by a large chair with soft cushions was not messy but nice looking, he thought, inviting. On inspection, he realized the room was not one but two. Pocket doors, two-thirds of the way down the length of the expanse, revealed a massive sideboard and a dining-room table large enough to seat a very large family. This put him off, made him sad maybe even a little mad.

Schreiber, appearing from somewhere like a phantom, laid a nice log on the fire and was leaning an extra piece against the hearth. As the room filled with men, he signaled the dogs with a sharp whistle, and all three retreated through a swinging door on the dining end of the room.

"Are we being arrested?" Rhys mouthed silently as she faced toward Richard, keeping the others to her back.

"No." His mouth and eyes perfect *O*s.

Rhys giggled, causing Richard to cough nervously into his fist.

Richard coughed often in Rhys's presence, usually as a warning. This one was an attempt to forestall a bout of what he thought of as their blooming idiocy. They could become a bit silly when nervous, giggly, patting people they didn't know well enough to pat, and he, especially, was always too chatty. This tendency, inherited from some mutual ancestor neither of them had ever known, was not an inability to take serious things seriously, but too often it was interpreted by others as shallowness. He was sorry about that; he was not shallow, and neither was she. To be fair, it was because they took serious things sometimes too seriously that he found himself reacting from time to time like a modern-day Bertie Wooster.

Seating her guests, Rhys pointed toward a large-bottomed library chair next to the sofa. "Mr. Tick, if you'll sit there, you can see all of us easily."

"Young man." She nodded to Pauley. "Richard." She motioned to a pair of cream-and-blue seventeenth-century wing back chairs on either side of the stone fireplace.

"Now then"—she peeked at her watch—"may I offer you refreshments? A whiskey perhaps? It's five o'clock somewhere, Yerba, Kuala Lumpar." Rhys, equally as comfortable acting the host or coquette, made Pauley's skin crawl.

Tick chuckled. "No, thank you, ma'am. It's a little early in the day for me and Pauley here. We don't mean to be a bother to ya. We're just gonna be here a couple of minutes." The officer's voice rumbled deep from the well of his barrel chest. "We're not here for another social like we had out at Mr. Fordyce's place this morning."

"Was that this morning? It seems eons ago," Richard said.

The policeman smiled at Richard. "Not that it wasn't a mighty fine spread, Mr. Fordyce. Much obliged to you." Tick nodded amicably. "But we need to get moving, so we won't be tying up your entire afternoon."

"Or Monday," Richard added.

"Or Monday, that's right." Tick started working the brim of his hat. "I guess you're wonderin' why we drove out here, Miss Rhys? Well, we need to ask you if this little thing"—Tick motioned toward Pauley—"if uh." Tick searched for a word unknown to him. "There's this here vase-looking thing, only it's too small to my mind to be a vase, but we was wonderin' if it might belong to you folks, or Miss Rhys if you might be able to tell us what it is. Mr. Fordyce, when we showed it to him when we was downtown—he din't seem to know what it was or even if it's y'all's. He says you"—he nodded to Rhys—"might know." He motioned to Pauley. "Go ahead, son."

Pauley pulled a five-by-seven manila envelope from inside his shirt and handed it to Rhys. There were three color photographs inside. Surprised, and surprisingly relieved that the content of the packet hadn't magically manifested into a discussion regarding the whereabouts of the diary, Rhys plucked the photographs from the envelope.

"What are they, Rhys?" Richard came toward her.

"Do these photos have anything to do with Raggedy Ann, Mr. Tick?"

Richard coughed another warning.

"Richard." Her eyes flashed. "Would you quit coughing at me? Are you ill?"

The two officers, surprised at this spurt of irritation from their seemingly airy hostess, wondered if she had the answer to any of the three questions on the floor: What were the objects in the photographs? What did it have to do with Raggedy's death? And was Richard Fordyce sick, and if so, was he contagious?

"A woman died behind our store last night, Richard." Rhys tempered her voice in an effort to offer an apology.

Her little outburst had sneaked up on her, rising out of buried emotions of which she was becoming only vaguely conscious. Seeing Tick seated here at the farm, in this living room after so many years, triggered painful memories.

"The police are here to investigate. They are wondering if this lachrymatory bottle"—she tapped the photographs—"belongs to us." Strolling to the windows for the best of the early afternoon light, she said, "These three are all the same piece? There is only one lachrymatory, right?"

"Yes'm. If that's what it's called there's only the one."

"Where is the real thing? The bottle?" She flapped the photos at Tick.

"At the police station," Pauley answered. "In the evidence room. That's where we keep evidence."

"Hear that, Richard?" Rhys, at last, dropped onto the sofa. "The man said *evidence* room."

"Is it a...a whad'ya call it?" Tick leaned toward her.

"Lachrymatory bottle. A tear bottle. I've seen either this one before or one very like it. I'm sure these pictures are representative of the actual size."

"Yes'm."

"Lachrymatory bottles can vary in size somewhat, but all are small, some very *bijou.* This one is no more than two, maybe three, inches tall. In the shape of a teardrop, very attractive and very appropriate, don't you agree? I recently returned from an estate sale. Were my fingerprints on it?"

"Kinda doubt we have a set of your prints on file, Miss Adler. You folks rarely show up on criminal charges." The misinformed perspective from which Pauley spoke was not lost on Rhys. Neither was his obvious aversion to her.

"You do have my prints, Officer McCrary. I was fingerprinted when my mother disappeared several years ago. You couldn't have known that. You probably were a little boy when that tragedy occurred."

"To answer your question, Miss Rhys, we haven't gotten the fingerprint report back yet," Tick said tactfully.

"How did the police come to have the tear bottle?" Richard asked.

"The morgue found it." This was all Tick had planned to say, but Pauley, eager to cover up his ignorance, jumped in, "In the victim's hand!

"That's interesting." Rhys looked at the photos again. The bottle was opaque and basically the sand-colored palette of the desert, although a greenish luminescence seemed to glow from the surface.

"If my prints show up on it, we can agree that I have handled it. It seems vaguely familiar. But if it's not listed on our bill of sale, it doesn't belong to us. I keep detailed and accurate records. I recently attend an estate sale in Delaware. I may have seen it there."

"*You* keep Adler's records?" Pauley asked.

Rhys lifted an eyebrow ever so slightly. "Perhaps I will drop by the police station tomorrow and kill two birds, Mr. McCrary. You may show me the real lachrymatory bottle, if you can locate it in your evidence room. And you can determine if I need to be fingerprinted again should you people have misfiled the original set."

Rhys held up a finger to stop any rejoinder.

"Please, I haven't been to the police station in many years by choice. And what I am about to say may come as a surprise, but I would like to be invited to assist the police with your investigation regarding Raggedy Ann, and I will begin with seeing the lachrymatory bottle. I want to see something other than photographs."

Amazed at the audacity with which she made this pronouncement, Pauley giggled, and Tick, being dealt speechless, gaped at Richard for male assistance.

"I can see you disagree, Mr. Tick, but I believe the mystery surrounding my mother's disappearance would have been solved if the police had been willing to investigate every scrap of information that came to them from the people, from our town, the people who knew her, who knew her ways, her habits, but..." Rhys's hesitation was dramatic. "But she was an old lady, and that was the prevailing attitude at the police department. 'She probably just wandered off.' You, yourself, said this to me as if that explained the department's ineptitude. 'We'll find her,' you promised. Well, she didn't just wander off, and you didn't find her. And now we have another old woman who died. And I believe that makes a viable reason for me to participate."

"Why...Miss Rhys," Tick faltered. "We did all we could back then. We listened to what everybody had to say. We talked to everybody who might know something. The public don't understand how we go about working a case." Tick looked down at his hat. "I don't want you to take offense, Miss Rhys, but I'm afraid, you don't understand either."

"Perhaps, but you can teach me. I believe someone in Riversbend knows what happened to her."

Tick paled as if he had seen a ghost. "Yes, ma'am," he acquiesced, not knowing exactly which old lady she was talking about. The room was silent for a moment except for the echoes of Rhys's pain and determination.

"Officer McCrary."

Pauley started at the sound of Rhys's voice.

"I had recently graduated from college when my mother disappeared. About your age now, I imagine. And I'm sure I didn't fully understand the art of investigative science, and I doubt you do either. Regardless, I still harbor reservations about the thoroughness of our law enforcement. I hope as an ambitious and freshman to the force, you will be assiduous in your efforts for *this* old woman."

Rhys turned to Tick.

"I'm sorry, my friend, I have no reservations about you. You are a fine man and a good policeman. You are, and always have been, kind and serious about your work. What you said about the general populace not understanding the work of the police is true, but it doesn't follow that no one in Riversbend knew what happened. And whoever this person is, he or she was never found or questioned, or maybe they were dismissed as unimportant. I don't blame you personally. You were young too, and you were not in command." She smiled at him. "Circumstances may have turned out differently had you been." Rhys sighed sadly. "But that's water over the dam isn't. Perhaps if I am to heal, I must quit picking at old scabs. Let's start over with the reason you came to see us?"

There was a murmur of accord as all leaned back in their chairs, waiting to see if the détente would last. Tick had managed to skirt issuing Rhys an invitation to join the hunt. Behind a stiff smile, he pondered how to keep it this way. He doubted it was over.

Cheeks flushed, Rhys opened the conversation, "Do you believe Raggedy's death was natural?"

"She was old. More'n likely it will turn out to be natural causes that killed her. We can't know much until we get the autopsy report."

"Ah, yes—old—natural causes." Rhys glanced at Richard who offered her an almost imperceptible nod of sympathy. "Okay, let's go back to the lachrymatory bottle? I'll need the invoice or my purchase list to answer your question as to ownership. I *want* to say if this one in the photograph is from the Carlton Estate, it must not have been for sale. Had it been, I certainly would have purchased it for Adler's Antiques, or for myself, depending on the price. It's quite remarkable."

"How much would it cost?" Pauley asked, seeing an avenue for a motive.

"They can be quite valuable, easily up toward two or three thousand dollars if you find the right market. Much more, of course, if it has a history, an important person attached to it, or a story, so to speak."

"When can you check your inventory?" Pauley ventured, hoping there were no embedded insults that might set her off again. He chanced a smile, hoping it could persuade her to find her inventory so she could answer the simple questions they came out here for: Was it Adler's or not?

Tick had known these people for a long time, but what did they really know about them? Either of them? He'd meant what he'd said about them probably not having fingerprint records. But he didn't believe their fine ways, and big word, and this rambling house made them innocent. But it did mean if found guilty, the police would have a hell of a time getting them to trial.

He tried to remember from police school what to watch for when interviewing a suspect. Shifty eyes. He looked at Rhys and then at Richard. Their eyes seemed okay. A guilty person often couldn't make eye contact, the manual had said. Something about jittery. Pauley continued his mental recital. Was jittery the same as nervous? Neither of these people struck him as being nervous about anything. In fact, the only really jittery person in the room was him and that big fellow they called Schreiber who'd disappeared.

"If it's a fake, it's done by a craftsman with an incredible gift for knocking off a piece."

Her voice, her words brought Pauley back from the police manual and into the room. She was pointing to one of the photographs.

"It's quite remarkable. The color and sheen are significant. It has been either burnished by a thousand years of desert sands or aged by a skilled hand, rubbed patiently for hours to create this patina of antiquity. If it is authentic, and as old as I think it is, it's very expensive. Look at the edge here," she said, walking over to Tick.

Her voice, low and as lulling as a lullaby, faded into the crevasses of Pauley's brain.

Swallowing a yawn, he popped to the front of his chair and glanced at Tick. "Looks to me like we've done about all we're gonna do here, Lieutenant. Like you say, we don't need to keep these people any longer." Pauley started to rise. All this talk about that little doohickey was wasting their time.

"Sit back, McCrary," Tick said firmly.

Pauley obediently fell back into his chair just as Richard rose from his. "Say again what'd you called this vase?" Richard reached for the photographs.

"Lachrymatory bottle. Tear bottle is the common name. Collecting tears in these tiny bottles during periods of bereavement has been a long-held custom in the Middle East."

"Amazin'! I am speechless, dear cousin, at the bits of knowledge you have cottoned onto, particularly weighed against the vast fields left untended." Richard chuckled.

"I imagine fewer are found today. Most of the sites have been cleared out by either professional archaeologists or robbers." Undeterred, Rhys continued her peroration on the tiny treasure from the dessert. "Depending on who gets them, the treasures are either in the museums or have been sold illegally to some private collector. Regardless, the most important finds, and this one could be one of them; it would be impossible to know without proper research, but it could be one of the ones found in the Qumran Caves. Remember the Dead Sea Scrolls?"

Drowsy, Pauley rubbed his eyes.

He decided to listen with his eyes closed for a minute. But in doing so, he hadn't heard her say, "Here's my purchase journal." Rhys had extracted a thin, multiringed, black binder from a desk drawer. Flipping through it she found the section and date she wanted.

Running her finger down a handwritten column with no apparent success, she walked over to Richard to exchange the purchase binder for the photos. "You look, Richard. I don't see the lachrymatory listed, but maybe it doesn't want to be seen just yet."

Richard's laugh was tender. "That's one of our Grandmother Adler's sayings," he explained to their guests. "When we were growing up, if something was lost and not immediately found, Grandmother would say, don't fret children; it isn't ready to be seen just yet. She believed it too."

"She did believe it," Rhys, thumbing along a wall of books behind the sofa, said. Then she added, "I should have something here about lachrymatory bottles." As she selected a small collection of books, she began building a stack they could research on the coffee table. "She was probably right too. Grandmother was. Take scissors. How many times have you searched for a pair in the same, identical place and found them on the second or third try? One would argue that you didn't look thoroughly the first time, but I wonder."

Tick, buried in the wings of his chair, wondered if the coffee she'd mentioned was ready. He sniffed the air not smelling any.

Richard stifled a yawn. The blood-rust stone of his signet ring, catching the light, sent a shower of prisms glancing about the room. Easily amused, he flexed his wrist this way and that. He heaved a sigh. Not often, but every now and again, Richard wondered if his aunt Dory might one day show up, even after all this time.

"You say Raggedy had the tear bottle in her hand," Rhys's voice broke into the spell of Richard's daydream. "Do we have any ideas about why?"

"Could someone have put it in her hand after she died?" Richard said, "To hide it, say?"

"Why would anyone do that?" Rhys asked.

Tick's face opened in interest. "That's possible."

"Why *would* anyone do that?" Pauley, stirring, sat up.

"But we're not here to talk about the dead woman, folks," Tick said.

"Of course you are. How can I help you if we can't be honest with one another?" Rhys thought of the diary and should have blushed; only Tick reddened for her.

"We just need to know if this here vase is yours. That's all. That's all we need to know."

"It is not a vase. You haven't been listening."

"I'm listening. You've just got a lot more to say than we thought. Is there anything else?"

Maybe it was the luminous winter light flooding her face, or maybe it was remembering his aunt Dory, but a flush of affection for his cousin swept over Richard. He looked at her for the first in a long time, realizing something about her that she didn't know. Age, his bête noire, would escort Rhys into the most attractive time of her life. She would come into her own. Her fine intelligence would appear less smug. Her sarcasm would soften into witticisms. As to her appearance, well, it remained to be seen, didn't it? She had never been what one could call beautiful, striking certainly.

"Here are some other pictures." Rhys turned to the index of a book she'd taken off the coffee table. "Richard, I'm surprised you didn't recognize it. We saw some of these on display in the Metropolitan one time."

"Yes, indeed!"

"Do you remember?"

"Not really."

He could see her as a child. A skinny, scraggly girl child, hair in her eyes, running beside him, often shouting at him, "I can too; I'm a tomboy," whenever he attempted to superintend her. He was older by a year, which, he assumed, gave him prerogatives, but he was just a plain boy, not a tomboy, which in Rhys's eyes was a liability.

To make her point, she learned early on to pee standing up. Richard never knew if she was successful or if she tinkled in her shoes on occasion. He smiled. Were they too old, he wondered, to reopen this topic over sherry some afternoon?

If Rhys was not as handsome as he, she was more interesting. A trace from the ancient line of Ben Adler's blood marked her undereye with a smoky smudge. When she was tired, it was noticeably darker; otherwise, it made her eyes look sort of sensual. But the smudge was exactly where sexy and Rhys Adler parted ways. She was the least sexy woman he had ever known.

She had an old-fashioned face. In another era, it could have been a contender for a cameo. But her cheekbones were a little too high, her chin too sharp, perhaps, and her dark chestnut, slightly curly hair still had a tendency to hang in her eyes if not controlled by a good cut or pulled back. Lovely eyes, though. He had never been sure if they were dark blue or dark gray, but they were bright, and they smiled, and at the moment, they were magnified by the glasses she had slipped on when her back was turned as deftly as a sleight-of-hand artist.

Bent intently over the photographs, he watched her shuffle them over and over. Her glasses had worked down to the tip of her nose.

A nice nose, Richard conceded—straight, with a thin flair at her nostrils. Aristocratic, he thought; snooty, some would say. He wished he had it. He had a common nose.

"Look at these." Rhys took another open book over to Tick. "Do you see what people are paying for them today? Even more than I thought."

Tick saw the figure and whistled. "I'm glad it's locked up. I'd hate for it to get broke."

"Damn tootin'. Did you find it listed, Richard?" she asked.

Richard reached for inventory register but was saved as the door from the kitchen swung forward and Schreiber backed into the room, carrying a tray with china cups, a silver coffee service, and a plate of cookies.

"There you are, Schreiber. If you can wedge the tray right on the coffee table between those books, I'll serve everyone."

She turned to Tick.

"So, let's be honest—you're here because you believe there's a connection between the lachrymatory bottle and Raggedy Ann's death?"

The policeman's response was quelled by a sudden and startling clatter followed by a shocking crash of fine china. All leaped to their feet only to stare helplessly at the mess on the floor. Rhys grabbed the stack of books still on the table, saving them from what would have been a milky bath. "My fault, Schreiber."

"I'll get Matte." Schreiber's face was gray. He disappeared to return in seconds with an armload of towels, a broom, a dustpan, and Matte puffing behind him with a damp mop.

All watched as the two threw the towels over the puddles, scooped up broken shards of china, and swept soggy cookies onto a dustpan, carrying it all to the kitchen without a word.

"I'm so sorry. This hasn't gone so well, has it? Have we said all we need to say? I can't find the lachrymatory listed, and until I see it tomorrow, I can't tell you anything more. " Rhys stood, signaling the end of their meeting. "Should I call before I come to town, Mr. Tick? I hope you'll be in when I arrive. I have a hundred questions. For one, unlike you, sir, I have a difficult time believing it was Raggedy Ann's heart that killed her."

"Me too!" Pauley cried out and instantly wished for a rag to shove in his mouth. "But that's speculation, right, Tick?"

Tick held up his hand. "Until the autopsy report is back, we won't know how she died."

Maneuvering his jacket off the coat rack in the foyer, Tick took Rhys's elbow and walked out onto the veranda, guiding her away from the others. "If you know something that could help us, Miss Rhys, I'm ready to hear it. Just like you said, you never know where the piece that fits is gonna come from. Call before you come, and I'll try to be there."

Rhys smiled. The change in Tick's attitude surprised her. She accepted the remark as an invitation to assist them. She thought of the diary tucked away in a drawer not five miles from him. "You'll be amazed at how helpful I can be, Mr. Tick. I'm freer than the police to roam around Riversbend and talk to people without being conspicuous, and I'll certainly tell you if I pick up on anything useful to us." She said all this, knowing that if the diary revealed an important treasure trove of information, she certainly would tell him—in good time. "One more question, do we know how she got herself in the Dumpster? I know I'd have to stand on something, like her grocery cart. Or a box or some kind of conveyance, a car, or truck—a ladder, maybe. Or someone could have helped her, or someone could have killed her and dumped her."

One man, half grinning, tried to imagine Rhys lobbing dead weight into a Dumpster, her long, skinny white legs all forks and corners. But the grin faded when he remembered the grocery cart still had to be dealt with.

Another man, less interested in Dumpsters and more interested in a plate of cookies, was wondering if he could slip back to the kitchen and asked Matte for a cookie and a glass of milk, and if he was lucky, maybe finagle an invitation to supper.

The third man said, "Hard to know how she got in it. It'd rained. There were no tracks. There was no ladder."

"May I be so foolish as to mention that damned little bottle for just one more time? Please, no more encyclopedic in-puts, Rhysie." Richard shrugged apologetically to the other two men. "But let's assume the lachrymatory bottle was wrapped in newspaper from the Delaware shipment, and it was still in the shipping boxes, and I, while unpacking, simply missed it. It was tiny.

Then later Raggedy found it. Maybe how it got in her hand is that simple."

"Boxes?" Both policemen looked baffled. "We only saw broken-down cardboard," Tick said.

"Raggedy could've broken 'em down. Tucked 'em in the sides of the grocery cart." Rhys didn't realize she'd given herself away.

"Cardboard makes good housing under bridges," Pauley said. When no one commented, he added feebly, "So, since the tear bottle doesn't show on your inventory, we can't make a case of *where* she got it, but we can suggest that there's a possibility she found it wrapped in newspaper, like Mr. Fordyce said, and broke down the boxes for shelter, which means she thought she had a future. She didn't know she was gonna die." He turned to Richard. "That was good thinking, Mr. Fordyce."

Richard shrugged modestly. "We may not know where it came from, or whom it belongs to, and we have no idea what she was going to do with it, but—"

"Does it matter? She's a junk junky," Pauley interrupted. "Who wanted her dead is my question?"

"Of course it matters," Tick barked. "If we knew whose it was, or what she wanted with it, we might know who would want her dead."

"I imagine she wanted to sell it," Richard suggested. "She did that you know. We were in the same business, of sorts, selling other people's stuff." They all sniggered at the absurdity of his statement. But it was true, wasn't it? Richard knew. Strange.

"Or hock it."

"Or she was hiding it."

That stopped the talk for a second. "From whom?" Rhys asked.

"Whoever put her in the Dumpster, maybe?"

Tick waved his hands to halt their idle guesswork. "Folks, we gotta be going. We could spend the rest of the afternoon playing games about who killed her. Go get the car, Sergeant."

"I thought you believed she died of natural causes," Pauley was saying as he turned to go.

"Did I say she was murdered? People can be killed without it being murder," he growled. It coulda been an accident. Maybe she fell."

Pauley was shaking his head. "You said hiding it from whoever put her there. That suggests another person. Some man she was meeting. We don't know."

"Or *woman*," Rhys said.

"Hit and run?" Richard threw in. "Dumped the body?"

"There you see how ridiculous all of you sound." Tick's craggy brow furrowed further in his disapproval. "Get the car, Pauley."

"Are you riding back to town with us, Mr. Fordyce?" Pauley asked.

"No, think I'll stay around awhile. Would you like for me to stay for supper, Rhys? You could run me home later. We could discuss the lachrymatory some more. You know, maybe I *have* seen one somewhere."

Pauley, laughing, silently moved into a slow trot toward the patrol car. He could put money on who would win this round. One thing for sure, he didn't have to worry about the bossy woman joining their investigation. He could tell Tick didn't cotton to that idea, any more than he did.

Slouched at the kitchen counter Sunday evening, Price Latimer stared at the boxy, old kitchen TV that sat squat on top of the refrigerator. He was making an effort to watch the six-o'clock news and weather but absorbing little of what the anchor was saying. He watched her tongue instead, which touched her teeth like a lisping child's. Tetchy, fidgety, Price slouched alone. Janine had escaped to the back of the house. He wished he could join her, chill out for a while before sleep, but his mind refused to unwind.

He wandered into the dining room and crouched in front of the credenza. Locating a fifth of Oakwood Reserve, he took a clean juice glass from the top rack of the recently run dishwasher and splashed a double shot into it, tossed it back, and poured another. To the third one, he added a cube of ice and returned to the TV to sip in leisure. He was dog tired and more than a little troubled.

Ordinarily Riversbend was a peaceful town, leaving Latimer untouched by grotesque old women turning up dead in inexplicable places, particularly when the inexplicable place happened to be on one of the Adler family properties. Price Latimer didn't like complications. He didn't like hoity-toity people or anyone raised with a silver spoon in his or her mouth. Princes or princesses, he called them, born horses' asses, the lot of them.

He'd had a bellyful of troublemakers in Bayou Bleu. Let some stink get on you, even if it wasn't your fault, and everyone in town suddenly wanted your head. "Dem findin' dat old bag behind Adler's is gonna be trouble, sister." He pointed to the weather advisor on the TV screen.

A few ounces of whiskey always let Latimer slide into his mother tongue.

Maybe it was the woman's voice, or maybe the familiar cadence of the Louisiana dialect, but Price's slippery thoughts slid back to that morning's anonymous phone call. He tried to pin a name to the voice. He could hear it, the soft lilt of the South Louisiana tongue. He could almost grab it. She'd invited him for a drink. He remembered that. She'd tried to stick him to Raggedy Ann's death like sticking a bug on a piece of flypaper. Latimer moaned. The old bag woman's death had to be dealt with before someone pointed to him. "Memory is long and vengeance is...sweet. Yah, I reckon, sweet."

He peered into his glass and swirled the golden elixir.

"Cain't mess up this time. Cain't let Tick get wind of dat phone call. That's all he'd need. He never wanted me here. He never liked me, tried to turn the men against me after I beat him out for sheriff. That was a jolt." Latimer chuckled. "Arrogant sob, never saw it coming."

Latimer squeezed the bridge of his nose.

"Less'n twenty days. I need to get him outta the office. Why cain't I give him the rest of December off...with pay...a kinda Christmas bonus for his long and faithful service." Latimer closed his eyes, trying to think how he could pull this plan off without drawing too much attention, but the sporadic flashes of light from the tube began to make his head hurt.

He tried to concentrate on the weather woman's voice. Soothing—calm. "There would be more sexy snow in Buffalo," she said, or someone said. He opened his eyes to see a man in rain gear, pointing at a drainage ditch.

"Sonabitch, what'd y'all do with the girl?"

Not always, but this time Price Latimer's special bottle of Oakwood Reserve was pulling him down. He didn't have any friends. No one he could trust. He didn't like Riversbend. He never would belong here. Whenever he was in the dumps, it wouldn't be long before his past would float up before him like a dead fish. It always did.

Price brought the last sip of bourbon to his lips. He was sure Tick knew too much. Maybe knew all there was to know about Price Latimer and Bayou Bleu. Scandal travels on short roads. And his scandal had been a real, above-the-fold headline.

His first wife, the love of his life, had cost him his reputation and nearly lost him his job. His career could still be in jeopardy if the disgrace surrounding her followed him to Riversbend. As it turned out, her screwing around on him had been the easy part. Humiliating but not devastating. Then she'd screwed him by slipping drugs to his jailed inmates. This had made Latimer, in the eyes of Bayou Bleu, not only a cuckold but also a joke, and totally unelectable. Then she turned up dead, in a cell, without a stitch of clothes on her sorry ass. Price rubbed at the sandpapery whiskers on his chin as if he desperately needed to rearrange them.

It was ruled a drug overdose, death by her own hand, but Bayou Bleu never acquitted him in their hearts. She was stolen goods, another man's wife, they said—so young, just a little girl off the bayou, way in over her head, running around with the sheriff before she was even divorced. Latimer's head sank into his palms. All he knew was the whole miserable mess almost sent him to the state hospital.

Latimer stuck the tip of his tongue onto the edge of the juice glass and let a last drop of amber roll onto it. In his unsteady efforts to get another drink, he tipped the bar stool, and it crashed to the floor. He listened for Janine. When she didn't holler as to what he'd broken, he thought he had escaped, but the telephone rang.

"Yeah...who's dis?" He'd grabbed the phone.

"Dr. Petitjean at the state morgue, remember me?"

"Hey! Yeah, sure I know who you are!" Latimer laughed on a wave of relief.

"I need to talk to Detective Lieutenant Quinn, and I haven't been able to reach him. Do you know where he is?"

"I guess you tried headquarters. You tried his house, his mobile phone?" Receiving affirmatives to both questions he added in a syrupy voice, "Well den, I cain't help you, baby. What else you got on your mind?"

"Only locating Tick. If you see him, tell him to call me. It's important."

"Tell me, sweet face. I'm the sheriff."

Then Petitjean began tossing out medical terms like a croupier with a hot deck of cards in hopes the sheriff's endearments didn't make her puke.

"Slow down, sugar. Lacerations, huh? What else?"

He wondered what was so urgent? So far everything she said was in the coroner's report.

"Back of her head…yeah…blood…Okay. No bruising on her throat, but a small bruise on her chinny…chin…chin"—he giggled—"and another on her hip. Okay, but dat doesn't rule out natural causes, does it? Cause dat's how she died." He tried to muffle a yawn. "No, I'm fine. Go on."

He listened without interrupting for a couple more seconds. He wished she would get to the point. Something about Tick coming or going back to somewhere or other. He wished his head had been a little clearer and his ears not roaring.

"You FedExing us something…Doc…Doc…" Latimer belched into the receiver. "You betcha, baby. Petitjean, I remember. Doc Petitjean. You're gonna FedEx the autopsy? Zat what you sayin'?

"No, you din't wake me up. I'm drunk, baby doll, and whatever it is you trying to tell me, don't seem to amount to a pinch of shit. Tell me again what it means to you, ma chere?

"Yes, ma'am. Doctor. Who could forget Petitjean, sugar?"

Still smiling minutes after their conversation had ended, Latimer was wondering if the doctor was hinting for him to drive down to Little Rock tonight. He thought she was saying Raggedy's death was a homicide. If he did go, maybe he could get Doctor Pussy to go have a drink with him. He looked at his watch. Naw, he was too far gone.

Besides, he didn't know if the bars were open on Sunday in Little Rock. Damn backward bunch of yahoos. He grew up in Bayou Bleu. He couldn't imagine folks not being able to get a drink when they wanted one. Hell, in Louisiana you could order a drive-through daiquiri on your way to Sunday school if you wanted one.

Atop a plump pillow at the other end of the sofa, Old Bay slept, huffing a quick, clipped line of woofs as dogs do when they dream. Jolly, belly up, ears spread-eagle, paws flopped at the first joint like tiny hands in furry mittens, snoozed in one of the wingbacks. Rhys pretended to read the Sunday paper.

Rehashing the Tick's and Pauley's visit left her with a preponderance of questions. Had any conversational missteps occurred that she had missed? Was there more to their visit than who owned the lachrymatory bottle? She was disappointed that Tick had not been more forthcoming. She supposed it was his prerogative, but it was not helpful if she was going to assist with investigation. If the bottle had been found in Raggedy Ann's hand, then it stood to reason that the owner, whoever that might be, could have a connection to her death. Was Pauley being honest regarding Rhys's fingerprints? Regrettably, if they did show up on the bottle, it would be one more tie she and Richard had with Raggedy's death.

Ah, Richard. She remembered Pauley's laughter as she had hustled her cousin into the patrol car. It hadn't been easy. She'd finally had to slip her arm through his just to get him down the steps. She had whispered, "Tomorrow," to his, "We need to talk about the lachrymatory bottle."

It was a bad decision. Now she wished for Richard's company. Today her normally well-ordered life had become a tempest. It started with Kate's call and impending visit, then the discovery of the diary, not to forget the bearded stranger, and then the police and the lachrymatory bottle. Exciting? But what did it all mean? And she had sent Richard away. There was no one but Richard she could to talk to in that special way she and Richard talked. He was the wall she could bounce her thoughts against.

She was bored. She needed to move, to begin solving the mystery, to do something more than just sit on her behind, asking herself pointless questions when there was no one to answer them or even to discuss them with her. It was Sunday evening, and as far as she could tell, she might be the only remaining human on earth. She couldn't hear Matte or Schreiber futzing around. She folded the newspaper. She could cook something, but she didn't really want to cook. She could telephone Richard, she supposed. Where was Kate? She should be here by now.

Rhys had been convinced for years that Kate's tendency to run late was a passive-aggressive ploy to gain control of Rhys's life. "Like I don't have enough controlling my life. Tennis on Tuesdays, duplicate bridge on Monday nights," she grumbled at Old Bay and Jolly, who were not really listening but who did open their eyes out of courtesy. "Don't look so innocent. You guys are as demanding as everyone else. Who is it that gets me up at daylight for a walk every day except Sundays and sometimes on Sunday, huh? Rut, rut, I say."

Rhys saw her months like a calendar in an old film. Days and weeks, page after page tearing away and flying off. Foursomes on Wednesday and Saturday, dinner at Par Green, *every* Friday night! Hair trims, manicures. College Board meetings the first Monday each quarter, church every Sunday, most every Sunday. Rut! Rut!

When she'd come home to Riversbend from the university, she'd dumped a load of suitcases and boxes in the middle of her bedroom floor, boxes brimming with the remnants of her youth. That May tired from exams and moving home, she was full of summer plans. It never occurred to her once that digging ruts was how her life would be?

Rhys leaped to her feet and marched into the foyer to peer through the beveled glass sidelights on either side of the front door in hopes of manifesting a Kate bumping along the drive. When she didn't see anything, she marched up the back hall into the kitchen, where she spun around a time or two, wondering why she was in there. Returning to the living room, she stood in front of the french doors staring out. Defeated at manifesting Kate, she returned to the sofa.

Why was she coming to Riversbend anyway? Rhys couldn't remember exactly. The occasion for the visit had seemed feeble, concocted. But that was Kate, engaging on the one hand and upsetting on the other, and never without a good story or excuse. Kate would spin a yard of yarn to sew on a button. And yet if Kate, who Rhys had known since childhood, was a riddle what could be said about Raggedy Ann? The other soul who had succeeded in thoroughly disturbing the monotony of Rhys's ruts? Who was she before she was Raggedy Ann? Rhys shivered.

Tomorrow she was going to drop by the sheriff's office. Maybe she could get Pauley McCrary to talk to her. Maybe together they could get the questions out in the air.

Good. Tomorrow she would begin. Good. She scratched the top of Bay's head. "Come on you two. Tomorrow's a new day."

Dachshunds respond well to routine, so when Rhys opened the door for the pair to dash off the veranda and make their way to their stable beds, she should have noted Bay's deep growl and her reluctance to leave the kitchen.

"Go on. It's your bed time." Rhys also failed to see the hair bristling on the back of Jolly's neck.

Shutting the door, Rhys veered toward the refrigerator to scope out Matte's cache of leftovers. Suddenly she felt hungry. She loved to stand in front of Matte's fridge and take bites or pull off small corners of some delectable sweet when no one was looking. But after a few minutes, not finding anything recognizable or very appealing, she kneed the door shut, permanently assigning some unknown morsel to obscurity in the back of the climate-controlled interior of their ice box that groaned like an aged bear in the quiet of the house.

In her defeat to find anything appetizing, chocolate sprang to mind. Fudge. And she didn't even need a recipe. She'd help

Matte make fudge for years. "Yep, Rhys old gal, beating a batch of fudge might be slightly better than laying waste to Kate when she finally arrives."

Upstairs, the television was turned low. Matte, nose always at the ready, sniffed once and then again. "Chocolate," she groaned. Matte had lived with Rhys long enough to know that when the girl cooked, something was simmering besides whatever was burning in the pans. She turned off her bed light and plugged her ears in defense against the freight train snoring at her side.

Eyes closed, she prayed that whatever was bothering Schreiber would be over soon and whatever tomorrow had in store would bring—but she never finished her prayer, because she too fell into the innocent sleep of the saved. The white light of the television flickered about the room unseen.

Downstairs melting butter, Rhys, too, was thinking about Schreiber. Accidents happened, of course, but more alarming to Rhys than the tray tipping, which was partially her fault, was the color that drained so quickly from his face. It should have been a flush of red, embarrassment at spilling the coffee, but his face was ashen more like shock. He'd been as surprised as the rest of them when the coffee and cookies had fallen. She tried to recall what they'd been saying when he walked into the room.

Cocoa added, she stirred, and watched the chocolate and sugar and oil marry. This forever stirring part of fudge making was the part she had a tendency to rush. But rushing, Matte had warned her, could ruin the batch. Rhys held up the spoon, letting the thin line of chocolate stream back into the pan. She was looking for the syrup to thicken. The aroma of chocolate was so strong she would like to have given up on fudge and just spooned the hot syrup into a bowl with some vanilla ice cream. But, obedient to her goal of helping Matte, she waited for a soft ball to form. She stood before the stove posed on one leg, like a stork.

Earlier that evening, after supper, when Schreiber had stepped out to "check on the weather," which was his euphemism for sneaking a smoke, Rhys had wanted to follow him, to ask if he was okay. But she hadn't. It was understood between the three of them that neither she nor Matte knew he still smoked.

When he'd strolled back in, the smell of tobacco still wafting about him, he'd attempted to cover his transgression with chatter. He started with, "I went ahead and fed the dogs. It's not too early, do you think?"

"I'm sure they appreciated it."

"I think after I lock up I'll go on upstairs if there isn't anything more you need for me to do."

"Nothing more. I'll let the dogs in after they eat so they can read the paper with me while I wait on Kate. I'll put them out later."

He nodded.

"Schreiber?"

He cupped an ear.

"Are you upset about something?"

"You women, always a worrying. Tired is all I am. I'm an old man," he said but not with conviction.

"Matte, why don't you both go up early? I'll help Kate when she arrives. I can lock up the house."

She shouldn't have mentioned locking up. That was Schreiber's domain, locking the house, securing the family. A man thing.

"Now who's worrying? I can do it just fine, old man." More words and further assurances took more time than Rhys would have thought necessary.

Thinking Schreiber was settled, she assured Matte that she wouldn't eat the beautifully browned rhubarb pie still warm and sticky with sugar before Kate could see its perfectly fluted edges.

Back to Schreiber, who palmed the banister at the bottom of the steps, fretting about Kate's arrival, Rhys assured him that she would be plenty strong enough to get her friend's luggage into the guest room. Actually, Rhys was quite proud of her strength. She worked out at the gym regularly—another item on her long list of ruts.

"Missy, are you listening?" Schreiber, having abandoned the banister rail briefly, was back, fiddling with the door. He stopped fiddling with the lock to look at her.

"Sorry, Schreiber, I'm listening." Rhys watched as he lifted the door slightly in order to secure the dead bolt.

"You have to pull up on the doorknob like this, don't you see?" he said, his voice in a strain at the effort. "Not so good for the knob, but the bolt don't ride into place right if you don't." He slid the dead bolt back and forth to demonstrate. "There now. It's locked." He said with satisfaction but then added, "Now Missy, after that girl gets here, don't forget to lock the front of the house too. No lifting the knob like back here, just lock it."

"You're the boss, my friend."

"I've got this door on my list of things to fix before spring."

"That'll be good."

"And should you girls have a mind to add more wood to the fire, remember little pieces. No more than can easily burn up before you go to bed, and be sure to shove any logs still smoldering to the back of the fireplace."

"Good night, Schreiber. Good night, Matte."

Smiling tenderly in her recollections of this pair, who were to her like family, Rhys lifted the spoon from the fudge. The thin stream of chocolate curled into a ball in her cup of cool tap water. It was ready.

As she lifted the pan off the heat onto the marble counter, a shadow caught her eye, a slight movement, more like a darkening at the door. Carrying the saucepan with her, she peered out onto the veranda. The kitchen, all bright lights and gleaming surfaces, reflected back in nine panes of wavy glass. When you live out in the country, you have all sorts of neighbors—some two legged, some four. She was safe; the door was stout, the bottom half solid oak.

If the shadow was not a deer crossing under the outdoor lights, it most likely was a bird, a blue heron maybe. They weren't that far from the Wachy River. She had heard a heron call as it flew over the house a few nights back. Rhys vanished into the pantry to get the hand mixer.

When she came out, a man's face stared at her through the window.

The mixer crossed the counter in a fling and slide, knocking the telephone from its cradle.

The pan of fudge in her hand hit the floor. Rhys screamed. She saw alarm animate the nameless face before it vanished.

Terrified, she ran back into the windowless pantry, her heart pumping wildly. Fully aware that she had cornered herself in the pantry with no escape, she listened cautiously for the back door to open. She listened for a turning knob, or breaking glass, but there was only her breath. Had she imagined a face? *It could have been a mop, a broom, a...a...something ordinary that had become...un-ordinary*. She peeked around the pantry door. *You didn't make him up. He wasn't a mop. Someone had been there*! She could still see his face mashed against the glass. Goose bumps crawled over her skin. Mustering a modicum of courage, she darted from the pantry's shelter into the back hall. The doors were locked. Thank goodness for Schreiber!

Oh my Lord! Except—she could hear Schreiber saying it, *"After that girl gets here, lock up front."* Courage bolstered by her more-or-less meager petition for divine intervention, she resolved to stroll to the front of the house and the front door.

Teeth clenched, shivery, and weak in the knees, Rhys doggedly restrained her gait as she approached the dimly lighted foyer.

Get hold of yourself, girl. Not every stranger grinning at you in the dark of night is a serial killer. Reinforced by her inner palaver, she quickly turned the front door lock. He probably wanted to see Schreiber about something as mundane as hay. Rhys was a level-headed woman, most of the time. She walked into the living room.

I bet I scared the squat out of him carrying on like I did in the kitchen. Throwing that pan of fudge across the room. He probably thought I was the mad wife who lives in the attic.

She consciously turned to each french door, locking, locking, locking as she moved along the wall of glass. Moving methodically, the shiny surfaces reflected the lighted rooms, blinding her to the black night on the other side. If the man in the window had been bad, if he had wanted in, she knew there was no way to keep him out of this old farm.

Where was Schreiber? Had he not heard her when she'd hollered? She did holler didn't she? Rhys knew her dear Schreiber was getting a little deaf, but Matte could hear some church friend's false teeth clicking two aisles over. And why weren't the dogs barking?

Was he still out there? The face through the glass panes had seemed unusually short for a grown man. Was he grown? An adult would have knocked if it had been a friendly visit wouldn't he? Or tapped on the glass like any normal person, maybe even tipped his hat? Was he normal?

He wore a hat! Her father would have called it a fedora. The face, triangular, with an extraordinarily wide, high brow, and a narrow chin, like a fox, had been framed in the lowest panes of glass, and the fox wore a fedora.

This man had unnerved her far more than the bearded guy from that afternoon. Yet the face did not evoke a taste or a color as had the first man. Had she not seen alarm cross the fox's face, she could have said his features were wooden, deeply carved, puppet-like. The grotesquery of her imagination hurried her into her bedroom, slamming her shutters as she passed them.

The doors were locked. She sat on the edge of her bed, listening. Rhys was not skilled at fooling herself, and tonight's ordeal was not over. She had to go back out into the house, Kate was coming.

Ten minutes passed and hearing nothing more than the sweet hiss of the radiators, she left the security of her room, picking up a porcelain figurine of a dancing girl from her dresser as she passed. She edged cautiously along the wall down the darkened hall into the kitchen. She was not thrilled; she would rather have stayed in the safety of her room, climbed into her bed, and stuck her head under her covers, but she had a fudge-sticky floor to clean up before morning. Not to mention, Kate, damn her sweet hide, who had not arrived. Summoning her last bit of pluck, she took a deep breath and stepped into the kitchen to see the back door standing wide open.

The ballerina lost a dainty foot when she hit the tiled floor. Rhys's scream was deafening. She karate-kicked the gaping door shut and ran into the pantry, grabbing the first weapon she saw. Out of the pantry and into the foyer, she bolted up the stairs toward Matte and Schreiber's apartment, as she took the turn on the landing a shadow moved over her.

"Land sakes, girl! What you after with that flyswatter?"

Nerves shattered, Rhys flung the flyswatter at the shadow. This time her shriek, shrill, overdue, and unanticipated, startled Schreiber. He jumped, swore, and stumbling backward in the commotion, shot a hole in the ceiling the size of a quarter. A shower of plaster dust rained down on both of them, just as Matte topped the stairs with a loud, "What the heck's going on in this house? Is it that Wesley girl causing trouble?"

It took a while for things to settle. The foyer was vacuumed, the police were called, and the grounds searched. Unable to find a short man, a macabre comedian, a puppet, or a fox in a fedora, Rhys and Schreiber, plus the two cops who'd been dispatched did find the dachshunds. They were in Rhys's truck, mildly sedated but breathing normally. Schreiber gently wrestled the animals from the cab, and Rhys, peering at her babies in his large-man arms, cooed softly as he carried them to their bed in the corner of the stable. Now they were curled together on a nest of straw and flannel blankets. Schreiber brushed his hands together in a gesture of satisfaction.

"Much obliged to you for coming out here again." Schreiber had followed the pair of county officers back to the patrol car. "If we have any more trouble, I'll let you know. I ain't expecting none. We've had enough excitement for one day."

"Thank you so, so much," Rhys said, waving them down the drive.

Back in the kitchen, after a brief puzzling with Schreiber over who the man in the window might have been, she announced that, after a cup of tea, if she had any hopes of getting the plaster dust out of her hair, a nice shower was in order. Otherwise matters weren't too altered. The dogs were okay. The ceiling wasn't too badly damaged. What would it take: a tall ladder, a plug of plaster, and a can of ceiling white?

"Who all wants a cup of tea?" Matte asked.

"I'll tend the kettle," Rhys volunteered happily, relieved to participate in the normality of a favorite ritual.

"None for me," Schreiber called back over his shoulder. "I'm going back to bed.

"Thank you, Schreiber."

"Accepted." He paused with perfect timing before he added, "You know I learned something new today. I'd never learned till tonight you could hit a ghost with a flyswatter?" He disappeared up the steps, but he was smiling, the women could hear it in his voice.

The water hot and turning amber in their cups, Rhys recited her adventures to Matte. She told her about the bearded man's visit even though she knew Schreiber had already done so. Then she told her about Raggedy Ann's, a.k.a. Francie Butter, grocery cart. She probably would have told her about the diary, except they heard a car turn onto the drive.

"Kate's here!" Both women sprang to their feet. "Let me wrinch out these cups and get on upstairs so you girls can be in here by yourselves for a good visit and a nice piece of pie before going to bed." Matte seemed almost giddy.

"Leave the cups, Matte. We'll wash up. Good night, Matte, and thanks. I don't know what I would do without you. You know that, don't you?"

Matte smiled. "Us too. Me and Schreiber feel the same. I'm wide awake if you decide you girls might need me for anything," she added with only a tinge of hope.

"We'll see you in the morning. Remember, no need to fix us any breakfast."

Rhys pulled her robe closer and walked out onto the front porch. Pressing her thumb and forefinger against her tongue and teeth, she produced a whistle shrill enough to rouse Morpheus. In a few minutes, Jolly ambled up, stretching and yawning. "Where's your mama, boy? Bay still got a hangover?" She scratched behind the pup's ears. "You guys want to sleep in my room tonight?"

Jolly stretched out his long body, yawned again, not caring a tittle that a string of flashing blue lights had turned into the narrow lane that led up to the house.

"What now!" Rhys watched for the third time that day as a short police motorcade came up her drive between the sentinels of white pine trees.

The blue-and-white pulled into the circle drive and stopped. Price Latimer emerged from the passenger side of the first car, followed quickly by Lockhart, his driver, who Riversbend had branded Latimer's rat. The rat was in the process of growing an unattractive mustache. The rat opened the back door. Rhys could hear a string of unfortunate words, which were followed by the emerging of a woman's leg, then a whole woman in a full-length fur coat.

"Sorry ta bother you folks, but this woman says she's stayin' with you." If Rhys hadn't known better, she would have thought the sheriff sounded a little inebriated.

"For God's sake, Rhys, tell these simpletons you know me." Kate flounced up the steps and over to Rhys. She pointed a finger at Price Latimer. "And don't forget my suitcase is in the trunk either."

Kate Wesley reached for her shoulder bag and fumbled around for some change, which she palmed off to Latimer as a tip.

"Have you done something different to your hair, Rhys?"

MONDAY DECEMBER 16

A True History of the Josiah Radley Family of Riversbend Arkansas

by Miss Isabella Jane Radley

Riversbend pioneers settled in an ideal location graced, as it was, by the Wachy River on its southern boundary.

Isabella Radley dotted the end of her opening sentence firmly. Easing her bony back into her father's old windsor chair, she gazed at the Belle Meade ceiling medallion that crowned the modest chandelier above the dining-room table where she composed her family history. The medallion didn't register in her thoughts because her head was crowded with visions from another time. This morning she worked on Riversbend's beginnings.

> Fertile on the south and east, the settlement nestled its right shoulder into the gently folding foothills of the beautiful Ozark Mountains.

Isabella Radley smiled. She loved it when she could turn a pretty phrase.

> Josiah Radley came to Arkansas in 1855 from Georgia with his cousin, Charles R. Radley. Both young men settled in what would soon become Quick County. Ambition drove their industry, and with their successes, they grew independent. From struggle, they learned to embrace a practical God, as well as to live by practical wisdom.
>
> Most of Charles's progeny would become farmers, a hard-working, frugal, conservative lot with a propensity toward downright muleheadedness. Josiah's sons, also farmers, invested further down river in the loess-capped fertile soil of the Wachy River bottoms. In time, and with true integrity, they married into well-established families and built for themselves, and for their descendants, easier lives.

"Easier." Isabella wasn't sure she liked her word choice. Easier, perhaps, but with good intentions, she felt confident. "Like young Ben Adler coming here from New York and marrying the McGuire money," Isabella said to a cardinal feeding outside her window. "I can still hear Papa, 'The Birdsong girl, only child, mind you, made a good marriage even if it was unconventional. The boy may be a Yankee, and he may be Jewish, but he isn't afraid of hard work. He'll add to McGuire fortune.'"

Miss Radley, the town's most revered historian and keeper of its collective memory, not to mention the founding mother of the local chapter of the DAR, capped her fountain pen and laid it across the sheets of fine vellum in front of her.

She could have told many stories from Riversbend's past. And yet, true to her father's teachings, she followed his advice scrupulously. "Sister, don't tell all you know. History can be a teacher, or an assassin." Her father's warning, though the man had been dead these many years, Isabella still found to be a prudent one. She savored the town's stories but kept most close to her chest. "History lives like a vapor all around us, unseen but present," she informed the red bird, who wisely cocked his head.

Isabella, elbows on the table, fingers steepled, was deep in thought. She was in a sticky situation. In remembering the Birdsongs and McGuires, she recalled another story. Trapped in the coils of time, her agile mind sprang to a series of seemingly unrelated incidents. Was it mere speculation, or had a crime been committed? Something terrible had taken place if her father had been correct. And it was this that created her dilemma. Unawakened remnants of history lingered in the human psyche, she believed—shapeless and nameless but capable of exploding into the present. Was it blood hatred, she wondered. She picked up her pen. It was just a fragment of a story, but there had been talk.

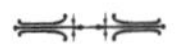

Frost as heavy and white as a light snow sparkled in the fields on Rhys's drive into town on Monday. She was in the Jeep. She was not aware of this idiosyncrasy to drive the Jeep when she was feeling adventurous, but she drove it this morning. Today she was going to do some investigating. First the diary. Raggedy's death was a police matter, but she'd already decided she would not offer the diary to Pauley when she went to be fingerprinted. He knew it existed. And he knew where it could be found if he wanted it. At the moment it was more important to her. If it had been Dora's, what was Raggedy

Ann doing with it? Rhys pulled the Jeep in behind Adler's, stopping as near the back doors as possible.

Downtown before seven o'clock, it was very quiet; Main Street's businesses were not yet open.

The yellow crime tape flapped loosely. Only a smattering of factory people on their way to or from work, shift people, gawked at their now-infamous Dumpster.

According to procedure, the tape could not come down until after the autopsy. But Rhys, grabbing her shoulder bag and scooting out the car door, knew nothing of procedure.

Accustomed to dancing around rules, she ducked under the tape.

⸻

As the highest-ranking officer in the homicide division of the metro police, it was Tick's responsibility to say when the crime tape came down, but when Pauley walked up to the lieutenant's desk Monday morning, he was greeted by Tick's complaints from around a thermometer sticking out of the side of his mouth. "I have a splitting headache," he said, which sounded to Pauley more like *spitting* headache. "And when I tell you to, you need to go take the tape down."

"Don't talk. It won't read right." Pauley put a hand on Tick's forehead much like Mrs. Robinette had done when Pauley was a boy. "You don't feel like you got any fever," he said, diagnosing. "You getting a cold? What you getting a cold for? I know why you're getting a cold, because you didn't let me drive you back to Little Rock after the morgue called you back, and you've wore yourself out. And what's wrong with your hand? Why've you got it stuck in half a sock?"

Tick grumbled before he extracted the slender tube and rolled it between his fingers, searching for the thin, almost imperceptible line of mercury.

"Here, let me see that thing. You too old to see it good." Pauley slipped the thermometer from Tick's fingers.

"Give me that. I can read it, and why are you talkin' like you're straight outta a cotton row this morning?" Tick snagged the thermometer, twirling his chair, turning his back to his partner. "See what'd I tell you. It's over a hunnerd." He glared as if it were Pauley's fault. "I want you to hang around so I can tell you when to take the crime tape down back of Adler's. You'll have to wait till after we hear from the postmortem. But until then, I want you to start asking questions. Someone put that woman in that Dumpster, and there's a good possibility someone saw him do it."

"How am I gonna do that if I'm hanging around here with you?"

Tick glared at him.

"You sure changed your tune all of a sudden. Yesterday you were all about natural causes, and now you're saying someone killed her? And I'm just saying you're speculating all over the place. It might not be a him who did the killing. Did you ever think of that?"

Tick shook his head. "All I'm saying is we don't know anything yet. But it's a busy street, even if it is a backstreet, and if someone knows what went on, we need to know who it is, and what in the hell they saw."

"Uh-huh, I hear you. So, someone really did kill her?" Pauley could hardly keep the excitement out of his voice. "And that's why the morgue wanted you to drive back down to Little Rock? I can't believe you sneaked off without me." He hit Tick's desk once for emphasis. "They need to get to know me down there."

"I was doing you a favor. I had to turn around and go back right after we got home from escorting the deceased to the morgue the first time."

"Uh-huh. Well, I could have been ready. Anyway, what'd they call you back for?"

"Quit asking questions. Just don't go goofing off somewhere I can't find you."

"So, what did they say?" Pauley tried.

"So, get going."

Pauley nodded. "Okay, I'm going. But I know they told you something you're not telling. I'm still your partner, aren't I?"

"They found a piece of chewing gum up her ass."

Pauley's eyes got big. "No kiddin'!"

Tick's big laugh was more a roar. "The point is, Brother Gullible, what difference does it make? You know how forensics is. They tell us what they think; we're the ones who've got to make it stick. And I have a headache. Go away."

Pauley framed by the door stared at his partner. He bobbed his head toward the socked hand. "So, what's with the sock?"

"I scratched it somewhere. Don't remember it happening. The sock is to keep Willa's antiseptic ointment on it." Tick looked up from his bandage. "Now go away. Make yourself useful. Go make a list of everything we have from Saturday night, including all the crap that came out of the Dumpster, off the ground around the Dumpster, and her grocery basket—once you had enough wits about you to find the damn thing. Should of found it that night."

Pauley paled. He hoped the grocery cart was still at Adler's. By the time he'd located the mobile unit in the carwash, the grocery cart was not on the loading dock when he'd gone back to get it. Mr. Fordyce must have put it in the stock room. He hoped Mr. Fordyce had put it in the stock room. Truth be told, after their visit to the McGuire farm, Pauley had forgotten the grocery cart.

"I knew a man who died of lockjaw once." He motioned to Tick's hand.

"Thanks."

"Why are you holding out on me?" Pauley took a step back toward Tick. "I know you are because the only material evidence we have is that little bottle thing, and I don't think they called you to come back just for that when they could have shipped it Priority Mail or FedEx or UPS."

"You're an expert on forensics now, are you?"

Pauley clenched his jaw.

"Go see if you can encourage Latimer to go have another cup of coffee across the street at the Coffee Cupp. Keep him struttin' around, and maybe he'll stay off our butts till this thing is solved."

Pauley didn't like being treated like a flunky. He turned half around. "Are you sure you want me helping on this case? There's no point in me hanging around a coming-on cold, if you don't want me here."

"Right now, I don't give a damn one way or the other. Right now, I don't give a damn about this case."

"What's wrong with you? I thought we was getting on good together."

"Pauley, I just gave you an assignment. Now go nose around, and, for God's sake, quit sulking."

"If you decide you need me, you'll have to come find me." This time Pauley did leave. Tick could hear him tromp all the way to the front desk.

"I'm going for coffee," Pauley grumbled a minute later to Gladys Gray, who was perched behind the information desk with a telephone receiver in both hands. "If his royal heinie wants me, come get me."

"Kiss my grits," she said.

"Maybe later."

Rhys flipped on the lights in Adler's stock room. A one-hundred-watt bulb high up in the ceiling, competing momentarily with a surprisingly bright morning sun that poured through the high windows on the north side of the workroom, could only throw a meager light onto the floor. Raggedy's grocery buggy, still by the lopsided bureau, beckoned like a lone piece of a devil's food cake. She hurried to the worktable and in seconds had dropped the diary into her pocket. Its weight was reassuring.

Task accomplished, she maneuvered the buggy in the crowded stock room. It was a manly chore, weaving it around boxes and dollies, rolling it between an upturned Regency chair and bolts of fabric; between shelves laden with assorted spindles and rungs, knobs and brasses, all carefully labeled and waiting to restore the odd highboy, tea table, or bureau, Rhys navigated a jagged course. And for a gawky, tall sister with long feet, she navigated it rather quickly. Once it was under the pathetic light, she scurried back to secure the double doors with a thick wooden crossbar.

"In for a penny, in for a pound," she hummed nonchalantly, yet betrayed by her fingertips, which were tapping together softly as she wove in and out of the stock room's jumble. Eager to be at her task, eager to be back to Raggedy's belongings, her plan was to inventory them. She felt just the merest guilt knowing that just any old body shouldn't go poking around in the grocery basket, taking whatever caught their fancy. But Rhys had not been raised to feel like just any old body. The lachrymatory bottle found in Raggedy's hand that could have come from the grocery basket—not to mention Rhys's precious diary—and these certainly could have bearing on the case. And from whom did Raggedy get these items? Whose trash told the story of these things? And there could be other clues from wherever Raggedy got these little jewels. That was a thought worth developing. The woman did have a penchant for snooping. She couldn't imagine why the police hadn't taken the basket. It was right there in plain sight.

Rhys, being smart, had remembered to bring gloves. She wiggled her fingers into them much like a surgeon. Eyeing a narrow shelf above the grocery cart, she removed the diary and propped it open. First she wanted to see if there was mention of—or a listing of—or for information regarding from whose trash barrel she had rescued this or that item. For instance, wouldn't it be interesting if the diary would tell her Raggedy had found her red vinyl purse in such and so's trash, it would give her an opening of where to start asking questions. What's to say the diary itself couldn't have come from the same location?

As the early sun, ever faithful this morning, continued to light the stock room, Rhys saw that the diary's brown leather was slightly stressed, and the stitching at the spine was loose, holding the pages more precariously than she had at first thought. In the daylight, she could see that it also was soiled. Picking it up she blew on it—her preferred method of dusting. She blew at easily imagined germs, sending legions of dust spores and miniscule feather mites toward her sinuses. "Aghh!" She sneezed loudly once, twice, but after a good nose blow, and determined to inventory, she pulled up a stool to the front of the grocery basket. The first item out was a gray sweater that she lifted by a holey elbow. Neiman Marcus! Now that was telling. There were only a handful of people who she knew who might have owned a sweater from Neiman Marcus.

Half an hour of emptying Raggedy's grocery basket and finding no associative clues in the diary, Rhys returned the diary to her coat pocket. Watery eyed from dust particles swimming in a wayward ray of sunlight, she walked briskly out onto the parking lot. Inhaling the crisp morning air deeply, she hurried to her Jeep to stash the little chronicle before Richard could arrive and catch her. The fragile journal fitted easily into the glove compartment. One last sneeze, forestalled until now, sealed her sense of purpose.

Returning to the stock room, she buried the grocery cart under a swag of silk velvet, real velvet, that Rhys pulled from a coat hook, where it had been hanging for at least a decade, waiting to be tossed into the Dumpster. It was too old and damaged to upholster even a vanity chair, but Richard, having an almost lascivious lust for the lusciousness of the supple Blue Boy blue velvet, didn't have the heart to dispose of it.

Satisfied that no one would notice the draped cart until she could decide what more to do with it, she set her mind to concentrating on at least one honest task she'd promised Richard. She began unpacking one of the crates from Delaware. As she worked, she planned the remainder of her morning. She wanted to go get fingerprinted, and while there, she hoped to make a fresh beginning with young McCrary. She was fully aware that he didn't like her, but she needed his approval if she wanted to be involved in the case. Not that he would be aggressive on her behalf, but he was little more than a boy, and certainly unwise to the wiles of a woman like her.

As she unpacked, Rhys's thoughts returned to Kate and the evening before. She relived bits of conversation and laughed again at some of Kate's shenanigans. She was pleased, too, at how interested Kate had been in hearing more about Raggedy Ann, about finding her behind the store in what she began referring to as the infamous Adler Dumpster. The two stayed up too late, talking and hatching plots for how Rhys could inveigle herself into service despite a reluctant pair of policemen.

This morning Rhys had left Kate to sleep off her portion of last night's single malt and to enjoy a leisurely breakfast. But later today, Rhys's sweet, butter-won't-melt-in-my-mouth, southern-hostess considerations would briefly have to be set aside. Like it or not, she was going to question Kate once again but more thoroughly about her peculiar arrival in Riversbend that resulted in a police escort to the farm. Kate's was a convoluted story, and Rhys knew Kate well enough to know she was a person who, occasionally, preferred fibs to truth especially if the fibs offered her an advantage. When Rhys got home, her task was to find a comfortable explanation and also to figure out why Kate needed an edge. What advantage she was after. Her account of the police confiscating her car and then driving her out to the farm didn't quite gel in the clear light of day.

Six smaller boxes and a large wooden crate from the estate sale in Delaware were stacked, waiting in one corner of the stock room. Finding the box cutter, Rhys slipped the blade between several tightly drawn yellow plastic strips of packing tape. Sawing energetically, she watched as they fell to the floor and coiled like pigs' tails at her feet. In minutes, all the boxes were unleashed, and their flaps pulled open. Eager again to caress the treasures she purchased at the Carlton estate sale, she removed the first layer of fat Styrofoam worms, whose sole goal in life, apparently, was to tenaciously cling to her blue fisherman's knit sweater.

She had unwrapped a small antique oil lamp when a sharp bang rang against the stock-room door. The lamp fell to the floor and shattered.

"Dammit!" Rhys whirled around expecting Richard. "Look what you made me do!" But it wasn't Richard, rather her woolly-capped intruder from Sunday stood at the far end of the stock room. He held a tire iron in one hand and a long piece of the yellow strapping tape in the other.

His image was bathed in sunlight that streamed through a high window to lend him an angelic aura in its gilt-and-golden brightness. These colors, Rhys knew, were not related to synesthesia. In this halo of light, he was even younger than he had appeared to be the day before. She didn't think he was twenty. How could she be afraid of a boy-saint who faintly smelled like an orange?

Seeing the broken glass at her feet, Rhys felt her anger rekindle. "Damn your hide!" she roared. "How'd you get in here?" He stumbled backward at the force of her outburst. "Why are you following me?" Hands on her hips, Rhys plastered a no-nonsense look on her face. The boy turned toward the door he'd entered only moments before. "Oh no, you don't! Don't you move a step, little mister, and don't you ever bang on my door or any other door like that again. You frightened me."

The almost emptied box she had been unpacking was useless as protection, but it was all that stood between them. She shoved it, sending it scooting across the concrete floor and provoking the angel to flight.

"Stop running. I'm not going to hurt you." She started toward him.

Close now, she grabbed the sleeve of the same fatigue jacket he had worn on her veranda the day before.

"Come on. We're settling this once and for all, buster. And give me that thing 'fore you break something else with it." She seized the free end of the tire iron and gave it a jerk. "Now! I want it now!"

She looked directly into his eyes for the split second he would allow it and was amazed when he released the iron.

"That's better." She bobbed her head and pointed to the strapping tape. "Unless you're planning on shipping a package, throw that tape into that empty box."

Rhys dropped his sleeve but thrust a commanding chin in his direction. "Come on." She motioned to the double doors. "Outside." She could have kicked herself for removing the crossbar when she'd gone out to return the diary to her Jeep. The twosome goose-stepped toward security, each relishing the glorious safety of being out of the darkish stock room and into the open. Cars moved slowly past the crime tape as Rhys Adler flopped down on the top step.

The drifter, if he was a drifter—she really didn't know what he was—stood in the parking lot, not exactly looking at her, but not, *not* looking either. She patted a spot on the step beside her. "Come sit down."

His eyes slid about, lighting briefly on her shoes, then on a piece of gum stuck on the under lip of the loading dock, and then he looked at his chest as if for crumbs. He worked his thumbs, sliding them over his index fingers in the universal signal for money.

"Please. We can't talk with you standing down there and me sitting up here." She moved the tire iron to her other side.

He sat. In closer proximity, he did smell like an orange, a real one, and like clothes that needed a good scrubbing.

"Do I owe you money?"

He turned his head away from her.

"Are you a burglar?"

Gazing into the distance, he continued to ignore her questions.

"What are you doing with your thumbs? What's your name? If you're trying to rob me, which I don't think you are, why are you here? What do you want, besides just popping up like a Jack-in-the-box and scaring the pants off me?"

The young man giggled and blushed in an amalgam of emotions graced with boyish charm.

Rhys returned the smile. "Now see. This isn't so bad."

She was probably being naïve, but she didn't feel this young man was dangerous. There was something wrong with him, though. He wasn't—she could say more about what he *was* than what he *wasn't.* He was edgy, and his body language was jerky. He was agitated. She wasn't sure what it added up to.

"You can hear me okay, can't you?"

He shook his head.

Rhys had been absently monitoring the traffic but now turned to look at him. "You can't hear me?"

Again, he shook his head.

"Now can you?" She was whispering.

He grinned but again denied he could hear her.

"You're teasing, and I don't like to be teased. You can hear as well as I can. What's wrong with you?" As soon as the words tumbled out of her mouth, she was sorry, because that was exactly what was wrong with him. He couldn't speak. He may not be deaf, but he was dumb. Was deaf and dumb pc, she wondered.

He bounced up and started humming. Not a tune, more a drone.

"Here, want one of these?" Rhys found a new package of cinnamon breath mints in her purse and offered them to him. "They're hot. Have you had one before?"

He shook his head. Fiddling with the small tin, he quit humming.

"You can hear me, but you can't talk, right?"

He continued to tear at the cellophane that wrapped the unopened breath mints. The concentration seemed to calm him.

She patted the steps again. "What's your name? Here, let me help you. I have longer fingernails." And cleaner, she could have added.

He jerked the tin out of her reach.

"Okay, okay." She sat quietly, watching him labor, thinking she could outwait him.

"You want the diary?" she asked. There was something nice about talking to someone who couldn't talk back.

He popped a mint into his mouth. In a moment, his eyes got big, and he spit it out on the step between them.

"I told you they were hot. And please, don't leave the one you spit out on the steps. Richard will step on it and blame me." She stuck her hand out to take the remainder of the package, but he refused to give it to her. He did pick up the expectorated cinnamon mint and stick it in his pants pocket.

"Okay. So, do I have something you want? Is it the lachrymatory bottle?"

Rhys thought she knew what he wanted, and possibly why he'd come out to the farm yesterday. The only things that didn't belong to her that she, sort of, had possession of, or at least he thought she had, was the grocery basket. He hadn't responded when she'd asked about the diary. "I'm not going to keep the grocery cart," she said. "But I'll have to give it to the police before you can have it."

This last comment was fair, Rhys thought. It could have been the beginning of a more productive conversation. Can a conversation be called a conversation if only one person talks? She was wondering just as Pauley McCrary, right at the wrong moment, wheeled into the parking lot, vaulted out of a mobile police unit, and advanced on them like an All-State linebacker.

"Where is it?" Pauley would have been less menacing if he had shouted.

And had Rhys been less guilty. She leaped up, bumping into the boy, and stumbled into a sort of awkward sit-down, while her friend, to keep from falling down the steps, had to choreograph a spring-and-twist combination any Alvin Ailey dancer would have celebrated.

Rhys regained her self-possession first. "Good Lord, McCrary?"

"It was here yesterday. I parked it myself," he said.

"And what is it you've lost? If it's the grocery cart, I am almost positive it is Raggedy Ann's."

"Mmm...m...m...mine," the strange boy stammered enigmatically.

Determined to keep his cool around this woman, Pauley garnered enough oxygen for a deep breath and then stuck his thumbs in his belt loops and let his fingers splay low along the flats of his pelvis. "Miss Adler..."

"At your service."

"Are you operating under the misconception that I am a dunce? We are investigating the unexplained death of a woman found in your Dumpster. And I wish for you to consider the grocery cart and this parking lot as police property for a few days."

"I don't have it."

"I parked the cart up there yesterday"—he pointed to the loading dock—"behind that ridiculous staircase. Your friend helped me."

Rhys looked at the boy like she'd never seen him before. "Him?"

"Mr. Fordyce."

"He's not my friend. Richard's my cousin," she supplied.

"We put it up there, and I left to get a bigger vehicle, a mobile unit, which would be large enough to load the basket into, but I got waylaid, and by the time I got back, the cart was not on the dock. And it is not on the dock now. Do you know anything about that?"

"Why do you assume I moved it?"

Pauley blinked. "Because it's the kind of thing you do and because it is written all over your face that you did."

"You should be more careful with evidence, I should think."

Pauley stared at her, struggling to keep his voice level. "Is it in the store? Good morning, Hummer."

"Hummer?" Rhys grabbed Hummer's sleeve as if she'd just discovered the cure for cancer. "Well"—she smiled at Pauley—"Hummer and I were discussing why he keeps showing up in my life at odd times and places."

"You know each other?"

"Not really. This is the man-child, who appeared out at the farm yesterday afternoon, before you and Mr. Tick showed up. We reported it." She looked her bearded adversary fully in the face. "Who this young man exactly is, is hazy." She glanced at both her accusers. "I sort of do know him, though, don't I? I've seen you before. I saw you yesterday, before you came to my house." She pulled her mouth into a quizzical moue. "We've never been formally introduced. I'm Rhys Adler." She stuck out her hand, and Hummer looked at it as if an empty hand was worthless.

"May I do the honors? Hummer's real name is Isaac Newton. He's a pretty good guy most of the time. He lives down at the Searcy Hotel. He's one of the Quick County Group Shelter residents."

"Isaac Newton? You're kidding me, right?" Rhys's face brightened with her laugh. "Is he related to Sir Isaac?"

Pauley turned to Hummer. “What you up to, man? I thought we had an understanding. You could be charged with harassing if you don’t quit bothering people. Did you forget what Officer Quinn told you and Toad just early this morning?” Rhys’s ears perked up but, to her credit, she didn’t speak. “Am I going to have to lock you up?”

“Oh, please, don’t do that.” Rhys could contain herself no longer. “The grocery basket is in the stock room. I believe Mr. Newton dropped by to get it.” She looked at Hummer. “Right, Sir Isaac?” She giggled.

“So, where is it?” Pauley turned to Hummer.

“I didn’t say he had it. Look, it’s quite simple, really. I saw it yesterday. I knew it was Raggedy Ann’s. She must have had it with her Saturday night. The baby-buggy wheels identify it, you see.”

“Mm…m…mine.” Hummer’s claim, soft and flat, surprised Rhys this time. “You can talk.”

“Okay, so where is it now?”

Sometimes timing is everything, and as was so often the case with Rhys, she missed her opportunity. This was the perfect moment she could have told the truth about the grocery cart and so easily mentioned the diary and thanked him for seeing that Richard got it. But by the time she reviewed her options, Pauley was convinced he couldn’t trust her, and that she probably was immoral.

“I understand why you didn’t take it when you could have. I’m sure you thought the grocery cart was ours.” Her voice was pure liquid persuasion. “It would be only natural to assume we used it for trash. It was on our dock. It was crammed with broken-down boxes and a mishmash of junk.”

“N…no!” Hummer’s contributions were minimal but loaded.

Rhys wished desperately she could slap herself into silence before she said too much. “I just meant that it was not from the brigades of baskets being used over at the supermarket.” She felt herself smile and knew her mouth was as frozen as a snapshot.

"R...r...ra." Hummer nudged her with his elbow.

"What are we really talking about here, Miss Adler?" Pauley asked.

"It's m...m...mine; it's mine, s...s...s...she, she, she...F...f...f... fuck!" Midsentence, Hummer remembered Toad had told him not to tell anybody anything. He began to hum again, loudly. If he was not into well-structured sentences, he was very competent in driving a point home.

Pauley, however, accustomed to the unpredictable behavior of this hapless young fellow, placed his hand lightly on Hummer's shoulder in hopes of stopping him from repeating the string of words, in which he all too likely would become entangled. "Hang on a second, pal. Go on, Miss Adler, the grocery cart? You were saying?"

"I saw the sleeve of a sweater, sleeping paraphernalia possibly, a plastic something or other, a plate, a cup, picnic ware. I touched nothing, barely touched, mostly looked. And I don't know where it is now." She had almost convinced herself of what she was saying.

"Barely touched." Pauley was annoyed with her and with himself. "Why didn't you mention this grocery cart yesterday when we were out at your house?"

"Ch...ch...chi...mmps." Hummer had begun working his thumb and index finger again. "Sh...she stole 'em. Stole 'em. Stole 'em. Stole 'em."

"Chimps! Are you insane?" Rhys glared at him. "Hush that up, or I'll have you arrested for stalking me."

Pauley McCrary laughed. Hummer added pacing in circles to his humming.

"Oh, hush, and be still." Rhys scrabbled among the items in her purse much like a mother looking for a compact or car keys to distract a whining two-year-old. She handed Hummer the first thing that caught her eye, her mobile phone. Willing his cooperation, she gave him the snake eye and turned to Pauley. "Perhaps if you find it, and after you have gone through her things, Mr. Hateful Newton can have it. I don't want it." Rhys's expression was unreadable.

"Is that door unlocked?" Pauley tipped his chin toward the stock room.

"I'm sorry. I don't have a key." Dear reader, please teach your children not to lie to the police.

Much earlier that morning, before daylight, before Rhys and Hummer and Pauley argued in the parking lot behind Adler's, a face had peered down from a third floor window in the Searcy Hotel. It was a single window but a good one, opening, as it did, over Main Street. In the 1880s the hotel had been home to an opera house and had played host to a fashionable clientele. A hundred years later, by the 1980s, the building, like many of Riversbend's historic structures, had deteriorated, and it now was used as a boarding hotel. Humbled by time, the building still contained in its wooden ribs the grace of line envisioned by its architects.

In need of a good scrubbing and a new coat of paint, and with its prevailing disposition toward a leaky roof, clanging radiators, heat-stuffy rooms, and the stench of mice, the Searcy Hotel suited Toad Potter. Here on the forgotten end of Main Street among Riversbend's fringe, he fit.

An early riser, Toad stuck his good leg into his trousers, lighted a cigarette, poked his hat on his head, stuck his other leg into the short side of his pants, and hobbled to the window as he zipped his fly. Wrestling the bottom sash up as high as he could, he stood open to a world still dark and not fully awake. Dwarfed, a back humped and lumpy like a loosely packed sack of potatoes,

Toad didn't stand as high as the middle sash. Framed in the narrow window this early Monday morning, he inhaled raggedly until his smoky lungs exploded into a fit of coughing, wherein he snorted and spewed until he recovered sufficient air to spit onto the sidewalk three stories below.

Toad liked monitoring this oldest part of Riversbend from his aerie. Unlike Raggedy Ann and his young friend Hummer, he was not a resident of the Quick County Group Shelter. He prided himself on being a third-floor, paying resident of the Searcy Hotel. Most of his disability check went to pay for his room and the one meal a day taken in the dining room. Disabled from his kyphosis, Toad's greatest fear was that he would one day be left completely immobile. A resident had to be physically able to walk and climb stairs. Meals were not brought to rooms, not even to a paying guest.

In hopes of becoming indispensable, Toad earned a bit extra, ingratiating himself to various members of the community. One of whom was the resident manager of the Searcy, Mr. Runsick. Toad volunteered frequently for small jobs. He ran errands, or he might sweep the sidewalks, or mop the kitchen floor. When Mr. Runsick was going to be gone for a few days, Howey, the manager's son and second-in-command, would often ask Toad to keep the desk for an afternoon so he could drive out to Pearl to spend a leisurely few hours, courting his girlfriend. Howey never admitted his activities to Toad, but Toad knew by the sweet musk that accompanied the boy home. Toad never failed to record the dates and times he filled in for Howey in a small notebook, should he need to refresh Howey's memory someday.

But Toad's favorite job was detailing impounded vehicles for the police department. Small in stature, he often was called to climb around on the various cars, trucks, vans, motorcycles to help find and then to bag his findings. Often nothing came from it, but there was always the hope that he would find the piece of evidence needed to convict. Toad was thorough. He took pride in his work.

Howey wasn't the only young fellow Toad took interest in for an extra dollar or two. He also nurtured Hummer. Not now, perhaps, but Toad wasn't blind to Hummer's polish. The boy wasn't born to reside in a derelict boarding hotel. The kid had potential to become a lucrative asset one day, some day in the future.

There was a rapid succession of raps on the door. Speak of the devil. "Come on in, Hummer. The door is open," Toad hollered. He had been expecting him.

Hummer, always bundled up for cold weather whether he was indoors or out, stepped into the room with his brown wool cap pulled low on his brow and a scarf wrapped to his chin. "D...did you do it?" he asked.

"I went like you asked me. Think she might've took a shot at me." Toad chuckled. "I was a good half a mile down the road when I could have swore I heard gunfire."

"She h...h...hazit."

Toad agreed. "And I'll help you get it. Did Raggedy have money stashed somewhere? I bet she's got a pillow tick full in that cart." Toad looked at Hummer for verification. "Anyhow, I'll help you, so don't go getting yourself all in a lather."

"It...t's m...mine."

"I know. But you'll have to tell me everything, Hummer." Toad looked straight at the boy. "You hear me?" Hummer's nod was not too encouraging, but Toad saw it. "Have you eat your breakfast? What'd they serving this morning, runny eggs or warm gruel?" Toad's smile was lopsided.

Hummer shook his head. Toad was aware the boy was more agitated than usual this morning. His breath was quick and shallow, like a baited animal's.

"Take a seat, Hummer, so we can discuss the problem you got with people taking the stuff Raggedy left you? Fer instance, is it writ down somewheres that she gave it to you? 'Cause her just saying it doesn't make it so. It needs to be legalized, like in a will. Some piece a paper that might stand up should we end up in court." Toad spoke softly.

He pointed to a chair, knowing his young friend didn't do well with too many orders or questions bunched together.

"It's warm in here. Take your coat off, son. You can throw it on the bed yonder."

"No, n…no." Hummer wagged his head. He tugged fitfully at a thread that seemed to be annoying the cuff of his fatigue jacket.

"Well, sit down, then?"

Hummer sat on the edge of the only other chair in the room, a chair with a history, a metal chair with a slightly skewed frame, salvaged from the alley behind the Searcy. Hummer sat across from Toad—a step stool stood between them. The stool, like most of the room's simple furnishings, might not have been exactly a principle of Feng Shui, but it was multifunctional. It served as an end table, a desk, a ladder, or as needed, an extra seat.

"I b…brought you an o…or…orange." Hummer pushed the bright fruit toward Toad. "And some…m…m…m…m." Lips tightly pressed in the paralysis of a stutterer, Hummer pulled a small red-and-white waxed carton of Mack Farm Dairy milk from inside his jacket pocket.

Toad nodded his appreciation. Retrieving an old newspaper from a stack by his bed, he sat, legs dangling, and spread the paper across his lap. Working his knife out of his pocket, he waved it at Hummer.

"You got one of these? Best tool a man can own."

Hummer shook his head, and a sad look came into his eyes. He didn't like lying to Toad, who was his best friend. Toad and Raggedy, but Raggedy was dead, so that made Toad his only best friend.

The police had taken Hummer's first pocketknife. He found another one sometime later. It had been used as a putty knife. The soft sealant was stuck to the blade when Hummer found it forgotten on an outside window ledge of one of the houses in town. Hummer had a penchant for peeping in houses at night. He'd never been caught at it. Had he, he would not have been allowed to reside at the Searcy. His jail time had not been for peeping. He was jailed most often for erratic behavior that to the police appeared as disturbing the peace. In truth, Hummer was mildly autistic and easily agitated.

He was afraid to carry his knife. He'd scraped the putty off it and pushed it up under the cushion of the armchair in his room.

"You did a...a...a...ask her about the b...basket?" As he relaxed, Hummer's mind had wandered back to his reason for coming to see Toad in the first place.

"Nope. Would have, but I scared her, and she dropped a pan on the floor." He glanced from his orange to Hummer's attentive face. "But first things first, right?" Potter peeled the rind in long, thin strips. "First..." Hummer's foot began to swing, in contrast to Potter's intentionally calm repose. "Like I said, it's important that I know the whole story, Hummer. 'Cause if you've done something wrong, I need to know it." Toad let the sentence linger.

Hummer was unpredictable. One minute he could be open, easy to get along with, and the next he could clam up or become belligerent, or even aggressive.

"I can't get myself in trouble, son. I can't afford to get kicked out of my room here, and I won't go to jail for you. Yesterday, you said Saturday night you were looking for her, but when you found her, she was dead. Ain't that right? Now where was it you seen her?"

"In th...the Duh...Duhh...Dumpster."

"Behind Adler's. All the backsides of them stores look about alike. Are you sure it was Adler's?"

Hummer traced an imaginary vision in the air with his finger. "Th…th…them stairs that g…g…go to that room where she s…s…sleeps s…sometime."

"And…go on." Toad Potter rolled his wrist like a movie mogul, urging Hummer to continue. "And she was?"

"D…d…dead," Hummer said, annoyed, as if this grotesque little man who had risen to best friend less than forty-eight hours ago might have missed the point. Hummer took a deep breath. "S…s…she…I could h…have all her p…p…prrop, all her s… stuff…in her cart, at the h…hotel or over there"—he thumbed absently over his shoulder toward the Adler's back stairs envisioned in his mind—"and under the b…b…bridge."

"Umm," Toad purred.

Hummer's potential was growing. The boy might need his counsel.

"You're saying all her stuff was either in her cart, her room here, or under the bridge? Do you know where under the bridge?"

Like the cat that ate the canary, Hummer's countenance became smug. He cocked his head but didn't say anything.

"Was she in drugs, Hummer? Because if she was, you'll want to stand clear of that business, or you'll wind up in the state pen, or worse." Toad wondered now, as he had before, if Raggedy had been peddling. If so, her fortune could have grown exponentially. "But we'll deal with that when the time comes.

"Let me ask you this. Have you seen what she had, or just been told what she told you she had. Like what was in her basket? Or what about someone else? Does anyone else know what you know?"

Hummer closed his eyes, dismissing the multiple questions.

"You didn't kill her to get her stuff, did you?"

Hummer growled to the negative. He gritted through his teeth, "I…I was like her son, and I don't like you anymore, Toad."

"I had to ask."

"She said when she died, I c…could have her e…estate."

"Her estate," Toad echoed. He would have laughed had it been anyone but Hummer. Hummer's words were serious. He didn't joke, didn't get jokes, and would take offense if anyone laughed at him. "You need to keep this to yourself until we know what happened to Raggedy Ann," Toad said. "Don't go telling the police or anyone else what you're telling me. They're liable to get the wrong idea."

"She told me she w…w…wa…"

"Yes, I know; I know." Toad Potter waved his hands a little impatiently. "Don't talk; I'm thinking."

He didn't know what part, if any, his naïve young friend might have played in Raggedy's death. Hummer was vulnerable; he could be led.

Potter stood up. "Just don't you go spreading this business about inheriting. Know what I mean? We'll get your grocery cart, and the other stuff too, but we got to be smart about it." Potter tapped the side of his head.

Hummer understood; Hummer understood things no one else did.

"Give me a couple of days." Potter thought he had the boy's attention, but assurances with Hummer were ephemeral. "I've got friends in the police department." Toad picked up the half-peeled orange. "Are you ready for a piece of this here orange you brought me? It looks mighty good." He held out a section.

"I've g…got to g…go."

"Where to? I think you ought to sit tight and let me do some snooping. If you go blabbing to people about your inheritance"—Potter pointed the peeled orange at Hummer—"there's some who might think you was the one who dumped her in that Dumpster. Not everyone understands you, and most people don't care to, neither, Hummer. People like us gotta stick together, buddy."

"S…stick together," Hummer echoed.

"That's right, and here's three things you gotta do for the next couple of days. You gotta stay in your room, or mine, and go to your meals, and keep your mouth shut. Don't talk to anyone about this."

Hummer's blink showed displeasure.

"One more—stay cool. When you are easy, Hummer, you do fine, but when you get all crazy acting, like I've seen you do, it makes people nervous and they might go after you. People don't like different. I know what I'm talking about." He tapped his bunched-up shoulder. "Now here, have a piece of this orange while we work out a plan?" He waited as Hummer reluctantly returned to his chair.

The older man took a bite of his orange. The juice trickled into the cleft of his chin and then hit the newspaper in a soft pud. "Ummm, ummm." His enjoyment was audible. "Hummer"—he smacked—"the Rag Doll was in the trash business. She was in and out of trash cans all the time. So do you think she was just going about her business last Saturday and had a heart attack or something? Or do you think someone killed her?"

Hummer wouldn't look at Toad or the wall his friend had covered in pinups, so he stared at the window, which was dingy with dust and pigeon droppings and streaks where rainwater had run. "You need to w...w...wash your w...w...winder," he said. But then he added, "S...she got herself k...k...killed."

Toad's eyebrows arched. "Did you see something?"

"P...p...policem...m..."

"Right." Trying to have a conversation with Hummer was like shoving little black squares around a palm puzzle only to find the last number in the wrong corner.

Still, Toad sensed Hummer knew more than he was telling. Maybe he kept his secret because he, like Toad, couldn't get the pieces aligned in the right order, or maybe he was being cagey. Hummer wasn't dumb.

"You know if she wasn't in that Dumpster on business whoever put her there might have seen you hanging around." It wasn't a real worry so much as Toad thinking out loud, but before either of them could follow the thought through, there was a loud rap on the door.

A deep voice boomed, "Toad? You in there?"

Toad put his finger in front of his lips to remind Hummer to let him do the talking. He motioned for Hummer to sit back down. "Door's open. Come on in."

Tick Quinn stepped into the room. "Morning, Toad, Hummer. Thought I'd stop by on my way to work. Got a couple of questions for you. We got a call from out at the old McGuire farm last night. You two know anything 'bout that?"

The fragrance of orange filled the silence around the goofy grins on the two anomalous faces.

It was after one o'clock before Rhys pulled off Blue Creek Road onto the drive that led to the farm house. Dense with pine needles, her route was more a path than a driveway. Past the sentinel of stately white pines, the road branched. To the left, she would have gone onto a paved blacktop that circled in front of the old McGuire farmhouse, but she veered slightly to the right onto a utilitarian path that midway bent like a dog's ankle. Rhys skirted between the twiggy December rose beds and the house to the horse-stable-cum-garage.

Hungry and feeling right proud of herself, she raced toward the stable faster than Schreiber would have advised. A small dust storm followed in the car's wake, only to settle and sift lazily into the many cracks and chinks of the poorly insulated house.

Her mind as usual on food; she thought she'd take Kate to the country club. Now she wished they were having lunch at home.

With company in the house, she hoped Matte had spent part of the morning baking. Dessert, when there were guests, was not only nice but also essential in Matte's view. Rhys was hoping for something chocolate since her fudge making had turned into such a debacle.

She maneuvered the Jeep into its slot in the stable, the third in the row of four stalls. In the first, she kept her predatory silver Jaguar, and in the second, her grandfather's truck, as red and shiny as lipstick; neither vehicle was in its relegated slot. She figured Schreiber was washing or buffing or changing the oil someplace other than the garage. The fourth slot was always empty except for the dogs' bedding. The last time Rhys saw her mother, Dora had been backing out of number four, presumably on her way to town.

Rhys stretched across the seat to retrieve the diary. Until she had time to read it thoroughly—and who'd had time since Kate's arrival—she was confident it was hers for a day or two.

Unlatching the glove compartment, she reached inside, expecting to touch it, but didn't. Scooting across the seat, she began disgorging things, maps, an ownership manual, a pink slip, and AAA papers. The last item out was a plastic ice scraper. It flew over her head, landing in the back seat just ahead of a string of obscenities her grandmothers wouldn't have recognized a century earlier. One would have recognized her temper as McGuire Irish. Rhys banged the dashboard with her fist. Hummer might not be as finesse able as he appeared to be. The diary was gone. He must have stolen it from her Jeep before he stormed the stock room. No wonder when she mentioned it to him he showed no interest.

Stomping into the kitchen, Rhys threw the car keys at the counter as Matte pulled a pan of brown bread from the oven.

"I heard you coming down the drive. I thought someone was after you."

"Son of a bitch!" The remainder of the sentence was lost in the long green-and-navy tartan muffler she unwrapped from her neck. The only words Matte could decipher were "half-witted" and one that sounded similar to a word Matte knew Rhys's mother, Dora Adler, would never have said, and to her way of thinking maybe experienced only once.

Matte got a carton of milk out of the refrigerator and began pouring some into an ice-cold ironstone pitcher. "Your mama wouldn't like you talking ugly," she said, not looking up but knowing Rhys heard her.

Rhys deposited her navy pea coat in the hall coat closet and reentered the kitchen with her hands on her hips. "I might as well be slaughtered as a goat than as a lamb. Apparently, I'm too stupid to live. But just so you'll know, Matte Schreiber, this skirmish isn't over yet. Not by a long shot."

"Sheep."

"What?"

"Sheep not goat, and hanged not slaughtered. And quit banging around, or you'll make this hot bread collapse." Matte was bending over her loaf protectively.

"I have been outsmarted by a lunatic, a liar, and possibly a murderer."

"That happened to me once," Matte said.

Rhys got a crock of butter out of the refrigerator and, picking up Matte's cheese board, carried both into the dining room. She hollered back through the open door between them, "Kate up yet?"

"Up and gone. Got up right after you drove off this morning. Ate the rest of the pie for breakfast! That Kate. I told her to let me make her a real breakfast, but she said the pie was the best she had ever tasted, even better than that old Consuela's who use to cook here."

"Did she say where she was going?" When Rhys came back into the kitchen, she was eating a wedge of cheddar cheese.

Matte slid the hot loaf of brown bread off the baker's peel onto a cutting board and handed it to Rhys. "Think you can put this on the sideboard without pinchin' off a piece? It'll mash down flatter than a flitter if you let the air out hot as it is.

"She ate two pieces of my pie too." Matte picked up the thread of her soliloquy on the virtues of Saint Katherine. "Don't see how she's such a little thing. You'd make two of her."

"Thanks."

"She told me about living up there in Delaware. Did you know she grew up a poor girl right out there past the Gatesboro turn-off? Her dad left them when she was a baby, her and her poor mother."

"Where is she now?" Rhys asked, chewing on a stalk of celery Matte had lined up on a relish tray.

"Dead, I guess."

"Not her mother, dear heart, Kate."

Matte chuckled. "Town, I reckon. Said she had some business to tend to."

"Should we wait on her for lunch?" Rhys looked at her watch. It was moving toward half past one. "I don't think I can wait. She's probably had a sandwich in town. What else needs doing, Matte?"

"Sorghum. I'll get it. Go wash your hands. Maybe she'll be back 'fore long."

Obediently, Rhys turned toward the sink. "Schreiber drive her in?"

"No. She said you wouldn't mind if she borrowed your little car for a while. She said you had let her drive it before."

"My Jaguar! She's driving my Jaguar?" Rhys stormed into the pantry, intending to get the jar of sorghum. "Kate Wesley will lie when the truth fits better. She'll smile to your face while jabbing you in the back with your own knitting needle, if it suits her." When Rhys came out of the pantry, with a box of lemon squares mix and a package of powdered sugar rather than sorghum, Matte had a stricken look on her face.

"Morning, sweet baby." Kate was standing in the kitchen door in a bright red wool suit with a stylish skirt, a cropped, Chanel-type jacket with a black velvet collar, very high black-leather boots, and a black-leather purse with brass fittings. The purse was more the size of an attaché than a handbag.

"Schreiber isn't back?" Kate asked. "I need him to drive me to town so I can rescue my car from impoundment, and Sheriff What's-his-name better hope to Jesus there's not a scratch on it."

Matte's eyebrows looked as if they might need to be pulled down like window shades. She retreated to the dining room with a handful of napkins and placemats.

"Why do you need Schreiber?"

"Your fancy Jag ran out of gas?"

"All by itself?"

"Because it only had a thimbleful in it."

"Where did you leave it?"

"Where is that marvelous smell coming from?" Kate clicked her pencil-heeled boots over to the swinging door, inhaling deeply. "Lovely, this aroma"—she made a curlicue gesture into the air—"reminds me of something my grandmother used to bake."

"Holy cow, Kate. You never had a grandmother."

"Everyone has a grandmother. Presumably, two of them I understand. But unlike you, sweetness, I was not surrounded by loved ones, as we call them in the obits. Except for Mama, I had to imagine a family."

"Good grief. Or should I say good theater, and you with such a small audience. Frightening, really—diverting too—which brings me back. Where'd you leave my Jaguar? How'd you get back here?"

"In the garage."

Rhys, pointing toward the stable and looking a bit stupid, said, "It is not in the garage. I was just in the garage."

"Rhysie. It's no big deal."

"You girls go wash your hands, and when you come back, I want you both to hush up this squabbling." Matte pointed toward the half bath in the back hall. "Go on."

Matte waited, arms folded across her chest. Rhys was back first. Kate, her nose freshly powdered, was next. Matte followed them into the dining room. She had no intention of missing a word.

"Okay, sorry. You've parked it in the garage." Rhys's sweetness reeked of sarcasm.

"Not exactly. It's in town. I backed into a tree. I didn't see it; it just jumped up out of nowhere."

"Oh Lordy," Matte groaned and hurried into the kitchen.

"A tree!" Rhys, half-seated, rose. "My Jaguar!"

"There's a dent in the passenger-side rear bumper and a taillight is busted. Mr. Languille said he could beat it out easily, dab a bit of paint, replace your taillight, and no one would know the difference."

"Languille? Ian Languille?"

"Ian? Is that his name?"

"Of course you'd take my car to Ian Languille. Of all the mechanics in Riversbend, whom would I most not want you to take my Jaguar to? Ian Languille." Rhys's color rose dramatically.

"Do you two have a history?"

"No! I don't know him!"

Kate rolled her eyes. "Oh, that's obvious."

Rhys hiccupped.

"Maybe you misjudge him. You have a penchant for misjudging people. I thought he was very gentlemanly. He offered to drive me out here, before I even asked."

"No doubt!"

"He smells like clean laundry."

Rhys's gray eyes grew wide. "Laundry! Ian Languille smells like laundry!" Rhys flushed again, as if Ian Languille smelling like clean sheets was indecent. "Kate! You took my car without permission, to a mechanic I do not use, and you lied to Matte. And if that is not enough, you ran my Jaguar out of gas, and into a tree, and..."

"And I'll pay for it." Kate smiled. "You said you didn't know him."

"I don't."

Kate rolled her eyes. What was the story with this hardheaded woman who denied knowing Ian Languille. She not only knew him but also knew him well enough to react at the mention of his name. It was like he was an allergen, and she a sneeze. "Girl, I don't know whom you think you're fooling, but I'm hungry. Let's eat?"

Matte, who had suctioned her ear to the door, now backed through it with the ironstone pitcher in one hand and two bottles of Coca-Cola held by the necks in the other.

"Rhubarb pie doesn't stick to your ribs, does it, Matte." Kate said.

"Sticks to my ribs well enough." Putting the drinks on the sideboard, Matte patted her roly-poly round behind.

Two of the trio of women laughed, but not Rhys, who continued to smolder. "Here." Kate reached toward the bread. "You need a hunk of this slathered in real butter, and you'll get your sense of humor back."

Matte jumped, protecting the loaf with a hovering hand. "This bread don't hunk; I'll get my bread knife. You girls just be still," she said with an authority that belonged to the baker.

Rhys, sitting rather rigidly on the edge of her chair, took up the interrogation, "And you took my car, choosing not to ride into town with Schreiber because?"

"I wasn't sure when he planned to come back. I didn't want to keep him longer than necessary."

"You didn't go to town solely to get your car, did you?" Rhys watched Kate closely. How many seconds it would take Kate to generate a story?

"I drove out to our old house. The place is a wreck. Houses have souls, you know. When no one lives in a house, the spirit dies. It becomes boards and nails."

"Bull!" Rhys turned to Matte, who came through the door with a bread knife. "Matte, pull up a chair. Join us for a live soap opera."

"I'll wait for Sam." Matte removed the lid from the tureen of chili and ladled some into two bowls to let it begin cooling. "Y'all give me indigestion."

The aroma of spicy cumin reminded Rhys that she hadn't eaten since 6:30 a.m.

"There's slaw, and a relish tray, a cheese board, and a foot-long dish of olives." Matte wiped her hands on her apron. "What can I get you to drink? Coke? Milk?"

"I haven't had a real Coca-Cola with ice crystals since Consuela worked here."

"It don't take much talent to put a soda in the freezer." Matte flipped around and marched into the kitchen.

"We don't use the *C* word in front of. Matte. She lives in a state of perpetual competition with Consuela's ghost."

"Uh-oh."

"It's just a tiny jealousy. Except for Consuela, Matte is a down-to-earth, sensible pragmatist. Don't fret; she likes you. Mostly, you say all the right things. She likes compliments and nice manners. Though both of us are on her list right now."

Kate smiled. "It's your fault."

"I don't think so."

The two began to eat, occasionally eyeing one another over their spoons. "I'm sorry about the tree, Rhys." Kate cracked first. "I knew you would be angry. It was an accident. I'm sorry. Maybe coming back to Riversbend wasn't such a good idea. You're mad at me, the sheriff would like to kill me, and now Matte thinks I'm white trash, which I am."

"Why did you come back?" Rhys asked, holding her spoon aloft.

"I'll tell you after you apologize."

"Me? You're kidding, right?"

"Yes, you."

"Okay, I apologize for letting you wreck my car."

"Nope. That won't do."

"Okay, I apologize for saying you would lie when the truth would fit better. Although on occasion..."

"Yes, I suppose that is true." Kate resettled herself. "Go on."

"I can't remember what else I said."

"That I was a liar..."

"We've established that."

"It's a hateful word."

"What would you prefer that I call your particular malfunction when it comes to speaking the truth?"

"'Fibbing' would be okay."

"Okay. You're a fibber. A gifted fibber, I might add." Rhys and Kate looked at one another steadily to see if they were making progress. Rhys's eyes twinkled. Now that she knew her car wasn't totaled, she enjoyed the occasional spiff with a worthy challenger capable of choice cuts.

"Go on," Kate prompted.

"I'm not going to say you're a good driver, because you're not. I think that's pretty obvious, don't you?"

"Okay. What about the knitting-needle thing? That was mean-spirited."

"Figurative language. I do know you wouldn't deliberately hurt anyone." Rhys looked up from a spoonful of chili. "You wouldn't, would you?"

"I'd like to knitting-needle the sheriff. You can blame him for the turn this trip has taken, him and possibly Barney Fife."

Rhys, sensed Kate was about to talk, and fearful of derailing the train, asked cautiously, "You mean Pauley?"

"Lennie...Leo. A slimy bit of manhood." Kate giggled. "All I know is he kept accidentally bumping into me, rubbing against me, if you know what I mean. I'd hate to be locked up alone in a jail cell with him in charge, and in possession of the key."

"Lockhart?"

"Yeah, the worm" Straightening the napkin in her lap, she said, "What about you, Rhys? Could you kill someone?"

"Not with a knitting needle."

"What would you use?"

Rhys pondered for a minute. "Poison."

"Bloodless."

"No blood."

"That would take premeditation. You would be executed if caught."

Each in her own reverie, with the clinking of silver on china bowls and an occasional smacking of the lips over Matte's fine smorgasbord of flavors, Rhys and Kate moved toward finishing their lunch in peace.

"Rhys, do you know what I've always loved about you? Besides the fact that you are the weirdest person I've ever known. It's that you know me and like me anyway."

"And do you know what I like about you, Kate? You don't hold grudges."

"A foolish waste of time."

"Agreed." Rhys tipped her spoon at the bread board. "Want to split a tiny piece?"

"No, thanks." Kate scooted the bread toward Rhys, who sliced it as one would a soufflé.

"And while you're at it..."

Kate push back from the table, and Rhys grinned.

"While you're at it...would you get us some sorghum for this last bite? It's in the pantry under the 'Esses.'"

"Ha-ha."

And while you're at it, you can figure out what you're going to tell me when you get back, and I ask again, and for the last time, why *did* you come to Riversbend, and what was your business downtown this morning before the stores were even open?"

It was Kate's time to grin this time, a little, her bright red lips parted. "Why do I feel as though I am being interrogated?"

"Not interrogated. I'm just curious why you didn't want to ride in with Schreiber, get your car, and run your errands. That's what a normal person would do."

"Hmm. I seem to be out of clever answers just now. Let's say I misplaced something and was hoping I could find it before someone else did."

"Hmm," Rhys echoed.

"How little?"

"A little something that belonged to the museum."

"A lachrymatory bottle by any chance? If so, you don't have to search any further. The police have it. It's a piece of evidence involved in Raggedy Ann's death. What's going on, Kate? Are you in trouble?"

"Not yet, baby doll." Kate tapped toward the swinging door. "Not if I can help it."

Rhys watched as Kate disappeared into the kitchen. She didn't know what to make of "Not yet, not if I can help it." This didn't bode well.

And Ian Languille. What's up with that? Rhys had been all too aware of the thud in her chest when Kate said she'd taken the Jaguar to Languille's garage. Did Rhys know him? Oh yes—but not really. Her current, favorite fantasy began at least a year ago. It started at a Riversbend High School football game. She'd seen Languille climb to the top of the stadium to the press box. She spent most of the game glancing over her shoulder, hoping to catch another look. He was tall, lean, with sandy, baby-fine hair that curled up onto the back of his baseball cap. In her Walter Mitty-ish frame of mind, he winked at her.

"You here by yourself?" she supplied him with words and a deep voice.

"Waiting for Richard. Sit down." She patted the bleacher beside her. And he sat, bending to kiss her lightly on her cheek. In her fantasy, he stayed with her the entire game, even after Richard showed up mid first quarter. Her hair looked great, darker, glossier, and with more lift than was normally hers. Would he like her best in slacks, or a skirt? She dressed and redressed herself in an imagined assortment of outfits. She dressed and redressed him too. He ate most of her popcorn, and he smelled like butter and salt.

"Sam's home. Do I need to reheat the chili?" Matte hollered from the kitchen.

"Not hot enough," Rhys, licking her lips, smiling, hollered back. The sound of the truck negotiating the driveway brought her back to Kate and the sorghum. "Did Kate find the sorghum?" She tipped her bowl to spoon up the last bites.

Two, three minutes, four minutes later, when Kate still had not come back into the dining room, and Rhys had not heard any conversation coming from the kitchen, and Schreiber had not come swinging through the door for lunch, Rhys walked into the kitchen to Matte's big-eyed innocence informing her that Kate was gone.

"So, what you reckon she's lost this time?" Matte had a funny look on her face. She turned back to the sink. Rhys shook her head. "It wasn't Schreiber?" Matte motioned to the back door. "She left in a hurry about something."

Rhys glanced at the key rack by the back door, and suddenly she knew. She started for Kate's room. Kate was gone.

Rhys didn't have to go all the way out to the stable to know the vehicle she and Matte had thought they'd heard wasn't Schreiber returning, but the Jeep leaving.

Slumped down on unopened sacks of potting soil, Rhys recalled their recent conversation. Kate's righteous claim that they accepted one another faults and loved each other anyway. It had been understood that Kate was Kate, and Rhys was nothing if not trustworthy.

"Not yet, not if I can help it." Where had she gone? Was she in danger? Should she notify the police? What would she say? Kate wasn't really missing, more AWOL. She hadn't stolen her Jeep, exactly. Surely, she was not in serious danger, not resilient Kate.

Helpless with no Jag, Jeep, or truck, Rhys stared into nothingness. The familiar dusty, grainy, doggy smells of the stable cum garage calmed her, allowed her to think. She could contact Ian and ask about her car, get an estimate of the damages, and assure him that she, not Kate, would be responsible for the repairs, and in the guise of transacting business she could ask him to call her if Kate came by.

Old Bay, sensing rightly, as old dogs do, that Rhys was half-sad and half-angry ambled over and nudged her furry head up under Rhys's hand. The old mother dog knew a good scratch behind her floppy ears would make Rhys feel better and think more clearly.

It was partly true. Yesterday's vague premonition that her life was out of kilter became clearer. The riddle surrounding her for the past few days was thornier than she had imagined. With Kate's erratic behavior, the lost museum lachrymatory bottle, plus all this crazy car swapping business, Rhys's problems were becoming increasingly more alarming.

Incidents kept accumulating, first Raggedy, then Hummer, and then the dwarf in the fedora. Incidents that were dangerous enough that her pets had had to be drugged. Kate hadn't actually said it was the lachrymatory bottle she'd lost, but Rhys knew it was.

Not clad for a long winter think even in the comfortable stable, Rhys began a slow walk back toward the house. Last night Kate had smoothed over her unfortunate arrival by reciting some drivel about speeding traps and losing her driver's license. And even as she nattered on, Rhys sensed her friend had been blowing smoke. She blamed her inattention on the single malt. How many lies were in the pile Kate was amassing?

If her visit to Riversbend did have something to do with the lachrymatory bottle, Kate may well be nervous. The lost item she'd come to find had been found all right, in a dead woman's hand.

She heard the truck before she saw it. Schreiber really was back this time. Rhys met him at the truck's stall. She helped unload three bags of dog food, and before the two of them walked together to the house, he grabbed a can of ceiling white and a small bag of plaster from the red truck.

"I guess you didn't pass the Jeep coming in?"

"No'm," he said, a deep frown formed under the brim of his Stetson.

As they walked, they talked, their heads bowed in concentration.

"Have you had lunch?" Rhys asked. The scent of brown bread enveloped them when they opened the back door. "I'll sit with you and tell all while you eat."

"Let me grab a bite then we'll go look for Miss Wesley."

"You know me pretty well, Schreiber."

He smiled, agreeing. Seated, he removed his hat before bowing his head. Grace, privately intoned, was returned, and his weather-beaten hand reached out for the brown bread, looking at the same time toward the steps.

"Matte must be napping. Would you like some chili? I'll reheat it."

"That'd be nice. We got any sorghum?"

Rhys stepped into the pantry and returned with a jar of blackstrap sorghum molasses as dark as crankcase oil. When he looked up to thank her, Rhys saw the saddest face she'd ever seen.

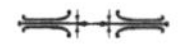

After lunch, Pauley left headquarters to find Hummer. Another chat about Raggedy's grocery basket was in order. Pauley felt

Hummer knew more than he was saying behind Adler's yesterday. Who could blame him? That woman had been a basket case. Pauley laughed at his unintended pun. But basket case or not, it wouldn't hurt him to know what part she played in Raggedy's death. For some reason she was all over it. There was the lachrymatory bottle and Raggedy's basket and Hummer going out there on Sunday. *Maybe if I'm smart enough, I can play them against each other. Miss Adler, Hummer, and Mr. Fordyce too.* He'd been awfully interested in the grocery basket Sunday morning when Pauley had pulled it up from the bayou.

Pauley raised his hand to knock. There were voices coming from inside Hummer's room. Raised voices, like an argument. Pauley listened.

"When?"

"Wh…while ago. It wasn't h…hard git'n in. They don't l…l… lock those doors in the day time. I…f…finding the…"

Pauley couldn't make out what Hummer couldn't find. The voices had faded, but Pauley recognized the second voice. It was Toads; he was sure of it. The Hummer was probably pacing about in true Hummer fashion. His voice would rise and fall in waves. He garbled something, Pauley thought, about baking, maybe about dough or rolls, chips. Were they arguing about poker?

This time Pauley did knock, loudly enough for the voices to fall silent.

"Hummer? It's Pauley McCrary."

There was a murmur, and in a second the door opened, and Toad, smiling broadly, stepped into the hall. "Afternoon, Officer. I was just on my way out the door."

A few minutes later after Pauley had greeted Hummer and they'd engaged in a polite exchange of meaningless trivia, Pauley asked him if he knew anything about where the grocery cart might be.

"Sh…she k…knows. Ask her."

Hummer started to pace until Pauley slapped a hand on the boy's shoulder, which seemed to settle him. "Have you and Toad been involved in an illegal poker game? If you've got yourself in trouble with the wrong people, Hummer, you should know there's a code on gambling debt and losses in Arkansas, but you have to apply for judgment within ninety days." Hummer looked lost until Pauley explained that he'd heard them arguing about money and poker chips. Hummer giggled.

"Me and T...Toad p...play a little p...p...poker, and I'm not g...g...g...going to t...take him to c...court."

"I'm going to Adler's. The damn grocery cart is in that store somewhere, and I'm gonna get it if I have to get a warrant," Pauley mumbled to a giant red-and-white striped candy cane walking down the street on his way back to headquarters.

Connie Becker systematically worked all the pharmacies in Quick County. His system was simple: he worked alone, and he was dodgy. No trackable routine would trap him. Dodgy was Connie. Granted, things had been easier a few years back before the government took pseudoephedrine off the shelves. No easy OTC when he first started. But in some ways, he enjoyed his government-controlled shopping sprees more. Back then, all he'd had to do was buy the stuff or slap some falsified prescription down. Tonight, he'd have to show identification and sign his name in a record book. This was more of a challenge. He had to be smarter. His main job was to remember which name he was using.

Scanning the shelves of the over-the-counter medications, he pretended to read the labels while he eavesdropped on the woman in line ahead of him. She was a looker. Old enough to be his mother, but what'd he care. She'd have experience to go with that great butt.

The pharmacy chick leaned toward her. "What's your birth date, Miss…Mrs.?" Connie strained to hear. Mrs. Who? Nervously fingering a tin of throat lozenges, he crammed them back on the shelf and sauntered over to a blood-pressure machine. Leaning against it he crossed his arms in an easy slouch. She'd have to see him or step on him when she turned to leave.

"These outta fix you up, Mrs. Wagner." The pharmacist's assistant handed her a package.

"I'm using a credit card." The woman's voice was husky. It excited Connie. When she finally did turn, she was busy returning the credit card to her billfold and wouldn't have seen him except he unwound his body and deliberately stepped into her path forcing her to brush against him.

"'Scuse you, lady. Here…" He caught her by her arm. "Le'me git that package for you, Miss Waters?"

"Mrs. Wagner," Addie said, but she smiled like a woman used to being pressed into tight places.

"Who's your husband, darlin'? I know some Wagners. Where you folks live?"

Addie smiled. "None of your beeswax, darlin'."

"Aw now, Mrs. Wagner, you oughta be nice to me. You might just like me if you got to know me."

"In your dreams, baby face."

Connie watched her until she disappeared around a corner. She made him fidgety. He wanted to follow her.

Connie would have been in line next except for an old codger who had slipped in front of him while he was engaged with Mrs. Wagner. The elderly man was slapping his cap against his trouser leg, telling the assistant about his wife's constipation.

Being asthmatic as a child, Connie knew how to feign illness. He was savvy enough, however, not to use asthma too often. Professing to a card catalog of allergies was his best bet. In the chicken-processing capital of the world, he could always use a vague allusion to his stuffy sinuses. Not to forget hay fever in the fall when ragweed and tree pollens were doing their thing. December was a bit more difficult, particularly after a good freeze. There was flu, of course.

The old man paid for his package from a roll of bills and shuffled away, whining about how the pharmaceutical companies were all filling their pockets off the backs of poor, sick people. Now, it was Connie's turn; he stepped up to the counter.

Sometimes, when he was feeling particularly plucky, he would play a game. He would see how long he could stand before the druggist without saying something. He would not offer an illness or a complaint. Instead he would pantomime, point at his nose, then at his forehead just above his nose, and then pucker his brow in pain. His objective was to prove how easily he could beat the system. But this morning he was in a hurry. "Cornelius P. Becker's my name. My friends call me Connie." He handed the druggist's assistant the card he'd pulled identifying the drug he wanted to purchase. This morning, the gullible young girl was unusually pretty.

"I'll need to see a photo ID."

Slipping his wallet out of his hip pocket, he handed her his driver's license. He hadn't used his own name at this grocery-store pharmacy for six months.

She looked at his photo then at him and, smiling, turned away to get the drug from somewhere in the secret depths of the bottle-laden shelves. "If you'll be signing right here." She pushed a logbook toward him.

While he wrote his name and the date, the pretty young assistant glanced at his hand to see if he wore a wedding ring.

He pushed the logbook back. "Yeah, well, I hope this does it." He ran his fingers into his longish bangs to enhance the boyish sweep that had fallen onto his forehead. "I've been messing with my sinuses since October." He reached for his wallet and handed her a twenty.

He noted she didn't compare his signature to the one on his driver's license, although it would have matched.

"Here's your change. I hope this fixes you up," she said as if she knew it would. "Mama used to say it takes two weeks to get over a cold, but if you take medicine it takes only fourteen days." She laughed until she realized Connie wasn't. "Get it? Two weeks, fourteen days? Anyway, it's a silly joke. Hope you get to feeling better soon."

Connie winked at her. "See ya." He cocked his index finger at her like a gun.

Sack in hand, he forced himself to walk slowly away from the counter, although he wanted to run, to skip, to holler. Cool it, Dude. He wondered if the people around him could hear the blood pulsing in his ears.

Connie was an astute observer of people. He watched and listened to folks all the time, particularly men he thought were cool. He'd watch, and then he'd steal a gesture or borrow a line. He told himself he could have been *somebody*, if life had given him a break. He could have been on stage, in a rock band maybe. He was handsome enough.

He was also a master of deceit. Connie had discovered years ago that a single drop of a very mild saline solution from a nose dropper into his eyes just before he entered a grocery could make them red and watery for the pharmacist, and a thin smear of clear nail polish around his nose, dried and scratched up a bit, could create a perfect illusion of raw nostrils.

He had needed to do neither, this morning, because he knew he was safe, but he'd have to change drugstores tomorrow or the day after. He wasn't going to cook a big a batch tonight, just enough to keep his main people supplied. It was getting tougher. A lot of the stuff was coming from off. Chili pepper, he called it. If he had a profitable winter, he might get out of the business for a while. If he saved his money, he might go back to school. He could become a druggist. Connie chuckled. He'd be good at it. No one would get by him.

Connie glimpsed his reflection in the refrigerator case as he passed between the ice cream and frozen dinners. He wore hunter's camouflage and thick-soled hiking boots that on his small feet looked like mud tires on a four-wheeler. His paper bag of pseudoephedrine was clutched tightly against his chest. He relaxed his arm, letting it drop into a natural swing. It wouldn't be too cool to look like he was in love with his little sack more than that fat woman ahead of him was in love with her giant bag of pork skins, now would it?

The flaming sunset that had infused the late afternoon when he'd gone in had faded to a disappointing mauve as he stepped out into the parking area.

Lightheaded, twitchy, needing a blunt, Connie danced to his truck and locked the door. He saw the old man in his rearview mirror probably waiting on his constipated wife. Connie keyed the ignition.

He watched a young girl cross in front of him. Her jeans were tight and her legs so thin he wondered if she'd even have to spread them apart. He wondered if she had on any underwear, a thong, maybe. *Chew it, baby; chew it.* The old man forgotten, he watched the girl until she disappeared into the store.

A bright moon, rising, floated in front of him. Maybe he wasn't quite ready to go out to the trailer, not just yet. Maybe he'd cruise around before heading out. What was his hurry? He'd have the crank cooking by midnight.

He'd forgotten about the few pieces of junk in the seat beside him, a pair of worn yard gloves, and a pin knife. Most of the Dumpster dipper's stuff was junk. He gathered them up and stuck them in the console. If he'd been thinking clearly, he could've taken the blanket before he shoved her cart down the precipice toward the bayou. He could have used that. *Ah well, if the fuzz don't find the buggy, I c'n go back. I got my Coleman stove out at the trailer. I'll be warm. A few cans of beans and half a loaf of bread. A little snort after dinner, and I'll watch stars and moons that ain't even there.*

Connie swung wide at the corner of the Goose and Gander. He checked his speed as he passed a string of parked cars and kids rowed up, hanging out. He saluted a group of boys he recognized. He'd liked them knowing he was around town, and that he might be available tomorrow, just not tonight. Tonight, I'm gonna hang at the pharmacy. See when that silly little girl gets off work."

He liked silly little girls. They were easy, and he didn't want to have to put out too much effort tonight. They could go hang somewhere afterward. Maybe go sit across the street from the courthouse and watch the police, who would be strutting around all over the place, trying to look important. Watching them spin around like hamsters on a wheel. He laughed. He was glad the old woman was gone. He wouldn't have to worry about her poking her nose into his business.

It was past midnight, and Rhys couldn't sleep. Vacillating between anger and anxiety, the twin sisters of sleepless nights, she sat wrapped in her blue silk duvet on the edge of the bed, staring at the telephone. Kate hadn't come back, nor had she called since she drove off in the Jeep. It had been long enough for Rhys's imagination to arrive full gallop at the edge of the cliff where she envisioned the little shit upside down in a ditch, bleeding, broken, and screaming lawsuit.

She wasn't sure why she expected Kate to call. There was nothing about Kate that suggested she would give a whistle at Rhys's worries. Wouldn't you think common courtesy would demand it? She questioned the familiar shadows of her darkened bedroom. In half an hour, and I'll call the police.

In an act of telephone procrastination, Rhys in robe and fluffy flip-flops flapped into the kitchen, seeking a glass of milk and lemon squares. At the half hour, she was perched on the edge of the harvest table, the old worn-smooth table that served the household well for a quick meal, or as a worktable. If one felt alone, as Rhys did tonight, one might think of it as a kind shoulder, an old friend who had listened for generations in the middle of a sleepless night to the troubled souls of Birdsongs and Adlers.

Tonight, Rhys read the labels on all the cereal boxes Matte had alphabetically rowed up on the table for easy breakfast choices. As she squinted at the nutritional info, she subconsciously listened for the Jeep to come bouncing down the lane, but the silence was loud.

Fortified with her snack, she was back in her bedroom just short of the hour.

The number for the sheriff's department was on the first page of the telephone directory. Her finger, poised to dial, faltered. She didn't want to talk to just any old body; she wanted to talk to Tick. She knew she shouldn't disturb him at home, but she didn't want some junior officer at the sheriff's department, who she didn't know—and, more importantly, who didn't know her. She fanned the pages of the directory to the *Q*s. "Qualls"..."Queary"..."Quearry"..."Quinn."

When the need came to mention her family's surnames for favors, Rhys could do so on a turn, but she was never quite comfortable. The Birdsong, McGuire, and Adler reputations—longstanding even after most of the ancestors responsible for the good repute were dead—still held a place of respect in the Riversbend's memory. All of them were rooted in the soil of Quick County, and they never forsook their roots.

Rhys remembered their grandmother's saying once that spoiled children, like spoiled meat, reeked of rotten. Then Grandmother McGuire would pinch her nose as if to quell the stench, causing Rhys to giggle. *"Darling, should you ask someone to do you a favor, be sure you are willing to return the favor when the request comes—and it will come."* Rhys dialed Tick's number and listened to what seemed like endless ringing.

Rhys, loved her grandmother, and when choosing to follow her advice, she'd found it to be sound. Rhys had had to hone her skills in seeking help and if need be favors during those early days after her mother's disappearance. And in her need she'd run into a few surprises. People are suspicious of the affluent, often they are not liked, and usually for no other reason than they are well off. It wasn't fair, but Rhys had learned that when one is born to a silver spoon there was need for extra sweets. Despite her anxiety with this pending call, when Tick answered, she was obligated to have a kind voice, a straight approach, and to show her genuine gratitude.

Theirs was a funny world. The same mantle of obligation drilled into him sat more comfortably on his shoulders than on hers. Rhys's world was too often filled with contradiction.

"Quinn, here." Tick sounded surprisingly awake, as if he'd been waiting.

Tonight, on the telephone, she reminded him of who Kate Wesley was. "So, you see, with her car impounded, she borrowed my Jeep for what I thought was a short errand, but she's not back, and that was twelve hours ago. I hate bothering you at this hour, Mr. Tick."

She could tell he was poised to say something, to tell her to call the sheriff's department, or to go butt a stump.

She hurried on. "But I was wondering since you remember Kate, and none of the others have ever heard of her, if you might have more interest. I suppose what I'm trying to say is, will you help me find her?"

His response was not what she had expected. Rhys thought she had misunderstood him. "You say it was not impounded?"

A scowl crossed her forehead. "Never?"

She was smiling. It was a trick she'd learned from Richard, who believed people can hear you smile over a telephone.

"Maybe we should be looking for her car as well as my Jeep, then, huh? And my Jeep, by the way, is a black Cherokee. And she drives a Mini Cooper. It should have a Delaware license plate."

Rhys listened calmly to Tick's assurances, but she would have preferred to have a small fit. Kate had lied about the impoundment! Rhys gritted her teeth, barely managing to refrain from blurting into Tick's ear that not only had the woman highjacked her Cherokee, wrecked her Jaguar, and spent the best part of lunch lying through her teeth, leaving Rhys wildly suspicious that Kate could be involved up to her eyeballs in all the insane things going on in Riversbend.

"Tick, I'm in your debt, dear friend. Thank you so much. I'm forever grateful." It was funny, as her conversation with Tick ended, Rhys did note she felt better. She took the aspirin he'd suggested along with his advice to go to bed. She felt sure he would tend to it.

TUESDAY DECEMBER 17

About an hour before daylight, when Mars, Mercury, and Jupiter in a fine planetary conjunction rose above the gentle hills behind the McGuire farm, Rhys was buttoning her 501s. Over her head she pulled a sweater, over her feet, heavy socks and hiking boots, and thrusting her arms into the geisha-red Patagonia jacket she'd given herself for her birthday, she was ready. She whistled Old Bay and Jolly up from the stable and their warm, doggy-smelling flannel and sweet-straw beds, and they began their early morning walk. She hadn't heard from Kate or Tick.

Gone about an hour, the three were on their way home from the low hills behind the farm when Richard made his wake-up call. In fact, they were nearing the stable when her cell phone's tinny arrangement of "Jesu Joy of Man's Desiring" sang forth from her jacket pocket.

"Morning, Dicky."

"Don't call me Dicky. I'm a grown man."

"Know anything interesting to chat about this morning?"

"What are you doing?"

"I'm watering the dogs. You're late. I expected your call ten minutes ago."

"I was enjoying muffins and licking the cranberry-chutney spoon."

"Could you come pick me up in twentyish minutes? I'm without transport," Rhys said and then added dismissively, "Kate wrecked my Jag and stole my Jeep."

"Of course she wrecked your Jaguar and stole your Jeep. Awful things happen when Kate comes to town."

Fresh water plummeted loudly into a metal pan. Her mobile pressed to her ear with chin and shoulder assistance, she turned off the faucet and watched as the dogs lapped greedily at the fresh water.

"Don't fuss." She turned her attention back to Richard. "Besides, that's not the whole story. Her car was never impounded. I know you don't love her, Richard, but this is not like Kate. These offenses are not her usuals. Anyway, I don't want to talk about it right now. I'll tell you more when you pick me up."

"Pick you up?"

"Uh-uh. Don't argue. I take it from your breakfast menu you made chutney yesterday." She rolled her eyes at Old Bay, who was dripping water off her long ears onto Rhys's boots and seemed pleased about it. "And that is excellent because now you are free to pick me up so I can leave the truck for Schreiber."

"I'm not finished putting my Christmas chutney into jars."

"Richard, dearest, if you want Schreiber to help with your little herd of cows that you keep out here—free of charge I might add—we have to keep a vehicle at his disposal. But if you simply cannot join me on my adventure, may I *borrow* one your cars?"

"I pay for the hay."

"As we agreed, but I pay for the labor, and the land is half mine."

"But the cows are not."

There was a pause. "So, will you come get me?"

"No. You're being hateful. Besides, Beau is detailing my car for the Christmas parade tonight. Miss Riversbend is riding in my convertible."

"Tonight? We just had the Christmas parade a month or two ago."

"A year ago. Time flies."

Rhys stretched and inhaled deeply.

"What are you doing?"

"It's the morning air. Lovely stuff." Then she let the lovely stuff out on a relaxed sigh before adding, "Why can't you wash your convertible for Miss Riversbend's tiny ass this afternoon? Beau will be the one to do it anyway." She pulled the receiver back from her ear so she would have to listen to another of his lame excuses.

"Richard, I must, must, must retrieve something someone stole from my glove compartment, and…no, not Kate, someone you don't know…"

Richard discharged a rather complex arrangement of sentences that Rhys wouldn't have been capable of recreating even if called upon, but she got the gist.

"Unsavory friends stretches it a bit, but speaking of unsavory I must, must, must go to the Searcy Hotel and find a man who has taken something valuable from me." Rhys waited, knowing she had her cousin nibbling.

"What's missing? If it's your virginity, you should know that's not that valuable." But his interest was undisguised.

"Mysterious, isn't it, and if you'll be out here in twenty minutes, I'll tell you what. You're going to be amazed at the turns this case is taking." She grinned, knowing he'd bitten.

"Oh, and Richard, you may want to bring your billy club. I know it's not legal, but you have one, so bring it." Rhys pushed the back gate open to let the dogs through.

"Okay, I'm hanging up now, and Richard, don't be late and wear rough clothes, more Walmart and less Abercrombie and Fitch. One more thing: Don't you have one of those little Scottish daggers you tuck in the top of your knee socks? Bring that too."

Richard and Rhys eyed the lobby, each recalling the Searcy Hotel from childhood when it had been a real hotel, rather plush where visitors found lodging and locals gathered many Sundays after church for lunch. She remembered Miss Johnnie's famous slaw. Rhys was surprised how small the lobby seemed and how seedy the hotel had become. A single lopsided love seat wedged into a corner scattered with last Sunday's newspaper was the only place to sit. On top of the newspaper a coffee can, demoted to spittoon, lay on its side. A dark amber puddle seeped onto the comics.

Richard hit the desk bell with his palm, and in minutes a pear-shaped man with a drifting eye came through a door from what had once been, and perhaps still was, the dining room.

The man stretched his chin as men do to adjust a necktie. "And how kin I hep ya?" he asked, coming around to the working side of the counter.

Richard, recognizing the man's face, stuck his hand out. "I'm Richard Fordyce, and this is Rhys Adler."

"Sure it is," the man said, but he said it in such a way that Richard was not sure if he was agreeing or if he didn't believe him.

"We're looking for Isaac Newton," Rhys said, grinning impishly despite her intentions.

The man, who misread the grin for a smirk, turned his attention from Rhys to Richard. "And might I ask what ya want with Hummer?"

"We want to talk to him," Rhys said.

"Hummer don't talk," the man said to Richard.

Rhys countered, "Well, he does actually. I've heard him." By now Rhys's chin was in the air. Richard touched her arm. "Is he in?" He asked the attendant.

"Couldn't say."

"Oh, I'll bet you could." Rhys turned from the counter and walked to the entrance of the dining area to peer inside. "Does he eat breakfast in here?" She asked from the doorway.

"Most mornings." Again, the man directed his words to Richard.

"How about this morning? Did he breakfast with you this morning?" Richard asked.

"Maybe he did. I believe he did."

"There now," Richard cooed. "That wasn't so difficult, was it? Did you tell me your name, kind sir? Our conversation will be so much more relaxed if we know each other. What is your name?"

"Runsick."

"Excellent. Well, Runsick, where were we? Ah, yes, here's one for you. Have you seen him leave the building since breakfast?"

"Can't say as I have, exactly..." Runsick's eye strayed toward the ceiling in the throes of indecision.

"Is that a *no*?" Rhys had wandered back to the counter.

"That's correct. I can't rightly say as I have or haven't saw him leave, but—"

"But, it's reasonable to assume he's in his room, wouldn't you say? And what room would that be?" Richard pointed to the ceiling.

"Three zero four."

Richard took Rhys's arm as they turned toward the stairs.

"Is he in trouble with the police?" Runsick asked.

"I guess room three zero four is on the third floor?"

"Third floor and just to the right of the elevator shaft."

"Oh, there's an elevator?" Richard's response was full of longing.

"It's broke." The man chuckled. "So's the escalator."

Richard laughed too. He liked it when someone could best him, and this man had done it easily. *Don't underestimate a man with a cocked eye,* he thought. "I know your face, Mr. Runsick. Did you use to sell popcorn at the movies about thirty years ago?

"Yes, I did."

"That is excellent. I never forget a face. You grew up here, then?"

"Nearby, Mr. Fordyce."

"We appreciate your help, Mr. Runsick."

"If Hummer's got himself in trouble, you can tell him to pack his bags. I've gave him his last warning."

"No trouble from us, Mr. Runsick. We're in your debt," Richard thanked him moments before eyeing the steep, narrow staircase, and seconds before Rhys pinched him on his arm as he grabbed the banister.

"Ouch! What was that for?"

"For being so agreeable this early in the morning to that oaf."

"Now, now. Be nice."

Athletic on the tennis court by the second landing, Richard's ascent had slowed. Neither singles nor his golf cart had afforded him much exercise this winter. The third landing was gained partly by pulling himself by way of the banister. Rhys waited at the top.

"Richard..." she started when he was about five steps from the top.

"Shut up. Don't say one word to me about my weight gain, or I shall smack you and leave you here without male protection."

Locating 304, Richard tapped as both looked at the door expectantly, but when there was no response, Rhys reached around him and gave the knob a twist. It opened. She stepped inside.

"Hummer!" He was sitting at a table, looking at a comic book. When he saw her, he stood.

"Remember me?"

He wasn't looking at Rhys but at Richard, who had stepped inside, careful to leave the door ajar.

"This is my cousin Richard Fordyce. Richard, this is the young man I was telling you about."

Richard stuck out his hand to Hummer, and Hummer took it, shook it, dropped it, walked out the door, and disappeared. Richard and Rhys looked after him with astonishment.

"Should we leave?" Richard whispered from the side of his mouth.

"Are you crazy?" Rhys searched for someplace to drape her jacket. She spotted a long nail holding a calendar. She hooked her coat on top of it and then dropped her purse on the only table in his room. "We're going to look for the diary."

"Ah, yes, the diary. Don't you think we should leave?"

"No. It's going to solve the mystery of what happened to poor Raggedy Ann."

"Francie Butter."

"Richard, I've never heard you call Raggedy Ann, Francie Butter until she died.

"I'm being respectful. 'What Would Jesus Do?' That's my new motto. I saw it on a decal the other day, on a new Lincoln, of all things. I thought that a little peculiar as Jesus seems to favor the poor, nonetheless—"

"Good heavens, Richard. You'll cause Father Burkett to seize up." Rhys was pleased that Richard, a tycoon type, who had stated less than an hour ago that he had to be at work, was clearly enjoying their adventure.

The couple began scanning the room for places Hummer might hide a diary. There weren't many. Richard lifted the edges of the mattress as high as he could to keep from running his hand under it—*filth, spiders.* "Doesn't the Brown Recluse live under mattresses?"

"I think so. Also, the male hunts at night."

"Achh!" Richard dropped the offending mattress as Rhys opened the drawers in a rickety bureau by the bed and peered inside. "And in drawers and closets, I've read." There was a scattering of odds and ends in the bureau, but no spiders and no diaries.

"Does he have no underwear?" Rhys wondered aloud.

The table, where Hummer had been sitting before he ran away, and where Rhys's big-as-a-breadbasket, compartmentalized, leather handbag now sat, had a narrow drawer. It contained a fork and spoon and several packets of salt and pepper and at least thirty hot and mild sauces from the local Take-a-Tamale.

There was a refrigerator with a carton of milk and an aluminum pie plate containing what at one time could have been a piece of chicken. There was also a small bag of organic baby carrots that appeared to be growing whiskers.

Hands on hips, Rhys turned slowly as if on a rotisserie. Hummer hadn't seemed uncomfortable leaving them in his room, which probably meant the diary wasn't here.

Either that, or it's very well hidden. About the time she spotted the overstuffed chair with the sagging lining, Hummer walked back into his room followed by a short, crookedly built man sporting a fedora. Rhys's heart bumped, and her jaw dropped.

Toad smiled. A confident man, considering his disadvantages in a world of much luckier people, he took off his hat, stepped toward Rhys, and introduced himself.

"I think we have met before, madam. My name is Clive Potter; my friends call me Toad. I hope we can be friends. I meant you no harm the other evening. I ask your forgiveness."

The "uuuhh" that issued from Rhys was untranslatable.

"When I realized that I had frightened you, I thought it best to find a better time to ask you about my young friend's property."

"I have nothing of Hummer's." Rhys had managed to generate enough intelligence to speak. She lifted her purse from the table and sheltered it under her arm as one might a small child or puppy.

"The police have the grocery basket, do they?" Toad said.

"How should I know? Grocery baskets around here seem to come and go at will." She saw Hummer risk a look at Toad. "Hummer has my diary. He stole it from my car. It was my...it belongs in my family...my mother's...possibly...probably."

Richard was the next to cut a look.

"It belongs to us. It could have been my mother's or Aunt Rachael's, or any number of our *great*-aunts, or *great-great's*." Rhys's assertion was partially successful, but Richard's confusion shimmered before them.

Toad grinned. "When Raggedy's grocery cart was not at Adler's Sunday afternoon, we was pretty sure you had it."

Rhys pointed at Hummer. "I'm interested in the diary, not the cart. He took the diary from me, not the other way around. And for your information, my glove compartment was locked."

With pleading eyes Hummer begged Toad not to abandon him to this woman who scared him so badly.

"Was it? Well, we have a diary. It was Raggedy's. But I will gladly pray to St. Anthony, the patron saint of lost things, if you wish to find your great-aunt's diary." Toad smiled playfully. "Please, won't you sit down?" When he motioned to the overstuffed chair with the sagging lining, Hummer rushed to it and plopped down before anyone else dared.

"Hummer! Don't you think the lady deserves the best chair?" The two men glowered at one another until Hummer relinquished the lolling beast of a chair as quickly as he had claimed it.

"Thank you." Rhys shouldered her purse and moved to the chair.

"There, Mr. Adler, if you'll make yourself comfortable at the table, Hummer and me'll sit on the bed."

"Fordyce. My name isn't Adler. Richard Fordyce—I'm Miss Adler's cousin. My mother and her father were siblings. And your name is?"

"Clive Potter."

"Oh yes, of course, Potter. You told us. I'm terrible with names. Never truly listens. It's a bad habit. I'm better at faces."

Toad, with a mug as malleable as Silly Putty, smacked his lips. "Are you, Mr. Fordyce? That's a handy talent. Some people aren't good at faces, you know." The little man hoisted himself up on the bed and patted a spot next to him to encourage Hummer to sit. "Now, why do you want the diary?" He addressed his question to either, but it was Rhys who spoke.

"The diary was in our junk room, found by the police and given to me." Thus acquitted, she looked at Hummer. "I thought it had, perhaps, belonged to my mother when she was a girl. I do not know how Raggedy Ann came to have it. And if, as you say, it was hers, I wonder when and how she came to have it. My mother mysteriously and tragically disappeared years ago. I do not take anything that may have belonged to her lightly."

Rhys stopped long enough to take a deep breath before continuing.

"That aside, I have another interest in it. I deal in antiques. So initially the age of it, the possibility of it coming from an estate sale and, perhaps, having originally belonged to someone of importance attracted me. But this aside, regardless of who originally owned it, in the end, the diary had been Raggedy Ann's. And I've become interested in her for not very noble reasons, I'm afraid. Curiosity is at the root of it."

Toad scratched his ear. "What is the nature of your curiosity?"

"Personal interest. Human interest." Rhys's tone had softened. "I wonder who the lady was before she was homeless. Who was this Raggedy Ann, whom we have seen for several years now around Riversbend? I hoped the diary could tell me. One hears stories, you know, but rarely does one have access to the truth."

"Did you find the truth?" Toad asked.

"I had not time to read it thoroughly before it was taken from my car." Rhys glanced at Hummer.

"Raggedy was living here when I came to the hotel," Toad said. "People don't ask too many questions down here. We might tell you who we are one day, and the next we might tell you we're somebody else." He laughed lightly. "We mostly go by nicknames. People down here are on the run sometimes or hiding, mostly surviving. So to keep from hurting someone or getting hurt, our philosophy is simple, but it works, 'Live and Let Live.'" Toad twisted his body toward Rhys as if he were trying to determine if she understood, and if he could trust her.

"Not Raggedy, apparently," Richard joined in. "She wasn't allowed to *let live.* Are you suggesting she may have said too much to the wrong person?"

"We don't know any more than you do, Mr. Fordyce. Are you suggesting she was killed by someone here at the Searcy?"

"No, I'm just following your lead, Mr. Potter."

"Call me Toad."

"Mr. Toad." Richard's sense of humor tripped; he put a quick hand to his mouth to keep from seeming rude. "Toad." He cleared his throat and tried again. "I'm sorry; may I just call you Potter? Mr. Toad reminds me of...someone...from my childhood."

"*The Wind in the Willows*?"

"Ah, yes! Then you understand there can be only one 'Mr. Toad' in a man's life, right, Potter?" Richard beamed.

Toad nodded agreeably.

Surprised but not waylaid, Richard continued, "We're speculating like everyone else. Our interest in the diary is fundamental. We wonder if there is anything in it that would help solve the puzzle of what happened to Francie Butter, or Raggedy Ann, as we seem to keep calling her." Hummer slid off the bed and began to pace. His low hum could add threefold to the tension already in a situation Rhys had discovered on Monday.

"Go on, Mr. Fordyce," Toad encouraged.

"Well you see, Miss Butter was a friend of sorts." He glanced at Hummer to see what effect the use of her name would have this time, but the humming didn't intensify. "We transacted the odd bit of business together, and I found her to be a truly nice person. Her death doesn't sit well, does it, not for any of us. Too many unanswered questions. I would like to know how she ended up in our Dumpster. Is that significant? I would like to know how she died. The diary could hold clues."

Hummer meandered over to the arm of the chair where Rhys was sitting.

"Would you like for me to move, Hummer? I'll be happy to sit on the bed with Toad," she offered in a half rise.

"Hummer." Toad's voice was custodial. "Come over here by me so as I can ask you questions should I need to." Reluctantly, Hummer returned to the bed.

"Why does Hummer act proprietorial regarding the diary? Or the grocery cart, for that matter?" Rhys asked. "Was he related?"

Hummer and Toad exchanged glances. "They were friends. She gave him things," Toad began cautiously. "If anyone is entitled to her possessions, it should be Hummer. She would want it that way."

"Well, and that's as it should be. No hard feelings, Hummer, old sport," Richard said. "Still, if you would let us borrow the diary? Just for a few days? We promise to return it to you."

"No." All three turned to face Hummer. "N…n…no…no…no," he hammered doggedly.

"Mr. Fordyce is right. The diary could hold clues to what happened. If it does, don't you want to know it? Wouldn't you rather they have it than the police?"

Hummer was in a dilemma. He wanted neither to have it.

"Would you be happier if they read the diary here?" Toad asked his young friend. "You could be with them, help explain things better than anyone around here."

Richard pressed, "The police have shown little interest in the diary as yet." He looked straight at Hummer. "They haven't associated it with Raggedy apparently, but when they do they'll come asking questions. And you, young man, since you and Raggedy were *special* friends, and since you're the one who will eventually get the diary, at least according to Potter here, you'll be the first one they'll suspect."

"A…e…e…eh…ehhh—"

"Hummer!" Toad stood, stopping the boy from saying more than he should.

"I was going to say," Richard continued, "if you'll let us take the diary for a couple of days, long enough for us to see what's in it, we'll bring it back to you on Friday."

He glanced at Rhys, who was glaring at him. He winked in return to assure her he knew what he was about.

"We'll even tell *you* what we discover. And other than the four of us, no one else need know of your association with Raggedy." The four looked at each other. "And…if later on the police do show interest in the diary, we'll take responsibility for it, Rhys and I. We'll come get it from you, give it to them, and leave you *completely* out of the picture. It'll be to your advantage, Hummer, believe me." Richard's offer had the seductive ring of a confederacy.

Three recognized that they were considering some kind of agreement that was not in the best interests of a police investigation.

"We should go, Richard." Rhys stood. "It's an excellent arrangement. May we borrow your diary for two days?"

"N…n…no!" Hummer's face turned a bright red. "In the m… morning," Hummer supplied. "After b…b…breaaa…k…fffast. Up h…here in m…my room."

"What time will you be expecting us?"

"S…s…s…sssix."

"Six o'clock then. Coming, Richard?" Rhys approached the door.

"I don't get out of bed until almost seven o'clock, and I must have a real breakfast, and time to shower and dress for work," Richard said.

Toad turned to Hummer. "Don't you think it'd be okay if we met at ten o'clock?"

Hummer pursed his lips. He didn't like people coming to his room uninvited and then bossing him around. He caught Toad's attention and jerked his head toward the cousins.

Toad shrugged. "He ain't comfortable for long around people he don't know very good. After he gets to know you better, he'll act differ'nt. Let me get your coat, Miss." Toad slid from the bed and crossed the room to retrieve Rhys's jacket from the nail. "Miss Adler." He held it open. Then to Rhys's amazement, Hummer escorted them to the door with as much aplomb as any Riversbend host seeing his guests to the door.

"He lives by his clock," Toad said. "If you're late, he's liable to leave and take the diary with him."

As Hummer reached the door, there was a scurry of feet, as if someone had been right on the other side. A furrow of worry pulled on Toad's brow. Whoever it was had disappeared behind one of the doors in a long hall of many doors.

Disappointed that Hummer wouldn't let them have the diary and annoyed with Toad's subsequent negotiation, which had them coming to Hummer's depressing room at ten o'clock, Richard was in a fizz. His exasperation was apparent as he held the car door for Rhys.

By contrast, the morning's activities seemed to have met with Rhys's approval. "Would you like for me to take you out for lunch?" she asked.

"I don't have time. I have a business to run."

"Could I borrow your car for the afternoon? I'll pick you up at five and we'll go out to the farm for a drink, and a sandwich, and then to the Christmas parade." Her eyebrows raised in anticipation looked hopeful.

"The parade starts at six o'clock. There isn't enough time to drive out to the farm and have a drink and eat a sandwich in one hour. Besides, I will have to go to bed right after supper so I can be in that god-awful room tomorrow in the shank of the hour to start reading that blasted diary"

"No need. I have it."

"I'm not sure what we've just negotiated. Who decided it was important?"

"I did, and I have it."

"What do you mean you have it? Have what?" Richard swerved into the parking lot behind Adler's, almost hitting a light post. "You have the diary?"

Rhys pulled the little book out of her purse. "Not kiddin. Pretty little thing, isn't it? I had it buried in the depths of my handbag as the rest of you watched Hummer leave my warm side to sit on the bed. It practically fell into my purse. Truthfully, I was relieved when he wouldn't let us take the diary. I hadn't quite figured out how I was going to manage to shove it back in the chair lining, had he agreed to give it to us."

"Well done, my dear."

"So, what's next? Since I saved you from having to witness once again the aesthetically unpleasant misery of poverty, are you going to escort me to the Christmas parade?"

"My pleasure, you wretch."

No one in Riversbend knew that the Par Green Country Club Christmas float—with the sparkling angel enfolded in a wonderment of angel hair and fully unfurled wings rivaling the wings in *Angels in America*—had won (once again) first place in the Christmas parade. And not until KRBA announced it did Riversbend learn that when Edd Beane—the egg-and-chicken processing plant truck driver who had been coerced into driving the float in the first place, had stopped at the end of the parade route; the truck bed was full of water. Not that water in a truck bed stirred much interest. The radio audience also knew that Jennifer Berry had recently won the coveted title of Christmas Belle, which meant she would automatically become the principal figure on the Par Green float, but what they didn't know, and what did grab their full attention was hearing KRBA, in their ten-o'clock Special Report, saying that when Edd Beane hopped onto the flatbed to help disentangle Jennifer Berry from the exaltation of angel wings, that it was not Jennifer Berry who was entangled, but Addie Wagner, and that she was dead.

A generator powering a small electric fan purred softly. The light fabric of the white costume wafted about her face, stirring her hair, creating a sensation of movement, of life. But Addie's body was dead weight held upright by the wings in a marvel of theatrical illusion. Behind the ethereal trappings, her mouth bubbled. Edd could smell blood. In death Addie's hand still clutched an exposed section of raw wire. The townspeople, not knowing to come gawk, didn't see Edd Beane, a man accustomed to hauling crates of doomed feathered things, faint dead away in a pool of water and blood.

Addie Wagner's grotesque death on the heels of Raggedy Ann's made Riversbendians anxious. Fed on nightly doses of TV drama—real time crime, police procedurals, episodes into the minds of psychopaths—that were gruesome enough to make a simple murder seem benevolent, it wasn't long until the notion of a serial killer traveled up Main Street and spread rapidly across town.

Latimer started bouncing questions as soon as the news of Addie Wagner's death reached him. Edd Beane was easy to find at the

Razorback Bar and Grill. Shaken, chalky faced in the smoky atmosphere of the café, Latimer led him out to the patrol car. Edd knew nothing about Jennifer Berry. Said he wouldn't know her if he saw her so he wouldn't know if it was her who got on his float. He had no idea where the Berry girl might have gone off to. When Latimer asked him if he thought Addie was alive when she got rigged up on the float, his shudder was almost convulsive.

When asked who was hanging around before the parade started, Beane stated he'd seen folks milling, but he didn't know any of 'em. He'd been hired to drive, so he'd been content to stay in the cab where it was warm. He said he fiddled with his radio mostly. "I ain't naturally given to Christmas parades, don't you see? I'm a Jehovah's Witness."

"Is that a fact," Latimer said. "You never even looked out the window?"

"Wouldn't have seen very much anyway with them big wings and that floaty angel dress n'all," Edd added. "I heard talking, but not what they was saying. It weren't none of my business."

"In thinking back, did you see anything odd, any suspicious people who seemed out of place to you?"

Beane considered the question seriously. The man had spent a little time in the state pen once for armed robbery, and this business of someone dying on his float made him jumpy. "Nope. Most of the folks who'd been decorating the truck had went up to Main Street to watch 'fore we ever got started."

"Were there any unusual noises? Anyone hollering for help, or crying out?"

Edd took off his cap to rub his shaved head as if it were a crystal ball. "Like I said, I's listening to my radio. If I heard anything it weren't such as caught my attention. I did hear laughing maybe, but I couldn't even swear to that. Then someone slapped the cab that it was time to get rollin'."

Latimer instructed Edd Beane not to leave town for a few days.

Late that night in his ersatz coroner's lab, Castro, his nose almost touching the corpse, was engaged in a series of educated sniffs. The woman's body reeked of alcohol and puke. Other than the electrical burn across her palm, and minor bruises from the weight of her sagging body against the rigging, there were no signs of violence. In the morning he would tell the sheriff he could cautiously attribute her death to asphyxiation brought on by alcohol poisoning, possibly drugs, and by electric shock. Why she was holding the fan's cord he couldn't fathom. This too, he concluded, was probably a tragic result of gross inebriation. The death was an accident.

The next morning in the clear light of day when Castro took a second look, he discovered the corpse's mouth was crazed with tiny cuts, which he hadn't seen the night before and which he couldn't explain. He covered Addie Wagner's body and walked across the room to hang his lab jacket on the hook behind the door. Perhaps it was too soon for him to give the sheriff a decisive answer. He'd look at her again. Perhaps there were other questions. Another look at the float might be in order.

Edd was brought in a second time and asked about the electric fan, and if he knew how the spun glass, or angel hair as it had been identified, got in her mouth. Beane, wanting to be cooperative, remembered when he jumped up on the flatbed after the parade the first thing he did was unplug the fan from the generator because of the standing water. He saw the angel was holding onto the fan's cord, but he figured she was just trying to help him. "But, no, sir, if the cord had been hot before I unplugged it, I couldn't say. I do remember there was a funny smell—"

"And the angel hair?"

"No, sir, I don't know nothing about angel hair or how it could have got in her mouth." He sat on a chair inside the police station looking like a man who'd lost his center.

Sheriff Latimer located Dr. Anthony Berry's car at the Par Green where Berry and his wife, China, had joined friends for a post-parade drink and late dinner. Only minutes before Latimer's arrival, the news of the tragedy on the Christmas float had reached them.

Jennifer's parents were in the club entrance, struggling into their coats as Latimer, bullying the heavy doors against an insistent December wind, brought a chill into the foyer. After a brief exchange, the sheriff followed the couple home, routing them by way of the egg processing plant, but the float had already been moved to a police hold.

Minutes later the two cars rolled onto a circular drive in front of a two-storied Southern Colonial with the required six columns but a roof too shallow to uphold the owners' notion of their standing in society.

Inside, Dr. Berry poured a dram each of Scotch into two glasses, handing one to his wife who shivered on a red plush love seat near a cold hearth.

"I don't suppose you'll want a drink since you are on duty."

"One about like you've got would be okay. It's gonna to be a long night."

Berry splashed another scotch into a glass and handed it to Latimer. "What's your plan, Latimer? My daughter has disappeared. A woman who was where my girl should have been is dead." Not expecting an immediate answer, he selected a remote from an assortment on the coffee table, and following a series of clicks, a bouquet of flames bloomed from the cold fireplace. The doctor joined China on the love seat before he continued his query. "Is Tick Quinn on this case? Quinn's experienced. I don't want this to turn into some debacle."

"Dr. Berry, we haven't known about Mrs. Wagner's death much longer than you have. And we have no idea where your daughter is. So let's get started." Latimer managed to sound less defensive than he felt. "Couple of questions. Did your girl want to ride on the float? Did you even go to the parade? When was the last time you saw her?"

The short glass clasped tightly to keep the Scotch from spilling betrayed the fear behind Tony Berry's insolence. He tossed the liquid back, picked up his wife's glass that sat untouched on the coffee table, and downed that too.

"Todd Oakley and I drove Jennie to the parade grounds to help her get on the float. After a while I left to go get my wife. Todd's an engineering student at the U of A, and I figured he'd be able to help her get into that ridiculous angel contraption better than I could."

"That was the last time you saw her?" Latimer took a small notebook from his pocket and scribbled something on it. "You say Todd Oakley is her boyfriend. How well do you know him?"

"We've known him all his life. There's nothing wrong with Todd if that's what you're suggesting."

"As Par Green's Christmas Belle, your daughter was expected to ride on the float. Was she excited?"

"Oh, I should say so. That was all she could talk about after the cotillion. I'd never seen her so excited and so beautiful." China Berry seemed to come alive.

"We were on Main Street, watching the parade until Jen's float passed us, and then we left. We were very proud of her, weren't we Honey?" The doctor patted his wife's hand. "We were meeting people for dinner. We're not really big on Riversbend's little bits of pageantry, are we, China?"

"And it was your daughter on the float when she passed you? Could it have been Mrs. Wagner?"

"It was Jennifer, all right."

"Do the two look anything alike, would you say?"

"We thought it was Jennifer." A flicker of doubt echoed around Mrs. Berry's words. When the float passed the angel was looking away from us. I tried to holler, to get her attention, but with those big wings and her gown billowing and all—"

"We were already at the club when we heard about Wagner woman. That she was dead. That she'd been found on Jennifer's float...and that Jen was nowhere around. I was ashamedly relieved. I'm sure you understand."

"At first, we were relieved, but then we realized we didn't know where Jennifer was. Had she been kidnapped? So many strange things have been going on. Doctor immediately called home. When she didn't answer we called the Oakley's. No one answered there either."

Tony Berry leaned into his wife as if to steady her. "They could have eloped. Jennifer and Todd have been talking about getting married ever since he left for school."

"We said all the things you're supposed to say; you're too young; you have to finish your education. She's always wanted to be a doctor like her father." China began to weep softly. "I... she..."

Tony, accustomed to taking command wrestled a handkerchief from his pocket and handing it to her, continued her thought, "What my wife is trying to say is that Jennifer may be pregnant."

"She *is* pregnant," China said, "no might be, Tony."

Berry took off his glasses. "And you know what? Right now, I don't care. I hope she is. I hope my girl is with that sonofabitch Oakley at some Justice of the Peace's house getting married, pregnant or not."

Latimer, who was never comfortable in the presence of weepy men, stayed for a few more questions before he stood to leave.

"Get your rest, if that's possible. Should you hear from your daughter, give me a whistle. She might have seen something, overheard something when she and her boyfriend were at the float."

Rhys and Richard had cheered mightily for the Par Green float. Richard had been on the planning committee and had actually spent a few hours slathering a gluey-floury goop onto old newspapers so the theater people could teach the committee how to make papier-mâché angel wings. All said, done, and dedicated, the float was spectacular, with glittering cotton clouds and so forth, and though the wings bore little resemblance to what one would assume real angel wings looked like, the sheer vision of the float committee should have merited first place. Rhys's only comment as the float glided by to the tinny accompaniment of "Joy to the World" was her surprise that the Berry girl seemed to be sloshed.

She opted not to go out to Par Green, following the parade. She asked Richard for a rain check. Kate had returned. She had strolled in like Callas taking the stage, about the time Rhys was putting on her coat to leave for the parade. She hadn't asked Kate to join them, but she had asked for Kate to relinquish the keys to the Jeep.

Rhys learned of Addie Wagner's death almost as quickly as had Richard. On his arrival Par Green was a buzz with the news, and he was still standing when he telephoned her.

Rhys immediately regretted two things: one, making the too hasty decision not to go with him, and two, her comment regarding the inebriated angel. She also regretted that she had made so little effort to know Addie Wagner.

WEDNESDAY DECEMBER 18

Sleeping later than usual, the next morning Rhys awoke thinking of Ian Languille. She'd dreamed about him, again. Lingering lazily in bed, she tried to remember the fading images from her dream. What kind of man prone to tiny briefs and silky boxer shorts rigs a binder's twine clothes line across a bathroom the size of a broom closet to dry his rain-soaked underwear? Where were they in her dream? Dammit! Must he always and only appear in her dreams—or fantasies? Was there no solid flesh and bone to the man? The last time she'd seen him he'd been in Robertson's Hardware, buying a screwdriver. Of course, he was buying a screwdriver, and before he could spot her, she had ducked behind a ten-foot shelf housing nuts and bolts and screws.

Rhys's eyes were tightly closed. She, a woman barely sullied, still practically a virgin, was obviously lusting after the lanky, languid grease monkey. Ian Languille. If Kate hadn't mentioned him smelling like laundry, Rhys doubted she would be inventing a vignette starring the skinny-assed mechanic laundering his underwear. WTF was wrong with her.

Ian unbuttoned her shirt, and as her clothing began falling piece by piece to the floor, he pulled her to him roughly, not too roughly, and began…

"Coffee's ready!" Matte hollered on the other side of Rhys's door. "Are you awake?" The door opened. "You've got company." Matte toddled to the windows and pulled back Rhys's white muslin curtains, securing them behind ruffled tiebacks.

"You look flushed. Are you sick?" The cook moved toward her with a hand half poised to place on Rhys's forehead.

"No'm, not sick, just waking up."

"Well, get dressed. Everybody's waiting in the kitchen."

"Please tell them not to go away." She smiled at Matte and stretched her long arms. "Y'all go ahead. I'll be there shortly."

Matte seemed firmly planted.

Rubbing her eyes to complete the charade of a modern day sleeping beauty, Rhys sighted the remains of last night's clothes piled high in the chintz chair. She pointed to them. "Kate and I stayed up too late, and I've a couple of chores to finish before I can greet anyone. Not up to being hostess with the mostest at the moment." She had gone for silly.

"I won't start the eggs until you get there."

"Matte, please don't wait. I'll eat toast." She flung her legs from under the cover and escaped into the bathroom.

She heard the door close softly. Rhys did have a handful of small chores. Hers was the small hand laundry that needed doing, not Ian Languille's. Two pieces: panties and a chemise.

She ran lukewarm water into her sink for the third and final rinsing. She hadn't thought of Ian Languille in weeks. Okay, since yesterday, but prior to that, in months. Of course, she always thought of Ian, or someone equally as sexy, usually Ian, when she was approaching her menses. Obviously, she was a tramp.

She wondered if loose morals ran in some part of her family unmentioned.

"Why do I purchase the kind of lingerie the label instructs me to hand wash? I'm an old maid. I should be enjoying the comfort of cotton. Cotton breathes."

Rhys scooped the bits of obsidian silk from the lavatory, but rather than arranging the pieces on a warm towel, she laid them across the radiator for the purpose of drying; she threw the silks into the bathtub, where they lay defenseless like the watered remains of the wicked witch.

"I want a real man. Not a boy with little skill. I want a man, romance, love, someone to…someone I can…" She could only think the word. It was such an out-there word.

Perplexed that she was into Ian's underwear this morning, followed by the recurring jolt that she would be fifty soon, left Rhys with the surprising thought that she would never have a real man, certainly not a husband. Perhaps, all things considered, this was as it should be. She was set in her ways, headstrong. Was she happy, wasn't she? She had a good life. It was not, exactly, the life she'd thought it would be. She cupped her bare breasts in her hands.

A woman in her midlife was at her sexual peak, she'd read. Women with an abundance of hormones—hers with no regard for the sad fact that she was not married, getting old, and no beauty according to current standards, plus basically deprived of gratifying what appeared to be an insistent condition of horniness?

Horny! Another one of those words. "Flushed," she thought, would be better. "Horny" was undoubtedly masculine. Not a suitable word for a prude, even a prude who was really a tart.

Having lived alone for a good part of her adult life, she had to wonder what she'd do with a husband. She wouldn't do well with someone trying to boss her, telling when, and where, and if she could go or not go, buy or not buy, eat chocolate regardless of if she needed it or not. She wouldn't mind a jackhammer-driving playmate on the occasional weekend, though.

Resituating her chemise on the radiator, neatly this time, she disrobed and stepped into a deep, long, claw-foot tub of hot bubbly water. She sank to the bottom until nothing was left but an oval cameo of her face. She heard a burst of laughter from the kitchen. Taking a deep breath, she went under.

Out and dried, talced, and clad in a pale wisp of silk a while later, Rhys entered her closet to dump a load of walking clothes from yesterday on top of the hamper and to pull a pair of light wool, camel-colored slacks off her trouser rack. Yanking a cream-colored shirt from a hanger, she put it on, tucking it all around. Satisfied her midsection was smooth and flat befitting her athletic figure despite her daredevil attitude toward chocolate, she zipped her trousers and ran a darker leather belt through the loops. From off a shelf of neatly folded sweaters, she selected a forest-green cashmere cardigan.

Her hair slightly flyaway this cold morning, she stood in front of her mirror, gathering it into a short ponytail before twisting it into a twiggy arrangement she could pin on the back of her head with a pair of tortoise-shell chopsticks.

She listened, trying to distinguish some of the voices coming from the kitchen. Kate was talking. The smell of bacon and the cacophonic orchestration of Matte's clanging utensils made Rhys's stomach roll hungrily. Had she had supper? Suddenly the strange events of the night before came flooding back. Poor Addie.

She remembered last Sunday's lunch with Richard. He'd told her he'd shared a pew with the Wagners at St. James's, and how striking Addie had been in her black hat. The woman just had it. The thing all women wished for, sex appeal. She made men reckless. Her beauty stole all eyes, reducing men to putty and women to pale copy.

Was Addie innocent of her effect on people? Perhaps not, but she wasn't malicious. This morning Rhys felt the enormity of the young woman's dying. She also wondered if it was this enviable sex appeal that in the end had killed her.

Fully clothed except for shoes, Rhys grabbed a pair of argyles and lifted a pair of loafers from a shoe rack. Seated on the chintzy chair, now empty of strewed clothes, she drew one leg up, slipping her foot into the sock.

Less than a week ago, Addie Wagner was alive, also Raggedy Ann. A week ago, Kate had been safely in Delaware, behaving herself, or so Rhys had thought. Now Rhys had knowledge of a crime of some consequence involving her longtime friend. What *was* she to do? Where did her moral obligation lie, with the law, or with the unwritten rules of friendship?

No one would be *expecting* her to *do anything*. No one knew of her knowledge of Kate's story. Nonetheless…

She reached for a shoe brush and began buffing the tops of her loafers. *Any path I choose has the potential of being the wrong one. Kate will be prickly if I expose her. The law could be pricklier if I don't.* Rhys's moral sense in regard to the law or to friendship was thick with prickles.

What if the situation were reversed? What if she had done a wrong, committed a crime, and confessed it to Kate? There was no doubt here. Kate would never expose Rhys. Kate would go to prison for Rhys.

Rhys wished she could talk to Richard. Not likely. Sitting in the car after the parade and before Richard had gone to the country club, the cousins had watched Kate through the french doors. She was pacing, obviously anxious. Rhys had begged him to come in for a drink, and to serve as her second in the fracas that was brewing, but he'd declined on the excuse that fresh blood made him donsie.

"Rhys, people don't always turn out the way you want them to. Kate's not you. She's not like you; she was not raised as we were, and I doubt with the extended absence of the daily dose of McGuire you and your mother offered her, she is not even the girl we knew as a child.

"You don't know that."

"She changed."

"We've all changed, Richard." She reached for the door handle. Her words were charged, querulous, and echoed in the silence. She opened the car door, gesturing for Richard to stay seated. "I'm not stupid, Richard."

"No, but you are naïve. You're Aunt Dora all over again." Richard's shrug was positively Gallic. "You enable Kate's bad behavior, Rhys. Always excusing her, allowing too much, asking too little, forgiving too easily. It does not help her."

"Stop it, Richard! I don't want to hear what you think about my mother's gullibility or my friend's self-absorption. There are things you do not know. You're right in theory, but theories are simply theories and usually full of holes. And your condemnation of our oldest friend is not only unattractive but also hateful. I'm not sure what happened to you and Kate at the University, but it left a mark. At least on you, a mark, a scar."

He laughed lightly. "I'm on *your* side, Rhys." He pressed his finger to his lips. "But, say no more. Shhh. Save yourself for the battle ahead. Hop on into the house, and get on with it. And tomorrow, if you need me, I promise I'll disinfect and dress any wounds you may incur in the course of victory. Otherwise, dear heart, win. Family honor and all that."

He kissed the forefinger that had pressed her silence and tapped the tip of her nose.

"Remember, tomorrow when I get here, it's your task to keep her away from me. I fell in love with her in the fourth grade, and in my addled state of amour, she stole my yo-yo."

A tiny smile cracked Rhys's annoyance. "Your yo-yo, Richard? You quixotic old maid. Look at us. Two cousins virtually handed the family silver platter, which I think we'd both toss over for a simple yo-yo, for a normal life like Kate's, with overdrafts and car payments."

"Don't laugh. It was a Bat Mobile model, electric, and it flashed colored sparks. My father gave it to me."

Rhys was still smiling as she watched his taillights disappear down the long drive.

As the kitchen door opened, the scent of cinnamon sugar from a plate of still-warm snickerdoodles disarmed her. Matte's secret ingredient for world peace, she recognized at once.

But her mirth began to dissipate like underwhipped egg whites.

"She's not like you, Rhys." Rhys loosened the scarf from her neck. Where was the plucky girl with the springy mop of hair? Rhys shivered as Richard's words hit home.

Why is she here? Not to pay back taxes, not to visit me, not to see Richard. She still sees us from the eyes of a disadvantaged child. "Enabling...excusing...allowing too much, asking too much, and forgiving too easily." Rhys shook Richard's voice out of her head.

"I should have called," Kate said. "I've been terribly thoughtless, and I don't deserve to have a friend like you. Anyone else would have called the police." Kate had followed Rhys to the hall, where Rhys busied herself closeting her wraps.

"I did call the police." Her words were muffled, coming from the coat closet, but translatable and unmistakably cool. "You could be dead. You could have had a wreck. You could have rolled on the Turner Road curve. Riversbend roads aren't for city slickers driving unfamiliar and high-spirited cars. Why did you take your luggage if you intended to come back?"

"Rhys." Kate touched her friend's arm to stop her from walking away.

Her effort wasted, she followed Rhys into the living room, where fire danced and crackled on the andirons.

"Rhys, I'm sorry. You've every right to be angry with me."

Not willing to relinquish her anger just yet, Rhys drew her fingers along the back of the sofa cushions in a gesture of indifference. She paused at the Queen Anne table to straighten a group of photographs. Most of the faces, long gone from Rhys's life, were now ghosts who watched with interest for what would happen next. Some of them had known Kate, the child, Rhys's Raggedy Ann friend. Approaching the fireplace, she turned and looked at Kate for the first time since witnessing the satin and feathers of her dressing gown and slippers.

Rhys had never seen Kate cry before. Her arms opened to gather in her oldest, weeping, annoying, and perplexing friend. "If those tears are phony, I'll have you arrested," She said.

No, after last night, as much as she would like to consult with Richard, the possibility was out. With Richard, Kate wouldn't have been as honest as she finally was last night, or so vulnerable. Nor would Rhys have heard the truth about the lachrymatory bottle—supposedly the truth.

The story told, hither and thither as it was, placed Kate in a room at the Carlton house, packing the estate gifts for the museum. She held a lachrymatory bottle, one of several she'd been packing, when someone banged into the room unannounced, unexpectedly, and loud enough to startle her. Kate dropped the lachrymatory into one of the opened crates, the wrong crate, the one shipping to Adler's, she'd said.

She hadn't elaborated; she hadn't said when she was aware she'd dropped it. Nor had she explained why she was packing two boxes destined to go to two different places at the same time. She didn't say when or how she'd planned to rescue the lachrymatory bottle from the Adler box. She obviously knew it was in there. She'd come to Riversbend after it.

Mistake or inspiration? Fishy, but not impossible.

What was clear to Rhys was that Kate wanted the lachrymatory bottle and, when fate conveniently intruded, she dropped the small treasure into her best friend's crate. A crate scheduled to ship out of state that afternoon. It was so like Kate. Rhys sighed; it would be so easy to arrange an overdue visit to Riversbend and collect her bottle when no one was looking.

It wouldn't be difficult altering handwritten inventory numbers. A carelessly scribbled five could easily become a three, or a nine embellished could become an eight. Who would know? Kate had been trusted. She'd put in charge of the whole Carlton affair.

"Rhys, it was so innocent. In the museum collections, the bottle would have been merely one more," Kate had said. "The least important one. It was not the most valuable, or the most beautiful. But on my shelf in my house, it would have been the premier piece," she'd said. "I loved it for its intrinsic beauty, the sentiment, the history. I know you understand."

Rhys did understand. There were numerous pieces of antiquity she had seen through the years that she would have loved to own, pieces she had brushed with gentle fingers, recognizing the singularity, admiring the exquisite workmanship, the mastered beauty. Pieces she had bid for and lost. But steal? Never.

Kate had seen the disapproval in Rhys's eyes. "What are you going to do about it, Rhys? I wouldn't have done it except the whole incident was like I was supposed to have it. Whoever it was that opened the door triggered a reaction. Cause and effect, you know."

"Or how about divine will?"

Kate peered at Rhys. "I don't think I would have kept it forever, Rhys. I would have returned it one day. I would have slipped it in with the others and no one would have known. I was the only one who knew it existed. I was the one inventorying the estate. But then, I lost it. Anyway, not to worry. It's no biggie."

"No biggie!" Rhys had pushed back from the kitchen table. Concern etched her face, her spine unyielding. She stood up. "Is that a child's assessment? Biggie? This is not child's play, Kate. It is big."

Kate rose from the table as quickly as had Rhys. "My bad; I'll deal with it."

"Are you aware you could be charged with grand larceny? It's a very big deal."

"No one knows but you and me, darling. Are you going to tell? I'm sorry. I shouldn't have shared my burden with you."

"You've always known your boundaries, Kate. I've always trusted you in the long haul. Like Sunday night, I was curious, but more amused when the cops escorted you out here. But did my trust betrayed me? Should I have asked you more questions? Like why had the police impounded your car?"

Kate blanched, but quick to see an advantage, she admitted, "My car wasn't impounded."

"So I've heard."

Now Richard, Kate, and Matte were in the kitchen, waiting for Rhys. She had to join them, but she didn't relish the idea. Kate's claim of sharing her burden was true. It was a burden. What now was Rhys's responsibility? What should she do about Kate? What kind of friend should she be? What was her obligation to the police, to Tick? He and Pauley had brought the photo of the tear bottle to her, seeking her help. Was she obligated to tell them what she now knew? She wanted to let this little larceny go away. *If Kate promises to return the bottle to the museum collection, is that enough? Does that right the wrong?* Almost to the kitchen, Rhys made a decision. *I won't tell the police. Not just yet. I'll use my silence as a goad to ensure that Kate will do the right thing.*

But the plan was flawed. If Kate did return the bottle and gave the museum authorities her tricky story about why she possessed it in the first place, there still could be punitive consequences. Kate was going to have to face the possibility. Rhys knew Kate made better choices being forewarned than being blindsided. This surely was Rhys's morning task.

Just as Rhys reached the kitchen door, the french doors in the living room were flung wide, and Schreiber stepped through with a fresh, needle-tender pine tree braced across his shoulders.

"Have you decided, Missy, if you want this tree out there in the foyer like we had it last year or back in the living room where it belongs?"

"I'm with you, friend, I like it best where it belongs. Good morning, Schreiber." Momentarily reprieved she took a breath of cold air that came through the door with the man and tree. "How nice to envision Christmas trees for a few minutes."

"Yes'm."

Rhys followed the green expanse of branches and the big man through the door. She smiled when she spotted the Christmas-tree stand in the corner opposite the fireplace where the Christmas trees had inspired the Adlers and the McGuires for over a century. "Nice pine tree, Mr. Schreiber." She inhaled its sharp, resinous fragrance. "Don't you love the smell of green in the house?"

"Yes'm, I do. I've cut you some extra cedar branches for the mantel shelves, and if you're gonna make wreaths for the doors and windows, and something green to go around Baby Jesus in the manger, I got you some more pine. It's out back. If you're going to use it today, I'll just leave it like it is and my nippers too, but if you ain't, I'd better put the greens in a bucket of water and take my nippers back out to my toolbox so as they don't get lost." Schreiber, with good reason, was careful with his tools.

"Thank you. I'll get Kate to help me this afternoon." *Perfect*, she thought.

Schreiber shifted his weight. "Missy, I was wondering if I might have a word with you."

"Yes, of course. Where shall we go?"

Schreiber laid the tree gently onto a sheet of black plastic he'd spread to keep it from seeping its sticky juice onto the rugs. He nodded toward the library. Following her in, he closed the door behind them. He held his hat, a prop, with both hands in front of him.

"I oughtn't to be in here with my boots n'all, Missy. Got mud caked in the treads." He rolled a foot over to prove his point. "But I've been waiting to talk to you when no one else was around to hear."

"I see." Thinking this had to do with farm business, Rhys walked over to her desk and sat down. "Please don't worry about a little mud. Have a seat." She motioned toward an upright walnut library chair next to her desk. He moved forward slowly.

He'd been waiting to talk to her since Sunday. He'd been practicing how to say what he had to say as he layered leaves around the rose bushes to protect them from the cold, as he mulched the kitchen garden and watered the winterized plants. His actions had been rote, a relief from his deeper trouble.

Rhys pulled the ledgers from a drawer where she kept the farm and house accounts and put them on the desk. Looking up she smiled. The man's girth took up the library chair.

"The crocuses will be tipping up before we know it; did you notice new sprouts along the fencerow? Were they Nandina sprouts? I think we could have a few more over near the bird feeders, don't you? Birds love berries." Her stomach grumbled in complaint. "You've had breakfast. Would you like coffee?"

He shook his head.

Rhys leaned forward as if to rise. "May I take your hat before you twist the brim off?" she laughed. "You may have noticed I'm chattering. It's because you're so serious. I'm afraid you're going to tell me you and Matte are leaving."

"No'm, we're not leaving. You don't have to worry about that. And they probably wasn't Nandina. It's a mite too early. Late

February will be as soon as you see much new growth on them." It was Schreiber's turn to be evasive.

"Well then, we mustn't rush the season. Mama used to say, 'Don't go rushing your life away.'"

"Yes'm." Schreiber nodded as he sat delicately on the edge of the chair. "I didn't aim to speak to you in the kitchen, you see, because I was afraid Matte might hear us." He paused, trying to remember how he'd planned to start. "We've been married forty-some-odd years this coming June, Matte and me, and what I have to say she doesn't know nothing about," he blurted it out. His chin dropped to his chest as he thought about the next thing he had to say. He rubbed the side of his head where his hat had flattened his hair. "It's that woman they call Raggedy Ann," he said.

"Yes?"

"That ain't her name."

Rhys's eyebrows gathered. "I know. It's Francie Butter."

"No'm. Frank is her name. What I mean to say is she's my brother. Until that Raggedy Ann showed up a while back, I thought my brother was dead. I never told Matte any different."

The call from the morgue came to Tick's cell phone. He had asked Dr. Petitjean at the morgue to call him as soon as she had the autopsy, regardless of the hour.

"No autopsy yet, Tick, but we have finished the first viewing, and guess what?" The words poured out of Maryjane's mouth.

"What?"

"I thought it might be important."

"What?"

"A feather."

Tick was silent long enough for the pathologist to ask, "You still there?"

"I'm trying to remember sump'n' about a fan dancer. The old gal was a fan dancer." Tick liked Dr. Petitjean. He'd always enjoyed teasing women; it was easier than talking and often safer, but this little doc was a good tease, sometimes gullible and usually with a comeback.

"This may be important, Tick."

"Okay, go on."

"It was in her windpipe."

Tick was silent. "You'd think I'd of known if she had a feather in her windpipe."

"Why would you have?"

"Our medical examiner, old Castro, would have mentioned it."

"It was tiny. Maybe he missed it. She had vomit in her mouth."

"Have you talked to anyone else about this?"

"Not the sheriff, not today, not about this, and, if I have my way, never again. Your boss is a creep."

Tick chuckled. "You're the best, Petitjean. I'll tell you what though, maybe you should call headquarters. I'm home today, kinda under the weather. Put the feather in a bag when you get it back from the lab and save it, but then I want you to call Pauley McCrary and tell him. No one else. You understand? When you can't get me, he's your man. I'll give you his mobile number. Tell him what you've told me, what you're thinking, and ask him if there's a pillow in the grocery basket. He's a good boy. He was with me when we found the body. You can trust him."

"Have you gotten the fingerprint report back on that little vase we found in Raggedy Ann's hand? Do you know what it is?"

"Got that one covered, and I'll tell you when we've got an hour to waste. And no, I haven't heard from the lab." I'm about to retire you know. They may not tell me." Tick sounded grim.

After a few exchanges on the overdue autopsy, and her concerns and solicitations regarding his health, their conversation ended. Back in bed, Tick contemplated his next move.

A feather in her windpipe. Was she still breathing when he and Pauley found her? He had advised Pauley to go carefully over the stuff found in the Dumpster, and her cart. Maybe he should have paid closer attention to her.

He could hear Willa's heavy stride from the front of the house toward their bedroom. He heard the glass pretties she treasured jiggling on the shelf in the dining room in perfect rhythm to her tread. She'd be coming to check on him, to ask if he needed anything, and then she'd remind him he should stay at home tomorrow because he probably had a flu virus and was probably running a fever, and if he didn't want to have a relapse and be sick for Christmas, he'd better stay home and take care of himself.

He didn't have the flu. He did have a terrible headache. But he didn't have the flu, or a virus, or a cold, like he'd told Pauley on Monday, or a temperature like he'd told Willa.

Pretending to sleep, he pulled the quilts up and closed his eyes, but her footsteps passed his door and disappeared in the bathroom at the end of the hall. In a few minutes, he heard the shower.

Guesswork troubled Tick. He could draw a hypothesis quickly enough. He could make a case that she'd been smothered, especially if he could produce a pillow from her cart. But that wouldn't be enough he'd need to put somebody behind bars. A pillow but no killer wouldn't serve justice.

He'd learned a hard lesson about Riversbend a couple of years back when he ran against Latimer for sheriff. He had been the favorite, or so he was told, but unfortunately there had been a series of break-ins in residential neighborhoods, which he'd labeled as mischief more than serious crime. No one was hurt, no vandalism, nothing valuable stolen, mostly just chairs turned over, and drawers opened and upside down like someone was playing a prank. During the race Latimer had convinced the people that Quinn was too old to be sheriff and that he'd lost his nerve and become soft on crime. Maybe he had.

He didn't believe Raggedy had been smothered. The autopsy would find she'd died from a brain hemorrhage. He'd seen the blood on the back of her head, matted in her hair on the Saturday she'd died. Copious had been Petitjean's word for it on Sunday when he drove back to the morgue for the viewing of Raggedy Ann's old scars—the atrophied male genitalia.

"With head injuries blood can be copious," Petitjean had said, "but I believe we'll find these are superficial wounds."

Blood in the ear? That wasn't so damn superficial. Tick put his arm over his eyes to block the light.

And then there was the Dumpster. It didn't make sense to him how she got half in half out, but someone knew. He wished he had searched the second-floor landing with Pauley the night they found her.

He got out of bed and began dressing. He had at least twenty minutes before Willa would be out of the shower.

With Mrs. Wagner's death and Tick out sick, Pauley had thought Latimer would put Tom Drake, the second to Tick on the force, in charge of the Christmas-parade case, but he hadn't. Latimer had decided to handle it himself. The Wagner death, with speculation running amok, was attracting statewide attention, and Latimer was a USA prime hotdog. The man had been basking in the attention the press had been giving him for the last couple of days. Two dead women. Pauley couldn't imagine Mrs. Wagner's death an accident. Little town, big news, so big, in fact, Pauley suspected his boss had forgotten that Raggedy Ann's case hadn't moved forward in days, and that her case was likely to go unclosed, ignored, and underground if he didn't get some help.

Pauley, watching Latimer swagger across the street from the Coffee Cupp midmorning, had groaned with the rest of the officers as they hovered around the double bay windows that fronted the door to the department. They jeered as they watched a fresh wake of reporters circling around the sheriff like vultures with a bit of skin.

"The guy in the blue Tiger sweatshirt is from the *Commercial Appeal* outta Memphis," someone near Pauley whispered as the sheriff and his entourage trooped through the door.

The small entrance around Gladys Gray's desk was filled quickly with elbowing, pushy reporters hollering inane or sensation-driven questions. Pauley and his brother cops escaped down the back hall to the water cooler. They were pretty well hamstrung; they couldn't work knowing that as soon as the reporters left the officers would be called into the incident room to await briefing—information, instruction, suggestions so they could get on with their jobs.

Pauley, still amazed that he had decided to become a cop rather than to play ball or become a coach was proud to stand among these men. He liked listening to them. He longed for the day when he would be as seasoned as they. As he listened to their talk he was learning how to be a good cop.

After the briefing Latimer stepped into his office and slammed the door but not before Pauley had slipped in. He stood in front of the man's desk.

"Sir, I have never worked on a murder case; I need someone with experience to help me. Why not Tom Drake, sir, if you're not going to use him on the Wagner case."

Latimer was working to pry an obstinate plastic lid from a cup of cooling coffee.

"Sir, let me help you with that? I can pop it off with my pocketknife."

Latimer kept pushing around under the bottom edge of the lip.

"Sir, Tick has the flu. And as you know he's the experienced cop, and as much as I would like to stay on it, I don't want the important first days—"

"Don't you mean hours?"

"Yessir, hours; that's best for sure, but we're to days now, and I don't want any more to pass without a proper investigation being seen to. I need to work with someone who has done this before. I need direction. I am aware that we are shorthanded, and if you want to put me somewhere else and assign a more experienced—"

"I doubt he has the flu." Latimer's jaw was clinched in his ongoing effort to uncover his coffee.

"Yessir, and a fever. I'm not trying to be..." Pauley's well-planned request for help was squelched midway when the mulish lid popped off, creating a minitsunami.

Latimer leaped to his feet, brushing the front of his shirt. "McClain," he shouted at Pauley, "have you asked around? Have you found anyone who might have seen some unusual activity back of Adler's Saturday night? Have you done anything?"

The questions, addressed to the wrong name and coming so unexpectedly, caused Pauley to sit down in the small chair in front of Latimer's desk. "Like what, sir? And I want you to feel free to call me McCrary, anytime."

"McCrary, a woman in Riversbend has been violently murdered—a popular coach's wife—and I do not have time to nursemaid you on this other case. Go back to your training manuals. I told y'all I'd give ya one day. I've given you extra because your fool partner is sick, if he is sick, and I'll tell you something else, Quinn should never have been on this case in the first place. So take charge, boy, or quit, but don't come in here whining like some sucklin' baby with those big deer eyes looking at me like I'm your goddamn mother."

"But..."

"Get out of my office."

"Yessir."

Shaken, pissed, and feeling abandoned especially by Tick, Pauley was slumped at Tick's desk when the phone rang.

"Is this Paul McCrary?" a woman's voice asked.

"Pauley, Yes'm. How may I help you?"

"How would you like a quick trip to the city, Officer McCrary? This is Dr. Petitjean in forensics, and I've got something interesting to tell you."

In the dead of winter, daylight is gone from Riversbend by five thirty. Pauley pulled into the parking lot back of HQ, the feather Dr. Petitjean had given him in tow. Pauley had liked Dr. Petitjean. She'd treated him like he was more than a rookie turd. It had ended up a decent day despite its rough beginning. A razor-thin streak of red lingered on the horizon. He watched the blade darken to plum and melt off the edge of the earth, taking the last light, and with it the day.

Still sore after his meeting with Latimer, Pauley decided he wouldn't tell the sheriff he'd had the call from Dr. Petitjean. Since the sheriff had dumped Raggedy's death in his lap with zero support, Pauley felt he was under no obligation to mention the trip, the feather, or how he was going to kick Latimer's white ass all the way to Tunica after this was all over. He'd talk only to Tick. As he'd crossed the bridge into town, he dialed Tick's house, letting the phone ring until the answering machine pick it up.

Inside headquarters, the building was unusually quiet. At Tick's desk he unearthed a blank piece of paper. He didn't like this part of police work, filling out reports. But he wrote what he thought was important—how much can you say about a duck feather? After six more or less complete sentences had been written, he considered the report finished and reached again for the telephone.

As it rang, he fiddled mindlessly with a nest of paper clips, failing to untangle them he tossed them into a wastepaper basket.

He stacked some loose papers, and sleeved a couple of CDs, and scraped some stray pencil shavings into a Styrofoam cup. The surface of the desk cleared, he discovered a well-marked desk pad had been waiting under the piles. Tick was a scribbler. There were random, nonsensical words and numbers, even a drawing a six-year-old might have made of a heart with acne, or perhaps a strawberry. But nothing grabbed Pauley's attention. He tore off the top sheet in search of a clean one. If he couldn't talk to Tick, he had, at least, improved the order of his desk.

He picking up his report on the feather, reread it, made a copy, and slipped the original under the desk pad. In the morning he would file it with Gladys. He folded the copy, stuck it and the duck-feather baggie into a manila envelope, and started down the hall toward the evidence room.

That was then he saw the grocery cart. It was up against the wall outside the evidence room. Holy shit! What was it doing in the hall?

He unlocked the door and quickly rolled the cart inside. Who'd had it? It had been rummaged through. Things were topsy-turvy, not neat and arranged like it had been on Sunday. Never having cataloged its contents, he wouldn't know if anything was missing. Dammit!

He shoved the grocery buggy up against the far back wall in the evidence room, a.k.a. storage room, and was leaving when something, a gut feeling, a tingling somewhere in his body, made him walk back to the cart. The corner of a vintage World War II army blanket, poking through the metal grid on the very bottom of the cart, caught his eye. And he knew what called him back, a feather a second feather. He rolled the buggy under a light and began carefully unpacking it. Examining every item, Pauley made detailed notes for his very tardy report.

Working his way toward the bottom, a blanket surfaced. A woolen blanket, army drab, moth-eaten, smelling of dirty hair and dead skin, covered with fragments of stale food that left greasy spots when brushed away. Pulling the blanket out, he placed it on a table and began to unfold it. Slowly, cautiously, hoping for any bits of information the folds and rough fabric might contain. Curiously, he noticed the wool was damp and had begun to mildew. Pauley brought a bit of the food fragment to his nose and sniffed. Chips, maybe? Hard to tell, probably from someone's garbage.

The army blanket told a story all right, if he could just read it. There was a hole in the middle Jack Horner would likely have plumbed. Tick would be pleased with his patience and investigative skills because, embedded in the fabric, he found what he was seeking—more tiny feathers.

Pauley didn't know whether to laugh or cry. He wasn't sure if the cart in the hall was the act of an angel or a demon, but he emerged from his grocery cart debacle smelling like a rose.

Latimer was right. Pauley was going to have to quit acting like a kid. It was time for him to take charge, be more conscientious and more deliberate about his evidence. He had to quit leaning on Tick, for acting like a dumb-fuck rookie with no authority, who couldn't fart without someone giving orders. He was lucky this time, but next time?

"First thing tomorrow, baby," Pauley beamed. "I'm taking you and your beautiful feathers as my first solid piece of evidence to Little Rock."

THURSDAY DECEMBER 19

Rhys got up on the right side for the first time in days. The inexplicable complications that had recently beset her peaceful existence seemed to have gone away, poof, at least for the moment. She hadn't talked to the police in a couple of days. The issue of the diary and Hummer's insistence on having it within his reach seemed to have settled. As recently as yesterday, he had come pecking on her window with an alphabet of accusations, but after hemming and hawing, she had retained possession of the diary at the cost of a glass of milk, a bowl of leftover chili, and half of a chocolate cake.

And if her possessing the diary uninterrupted for a few hours wasn't gratifying enough, Kate had agreed to fly back to Delaware and face her employers at the museum. This had been Rhys's condition for keeping silent.

"Get it over with," Kate had said with a shudder. "If they don't prosecute, I'll fly back to Riversbend after the first of the year and pick up my car."

In the shower, out of the shower, back in her robe, and with all ten toes in clean socks within eight minutes, Rhys whistled an airy tune one might have recognized as a carol, if one were generous.

Rising later than usual this morning, and deciding not to walk the dogs until after lunch, Rhys and Kate, one in flannel and the other in supple blue velvet, had finished toast and juice in the living room and were visiting over a second cup of coffee when the doorbell rang. The absence of footsteps from upstairs or the kitchen indicated that Matte and Schreiber had driven to town to Christmas shop, which they had been threatening to do for days.

Brushing toast crumbs from her lap, Rhys started toward the door. "No one comes to the front door out here except trouble or strange people. If I'm not back in half a minute, come look for me." She waved a half-eaten piece of toast as she spoke. Pausing in the pocket door between the living room and the foyer, she added, "As soon as I've dealt with whatever problem is ringing our doorbell, we'll plan our day." The third ring sent her scurrying into the wide entry.

Through beveled sidelights, Rhys saw a man's back. She also saw her Jaguar parked beyond him, in front of the house. Turning quickly to a mirrored hat rack, she saw her own pale face, and she saw dismay surrounded by a tangle of hair that looked as though it could recently have been electropositively charged.

The merits of fight or flight popped into her head, but even as a means of escape surfaced, so did an insistent tapping on the glass. She opened the door, and Ian Languille's beautiful, blue eyes smiled at her. His straight, sandy hair needed a good cut. She loved the way it tickled his collar.

"I'm returning your car."

"Yes!" she managed to say before she slumped to the floor.

"The morgue called, so I drove down," Pauley explained reluctantly to Latimer. The sheriff had been in the hall when Pauley came out of the evidence room, carrying a large plastic bag. He took Pauley into his office when Pauley explained that he couldn't be found yesterday because he'd been in Little Rock.

"Why you?" Latimer asked. The question, Pauley thought, should have been "What for?"

"I imagine Tick asked them to. Like you say, boss, it's our case. My case, actually." Pauley felt a tingle of pleasure.

Latimer jerked. "Watch your tone with me, Mc...Mc Whatever."

"Just call me Mac, sir. You seem to handle that part of my name okay. I wasn't being a wise guy; I was trying to explain why I got the call and you didn't. The morgue has been in touch with Tick a couple of times. It is his case. Anyhow, the call, the trip, and a feather are duly cataloged and locked in the evidence drawer."

Latimer looked up at *feather*, but he didn't press except to say, "Have you told Quinn?"

"I suspect he's the one who had Dr. Petitjean contact me. We're trying to stay in contact while he's home." At least Pauley was trying. Tick didn't seem to be anywhere on the planet.

Latimer nodded something like approval and then leaned back in his chair, "So what'd you think about little Miss Hot Pants? Did you feel her up while you were down there?"

Pauley heard the words; he just couldn't believe what he'd heard.

"She's a nice piece of ass, huh?"

Pauley paled.

"Awww, don't look so guilty. We don't hang colored boys for screwing around with our women anymore—might ought to, but—"

Pauley didn't wait past "ought to, but." He sprang from his chair and was out of Latimer's office before he hit the man.

"You should have stayed around yesterday," Latimer hollered after him. "The autopsy report came in. I was in a hurry, but I read enough to know that the old bag woman didn't have a stroke or a heart attack, so we've got another homicide on our hands."

Pauley kept walking, and Latimer followed. "Says she got a good-enough bump on her head to kill her." Latimer stopped following. He watched Pauley reach the door. "But that's not what killed her apparently—Officer McCrary; don't walk away from me. Get your black ass back in here."

Every policeman, patrolman, secretary, and volunteer in the building followed Pauley with their eyes as he passed them on his way out. Even Gladys came out from behind the front desk.

"McCrary! You're fired!" Latimer bellowed.

Seconds later, Lockhart, breathless for an uproar, charged down the corridor after Pauley, hitting the back door before it could shut. "Someone smothered her. Have you read it, the autopsy?"

"No."

"Me neither. Are you gonna?"

"No."

"What's in that bag you're carrying?"

"None of your business! Now, back off, piss ant."

The first thirty miles on the way to Little Rock were spun out in anger. Pauley broke all the laws for safe driving. He flew down the highway, weaving carelessly in and out of traffic snarls, unaware of the alarm he was triggering among the Thursday morning commuters, travelers, and adventure seekers. Since he was driving a patrol car, no one questioned his actions. Everyone assumed he was in pursuit of some lawbreaker or traffic violator. He played out at least a dozen angry verbal battles with Latimer in the first thirty miles, winning them all. By the last thirty, he had cooled.

Now comfortable with the speed limit, the hum of the motor, the clacking of tires on the deteriorating highway, and with Mary

J. Blige, plugged into his ear, he thought about the crossroad he had approached. Why was he putting himself through this? He could walk out of law enforcement this very minute, if he wanted too. *I'll stick long enough to end this case, then I'll make Latimer* kiss *my black ass.*

Pauley stopped at the forensics lab to deposit the army blanket, so it was close to one o'clock before he got to the morgue to see Maryjane Petitjean. As luck would have it, Dr. Petitjean was gone. He had to do some fast talking to get a gangly white guy called Dockers, who was trying to leave for lunch, to hang around long enough to make him a copy of the autopsy report. He bribed him by offering to buy his lunch at a place called Burger Mama's out on Kanis Road.

On the drive back to Riversbend, Pauley called Tick again. Willa answered on the second ring, informing him that her husband was likely down at the sheriff's department, but that he shouldn't be. "He's sick and going to ruin Christmas for both of us. If you can't find him, he's out chasing criminals when he oughter be home in bed." Willa Quinn was from Indiana; her clipped accent made her sound all business.

She did suggest that if his call had something to do with that poor, old homeless lady who ended up in the trash bin behind the antique store, he should ask for Paul McCartney at the sheriff's department. He was her husband's young Negro partner. She said this with a solid finality and then more or less slammed down the receiver. She was gone before Pauley could identify himself properly.

One thing Pauley knew for certain was that Tick was not at the department. He wished he'd talked to Mrs. Quinn earlier. He began punching in Tick's mobile number, but then he stopped. Mrs. Quinn had said he was after someone. What if the ringing phone gave him away? Got him shot? *Lord, that's probably why I can't get him. I may have got him killed.*

⟝⟞

Midmorning Thursday, Rhys was ensconced with Schreiber in the library. Distracted earlier with Ian Languille standing over her grinning, and Matte and Kate fanning her, acting as if she'd fainted, when actually she'd just been surprised to see Ian Languille, and maybe she blacked out for a split second from catching her breath when she first saw him, and failing to take another. It could happen.

But now, everyone in another part of the house busy with their own business and out of hers, she'd was listening to Schreiber as he remembered his childhood and his brother. Rhys still could scarcely believe it. Raggedy Ann or Francie Butter was really Frank Schreiber, a man. If so, what was Frank Schreiber doing with the diary the night he'd died? The idea of Raggedy being a man unnerved her. The idea of Raggedy being a Schreiber unsettled her even more. Why did it matter? She realized she had been almost unconsciously holding on to a vague idea that Raggedy Ann might have known something about her mother's disappearance. She'd hoped the diary could. She wasn't sure what she hoped the diary could tell her. Raggedy Ann, the bag woman seen all over town, knowing something about her mother hadn't seemed so remote a possibility. But Frank Schreiber?

"Schreiber? When did Frank come back to Riversbend?" she asked, pulling her thoughts and his reminiscing together.

"I didn't know where he was for a long time. All I know is after Matte and me come back, he showed up one morning—in a skirt. That would have been a few years or so ago."

"Family, I guess."

"Almost never saw him."

Suddenly Rhys felt lighter. The question of if Raggedy Ann or Andy had knowledge of Dora's disappearance had quietly been resolved. Frank Schreiber had not lived in Riversbend twenty years ago. The diary might or may might have ever belonged to any of the Adlers or the Fordyces. Raggedy probably found it in someone else's trash receptacle. The diary had teased Rhys just because Raggedy had it the night she died, and it was found in their junk room.

A raucous cry rose from the kitchen. It rang through the house three times before ending with a victorious cry. *Razorback!* Richard had arrived and Kate, gushing like a geyser, had greeted him with the U of A fight song. Rhys giggled, imagining Richard's escalating alarm as he found himself trapped, once again, in his onetime lover's (or so Rhys surmised) magnetic field.

"Rrrrhyssss." She heard the door from the kitchen open. Richard was headed toward them. He sounded a little shrill.

Rhys squeezed Schreiber's hand. "We'll talk again later, Schreiber. Yesterday Richard and I had a date to begin our purview of the diary, but after you told me about Frank, I postponed his visit. So, if you'll excuse me. I don't want him to get all cranky." In a rush of affection, she added, "Should I keep Raggedy's secret? I don't want to intrude in any way other than to support you. You still haven't told Matte?"

"Not yet. She's gonna kill me. I should have told her years ago. You do what you have to Missy. "

"Yes. I imagine she will be upset, but she'll be your best support once she gets over the shock. I won't let it slip." Rhys smiled. "I'm sorry, Schreiber. Would you like for me to take care of burial arrangements? It could be done quietly. If you would like, let's bury"—her hesitation over which pronoun to use was barely perceptible—"*him* in the old McGuire cemetery here on the place. We can give him his name back. Frank Schreiber?"

Schreiber's eyes brimmed with tears, which brought tears to Rhys's eyes. He pulled a handkerchief from his back pocket. "I'd like that for Frankie." They could hear Richard squeaking down the back hall in his new Nikes.

"Rhys?" There was a knuckle tap on her bedroom door. "Get up, lazybones. You've got company."

"We're in the library, Richard."

"There you are! Don't leave, Schreiber." Richard entered the library. His nervous tension spiked the room like a glint off clean glass.

In a short time, the cousins managed to sequester themselves in the library with laden breakfast plates and hot coffee. They were taking turns reading the diary aloud. It was Rhys's turn to listen as Richard read excerpts. Her thoughts skittered between Schreiber's dramatic revelation, Kate's nefarious association with the lachrymatory bottle, as well as the yet-to-be-plumbed diary.

"You are not paying attention." Richard slapped the book with his palm.

"I am. Go on"

The excerpts at the beginning, which had been written in a spidery hand on January 1, 1930, were sketchy. There were two ongoing themes for most of the first month: an apology in the defense of giblet gravy and a discourse on the diarist's allergies to cedar.

"Do you remember anyone in the family having allergies to cedar?" Rhys asked, forgetting for a moment her recent pronouncement that the diary probably never belonged to any of them.

"Nor do I remember giblet gravy. My daddy wouldn't eat a gizzard if it wore a top hat."

"You're so witty, Richie. You create the most delightful images."

Richard glared. "I hate you." But then he began reading again. Minutiae mostly, trivialities from a string of dull winter days: the chill, the clothes, the smoking fireplace, the lack of friends dropping by due to influenza. The longer Richard read the lower Rhys sank onto her spine. Soon she was adrift in the free flow of drowsiness.

"Look at this?" Richard sat up straight. He rotated the diary toward Rhys. "Green ink. A new scribe. The color of jealousy" An elegant hand in emerald-green ink had possessed the diary in the spring. Someone's spring.

"These entries are recent, I'd say," Rhys said, leaning forward for a better look.

"Why do you say that? We know it was written on the eighth of December, but we don't know what year. The years are not recorded except the original entry in1930, and that diarist didn't even make it through February."

"Wonder if she died of the flu?"

"Stay on task, Rhys."

Rhys maneuvered the diary away from Richard, set her glasses on her nose, and began fanning through the section of pages written in bright green. "A second diarist," she agreed. "A woman—and she's from Riversbend—and we probably know her."

"How can you say that with such assurance just by fanning through some pages for less than a minute? You are so annoying." Richard grabbed for the diary, but Rhys was too fast for him.

Rhys's interest, bolstered by her firm opinions, returned to the diary. "Look Richard, the green-ink diarist begins writing on April first, April Fools', and ends abruptly, practically midthought, on November eleventh, just over a month ago. Listen. 'I can just see...'" Rhys began reading again, only to be immediately interrupted by Richard.

"You simply cannot disregard the fact that we don't know the year." Richard's attitude underscored his long-held view that one simple fact would always prevail over a basket of quivering intuitions. This attitude ordinarily would have laid Rhys's ears back. Fortunately, this afternoon her ears stayed in place.

She ignored him and continued to read until...

"Okay then. Who is she? Miss Smarty Pants?"

"Just listen, Richard and quit thinking." Rhys shifted her vision bifocally to read, "'Made an appointment at Clip 'n Cut.'" Rhys threw Richard one of those knowing looks he rarely caught. "'I'm considering a short cut, one of those spiky dos.'" Rhys laid the diary down. "Richard, have we seen anyone recently with a spiky haircut?"

Not fully clear on exactly what a spiky looked like, he considered the question thoughtfully before he admitted that he had not. "No. But may I point out that, unlike a man, a woman who is considering a new hair style may or may not actually get it."

"True." Rhys rolled her hand in the gesture that suggested it was only a quasitruth. "Still, keep your eyes open. Once a woman starts considering a new do, she's going to do something. It may not be quite as intense as spiky, but she'll do something."

Rhys continued reading.

"Blah, blah. Okay, here it is: 'I bought a delft-blue V neck at Wicket's Fine Fashions. Even on sale, I paid too much for it.'" Rhys scanned down the page. "'Saw ED on Tuesday.' Ah ha!" She looked at Richard. "She's seeing Ed someone. Do we know any Eds?"

"Edd Bean. I can't imagine anyone being interested in him."

"I hear he's very well endowed," Rhys said in the pretention of innocence.

"Shame on you!"

She shrugged. "That's what I'm saying. I don't know personally, of course."

"I should hope not—how well endowed?"

"Horseish."

"That's ridiculous. Impossible. Who told you?"

"I shouldn't say. If I did, every time you see her you would think about it."

"Then let's move on." Richard tut-tutted before moving on. "These entries don't suggest any single woman to me. A hundred women, maybe." He paused. "What is a spiky-do, anyway?" He plucked the diary gently from Rhys's hand.

"Clip 'n Cut is currently the trendiest hair salon in Riversbend," she said. "In fact, spiky is already passé. Straight and smooth," she said, "long to longish..." The sentence trailed off as she casted about, trying to recall something important.

Richard patiently put the book face down on his lap.

"Remember, I said I thought Green Ink was current? Well, I can prove it. Relatively current. Clip 'n Cut has been operating for less than three years."

"Ah," he said.

"That's right. And Mr. Wicket has a preholiday sale every year that runs from after Halloween until the day before Thanksgiving. Of course, he jacks his prices on the front end so he can offer a deep discount."

"Smoke and mirrors. Listen to this," Richard reads, "'Saw ED again today.' "Green Ink always capitalizes the *E* and *D*, wonder why? 'Saw ED again today. She pretended not to see me, but she did.'" Richard cocked an eyebrow. "Ah-ha, Miss Marple, my investigative skills are as sharp as yours. ED is a woman! Do we know a woman named Ed, Eddie, Edwina? Maybe it's not Ed anything, but initials. Who do we know, a woman, with the initials *E* and *D*?"

"We don't, but we know an Edie...Eeee Deee!" Rhys was triumphant. "Halliger! Edie Halliger!"

"Ole Edie! Maybe." The cousins clapped a clumsy salute to their success.

"Keep reading."

"'Red wool—eighty-nine point ninety-five dollars.' Does Edie go to Clip 'n' Cut? Do you know if she has a new blue sweater or a red wool something or other?"

"You're getting confused, Richard. It isn't Edie who bought the blue sweater. Edie is the person Green Ink saw. Edie is the one who pretended to ignore Green Ink. Green Ink is the one who bought the sweater and a red wool something, and who is having an affair."

"With Edie Halliger?" Richard was astonished. "I don't believe that for a minute."

"Not with Edie, doofus, with Larry. Edie ignored Green Ink. Why? Because Green Ink is having an affair with her husband, with Larry Halliger."

"You amaze me. You read four or five sentences and immediately know who is having an affair with whom? We should exploit your amazing talent someway. We could bill you as a soothsayer. Make a fortune. You could go on television like these televangelists. You could become famous, a star. Think of it, Rhys." Richard fanned his arms out into an arch: "Madame Adler Knows Your Deepest Secrets."

"Plug it, Richard. Let me see the diary." Rhys read silently for a moment, "Okay how's this: 'I saw him this afternoon in shorts!!!' which is followed by three exclamation points, if you'll note." Rhys glanced up to see if Richard reacted. 'I sure would like to know if that tight little ass is as hard as it looks.'" Rhys's frowned, a look of concern crossing her face. "Richard this is serious."

"How come?"

"Who is...was...the sexiest woman in Riversbend?"

"Addie Wagner?"

"Right, and who, besides Larry Halliger, our dear friend and coach who considers himself God's gift to beautiful women, wears shorts in the dead of winter?"

"A lot of people. College kids out at Holly Colly, health nuts, runners."

"Most anyone under sixty who has not yet turned into warts and lard."

"Oh dear." Richard pulled the cuff of his slacks up higher than the top of his socks. "So far so good. So...where are you going with this, Rhys?"

"I don't know. Nowhere, except that Green Ink could be Addie, and Larry has a tight little ass. And Addie is dead..."

"Yes, but is there a connection?" Richard returned to the diary, but with the turn of a page, Green Ink disappeared, and a new diarist appeared. This one with a stubbed pencil. "I think we've found someone else," he said, his voice distraught. The new hand writing was familiar. He slowly closed the diary. "This is a good stopping place. I've got to go to the store. Miss Viola has probably already started filling out insurance claims on me."

"Let me see." Rhys looked quickly. "You think this scribble belongs to Raggedy, don't you? Can't you stay a few minutes longer?"

"You keep reading. I'll drop by later and you can tell me what you've found."

"Why does Raggedy make you uneasy?"

"I'm just not sure I want to get involved. I'm not sure I want to know the truth. I like my Riversbend to be wholesome. Peopled, as I've always believed it to be, with decent people. I don't like questioning my friends, discovering things about them that I never knew, things that jar my own priggish value system. "

"Poor Richard."

"I know. I know. I'll called you this afternoon." The two walked into the hall and Richard slipped quietly out the front door to avoid Kate.

Rhys needed a break too; a glass of water, a short walk to help her think maybe, but the diary lay open, calling to her.

She read at random, hurriedly. There were a lot of numbers, none identifiable as telephone numbers, dates or times of day, social security, PINs, accounts, credit cards. Partial sentences, phrases, one about "goofy" with a small *g*, so it didn't occur to Rhys that "goofy" with a little *g* could be anything other than an adjective. There was a "Mick" or "Nick." Something about needing to find *H* followed by a series of numbers. Maybe a "Louise," but no "Thelma," definitely a "Daisy" but no "Donald." Rhys rubbed the back of her neck. Blunt Pencil was no calligrapher or orthographer. There were single initials other than *H*; there were pronouns in all caps: SHE and HE, or probable monikers like "Hooie." But mostly the entries were as meaningless as hieroglyphs to the uninitiated."

A couple of ragged edges suggested that pages had been torn from the diary, but in the end, there was no real proof that the writing was Raggedy's or Addie's. And as yet there were certainly no pointers as to who might have wanted to kill either one of them. Edie maybe.

Rhys dropped her head back against the soft chair. The diary, the gibberish, her failure to find a clue had given her a stiff neck. "Okay Raggedy, if you want to tell me who killed you, I'll give you five more minutes but you're going to have to be a little more open, sister." Riffling the pages in hopes Raggedy would speak, Rhys's heart skipped a beat when a torn, yellowed newspaper clipping, stuck between pages fluttered to the floor.

Reward

The family of a woman who has been missing from Riversbend f a week has offered a substanti reward to anyone who may have seen her, or who has informati as to her whereabouts. If you have information contact the po immediately.

⁂

One of the perks of being homeless (even theoretically homeless) is that you are invisible. Like with a snake, people forget you exist until you do something that draws attention. Hummer liked to follow people. An adept—he sometimes followed just for the heck of it. Sometimes out of boredom, but usually for fun.

In the dining room, over a plate of cabbage and potatoes, Hummer ate with little interest. He gazed absently out the window, noting that the bright blue-and-yellow morning, which had cheered him earlier, had gone gray, and with its oppressive bleakness so had his sense of well-being.

His stomach ached. He didn't blame his boiled dinner or the weather for his sour belly; he blamed Rhys Adler's imminent arrival. She was always nosing around, making his life miserable and often dangerous. He knew things; he saw things.

Steadfastness, not an attribute that carried much weight with Hummer, he finished his cobbler, which had the consistency of warm petroleum jelly with chunks. Then hurriedly transporting his tray to the kitchen, he slipped out the back door into an alley.

The west sky was low, a good weather prognosticator. Hummer wrapped his scarf around his neck, up to his chin, and over the top of his cap. There was a chance for light snow flurries if the temperatures continued to drop.

Exiting the alley, he wandered up Main Street, stopping at a display of twinkling lights and glittering tinsel in Ball's Department Store windows. A few loose coins jingled in his pocket but not loudly enough for him to go inside and buy himself a gift for Christmas. If he ever got the grocery cart Raggedy had promised him, things would be different. He worried that the money she'd recently bragged about, and safely squirreled away in the cart had been discovered.

Christmas tunes summoning shoppers further up the street caught his attention, and Hummer continued his walk toward a memory from his childhood. A band of three stood on the corner, two in dark hats one in a bonnet. They played carols on a brass horn, a tinny drum, and an accordion.

He hadn't been listening for very long when he saw a familiar figure exit from a pawn shop. Hummer ducked into the alcove and watched as the man stuck two packages, sacks, between his knees so he could wiggle his fingers into a pair of leather gloves. When the man began to walk away, so did Hummer.

Hummer knew the man was one of Raggedy's ducks—her own word. "Here comes one of my ducklings," she would say, or "Quack, quack," she might say behind a wry smile. She had obviously enjoying her latest entrepreneurial venture, but Hummer hadn't. "Someone's gonna come after you, Rag," he'd told her more than once.

"I'm just looking for a little down to feather my bed, honey," she'd said. "It's called getting' even, baby, and don't you go worrying about the Rag Doll. I know what I'm doing."

"How much does he owe y...you?"

Hummer remembered she'd smiled enigmatically. "His good name. Now don't go asking me a bunch of silly questions. Remember what you don't know can't hurt you."

The man, a block in front of Hummer, toted his purchases, one in either hand. Christmas gifts from the pawn shop? "Ch... cheap Eb...eb...eneez...er," Hummer stuttered. One package was pocket sized, and Hummer wondered why he didn't put it in his coat pocket. The other, rolled tightly in brown paper, dangled from his finger by a string. It had weight, Hummer could tell, by the way it bumped against his leg.

The man turned into a residential street, a cul-de-sac, and Hummer, sensing that he was more visible where he didn't belong, slowed his pace but continued trailing after him, letting the distance between them stretch. Pulling his scarf around to cover most of his face, Hummer watched the man approach a single-storied, pale-yellow brick house in the apex of the arch that crowned this neighborhood of attractive, well-tended homes. The man lingered briefly at his mailbox, collecting the day's post, and then without warning turned a sharp 180 degrees and waved at Hummer.

Hummer began running, and when the police car pulled alongside him, he didn't stop.

Rhys, with Old Bay and Jolly in tow, sneaked a peek into the dining room, hoping to see Hummer. Quickly eyeing the mostly empty tables and not seeing him, she easily concluded he'd either eaten earlier or she was late and he had returned to his room to wait for her. What did catch her eye was a lone soul slurping over a bowl of what looked to Rhys to be tomato soup. He smiled and waved enthusiastically, motioning for dogs and all to join him. Deciding on the side of wisdom, which suggested one should not engage a man with no teeth in conversation during his soup course, Rhys smiled weakly and scurried toward the stairs.

Minutes later, she knocked once, twice, listening closely for life on the other side. She'd foolishly brought the dogs as an unadmitted diversion-security tactic. Now they looked at her expectantly. She'd told Hummer she'd come right after lunch, which translated after 11:00 a.m. to him, 1:00 p.m. to her. The clock problem, not to mention the other vagaries of her morning: Languille arriving and Schreiber, and then the jolt from the clipping that had fallen from Raggedy Ann's diary, which had required a lengthy discourse from Richard who felt he must assure her that the clipping could have been stuck in the diary by anyone. "We don't know who the diary belongs to, Rhys, remember?"

Annoyed with life's little aggravations, she watched Jolly and Old Bay wander down the hall contentedly sniffing this new world of strange scents. She thought about scribbling a note and slipping it under Hummer's door, but what if he couldn't read. He wasn't worth a damn at talking. A week ago, she didn't even know Hummer, and now she thought about him daily and sometimes saw him as often. A week ago, Kate was still in Delaware and Rhys was happily ignorant about lachrymatory bottles mysteriously disappearing from lovely old, private museum collections. She had left Kate at the farm with instructions to call the airlines about flight arrangements. If things worked out, Kate's Mini would stay in Riversbend until she returned to Riversbend at the first of the year. On her return Kate would be washed clean and as pure as the proverbial snow.

Rhys tapped one last time before she corralled the dogs, and all three trotted back down the stairs. If the hateful Mr. Runsick was around, dare she ask him if he knew of Hummer's whereabouts? Toad would be her better choice, but she'd have to locate Runsick for that too. She couldn't very well prowl the halls, knocking on every door. She put a pleasant smile on her face, favoring a fruitful encounter rather than a snarky one when her cell phone rang. It was Richard.

He wasted no time alarming her. "The police are looking for you. You are to go to the jail at once," he said.

"Richard, about the clipping in the diary..."

"Rhys, did you hear me? The police are looking for you!"

"Why?"

"I was afraid to ask."

"Oh, Richard, don't tease. Sometimes I need to be taken seriously. Where are you?"

"At the store. Working."

"Would you come with me? I have the dogs."

"Not on your life. Should I call our lawyer?"

"Richard, listen to me. This clipping was in the diary. Doesn't that suggest it could have something to do with our family."

"There never were any claims made for a reward, were there? Not legitimate ones."

"No."

"So let's get back to your problems with the police."

"I haven't done anything. Have I done anything? Is anyone listening to you?"

"Viola Day, but she doesn't give a fig what you do so long as you pay your bill, which, by the way, is something you need to address when you are less involved with the police."

"Could I leave Old Bay and Jolly with Viola Day?"

"Hardy-Har-Har. No."

"Please meet me at the jail. I'm not even sure where it is."

"Where are you?"

"I'm at the Searcy Hotel."

"You do keep interesting company." Richard, enjoying his advantage, would love to have gone on, but Rhys cut him off sharply with her request for directions.

"Okay, go out the front door, turn right, and walk; oh, I'd say about six blocks, maybe five, and you'll come to the jail."

"I have the dogs. I can't walk. You do know, don't you, Richard, that I will not tell you what I found or what this is all about if you don't meet me."

"But you will, darling. I'll be the one you call to bail you out."

Rhys and Richard arrived at the jail about the same time. Rhys stood at the desk, talking to an attendant when he came up and touched her lightly on the shoulder. "Who is that man in your car with the dogs?"

"I hired him."

"Where did you find him?"

"In the dining room at the Searcy Hotel."

Richard shrugged between disapproval and indifference. "I had to come. We have always stood firmly together during our incarcerations. When was your last one? Remember the time you stole that diary from that poor old woman?"

Rhys's face turned the color of cream of wheat. She smiled weakly at the woman she presumed to be a warden. "Don't listen to him. The only thing I've ever stolen in my life was a watermelon at age fifteen from some farmer's patch, and I've suffered guilt ever since."

"Say your name again, sweetie."

"Eugenia Rhys Adler. *E-R-A.* Initials that spell something are lucky. People call me Rhys. You'll need me to spell that for you." She spelled it out slowly. A dark look came into the matron's eyes.

"*R-h-y-s*? Are you sure you ain't left out a vowel some'eres? And say again how you say it?"

"Like the Peanut Butter Cup. It's a family name. My wretched cousin, standing here behind me, said you wanted me to come to the jail." The woman looked at a clipboard long enough to find Adler. "Says here your name is *R-e-e-s-e*," the woman spelled it one letter at a time.

"*R-h-y-s.*"

"It says here *R-e-e...*"

"I don't care how you've mangled it on your...your clipboard. My name is spelled *R-h-y-s*, pronounced "Reese," like the Peanut Butter Cup, if you will."

"I gotcha. Like the candy bar." The matron was satisfied. "We have a guy here goes by the name of Newton?" She glanced at Rhys. "Like the cookie, I reckon."

Rhys giggled.

"He says he needs to talk to you. I'll take you back to the cells." The matron reached into a drawer and took out a ring of keys.

"Is that the best place to keep the keys?" Richard nodded toward the door. "What if there's a riot or a break out, wouldn't that be the first place a criminal would look?"

"I 'spect so." The supervisor didn't seem perturbed.

"It just seems to me—"

"Richard," Rhys growled. "Perhaps you'd like to run for sheriff next term, but until then, put a plug in it."

Following the matron, the cousins were moving toward a double-wide metal door directly behind the matron's desk when the door in the front entrance opened to admit a cold breeze and Clive Potter.

"Mr. Toad!" Richard called out joyously, as would any child seeing a favorite storybook character.

"Mr. Fordyce. I've been looking for you both. Miss Adler, I haven't seen you folks since you pinched Hummer's diary the other morning." Toad tipped his fedora. His gray whiskers sank into deep grooves as he smiled. "Speaking of our young Hummer, he's got hisself a little problem, I'm afraid. He's been accused of stalking."

The cousins were in unison. "What? Who?"

"He won't say who he was stalking, or why 'xactly. That's part of why he's still in jail."

"What's the other part?" Rhys asked.

"Running from the police."

"Oh dear, not good. Who reported him?" Richard asked.

"Anonymous. Some feller said his wife had seen Hummer and that he was acting weird. That she thought he might be on drugs."

"Where'd they pick him up?"

"Over on Oak Street, running back to the Searcy, I 'spect."

"If the caller was anonymous, then I'd think it'd be Hummer's word against his. Doesn't sound too serious. What does he want with Rhys? Bail money?"

"I don't think he has been formally charged. They can't keep him too long. I don't rightly know what he wants. By the way, Miss Adler, what's old Leaky doing in your car?"

"O'Leaky?"

"John Leary's his name. Leaky is just what we call him. Bladder's the problem."

"If y'all are coming, come on." The matron jingled her key ring at them.

The trio followed her through the double doors into a wing of the new jail. Feeling squirrely, Rhys and Richard walked quickly down the corridor that housed six intake cells on either side.

"Hey Toad! Didja come to get me out? Hey man!" Toad seemed to know and to be known by most of the current crop of the incarcerated.

"Macie. I been wondering where you was at," Toad said, his thumb bumping rhythmically along the bars of the cell.

The inmates were friendly or sullen or sleeping. The last cell was Hummer's. The entourage plus Hummer were escorted to an interior room with a table and four chairs. They waited until the matron left, and then all three began speaking at once. Hummer's hand flew above his head, and with a wave, he silenced them and dismissed two, the men. Only Rhys was allowed to stay.

Escorted back through the metal doors, Toad left, leaving Richard vetoed, banned, and feeling mildly sore about it, in no mood to chat with the matron, who was hunched in front of her computer playing solitaire.

He didn't like being excluded, and according to Toad's brief conversation with them prior to going back to find Hummer, it was clear he and Toad were in cahoots. And Rhys? Oh yes, she was right in the middle of it. He stood up to leave as Rhys came clanging through the metal doors.

In five minutes Rhys had handed Leaky a ten dollar bill and sent him up the street. Old Bay looked relieved. Jolly, on the other paw, watched suspiciously as the old man head back toward the Searcy. "Aagh!" Rhys waved a hand in front of her nose. And Richard, carefully eyeing the passenger seat, couldn't bring himself to lean over and sniff. He got in the back seat.

"So, what did he want?" Richard asked, irritated that he had to ask.

"He wants you to locate the arresting officer, find out if he is going to be charged, and if he isn't, then he wants you to help him get released from the jail as soon as possible."

"Me! He wants me to get him out? Why not you? You're his best pal, not me."

"I'm telling you what he said," Rhys declared, truthfully enough. "Please. It shouldn't be difficult, and if you're successful we have permission to keep the *you-know-what* all week. He gave me a tad of information that puts that tiny tome in a different light."

"Such as?"

"Our Hummer says the old girl was in the blackmailing business."

"I don't believe it!"

"Hummer said she was, and he said he wasn't stalking. He was following one of her ducks."

"Ducks," Richard intoned grumpily.

"But he won't say who the duck was. He knows, I think."

"Ducks! Quit talking about ducks. What are you talking about? That boy may be crazy, probably is. He may be making the whole thing up. He may just say whatever nonsense pops into his head so you'll get him out of jail."

"He's not lying. I trust him."

"I'm saying you don't know him."

"You're being hardheaded. You're not listening."

"I am not. I just don't understand why he told you these things and not me. It's because he knows you are gullible."

"He thinks I can understand him when he talks. He struggles, you know."

Richard's face softened slightly. "If he's not lying, then I'm sure you're aware that he should go to the police with this kind of information? You should encourage him instead of abetting him, Rhys. This kind of material introduces motive. This makes me extremely nervous."

"You've got to get him out of jail, before we can learn more. You're a man. Getting someone out of jail is man's work."

"Rhys!" Richard threw up his hands at the cheek of this woman. But he knew he was going to lose. "Dammit, woman! I hate this, but bring the diary to Cedars tonight."

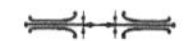

Lunch on Wednesday with Dockers had been a cool move. The two guys, contemporaries, had hit it off at Burger Mama's. Pauley was a couple of years older, but they were teenagers in the same decade. Same music, same movies. They trusted each other.

Dockers talked openly about Raggedy Ann's postmortem, boasting often. He was professional enough, being cagey sometimes, but enough tidbits were tossed out to make Pauley hungry to know more. So the second carrot came that evening when Pauley offered to spring for beers and pizza over at Gusano's after Dockers got off work.

Rolling down Ramey Mountain late and crossing the Wachy Bridge brought him back into Riversbend. One wide turn to the left, a couple of blocks on, then a right onto Library Street, and he was at police headquarters. After threatening all day, it was beginning to snow.

Confident that Latimer had gone home, his plan was to rush in, make some notes about his recently acquired autopsy report, and go home. He patted his inside jacket pocket. The envelope was snug against his chest.

He didn't question if Dockers slipping him a copy of Raggedy's autopsy was illegal because he didn't care. He had his copy, which meant he wouldn't have to go begging Latimer for the original.

If Pauley was going to solve this murder—and it appeared that if it got solved he would be the one to do it—then he was going to have to make his own opportunities and build his own network of people. Dockers and Dr. Petitjean were definitely high on his list and definitely were people he wanted to keep happy.

Inside the building, a telephone rang somewhere up the hall and a man's voice answered. It wasn't Price Latimer's.

Pauley started down the hall, his soft-soled, squeaking shoes, ratting on him each step.

"Whoa!" Tom Drake stepped out of the men's room. "Didn't mean to scare you, McCrary; didn't mean to make you jump. Sorry about that, pal. Speaking of sorry, I hated what Latimer did to you this morning. He's not bad, more like a jock itch."

Pauley smiled. "A real case of crabs."

Tom's face brightened. "Hey, I just remembered. The guys felt bad for you this morning, but we also appreciated your kiss-my-ass attitude. Anyway, we got you something. Sort of a consolation, you know."

"Not necessary, but nice. Thanks." Pauley was self-conscious in the glow of Tom's attention, but he was pleased too. "That's really nice."

Tom chuckled. "I'm not sure right now where we left it."

Pauley nodded. "That's fine." He watched Tom start around the corner.

"Go ask the new night dispatcher." Tom stepped back toward him. "She might know." As he rounded the corner the second time, he was laughing. "Girl magnet," Drake hollered back over his shoulder.

He was glad Gladys wasn't on tonight. He didn't want any conversation. He had decided on the drive home that he was going to become a lone wolf. He was going to operate without a pack.

He would think for himself. He was going to learn to be satisfied with his best whether it stunk or not. And he wasn't going to worry about what Latimer thought, or Drake, any of them, not even Tick.

"In the morning I'm gonna start nosing around and asking questions. Talking to people who work on Bayou Street. It'll be my new style. I'm gonna be getting in white faces for a change. Black too, but when I have to get in a brother's face I might be a little nicer. Yeah, and Richard Fordyce's too." Pauley didn't know what people thought about Richard Fordyce. He knew what he thought. He thought he was queer.

At Tick's desk he couldn't find a good place to stash the autopsy envelope. How long before he'd have his own desk, or a drawer that could be locked. He didn't even have a drawer. He did have a locker, a narrow metal affair with a lock that could be picked with an orange stick. He'd get a better lock tomorrow, but for tonight the locker would have to do.

Other than the hum and click of a nearby printer, suggesting some activity in the building, the only person in evidence was the new night dispatcher, who hurried past just as Pauley saw a note duct-taped to his locker door.

"Hey, Miss!" He started after her. "Do you know where..." he started to ask, but she had a Bluetooth stuck on the side of her head and was speaking into space. Her smile was expansive, though, as she pointed to the multipurpose room a couple of doors down.

The note was typed: "Your partner is napping in the multipurpose room." Pauley stuck the note in his pocket and crammed the autopsy report into his locker.

Barely containing his excitement, he opened the door and stuck his head into the room. "Tick?" He caught a whiff of something, a foul odor, dank but vaguely familiar. "Hello." He flipped the switch.

There was a shifting of weight and a short series of thumps, and then a short-haired, dirty-blond head peered out from behind a filing cabinet.

"What're you doing in here?" Never having had a dog of his own, Pauley was wisely cautious as he approached.

He was particularly wary of big, sad-eyed dogs who sagged in the middle and who, if human, would have been tagged slue-footed. But before he could explain it, Pauley was laughing out loud. He was not scared of this dog. Who would be? This dog was a joke. A half-breed for sure, predominantly retriever, with its dull-yellow fur, the ears of a hound dog, and a long ancestry of plain junkyard mixed in too. And from the way the body caved and splayed, it had to be old.

"Hey, boy. No offense, but you're just about ugliest bag of bones I've ever seen."

He clicked his tongue and held out his hand palm side down toward the animal that remained glued to the cabinet.

"Are you a boy?" Pauley peered under the dog's belly. "Tsk, tsk, you're no virgin. You've had a few puppies, haven't you, old girl? Too bad about that; I can't take you as my partner with a bunch of puppies for us to worry about when we're out on a case, now can I?"

The dog dropped her head to her chest as if she understood every word and that she had been rejected.

"Aww, come on. Be reasonable. Okay. Here's a compromise." He reached in his pocket for a coin; a silver dollar came out between his fingers. "Tails, I'll leave you here for those bozos to take you back to wherever you came from. Heads, I'll take you home and give you a decent meal. Maybe a bath. Fifty-fifty chance. That's as good as I can do."

Pauley flipped the silver piece.

"How you like your eggs?" He took a few steps toward the dog. "Aww shit."

He felt a soft squish under his foot.

"Aww shit." He rolled his boot over. "Now was that a smart thing to do on your first interview?"

The dog began to wag her low-hanging tail.

FRIDAY DECEMBER 20

The Concise Oxford Dictionary of English Etymology lists the word "sagacious" thusly: of acute perception, esp. of smell; gifted with mental discernment. XVII.

The hound dog's yellow coat, dull and reeking of sewage the night before, was deemed acceptable this morning, following a good, hard scrubbing with flea soap, and a second shampooing with a lemony-scented bar Pauley'd found in his medicine cabinet. The bath hadn't helped her sagginess, but the food had made her grin all the way back to her ears. He'd chosen the name Sagacious because she sagged.

Pauley perched on the end of his chair rubbed the loose-fitting skin behind Sagacious's ears. He was cogitating about her at Tick's desk when the phone rang.

On his way home the night before, he dropped by his grandmother's to mooch a piece of pie, but in truth to get her reaction to his new partner. Opal Robinette had made Sagacious stay on her porch, pronouncing her to be the ugliest animal she had ever seen, but by the time Pauley had finished his pie, she'd begun to come around. "There's something about her you like, though, isn't there?"

He and Sagacious were kindred spirits, he decided. Mutts, the both of them. When the two were leaving, his grandmother had actually cooed at Sagacious through the screen door.

"I'll take you to the vet after my church meeting tomorrow, if my grandson will drop you by." She looked up at Pauley to be sure he'd been paying attention. "And, if you behave yourself, I'll stop by the butcher's and see if Mr. Hawkins has a solid soup bone in the back of his shop."

"Would somebody up there answer the damn phone," a shout from the maze pulled Pauley back into the present. The telephone must have rung six or eight times during Pauley reverie.

"McCrary speaking."

"This is Willa Quinn. Have you seen my husband?"

"Mrs. Quinn, hello! Sorry it took me so long...I was...I have a new dog." Pauley grimaced, knowing his conversation sounded stupid. "This is Pauley McCrary. No, I haven't seen Tick. Have you? Is he coming in today? Is he feeling better?" Pauley spoke into silence.

"Who'd you say this is?" Willa Quinn asked.

"Paul McCartney." Pauley laughed lightly, shaking his head. What was so difficult about his name that people could never remember it?

"Paul. I can't find Tick. He hasn't been home for the past couple of nights."

There were seconds of silence before Pauley could speak. "He hasn't been home? At all?"

"Not at all. And he hasn't called."

"Tell you what, Mrs. Quinn. He could be here, and I wouldn't know it. It's a pretty strung-out building, lots of cubby holes and stuff. Let me do some checking around and see if he's doing something for the sheriff, and I'll call you back."

There was a pause, then, "It don't fit; I can tell you that." The phone clicked.

Pointing an authoritative finger at Sagacious, he said, "Stay." They eyed each other, Pauley waiting to see if she would, and Sagacious waiting to see if he meant it. Seeing he did, she did.

"Have you seen Tick this morning?" he asked Gladys Gray, the only woman working in the department, who knew what was going on 99 percent of the time.

"Not since"—she counted on her fingers—"Monday. Went home sick."

"His wife said he didn't come home last night."

"Okay," Gladys Gray said noncommittally.

"Is this normal around here?" Pauley looked distressed. "If the man's not down here and not at home—is this how he works usually? What if he's dead?"

Gladys looked at him wide eyed.

"I can check with the sheriff, when he comes back. I'll ask Tom Drake too"—she nodded at this good idea—"he's pretty up on things. In the meantime, why don't you go..."

"I'll go find Tom."

Gladys Gray liked Pauley. She knew she was old enough to be his mother, but she smiled anyway and shoved her glasses a little higher on her nose. "Latimer's still across the street," she said conspiratorially. "Special delivery brought a report from the lab. It's on his desk. You might want to take a look at it before he gets back. I'll watch out the window and holler if I see him coming." She motioned with her head, prompting him toward Latimer's office. "Go on in there."

The manila envelope, containing numerous photos of fingerprints and an accompanying report, was sealed, but not too securely. Pauley grabbed it and started down toward Tick's desk.

"When you've finished, bring it back. Latimer won't know."

"I owe you one, Gladiola."

"Yep. I'll collect, one of these days."

After the excitement of discovering the dog, the night before, Pauley had put off reading the autopsy report again until this morning. Now having it and the fingerprint information he'd just filched, he settled back in Tick's chair. Surely one or the other of these weighty documents would tell him something he could use.

He tapped the bottom of the autopsy report on the desk to align the pages and began reading. The report was not reader friendly. The language was stiff, scientific, specialized gibberish, and for the most part, unyielding. In moments such as these, he always thought of Tick.

Unclipping his phone from his belt, he jabbed familiar numbers onto the tiny keypad. Tick's message came on immediately for the first time in days. "Call me," Pauley said in a whisper.

Contact! Tick didn't have much to say. Just his voice on his answering machine, but it meant his phone was charged. He called Willa Quinn as he'd promised he would.

"Did his message say anything? I never could get him to answer."

"He said the usual, 'Can't come to the phone. Leave your name and number,' you know. Tick could be anywhere, Miss Willa." Pauley's voice rose with made-up hope. "When an officer is on a case, hunting for clues," Colonel Mustard, in the library, with a candlestick, he might as well have said. His words sounded as hollow as his heart. "I'm gonna go look for him, Miss Willa. I'll find him."

"Well, do what you can. None of you people down there have ever been very good at finding much of anything. I lost my umbrella once, and it never did turn up."

Pauley heard voices down the hall. In seconds, Latimer and Richard Fordyce came into view, heads down as though they shared a secret. He acknowledged Fordyce with a nod. "Let me call you right back, Miss Willa. I'll check around for Tick." He wouldn't have cut her off in the middle of her umbrella story except he had to hide the ripped-off reports before Latimer spied them.

He watched the two men pass. They never looked his way. He sighed, but his relief was premature. Latimer stepped back pinpointing Pauley with an accusing finger. "I want you to drive me to Mrs. Logan Wagner's graveside services at two o'clock this afternoon. Be ready."

"Yessuh, boss."

"And git that dog outta this office."

"Two o'clock, suh. I sho' be ready."

Minutes later and after a trip to scan a copy, the fingerprint information was back on Gladys Gray's desk. Pauley had only glanced at it on his way to the copier. Having a multiplicity of minions to do his work for him, Latimer was rarely in the room with the constant clacking and clicking of copiers, printers, scanners, and computers.

Until the coast was clear, Pauley replanted both reports in his locker, which reminded him he had scheduled today to buy a new lock. With unfinished business and mounting clouds of doubt over his head, he pulled the reports back out of his locker and stuffed them inside his shirt. He had to find Tick.

"Come on, Sagacious."

Connie Becker always approached the Searcy on foot. He didn't want his truck to be identified with this place, which offered shelter to some of the best of his sales staff and provided him with a hideaway. As he got nearer to the hotel, he saw a sweet, silver Jaguar parked in front. He kept walking until he was close enough to touch it. He wondered who it belonged to and what they were doing at the Searcy. Not fully recovered from the beauty of the vehicle and the envy that followed, Connie was blinded momentarily by a glint of sunlight on the windshield as the door of the hotel opened and a tall woman came out. He sauntered innocently away from the car and over toward the old hotel. Leaning indifferently against the building, he lighted a cigarette.

"Nice wheels," he said through an exhalation of smoke.

The woman smiled absently and climbed in on the driver's side. He watched as she inched her car away from the curb and drove west on Main.

Connie Becker was curious. There wasn't much on lower Main of interest to the hoity-toity, the old tire and auto yard, and the jail. Yes, he was curious as to why she was nosing around his haunts, and he didn't much like it.

He watched to see if she turned onto one of the streets running adjacent. When she didn't, pulling instead into the Quick County jail parking lot, Connie stepped into the hotel.

"Who's 'at woman was in here just now?" Becker asked, sniffing, his nose bone-dry from his party the night before. Runsick, pear-shaped and impervious, was standing behind the counter, peering at Connie.

"The Adlers ain't no concern of yours."

Connie grinned and pulled a small bag of whitish crystals from his pocket. "See this, old man? Tell me what she wanted, or I'll find your young Howie and send him into outer space for a few hours. He'll do anything I ask him to do to get a chance to go into orbit." Connie flapped the baggie back and forth in front of Runsick's roving eye. "He'll kill the Adler woman, if I asked him to."

Runsick's olive skin turned ashen. "I didn't say who she was."

"He's an addict, you know, your Howie. A crackhead, most people call him."

"You lie! I'll have you arrested! How do you think you can come in here, threatening me with lies? I could have you sent to the prison for years with that...with that..." He pecked a finger airy at the baggie.

"Do, and I'll bring Howie with me. Now, what did the Adler woman want?"

After hours of wheeling around the county looking for Tick, Pauley felt his tactics pointless. He was defeated, and angry, and he wanted to punch Tick who had deserted him in this unholy mess. He made a tight U-turn off Powhattan Road onto Highway 25 and headed for his grandmother's house.

"Sit." Sagacious sat, and Pauley loosely tethered her to a porch post.

Knowing he'd get a good tongue-lashing for doing it, he found one of his grandmother's cooking pans and, filling it with cold water, took it out for his dog.

Back in the kitchen, Pauley grazed the refrigerator. He ate a stray wedge of cheese she'd left in a piece of plastic wrap and the last sliver of pie she had been saving, as he moved his way toward last night's meat loaf. There was plenty for two sandwiches. Slathering mayonnaise and tomato jam on bread, he added the slices of thinly cut meat loaf, a few sweet pickles, even though he would have preferred dill, and some lettuce. Pulling up a tab on a cold root beer, he straddled a chair at the kitchen table.

His first sandwich devoured in six bites, recharged his energy. He shook the autopsy report from its envelope and spread it before him.

> Name: Francie Butter...(blah, blah)
> Address: (blah, blah)...Riversbend...(okay)
> Ethnicity: Caucasian.
> Age: Unknown, abt. sixty.
> Gender: Male.

"Whoa! Typo?" Pauley sputtered. Had he picked up the wrong autopsy? "Says here, Francie Butter." He read the first page again, this time more slowly and with no assumptions.

> Name: Francie Butter, a.k.a. Raggedy Ann.
> Address: Quick County Group Shelter, Searcy Residential Hotel, Riversbend, AR.
> Ethnicity: Caucasian.
> Age: Unknown, abt. sixty.
> Gender: Male.

He chuckled again. This had to be Dockers's handiwork. Until he saw

> atrophied scrotum. A 2.54 cm scar from an old injury to the penis artery suggests there was sufficient genital damage to render the deceased sexually dysfunctional.

Pauley lost his appetite. He opened the door and tossed the remainder of his meat-loaf sandwiches to Sagacious, who thought the sweet pickles were just fine.

Back at the table, Pauley read the report once again this time at length. It ended with Dr. Petitjean's succinct conclusion:

> cause of death...suffocation, preceded by head trauma.

Petitjean had penciled note at the bottom:

> Tick,
>
> The feather lodged in the upper trachea immediately behind the epiglottis suggests the deceased was probably smothered with something that contained feathers. The possibilities of what is open: a down vest or jacket, pillow, or poultry sack. Her head injury, though not fatal, could have rendered her weak, possibly addled.
>
> Just thinking out loud.
>
> Luck,
> mjp

Petitjean was wrong, and it was his fault for not getting the blanket to forensics sooner. Pauley knew how Raggedy had died. He just didn't know by whose hand. He took the autopsy to his grandmother's spare bedroom and stuck it in a bureau drawer. He kept the fingerprint document with him. Pointless or not, he had to go back out and find Tick. This case was wide open, and it was scaring the hell out of him. He didn't want no truck with nobody who had no respect for a man's genitals.

Dishes quickly splashed and stacked in the sink, he left Sagacious for his grandmother to take to the vet. Trading the patrol car he'd been driving for his own car—a graceful 1984 maroon Seville with a vinyl, toast-colored carriage top—Pauley stared out the windshield, his hands white-knuckling the steering wheel.

Where to next? Back roads? Washed out mud tracks? If Tick had gone underground, his truck could easily be hidden in the clutter of mutilated auto bodies strewed along the county's periphery in too many ill-kept chop shops. That morning Pauley had searched cheap motels, and the outskirts where most of

Riversbend's industry had settled. He had circled parking lots, driven up and down and between hundreds of cars and trucks, ideal places for a clever old truck to hide. But if Tick's truck had been in one of the lots, Pauley had missed it.

What the hell was his man up to? Why hadn't he taken him with him? What had they learned since Monday, the last time he'd talked to him, that had made Tick so cagey? Was he gettin' senile?

"Feathers!"

Pauley started the engine and headed for the river roads where the poultry plants were located. If Tick had gotten the call from Petitjean, the old man knew about the feather in Raggedy's throat, and the first place he would start looking would be where there were lots of feathers.

"Don't go jumping to conclusions" is what Tick would be saying if he were riding shotgun. "Look, you old know-it-all," Pauley growled as he wheeled off Riverwater Street. "I know the feather came from an old army blanket. I'm waiting for the report to come back to prove it. I'm driving out to the poultry plants right now to find you. Now hush the fuck up and let me think." *Just don't get yourself mutilated, running around like a chicken with its head cut off.* Pauley's pulse quickened.

He wished he had his dog.

Reel it in, boy. Facts. What are the facts? Pauley tried to remember exactly what the autopsy had said. Old wound, he remembered that. There was nothing in it to suggest Raggedy's injury had been caused recently by whoever killed her. It could have been, and most likely was, an accidental injury. A tiny smile chipped away at his jumpiness. Okay, so facts are less frightening—also, they are inconclusive.

Ten minutes later with no hint of the chalky, baby-blue-and-white, rust-eroded two-tone Ford truck at the Home Pride Poultry Plant, Pauley drove to Tick's house.

He didn't expect his luck to change, and, of course, it didn't. There was no truck in the driveway or in the front yard or on the two-wheel path that seemed to go to an open field behind the Quinn's house. Lowering his window, Pauley removed his sunglasses and gazed out across the field. Like generations of men before him, he speculated on what lay just beyond the horizon, past that thin edge where the earth falls away.

The Quinns had no garage. Around back, Miss Willa's Minivan, a sizable dent in the front right fender, was parked at a quirky angle under a metal roof. It looked as if she had attempted to enter the double-wide car shelter sideways. The van was nosed in toward the house as close as Miss Willa could get it without cracking the stucco.

Now that he was here, Pauley's impulsive act to call on Willa Quinn didn't seem so smart. She hadn't heard from Tick or she would have called Pauley. He squared his hat and got out of the car.

When the woman opened the door, he could tell she had been napping, or possibly crying. Pauley wouldn't have guessed her to be the type for either. He removed his hat.

"Miss Willa. I'm Pauley McCrary. I didn't get back to you about your umbrella."

She had a peculiar look on her face, but she led him into the living room, wiping her hands on her apron. "Would you like a cup of coffee, Paul?" He sat on a red-velvet love seat that didn't seem to fit the owners, or with the rest of the furniture. While she was in the kitchen, Pauley looked around. He'd never been in Tick's house. The living room was small. Two recliners, a narrow table between, a large television, and the velvet love seat almost filled the space. There were no photographs. A small painting of a mare and foal in a field was over the television. When Willa Quinn came back, she carried two mugs. She handed one to him and seated herself on the smaller of the two recliners.

"I hope you like it black. I'm out of milk. Sugar too. I don't want to go to the grocery store. I could miss my husband's call when it comes."

She seemed to enjoy his visit, but she didn't tell Pauley much he didn't already know.

Tick had wanted her to sleep in the guest room so she wouldn't catch his cold. Pauley did learn he'd left the house on Tuesday, returning with a sack Miss Willa thought was from the drugstore. When she'd asked if he'd seen a doctor, and what the doctor had said, Tick had said that he was not going to die.

"He always says things like that." Willa took a sip of her coffee. "He's always joking. Never takes things serious. He said, 'I ain't gonna die just yet,'" she repeated.

Pauley nodded. That was Tick, all right.

"He asked me to make him a pot of homemade vegetable soup. He ate a good supper on a tray in our bedroom." Willa went on to say she didn't think Tick had slept very well, as she heard him roaming around the house that night.

"Do you have any ideas where he might be?" Pauley finally got around to asking. "Some special place he likes to go?" It was not exactly a question one would ask about a policeman supposedly investigating a case.

Willa had caught the question within the question. "What kind of talk is that? He wouldn't find whoever killed that old woman out there."

"Where is out there?"

"His homeplace. We used to go out to his old homeplace on picnics when we were younger. He called it the shotgun house. I doubt it's still standing."

"Do you know how to get there?"

"Out from Pearl, near the river. We used to go looking for mussel shells."

The rest of the visit lasted only long enough for Pauley to drain the last drop of coffee.

She watched from the door as he backed out of the driveway. He glanced at his watch. He wouldn't have time to go back out toward the button factory this afternoon. There were a lot of brick houses that all looked alike, but no tumbledown shacks, to his knowledge. And if there was one road out from Pearl, there were a dozen. He'd save Pearl until tomorrow when he wasn't having to play chauffer to the sheriff.

Pauley tried to think where on the river the button factory had been, where mussel shells would have been gathered. He'd ask some of the old-timers. He also needed a decent county map. But before he got one, he stopped at a Breeze-By and grabbed a half gallon of milk and a five-pound bag of sugar.

Determined to postpone any confrontation with Latimer until after Addie Wagner's funeral, Pauley popped into headquarters and got an updated county map from Gladys and then ran back out to his car. If Latimer did show up, he'd assume Pauley's old car belonged to one of their inmates.

As he reached inside the glove box for the fingerprint report, an inexplicable sense of well-being swept over him, causing him to pat his dashboard. His Seville might be older than Methuselah, but her interior was enormous and very accommodating.

Maybe I don't need a desk of my own. I'll get me one of those padded lap desks like Gran uses to work her crosswords, and I can get me a metal box with a serious lock. Hell, I can keep my sleeping bag in the trunk and one of those plug-in coolers.

Pauley nodded in agreement at the happy prospect of his new mobile office.

Maybe I'll quit parking back here too. I'll find a new spot, convenient but undetectable, and Latimer will never know exactly where I'm at or how exactly the Lone Wolf strikes again to save Riversbend from harm. "Yay."

Revved, Pauley gunned his engine to go seek this undetectable place where he could park, and hide, and read the fingerprint report in the privacy of his fine wheels without feeling like Asshole was looking over his shoulder, just as Asshole pulled onto the department parking lot, blocking the narrow drive, thrusting two menacing fingers at Pauley, while mouthing something stupid like Pauley'd better be back in time for Addie Wagner's services, or his black ass was grass.

A temporary parking spot was behind the Coffee Cupp. The fingerprint report was brief. The lachrymatory bottle kept its secrets. There were prints, but only one set clearly identifiable, Raggedy Ann's. The others were either lab employees or unidentified.

Okay then, who could have had contact with the lachrymatory bottle besides Raggedy? Fact: her prints would have been taken at the morgue. So if the bottle was found in her hand only after *she had been admitted into the morgue, does that tell us anything? Not me. Doesn't tell me a damn thing.*

Okay, Tick or me could *have had prints on the bottle, had we seen the bottle the night she died. But we didn't. The morgue and lab people all had contact after they found it, obviously, but, fact two, they should all have prints on file, so why didn't they show up? Gloves.*

Pauley rubbed his head, trying to sort the mishmash into something reasonable he could work with. The lachrymatory vessel was a museum piece. It should be covered in prints. The murderer's prints among them, right? Not necessarily. There was nothing to prove the murderer even knew that Raggedy had the bottle in her hand. What good were prints if they could not be identified? Pauley wasn't even sure what questions he should be asking himself. Okay, if the prints were unidentifiable, wouldn't that suggest there were no previous records for comparison? Yes, that was a possibility. Okay. That was a start. But it was nearly time for Addie Wagner's funeral. He'd better get his ass in the door and report for duty. He locked the print report in his glove compartment-filing cabinet.

As Pauley passed Tick's desk on his way to locate Latimer, he spotted an envelope that hadn't been there earlier. Glancing around, not sure if he should take it, he stuck the envelope in his shirt pocket. He'd read it in the car while he waited for the sheriff to leave the funeral. Postponing this dummied-down assignment to chauffer the sheriff for as long as possible, Pauley chose to steal a few minutes in the evidence room would be a better use of his time. He wanted to searching for a piece of evidence that could be fingerprinted and that just might match the prints on the lachrymatory bottle. His case needed something. To date there was very little convicting evidence. The few things he'd gathered that night that had seemed like a good haul: the cigarette wrapper, a small piece of packing tape, and later a few of her clothes, her shoes, and later still significant items from the grocery cart added up to mostly zip.

Flipping the light on, the first thing that made his heart fall into his belly was the file drawer where the stuff for Raggedy's case was kept was unlocked and standing ajar. The second thing was to discover that the tear bottle was gone.

Pauley hugged the steering wheel in Number 11, the newest and most recently spit-polished patrol car. He watched Price Latimer, who stood hatless in a large mix of mourners and curiosity seekers. As he watched, he stewed about the lachrymatory bottle, wondering if it was another prank like Sagacious, but his gut told him it was not a prank. Nothing else seemed to be missing.

Isabella Radley, on the other side of the gravesite, watched Logan Wagner loosen the tan Burberry scarf from his neck before offering his arm to an older woman as they were ushered under the green funeral awning to be seated.

The Episcopal priest, in a black robe and a white liturgical stole, leaned toward Logan, appearing to whisper something that prompted Logan to partially stand and glance over the congregants. Miss Radley could tell he was looking for someone.

Family members, moving awkwardly, filled the row of chairs to the side of Logan's and a very somber older woman's. Her hands folded stiffly in her laps she barely acknowledged the others, or the mash of people who had begun to crowd in under the canopy. Then Isabella saw Logan's face brighten.

Interesting. Isabella edged her way toward the canopy to get a better view. A young woman who could have been Addie Wagner's twin had come in and had taken a seat on the back row almost hidden in a swag of the canvas. Logan exchanged a few words with his mother-in-law and then walked back to Addie's sister, Marilyn. Leaning down he kissed her cheek and whispered to her. She seemed hesitant, but then Logan took her hand, and she followed him. Her handkerchief was squeezed into a tight ball as the front row of grievers shifted to the right.

Riversbend, like all towns, enjoyed drama, and Addie Wagner's death had been the most sensational in nearly 150 years. The last comparable one was John Bailey's hanging in 1863. In the old days, school would be let out, so the students could attend a good hanging. A meaningful lesson for the little ones, her father had speculated, a gruesome deterrent from choosing a life of crime. *"Yes, death was seldom the end of the story."*

When the priest took his place beside the casket, Isabella stepped back. They were all there: Episcopalians and Baptists, students and teachers, doctors, judges, lawyers, policemen, even Marybeth Wagner, Logan's ex, looking successfully solemn, but Miss Isabella didn't step so far back that she couldn't catch bits of conversation from the murmurings around her. Most of it was what one would expect, the "so-sads" and "what-will-become-ofs," but some were quite tasteless. "Who'll be the next Mrs. Wagner? My money's...on that sister." Isabella was not the only one with eyes at that funeral.

Addie Wagner was not old family. She was not even a native of Riversbend, which had rendered her more or less insignificant to

Isabella Radley until her tragic death. Now Isabella scanned the faces of the people, wondering if Addie's killer was there, veiled in innocence.

Pauley, waiting in the patrol car, pondered the same question. He could have learned some things from Isabella Radley, but he knew her only by sight. He was a quarter her age and it never occurred to him that she had a kind of wisdom that could assist him in his investigation. In a short time, he would learn this, but today he only saw a withered old woman sitting on a canvas chair that had miraculously popped out of her walking stick. On the side of the grave opposite him, Isabella Radley watched him. She knew a great deal about Pauley McCrary.

Had she been asked, had she known Tick was missing, Isabella probably could have told young Pauley where his friend was hiding out. She shivered, looking at the sky for signs of more snow. Cold weather might cause her old bones to creak, but she'd never let that quell her interest in Riversbend's goings-on.

Isabella could also have told Pauley that if he'd look back just over his left shoulder he'd actually see his detective lieutenant. Tick wore a wide brimmed straw hat. He was seated on a bench beside the remnant of a large oak tree at Jimmy Quinn's gravesite. The grave was in the newer, less prestigious part of Peaceful Oaks Cemetery. He looked just like any other gardener or gravedigger in overalls, holding a shovel.

Getting Hummer out of jail took longer than either cousin had anticipated. As the weird and wonderful boy came slouching out the door into a light flurry of snow, Rhys was waiting in her newly washed and lemon-scented car. She motioned for Hummer to get in the front seat. She was surprised when he did without argument.

"Hungry?"

He nodded enthusiastically, which began a series of suggestions on her part, ranging from Hamburger Heaven's burger basket with real onion rings, to the Cupp's Blue Plate, to the triple-dipper banana split with whipped cream, nuts and a cherry on top still served at the old New City Drug soda fountain. All these were answered by thumbs down. Finally, Hummer, in a sparse five or so syllables, allowed that he would talk about Rag's diary only if Rhys would treat him to a T-bone at the Razorback Bar and Grill out on the old highway to Pearl.

"Don't press your luck, bucko."

"M…m…meeee…medium…r…rare."

"Damn, you're pushy."

"R…r…rare then," he said smugly. Rhys'd treat him to a whole roasted cow if he asked for one.

"May I ask you one question? Did Raggedy ever blackmail people?" Rhys knew Hummer wouldn't be direct. He was too cool for that until his T-bone bled in front of him. He gazed out the window rather than looking at her.

Rhys telephoned Richard. "You've got to go with us. It's a pool hall."

"Nope. Emphatically and unconditionally, no."

"That's not nice."

"I've planned to go to the club for dinner, and I am going to go. I haven't been with any of my friends since this town has gone crazy killing people, and we have a lot of catching up."

Par Green.

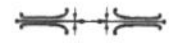

Every wine-warmed society-swell momentarily froze when Rhys Adler and Hummer strolling through the cedar-garlanded-red-ribboned double doors into the Par Green dining room. Brows crowned, eyes widened, lips (caught midsentence) ceased to move, creating for anyone quick enough to witness it, one of those marvelous moments when the world does, according to the poet, become a stage.

Passing each table, Rhys offered moue kisses to one or two, twittered her long fingers at others, and between gestures, she scanned the room for Richard.

Hummer, trailing behind her yet surprisingly urbane, was the first to spot him.

"Th...th...th...there!" He pointed to Richard who was perched on a bar stool amid a group of laughing people. Giddy with sensory overloaded, Hummer plowed into Rhys's back full bore.

Teetering on the edge of poise, pretending imperviousness to the many eyes watching, she regained her balance and continued in an almost slow-motion glide toward Richard, with her own personal Dickensian ragamuffin following on her heels, chanting monosyllabic nonsense.

Her advance was silent therefore without warning. "Richard? Hummer and I are hungry for a steak dinner. Want to join us? I'm buying."

"Good grief, woman! Here, have a seat. Hummer." Richard knew when he was bested, and when beaten, he could become extraordinarily inane. He rose on a wisecrack regarding his cousin's new career in private investigation, popped the olive from his martini into his mouth, and proceeded to introduce Hummer to his circle of friends. His hand resting comfortably on Hummer's shoulder, Richard launched the crusty, slightly stale-smelling young man into the midst of Riversbend society. Three men and two women extended their hands instinctively, but after Richard's sweeping gestures, the quintet quickly brushed their *bonhomie* against a skirt panel, a square of handkerchief, or a blazer pocket. Then with a brisk bow, Richard excused himself from his party.

Hauling the diary from an oversized coat pocket, Rhys handed it to Richard in a gesture of pacification.

They scanned the dining room for privacy, a spot where they could whisper. They found a quiet table back in the corner.

Tonight, Hummer, always a man of few syllables, was mute. He wouldn't answer questions, he wouldn't even look at them until after he'd dealt with the salad bar, a twelve-ounce steak, a loaded baked potato, a basket of fresh-from-the-oven sourdough rolls with a chunk of butter the size of a lemon. At last sated, he warmed to cooperation, pulling the napkin from his shirt collar, scooted his chair back, and belched effectively. "R...Rag wanted to stop. M...meant it to be the last t...time."

Rhys, who had begun to regret her bribe until now, said, "Wanted to stop. Last time for what?"

"Sh...she had one more p...piece of b...b...business that needed f...finishing." The cousins exchanged looks. This was the closest to a conversation they had ever had with Hummer.

"Blackmail, you suggested to Rhys, but are you sure, Hummer? I can't imagine. Who was she blackmailing?" Richard asked. "She wanted to quit, right? She was not a bad woman."

Rhys turned to Richard. "Would someone want to kill her for *not* blackmailing?"

"I knew her better than you. Perhaps she was someone's patsy?

"Patsy? What century do you live in, Richard?"

As Richard's continued to deny Raggedy's complicity, Rhys noticed their young man gazed at his empty plate. "Hummer?" Across the starched tablecloth, she touched his hand lightly. "I'll buy you dinner weekly for a month if you will answer our questions honestly and as quickly as you can. We don't have a lot of time if we are going to find who killed Raggedy Ann. For instance, in the diary she mentions an ED?" Rhys enunciated the initials singly and clearly, wanting to avoid imposing her suspicions on Hummer.

"Who writes with green ink?" Richard asked.

"Who is Mickey?" Rhys asked.

Hummer turned away, but a stream of word-like sounds tumbled out of his mouth as he did so.

"Beg your pardon?"

Hummer giggled. "I...I don't know about M...M...Mickey. B...but H...hooweeee." He rocked his head in a cadence.

"Sorry?" Rhys looked annoyed.

"Y...you r...r...r'member. M...M...Mickie n...D... Donldduhhh. R...rag's...duhhhh...ks." Hummer stretched his neck reaching for the *k*. "Ka."

"Duhk. Did you just say 'duck'?"

He nodded. "A...all of em. H...oowien-looweeand Dooo."

"Dewey, Huey, and Louie? The nephews?" Rhys jumped up.

"H...her i...i...insurance. Her f...four-oh-one *k*," Hummer beamed.

"Four oh one k. Raggedy's insurance, her ducks! You're talking about blackmail victims, right?"

Another smile, buried deep in Hummer's beard, pudged his cheeks, crinkling his eyes.

"Do you know his middle name?" Richard asked, not waiting. "Donald Fauntleroy Duck."

"Richard, is this information important, do you think? Really!"

"He's r...r...right, Miss Rhys." Hummer blushed. It was the first time he had ever called her by name to her face.

"Okay. Fauntleroy. I don't give a fig. Fauntleroy, okay, but please, let's get back on focus." Rhys sat down. "Now the nephews! What does it mean, Hummer? Who are they? Her blackmail targets, but who are they really. Richard, can you remember exactly in the diary what it said about Huey or Louie?"

"Are you serious? Are we really going to charge Donald Duck with killing Raggedy Ann? This entire conversation is ludicrous. Plain silly." But Richard chortled.

"Not silly, it depends who Donald is, doesn't it? Who are we talking about. Do you know someone here in Riversbend with three nephews or anyone with names that sound like Huey, Louie, Louise, or some such?" Rhys pulled her ear lobe like one does when playing charades. "How did she choose her victims? Where did she get her whip, so to speak?"

"T…trash. R…recycla…b…b…bles."

"Dumpsters," Richard added. "I feel silly, Rhys, but,"—he turned to Hummer—"Who might Dizzy Duck be?" His question sounded earnest, but his conviction that the trio was onto something significant was betrayed by the silly grin on his face.

Rhys leaned back in her chair to remember the first morning they had the diary. "It seems there may have been a Daisy."

"S…she never used r…r…real names," Hummer offered. "I…i…ini…ini…f…f…f…first ini…"

"I love it!" Rhys said excitedly. "We're making progress."

"We're getting nowhere."

"Listen Richard, 'Louie' would mean an *L* name and 'Huey' a name starting with an *H*?"

"Halliger!" Richard said.

"See! What did I tell you!" Rhys, always a little right, leaped on it.

Richard sitting sideways in his chair, long legs crossed gracefully at the knees, glanced casually around the dining room. No one seemed to be interested in them. "Okay." He turned to his companions. "This conversation is nuts. But if we're going to go with it let us pull together." He waved them to lean in across the table, and then for the next half hour, the three conspiring heads quietly dissected Larry Halliger's recent life. How many nephews he had? One. Was he having an affair? With Green Ink? Who was Green Ink? No one knew, or if one of them did know no one would say.

They agreed that *H* could stand for "Hummer," or for "Halliger," or for anyone else in Riversbend who had a name that began with an *H*. Richard enjoyed pointing out.

Hummer couldn't exactly explain the numbers in the diary. They agreed had to be dates or times, or money. There was one curious entry, a number twenty with a smiley face drawn into the zero. That surely meant something. It showed emotion.

"We've wandered off course," Rhys said, "Let's get back to Larry. Assuming he was having an affair, was he having it with Green Ink? The cousins looked to Hummer who blushed prettily, which was a dead giveaway that the suggestion of an affair was a possibility, but with Green Ink, not so much.

"Could Larry Halliger have been one of her ducks? Raggedy could have been blackmailing Larry Halliger?" Rhys was like a dog with a bone.

"Don't jump to conclusions, Rhys." Richard sat back momentarily. "Larry Halliger may be Romeo, but he wouldn't kill someone even if he were being blackmailed."

"Who else could it be? Hummer, I know you know more than you're saying."

Hummer shook his head.

"Was drug dealing part of her business? Did she work for that slime ball, I've seen hanging out at the hotel?" Rhys asked.

"Of course she didn't deal in drugs," Richard said.

"Beeec...Becker? N...no! Everyone stays away from him."

Rhys wondered if Becker could the Mick, Raggedy was concerned about? "Is Becker bad news?" she asked.

"Ye...es...s. M...Meth." Hummer vaguely waved his hand over his head.

"In Riversbend? We must report this."

"You don't have to tonight, Richard."

"Becker's gonna k...k...kill us!"

"He won't tonight, Hummer."

"So, who else was she blackmailing? Hummer, I know you know."

Hummer pushed back from the table this time and immediately began to hum. He hummed loudly enough that heads at other tables turned toward them. It was just as well. He was perfectly clear that he had said all he intended to for one meal.

Richard left them shortly after being assured Rhys was going to pay the tab. Pecking her on the cheek, he wandered back to his friends in the bar. Rhys, avoiding the bar, escorted Hummer out the front door. At the Searcy she thanked him and asked him to try and remember all the little things he knew about Raggedy's ducks. Rhys suspected he remembered far more than he was willing to tell. After all, he had a taste for fine food, and Par Green had a much better chef than the Searcy Hotel.

When they'd parted company, Hummer was jittery, and Richard troubled, but Rhys was excited, she had information. Sketchy, but enough: there were missing pages, they knew Raggedy was a blackmailer, they knew cartoon characters referred to real people, and there were numbers in the book that meant something. Now all she had to do was figure out what. *If we only knew if ED was Edie, if so, then we'd know the Halliger family was somehow involved in Raggedy's death even if they didn't kill her.* The answers were all there in the diary just as she had known they would be—there was the red dress, the blue sweater—the haircut. *And I'm sure,* Rhys continued her wordless convictions into the air around her, *when we discover who Green Ink is, it will be someone Edie knows, and runs into regularly. Riversbend is not a metropolis. Green Ink must be one of us! Besides—Larry has a hard ass. He's a coach; he wears gym shorts.*

It wasn't late when she walked into the kitchen, but the Schreibers had retired to their rooms. Coming up the drive she'd seen a light was on in Kate's bedroom. When Rhys poked her head in to say good night, she saw Kate had fallen asleep reading, or was playing possum. "Kate?" she whispered, but listening to Kate's light, whiffing snore, Rhys closed the novel that lay open on top of the quilted comforter and placed it quietly on the bedside table. Then she turned off the lamp.

Bone-weary Rhys was ready to give up her private investigation for some sleep, she stripped, slipped into her gown, washed and moisturized her face, turned off her bed light, and in minutes too short to count, she too was whiffing.

At peace with the ending of a successful day, she should have slept soundly until morning, but at some hour, she was awakened by a crazy parade of cartoon characters. In the haze between asleep and awake, she recognized what should have been obvious earlier.

"Goofy" with a little *g* was no adjective, Goofy was one of Raggedy's lucrative acquaintances. Connie Becker was Goofy. She didn't know how she knew, but she'd bet on it. Unfortunately, whoever the Mickey was that Raggedy had been worried about had not come to Rhys like a breakthrough. Who could Rag have been fearful of? Who would make a bag lady anxious? Was blackmail the same as extortion?

Rhys's eyes followed as beams from a cold white moon filtered through the window onto her duvet, but her eyes didn't knowingly see them, rather she listened to something Richard had said at dinner. Larry Halliger was not a killer. When you live in a small town, you know things about people, and Rhys too knew that Larry Halliger was not a murderer. Still...

She slipped on her glasses. It was 2:56 a.m., almost the witches' hour. Tomorrow she'd go snoop around in the junk room, looking for she knew not what, and then she's go question Hummer some more about Connie Becker. Wasn't there something about civil disobedience that had a positive ring? Richard was just going to have to hold his horses, for a day or two until she was ready for him to inform the police about Goofy with a little *g*.

Poor Hummer, he was in an awkward position as far as Raggedy's murder went. He would be interrogated by the police soon. His association with Raggedy demanded it. He was her heir, so to speak. And then there was Becker. How did he play into this? Was he as dangerous as Hummer imagined? Might he try to kill them? She didn't suppose Becker would be dangerous if *he* didn't know *she* knew about him. Regardless, she couldn't wait forever before reporting him to the police.

In the moonlight Rhys promised herself that tomorrow she would piece together all the information she could from the diary, and then she and Hummer together would take it to the police. They must do this for his protection.

Burrowing her head deeper into her pillows, satisfied that extracting information from people must be one of her God given talents, which surely warranted her using her talent for good, she wondered briefly if she should—the thought trailed away like Hypnos after Nyx.

Not prior to nor after Addie Wagner's funeral did Pauley mention to Price Latimer that the lachrymatory bottle was missing. He did, however, ask Gladys if anyone had shown any interest in it.

"It's not in the evidence drawer?" Her immediate response carried a wide-eyed panic over the tops of her bifocals.

Pauley flashed a sickly smile. "Aha! Just making sure you're onto what's going on around here."

"What is going on?"

"Nothin'. Just checking."

Gladys watched him strut away, but she could tell by his stiff neck that he struggled to keep from turning and looking back at her. A sure sign that something was up.

Pauley whistled as he passed Latimer's door back down the hall. Hell would freeze over before he would tell that pigheaded warthog anything about anything. Oink, oink.

He had left the building before he remembered he'd never read the fold of paper in his breast pocket. He climbed into the back seat his maroon and tan vinyl-roofed office and locked the door. Shaking the note free of its fold, it took seconds for him to see that it had been torn from a diary, a five-year diary with inch-wide divisions and no dates.

> How 'bout them apples. I saw you take 'em. Hand me what cash you got in that big pocketbook full of stolen apples, and I'll pretend I never saw you.

It didn't take a wizard to know the diary it was torn from was the little book he'd stupidly left with Richard Fordyce. Pauley's skin began to crawl. "Stupid!" He wadded the piece of paper in his fist. "Asshole! You give good evidence away and keep shit like all the shit in the grocery cart."

He unwadded the note and read it again. It wasn't signed, but there was a smiley face. Pauley looked at both sides of the paper and then at the envelope; "Fresh as a Daisy Cleaners and Flower Shop" was stamped in the upper left-hand corner. Out of the back into the driver's seat, Pauley spun out of the parking lot, seeking sanctuary from nosy eyes and finding it sooner than he thought. He pulled sharply into a seldom used alley-like double-rut across the street. Luckily situated at an odd angle and far enough away that if he rolled down his window and leaned as far to the left as he could, he could get a pretty good view of who was coming and who was going at headquarters. Looking his car, he jaywalked across the corner on Library Street to the Fresh as a Daisy Cleaners and Flower Shop.

Ten minutes later he had the name of the customer whose trousers pocket had made a blackmailer's note police property. Saluting Mr. Crayton at Fresh as a Daisy for helping, in another ten minutes, Pauley was ringing a doorbell a few blocks away. He double-checked the name above it. Almost immediately a small woman who must have seen him come up her sidewalk opened the door a crack.

"Mrs. Roach?"

"Yes." She peered suspiciously at him.

"I'm Officer McCrary of the Metro Division of the Quick County Sheriff's Department." Pauley showed his identification. "May I come in? I have something that I think belongs to you." Slipping the crumpled note from his pocket, he smoothed it against the doorframe as he watched all color drain from the woman's face.

"My husband is napping in the front room." Her distress on seeing the note overcame her first fear, which was having a colored man standing at her door, even one in uniform. She stepped out onto the stoop, cautiously closing the door behind her. Too crowded for two on the stoop, she whispered as if she told a secret. "That isn't mine." Her voice trembled slightly.

Pauley could have kicked himself. He should never have shown her the note until he'd gained entry into her little house.

"Mrs. Roach. I'm more interested in who gave you this note than in why it was given. Blackmail is a crime."

"I'm a churchgoing woman, Mr.…Mr.…"

"McCrary."

"I have done nothing. I am blackmailing no one, and no one is blackmailing me."

"The note was in the pocket of your trousers, Mrs. Roach." Pauley desperately wanted to keep her talking. "Please help me. We are investigating a murder—"

"No. You are mistaken. There is no need." Her smile was wobbly.

Pauley frowned. "No need?"

"God metes out his own justice. That paper has nothing to do with me…or my husband. I must go back inside. If my husband wakes up and I'm not in there..." She motioned toward some room on the other side of the closed door.

"Mrs. Roach, just one more question, please. How long have you lived in Riversbend?"

"I grew up here."

"Then you may have known Raggedy Ann. And I bet you know she was the woman who was found in the Dumpster behind Adler's last Saturday. Was it Raggedy who handed you the note that you stuck in your trousers pocket?"

Mrs. Roach's smile was not so wobbly now. It was hard. "My husband is the only one who wears trousers in this family, Mr. McCrary, and he is an invalid." The door closed quietly behind her.

"As I am a policeman's wife, Tick was always saying to me, 'Willer,' he always calls me Willer, 'don't go borrowing trouble.'" Willa Quinn, talking over the ache in her throat, coughed.

Pauley waited. At dusk, the loneliest part of day, he'd finally caught up with her on the telephone. He could hear her attempt to swallow her tears, the tightness.

"Don't go borrowing trouble," she managed to repeat. "But something isn't right. This isn't like him. He had a fever, you know. Did you go out to see if the old place is still standing?" Her voice was flat, coming from the dead zone of worry.

"I had to drive the sheriff to a funeral. I'll go tomorrow. He's never gone off this long without contacting you? Is that what you're saying?"

"Not without a word."

The day was gone with its cheery light when Pauley slipped into the evidence room. It would take him only a couple of minutes to see if the tear bottle was back. Grasping at straws earlier, he had decided that the bottle have been misplaced or misfiled. Now, as the day was faded, the doubts that had lain idle in sunshine began slipping loose to flutter up from his belly. He groaned.

He tugged at the drawer tagged as "F./Butter/ 121407" and began rummaging among the labeled bags of evidence. The feather was there, as well as a strip of yellow plastic packing tape. He ran his hand around the drawer's deep sides, feeling slowly toward the back, under the file folders. He peered inside the folders. The lachrymatory was very small; it could be hiding in one. It wasn't.

Buttoning his jacket he trotted up the hall to the front desk. Gladys Gray, head down, was sorting to file a backlog of reports from an overextended and understaffed department. Pauley knew if she didn't have the bottle, or know something about it, he would have to tell her it was gone. Missing.

After her initial reaction—which was that no *man* knew how to hunt for something lost—he assured her he'd searched through all the drawers, on every shelf, and in every file cabinet in the evidence room. He ended on a plea, "Would you check around for me, Gladys? I can't afford to be thought of as the cop who can't keep up with his own evidence."

The vulnerability of inexperience shone in his eyes.

"You know just casual-like. See if anyone has seen it, had it. If they have, get it if you can and hold it for me? Don't put it back in the evidence room, don't give it to anyone, and don't say a word to Latimer, okay?

"One more thing." Pauley turned back to her. "I don't guess *you've* heard from Tick."

"Not a grunt or a groan." Gladys's face was sympathetic. "I'll give you a buzz if I do."

"I don't care what time of day or night it is."

"Tom Drake's a nice guy. Talk to him," she said.

"Can't. Everyone's too busy on the Wagner case."

"You're doing all right. Hang in there, handsome."

Pauley stopped talking for a moment to look at Gladys. A slow grin moved up from his lips into his eyes, and he put his elbows on the counter and leaned in toward her. "Have I ever told you about my car, Gladys. First off she can sit a curve like a tank." Gladys frowned, but she was listening, leaning on her desk as Pauley began purring the most beautiful, nonsensical sweet talk she'd ever heard. "Easy, low ridin', roomy in the rear, holds the road. I'll take you for a ride one day." Pauley slapped the top counter resolutely and straightened up. "All she needs is a good lube job, but, unfortunately, I can't afford it right now."

"One day, baby. One day." Gladys was breathless.

"Thanks for the chat, Gladiola. Nothing makes a fellow feel as good as a little car talk. See you in the morning."

When he passed evidence room on his way out of the building, he rattled the doorknob to ensure it was locked. By the time he hit the back door, the lachrymatory bottle dominated his thoughts. Who would want it? Who did it belong to? Why was it in Raggedy's hand when she died? That was the easiest question. She was a Dumpster diver. It was the first two questions that stumped him. *If I knew the answers would I know who killed her? Maybe. Not necessarily. TV cops were always boasting about how if they knew this they'd know that. It didn't mean it was true. "Facts, son."* Pauley could almost hear Tick. "I hear ya man."

To focus Pauley began enumerating the facts as he knew them. *One, the tear bottle was found in Raggedy Ann's hand at the morgue. We don't know for an absolute fact that she had it in her hand when she was murdered. We just know she had it in her hand at the morgue*—Pauley attempted to separate assumption from certainty. *We don't know if someone put it there, and if so why.*

He frowned.

That's dumb, McCrary. Okay, two, we don't know who owns the tear bottle. We're not even positive that it's an antique. It may have nothing to do with Adler's.

Pauley stood on the steps at HQ, searching for answers in the deepening night.

Three, the tear bottle—or at least as recently as ten minutes ago—was not in the evidence drawer. This doesn't mean it was stolen. It only means that it's not where it should be. So, is there a useable connection between the disappearance of the bottle and the murderer? He exhaled in frustration. *Whoever took it knew it was in the evidence drawer. That's a fact. So it had to have been someone in law-enforcement, right?*

By the time he had reached his Cadillac, he had concocted several reasons why someone might want it. CIA. The bottle had something inside like a tightly rolled cylinder of paper, a note, film, international something. Or Medical. Drugs. Illegal. A vial, something as slender as a needle case, with or Terrorist Plot. Anthrax! Something powerful enough to destroy a city's drinking water supply, a drop from the vial potent enough to kill thousands. But in Riversbend? Suddenly, Pauley began to crave a drink of water. He started toward the water cooler. Or—and this made more sense—there was something on the bottle that worried the murderer.

"It's okay to be open to ideas, son. Just don't go marryin' every idea you have. Some of 'em are whores."

The last thought Pauley had regarding the lachrymatory bottle turned out to be the least creative. If it was an antique; you could get good money for it if you knew how to fence it. He and Tick roughly knew its value but they wouldn't have if Miss Adler hadn't told them (and told them, and told them).

He trudged across gravel to his car. Rhys Adler knew, though. She knew its worth, and she knew it was in the evidence room. He'd told her himself. She wouldn't need a fence either; she'd keep it, hide it in the clutter of all her gewgaws. That'd be pretty smart. Coming down to get fingerprinted and managing to finger the lachrymatory bottle. He could see it happen. She was a snoop. It was possible. She'd have to have someone on the inside help her, wouldn't she? Pauley pondered who for a minute. *It'd have to be the rat, Leo Lockhart. Nawh,* Pauley sighed. Rhys Adler couldn't sneak around anywhere without drawing attention to herself? She was too damn haughty—and gawky. If she tried to sneak here, she'd create such a racket everyone in the department would be following her around.

Pauley liked his idea of her hiding the lachrymatory in her house though. He'd like to go back out to the McGuire farm house and do a little sneaking around himself. He liked the farm, the land, the house, but he didn't much like all the odds and ends sitting around. Depressed him. Made him feel like he was gonna smother. His McCrary grandmother's house was crammed with the same kind of old stuff.

When he was a kid, he and his grandmother Robinette would be invited to the McCrary house for a visit every Christmas afternoon. Glass figurines, ornate vases, little plates, and tiny cups sat on every surface, gathering dust, just like his grandmother McCrary in her stiff-backed armchair seemed to do.

Pauley half laughed. He kinda felt sorry for Sarah McCrary. She probably was depressed all the time, living like a dusty, old, useless relic. For the first time in his life, all his hateful thoughts about the McCrarys and the Adlers and all the rich people like them took a turn, a tiny turn. He had been denied a place in that depressing, dying world, and unexpectedly today he was glad. A broad smile spread across his face.

Thinking of Lockhart Pauley remembered him telling about Miss Adler's guest calling Price Latimer a simpleton the night they drove her out to the farm. Kate Wesley, Wasn't that her name?

Pauley slid behind the wheel. What was she doing poking around Adler's on a Sunday night when all the stores were closed? What's up with that?

Pauley started the engine, but he knew as soon as he turned on the headlights that something wasn't right. He couldn't see through his windshield. There was light, a brightness, beautiful almost. It was weird like he knew what was wrong but at the same time didn't—and then he did. "Goddammit." He climbed out of the car. His windshield was smashed, shattered. The glass, like thin ice, was so thoroughly crazed he had to roll down both windows to drive. That was when he saw a pickup truck parked across the street at the courthouse, its motor idling.

Tick! Pauley revved his motor. Navigating through his open windows and assorted mirrors with the crisp night air in his face he felt alert, ready for whatever Tick was up to. Pauley revved his engine again, throwing gravel as he spun off the lot, twirling the steering wheel to what felt like a 360; he suddenly was sixteen years old, he was ready, and in his exhilaration, he remembered Boula Banjo. Now there was a man who could find him an old 1984 windshield. In the same instant, he thought of his old chop-shop buddy, he heard the pickup brake, then accelerate, change gears, and roar on ahead, leaving Pauley with the acrid smell of dirty exhaust. It was an old truck like Tick's, but it wasn't Tick's. Pauley's momentary elation plunged. He couldn't see the color or model of the pickup, but it wasn't Tick's. As he raced after the son of a bitch, a passing car's lights flared onto Pauley's shattered windshield, forcing him to the side, to the shoulder, to a stop. The truck sped away.

Unable to give fair chase, Pauley watched the taillights and exhaust roll down the street past the fire station, the flower shop, and the post office. It wasn't Tick. Whoever it was moved more slowly now, mocking him.

Every muscle tense, Pauley McCrary, for the first time in years, had tears in his eyes. He was so sure it was Tick. It hadn't occurred to him, until the truck defeated him with such scorn that the driver was the bastard who had smashed his windshield.

"What in the hell am I doing?" Pauley leaned into his steering wheel. "I've lost my partner. Tick needs me, and I can't find him. He needs me, and I can't think fast enough to grab a patrol car and go after the s.o.b. who smashed my windshield." Pauley jumped out of the Cadillac, and grabbing the first object large enough and hard enough to finish the job the truck driver had started, he destroyed what was left of the glass in his windshield.

Routing his way home by a series of backstreets, cold air hit his face hard now. The energy he'd expended knocking out his windshield began to sooth him. He was barely aware of the tiny shards of sleet in the air or of how the cold sharpness felt so fitting. He hadn't been hurt. That was a plus. He inhaled deeply, trying to recall whatever it was he'd been thinking before he saw his car, but all he could think about was Boula. Where he'd been hanging lately, if he was still alive? Boula Banjo was a friend from high school who had made a successful career on other people's hubcaps.

SATURDAY DECEMBER 21

By Friday, Schreiber had jollied up enough nerve to tell Matte about Raggedy Ann being his brother. Matte, as predicted, had morphed into a clump of ice, refusing to speak to Schreiber or Rhys. Most of Friday she'd spent upstairs thinking (sulking). As she thought (sulked), she knitted a line of gray yarn into a string several feet long. Rhys, on witnessing it, likened the knitting to prayer beads. She didn't believe the yarn was stout enough to work as a noose.

By Saturday morning, on Rhys's way out the door to walk the dogs, Matte asked her how she had slept, which indicated that Rhys had returned to favor—distant, cool—but to favor. Rhys suspected the melt had begun for Schreiber as well. He sat at the breakfast table with a bowl of oatmeal. Not his favorite breakfast fare, but nourishing.

Two miles later and back from a brisk walk, Rhys fed the dogs, scraped mud from her boots on the rough edge of the veranda, and had stepped into the kitchen when Matte sang out to her from the dining room.

"That...that a...uh, young"—the round, low-to-the-ground cook stammered in her search not to sound racist for the right identifier for a black man—"for that...nice, young police officer who was out here last Sunday..."

"Tick Quinn?"

"Nooooo." The "Ooos" rolled out in an elongated grumble. Matte ambled from the dining room into the kitchen. "The other one. He wants you to call him. He's down at headquarters." She said headquarters with an authority that suggested she had, maybe even just that very morning, been made a deputy.

"What'd he want?"

When Rhys returned his call, Pauley was vague about what he wanted except that he would like for her to come down and to bring Kate with her.

Pauley arrived at work early, earlier than usual, early enough that Gladys Grace was hanging her coat on the rack behind the front desk when he asked, "Has a package come with my name on it?"

"You think I'm your personal secretary, do you?" She was in a bad mood. Her coat, double-breasted with large, brown buttons on the tips of wide lapels, seemed to be watching as she wrestled the latest issue of the *National Inquirer* out of the wastepaper basket under the counter.

"Sorry. You're the only one I trust," Pauley mumbled.

"We're sorta creating an in-house conspiracy, aren't we, Officer Baby? You, me, and all these *let-me-knows* and *don't-tell-any-body-elses* you've been bandying about lately. You're gonna get me in a mess with Uncle Price, if I'm not careful."

"Are you kidding? Even Uncle knows you're the only one in the department who can find the coffee filters. He'll never mess with you, Mama."

"Humph," she said.

"Humph yourself, lady. Speaking of ladies—I've got two of them I need to talk to this morning. Don't want to talk to either of them exactly, but got to. Would you look up Rhys Adler's telephone number for me?"

"Humph."

Rhys felt confident, as they pushed against the heavy glass door decorated with a plastic Christmas wreath. Apparently, she was not to be arrested for obstructing justice since Kate had been invited too. Her smile was genuine as she asked the woman at the desk where Officer McCrary's office was located.

Gladys smiled at Kate's full-length fur coat. "Hello there. Hey, nice coat you're sporting this morning. Don't see many of those in Riversbend," she said. "If you get too warm, I'll be happy to keep it for you. We got a pen in the back." Grace laughed, pointing to a nonspecific space behind her chair. "Go on down the hall, ladies; you'll find McCrary easy enough. He's the one pacing the hall."

The two women started in the direction indicated. "Do you know each other?" Rhys quizzed as soon as they were out of earshot.

"I'm notorious, remember?"

"Ah, so you are."

As the women neared the hub of Quick County's law enforcement—based on the elevated buzz of quiet talk and ringing telephones—Rhys spied Pauley at a desk in front of a disorderly maze of desks. The expanse was divided into a few cubicles of eyebrow-high partitions that had been set edge to angle and constructed from what looked like a deck of giant playing cards. Between the cubicles there were narrow aisles. Inside the cubicles, desks were cluttered with normal office paraphernalia: Styrofoam cups, telephone directories, maps, and PCs. In the scrap of floor space remaining, a single chair waited near the edge of the desks, or out of place like an exile. Engorged file cabinets, some with drawers half-open, exposed the labeled tabs of a world of pain.

As second-in-command until his retirement, Tick's desk was front and forward.

Several officers were lost in their computer screens, but most were hanging around in groups of two and three, talking. All activity ceased when the two women walked into the maze.

The women were assessed and relegated to some obscure corner of each man's temporal lobe. Only Kate was comfortable enough to appraise back. Pauley, spotting the women and sensing the excitement of his fellow officers, sprang from his chair at the same moment Rhys was straightening her indignant spine to her almost six feet.

"Sorry." Pauley greeted them with an uncomfortable smile. "If you can accept ogling as complimentary, please do. It was meant as that."

"Have you met my friend, Kate Wesley?"

Kate, seeing Pauley clearly for the first time, melted into her throatiest, sexiest line filched straight from her favorite, blockbuster 1988 movie. "Oh my!"

Pauley, who ordinarily had been savvy with women and their responses to him since his puberty, discovered this morning that these two made him nervous. He shook hands and thanked them for their punctuality. He refrained from smoothing his shirtfront, or from running his hands over his hair as he stepped to the nearest empty cubical to cop a second chair. "Would you like coffee? It's not good, but it's brown."

"No, thank you. I'm driving Kate to the airport as soon as we finish. You said this wouldn't take long?"

"Shouldn't."

Kate had only spoken four or five words since arriving at the station. But in Pauley's presence, the cat relinquished her tongue, and she purred. "Ohhh, we're in no hurry, are we Rhys?"

"Is there a broom closet in this building where we can talk without being be heard and voted on by every cop in the county?" Rhys asked.

"Good idea. Follow me." Pauley led them down the hall to the arguable evidence room. It was a windowless, narrow room with multiple rows of metal filing cabinets and lockable shelves with cheap locks, which any yegg could tumble. The space held a metal table large enough to accommodate two people, and the room smelled like dog. Sagacious snored from a cushy dog bed in the center of the room. Pauley closed the door behind them.

"Scoot over," Kate uttered another pithy phrase as her heels clicked around the outer arch of dog and bed.

Awake but not moved to stir, Sagacious eyed the visitors, huffed once, struggled to her feet, stretched, yawned, raised her head in the air for a good sniff, and in hound-dog fashion ambled over to nose Rhys's dog-treat pocket.

"This is Sagacious. Sagacious can you say hello to Miss Adler and Miss Wesley. If 'Sagacious' is a mouthful, call her Sack as in sad sack. I'm afraid she's had a sordid life. She'll come to most any name."

Rhys had given the dog one treat before being introduced. Leaning forward, she extended her hand for the hound to sniff. "Hello, Sagacious. Is your name well suited?" Sagacious raised her paw and placed it on Rhys's skirt. "Well, I think it is. Here." She whisked a second treat from her pocket. Sagacious took it politely.

"She has very nice manners," Rhys said.

"I didn't know she could shake hands." Pauley beamed as would any master upon watching his dog take a first at a Westminster Dog Show.

"How long have you had her?"

"Not long. She was a joke." He straightened her ear that had gone topsy-turvy. "I don't know much about her, I figure she's a pound pooch. She's smart, though. Sit, Sagacious." The dog sat.

"Bed, Sagacious." The dog gazed up at Pauley. "Bed." Sagacious cocked her head.

"Stand," Rhys said authoritatively. Sagacious smiled but remained seated. "Up, Sagacious."

This time the dog stood and, as if the commands that had been circling between her ears suddenly made sense, she climbed onto her dog bed and curled down into a bony curve of yellow fur.

"She has a mind of her own. Not a bad thing in a police dog," Rhys said. "She's capable of acting independently, which could save your life one day. And I'll bet as soon as she has time to teach you her vocabulary, you'll make her a worthy partner."

Pauley smiled, relieved with the friendly turn of events.

"Sit." Pauley playfully pointed to the only two chairs at the table. Gooning obedience training, the women sat.

"Let's get started. That okay with y'all? Don't want to waste your time unnecessarily." Pauley walked to the other end of the table and half sat on the edge. "Miss Wesley."

"Call me Kate."

Pauley smiled. "Miss Wesley, what were you *really* doing behind Adler's Sunday night?"

The lingering lightheartedness from their play with Sagacious vanished. Kate's eyes stayed on Pauley, but her smile began to morph. "I was looking for something. I hope you have it, Rhys said you do. The lachrymatory bottle belongs to a museum in Delaware. I was to oversee the removal of some artifacts and items given to the museum from the Carlton estate sale. The last heir of this once-large old Delaware family died a few weeks ago. He had no family, no heirs. In his will he left a number of valuable pieces to the museum, wanting to keep them in Delaware. I lost one lachrymatory. The one you have here."

"That's a shame." Pauley nodded in sympathy. "Why would it be in Riversbend, or particularly at Adler's?" Pauley's tone was unaccusing.

"I was rushed, too hurried. The bottle was dropped, inadvertently." Kate paused, daring either of the two who eyed her so intently to deny her a fair hearing. "It's very small; easy to misplace."

"Yes." Pauley thought of his own missing bottle.

"When I couldn't find it, I believed I'd dropped it into a box going to Adler's. It was my fault. But as I said, it was unintentional. The bottle was exceptional. Even if I had all the money in the world, it is irreplaceable. I am desperate to find it."

Kate hadn't mentioned someone startling her, the catalyst for her dropping the bottle in the wrong box. Rhys wondered why not.

"Why was a box coming to Adler's?" Pauley asked.

"We had been invited to the sale. Don't you remember our discussion regarding the bill of sale on Sunday?"

"Oh, indeed I do. Yes." Pauley smiled and turned to Kate. "Miss Wesley…"

"Yessir?"

Kate Wesley at first noticeably relaxed, unlike most people in a police station, suddenly seemed on edge. He understood her concern over the loss of the bottle. He wanted to believe her story, but there was something that didn't feel right. She was too involved with the very thing that had been taken from his evidence file. It wouldn't take much, a little maneuvering the right person, a little luck and she could have been the culprit who took the bottle. He didn't know anyone who wanted it as much as she did.

"You knew the store would be closed on Sunday night."

"Yes."

"And you say you're friends with Mr. Fordyce as well as Miss Adler. You were in town, you had a car, why didn't you go by his house first?"

"I…" Kate crossing her arms at the wrist clasped her own fingers, a childlike gesture, almost guileless. She was capable of conjuring an explanation except the door to the evidence room opened a crack and Lockhart stuck his head around.

"Morning, Miss. I seen you two coming down the hall." Lockhart, nerdy and flirty, deficient and calculating truckled to Kate's beauty.

"Lockhart, do you need something?" Pauley snapped.

"Nope. Just thought I'd see if you needed any help."

"I don't. So, if you'll close the door behind you..." Pauley moved toward the man. "We're busy." The door closed, and Pauley locked it.

"What was that about?" Rhys asked Pauley but knew she should be asking Kate.

"He's the slimy worm who escorted me to your house Sunday night. I told you about him."

But it wasn't what the slimy worm said. It was the knowing eye he had given Kate. Whatever his intention, it had hit home, turning the pure tints of Kate's peaches and cream Irish skin to the color of skim milk.

"Can we get back to why you didn't contact your friends for help on Sunday night rather than snoop around behind their store?"

This time Kate crossed her legs at the knees. "Hindsight being twenty/twenty, you mean? But, I didn't, did I? I was looking for a miracle, for the elusive four-leaf clover. I had convinced myself that the lachrymatory was at Adler's, and that if I went down there I would find it." She shrugged. "I just knew I'd find it lost in the trash, it's so small."

"Are you serious?"

"I couldn't risk it being sent to the city dump. And you know what, it may be improbable, but it's not impossible that Richard could have been working late. Don't you ever get that off-the-wall feelings about something? When you just know something is true? He does sometimes work late. Sometimes it works, and sometimes it doesn't. It was a silly notion, but I'm in danger of losing my job."

"Why did you park behind Ball's department store rather than Adler's?" Pauley was unrelenting.

"Would you believe me if I said I thought I was in the right parking lot?"

Both Rhys and Pauley were amazed at Kate's quickness, the rabbit out of the hat, the bouquet of flowers from her bag of tricks.

"Listen, people, I know you think the center of the universe is Riversbend, but it isn't. When you haven't been here in a while, you forget things. It was night. In the dark, one parking lot looks very like another. As soon as I was out of the car, I knew I'd pulled into the wrong one, but I left my car where I'd parked it. Ball's lot isn't fifty feet from Adler's, right?"

"Right," Pauley said.

"Right," Rhys said, feeling sure Kate had dodged another scud. "Right," she said again, wondering what exactly Kate had dodged.

"How's your investigation coming along, Officer? Know any more?" Rhys asked, hoping to quiet her fears regarding Kate. "Why would anyone want to kill Raggedy? What could be in a Dumpster that someone would kill for?"

"According to Miss Wesley, an irreplaceable lachrymatory bottle," Pauley said.

"Blackmail, sister!" Kate said. "Trash cans hold all our secrets. Who we owe money and how much, our letters, our...our pill bottles, wine bottles, what we eat, where we shop, who's dunning us, or screwing us."

"Before we go off on some theory of blackmail, Miss Wesley, your museum bottle was in Raggedy's hand when the police found her." Pauley's voice was even, but his comment, hoping to unsettle her, did just that.

He hopped off the edge of the table. "Interesting, isn't it? Did you know Raggedy Ann, Miss Wesley? Have you ever known her?"

"No. She wasn't here when I lived here."

He turned to Rhys. "And what about this blackmail talk that keeps coming up?"

Rhys blinked. She had no intention of squealing on Hummer or of handing over the diary. Not yet, anyway. "Like Kate said, trash cans hold all our secrets?" The sinews in Rhys's neck tensed and her voice rose. "Like she said, it offers a possible motive for why someone would want to kill her."

"Miss Adler, I am disappointed in you. You are withholding information from me. You are aware, I'm sure, that this is a dangerous path for you to take. You may want to reconsider your options. Let's start with the little book I gave to Mr. Fordyce. Who has it now?" Pauley was astonished at this new bravado that he seemed to have pulled out of his sleeve. He liked it. A lot, in fact.

He noted Rhys's inability to breathe properly.

"I know you've said you want to help us. And I believe you, but I have to ask, is the book part of why Hummer and his friends keep turning up in your life?"

Rhys took refuge in her purse. She began rummaging through it recklessly as would an addict looking for a cigarette, which she wasn't. She'd never smoked. She hoped she looked foolish and not frantic. She didn't want to lie or to be accused of obstructing justice, and she sure didn't want Pauley to talk to Hummer.

"It wasn't my mother's. That's all I know."

She should have anticipated at this juncture that her natural skills at detection or in deception were wanting, and finding herself in the presence of two superior models, she should have considered seeking either guidance or rescue. But Rhys was Rhys, and, as her goal, ostensibly, was no different from Pauley's, she continued on her own regrettable path. She had made the decision to give the diary to the police—but not before she learned positively who Goofy with a little *g* was, and not before she could see if she could track him through the diary. And...

"Miss Adler, are you still with us?" Pauley was strolling around the table, watching her closely, he moved directly across from her. "You seem to be lost in your own world."

She held up a tube of lipstick. "Here," she said, and began applying it. "Where is Tick, by the way?" She pressed her lips together.

Blessed by the whimsies of fate, Rhys's impulsive question pushed Pauley off his game for the second time. He would like to have tied her to a chair, stuck a gag in her mouth, and rolled her down the hall into a broom closet.

"He's sick," he said too quickly. "Flu. Fever."

Unvarnished truth seemed to be in short supply this morning.

How would Rhys Adler react if he admitted he didn't have the foggiest notion where Tick was and hadn't known for days. "Home."

None of them were comfortable with their roles this morning or their responses. Tick's illness gave them solid ground.

"Speaking of illness, let's talk about drugs." Kate leaped at her escape. "Was Raggedy involved in drugs?

"She's not on any of our lists."

"You ever heard of someone named Connie Beckett?"

Pauley hunkered down beside Sagacious and began rubbing her ears. "What are you talking about, Miss Adler? I need to know whatever it is you know. Tick is not here to help, and the department has two unsolved murders."

The request for honesty was so clean and sincere, Rhys dropped her head.

"We need cooperation. The longer we wait, the easier it gets for Raggedy Ann's killer to cover his tracks, get out of town, and concoct an alibi."

"It's already taken longer than you'd like, I know. Believe me, I wish I could be more helpful, but I don't know anything, not really." Not yet. She was thinking of the diary, which was still basically a rune. "But perhaps I know something that could be… helpful." She was thinking of Schreiber's revelation. She didn't know if the knowledge that Raggedy was male was important to solving the mystery of her murder, or not. "Raggedy wasn't exactly who…"

Listening intently, eager to learn anything this woman knew, Pauley's mobile rang. He held up a finger, like a bookmark, to hold their conversation.

"Yes? Yes!" He turned away from the women and started toward the door.

"Don't go away," he said into the small phone, his voice up an octave. He pressed the cell phone against his chest and with a lift of his hand he signaled for the women to go—to leave.

He watched as they slipped into their coats and gathered their purses. The phone still pressed to his chest. He could only think that if they didn't speed up, he was going to bodily push them out of the room.

"Tomorrow," he mouthed to Rhys as she passed him. "I'll call. Remember what you were going to say, Miss Adler."

"Tomorrow," she confirmed.

He closed the door firmly behind them. "Tick?"

The line was dead. Pauley quickly redialed, only to get, "I am unavailable at the moment. If this is an emergency and you need a policeman, call nine one one."

Gladys watched Pauley jaywalk toward the coffee shop. Head bent low, he was talking to Toad Potter. She saw the little man reach into his coat pocket and hand Pauley something. Pauley laughed, but then the men stopped midstreet while Toad informed him about whatever it was Pauley had slipped in his own pocket. Toad had been a friend to law enforcement for a few years. She was pleased to see the young policeman talking to him. Toad Potter knew more about what was going on in the lower end of Main

Street than anyone. The men disappeared into Fresh as a Daisy Cleaners and Flower Shoppe.

A few minutes later when Pauley came back to headquarters, Gladys plopped a big package on top of the counter. "This came for you." She pressed it with her hands. "Feels soft."

"Shhhh." Pauley put a finger to his lips.

Gladys tilted her head toward the Coffee Cupp. "He's still having lunch."

Pauley peered at his watch and then out the window toward the café. "That's good. Better safe than sorry, huh." Taking the package and the attendant report to the evidence room he read hurriedly. The feathers on the blanket did match the one found in Raggedy's throat.

"Smothered." He poked the blanket with his finger.

The more recent stains on the blanket were blood. Two types: A positive, identical with Raggedy Ann's, and O, the universal donor. A note addressed "To Whom It May Concern" read,

> An in-depth analysis would have been made on the blood if the requesting officer had asked the lab to run DNA samples rather than BPA samples.

"Damn." Pauley slapped the report against the file cabinet.

> Normally this further work would take five to ten days. At present it would take a minimum of two weeks.
>
> Snowed Under in LR

"Two weeks? We can't wait two weeks." He punched the army blanket. But not a man to be outdone by a mean-spirited world, he took the blanket and the report out to his Seville. There was more security in his newly "air conditioned" stud-mobile than in the easy-in-and-easy-out evidence room. "In fact, Scooby Doo, I'm gonna clear out all the evidence in the case file and stash it in my fine vehicle. Boy Genius cracks the case single-handedly!" Pauley could smell the headlines.

The lab report folded and wiggled into his bulging glove compartment, he swathed the blanket in a piece of plastic, and poked it into the tire well in the Caddie's massive trunk. Pressing his full weight on the lid he pushed until he heard the trunk click and lock. Assured of this new security, he trudged back into the station. His spirits were lighter. He had something to work with and it started with two questions: One, how did the blood get on the blanket? And two, who was type O?

Intuition or second sight, he didn't know, but a frisson of dread ran across his scalp. He went up front to find Gladys. "What are my chances of borrowing someone's personnel file?"

"Nonexistent."

"Gotcha."

Killing time until he could enact his plan, he began printing ID tags for the new evidence, and penciling a few notes for his memory.

It was twenty-one minutes and nineteen seconds before Gladys came trotting down the hall toward the john. He watched her disappear around the corner; he heard the restroom door hiss on its hydraulic closer. He figured if he was lucky he'd have less than five minutes. He prayed she'd take time to fluff her hair and put on some lipstick.

The personnel cabinet was in the small records room behind the front office where Gladys guarded the files like Cerberus. He quickly found the cabinet and began riffling through the *B*s. He didn't recognize the name when he first saw it, but second time through, there it was: "Quinn, Tilman—O."

Following a late lunch at the Capital Hotel, Rhys left Kate at the Bill and Hilary Clinton International Airport with minutes to spare before passenger boarding. Kate had flown away in high spirits, ready to face the Brindlewick curator. She was full of confidence, feeling she would come out of the lachrymatory ordeal on top. "See you in January if I'm not in the tank." They had cheek-kissed.

Rhys spent the first half of the drive back to Riversbend, devising and perfecting a scheme that would require Hummer. From the conversation at the country club regarding drugs and dealers of drugs, she was fully aware that the potential for danger had doubled. Rhys needed to meet the enemy. Not exactly face-to-face. That would be foolish, but she could snoop around and maybe find answers to some of her questions.

As a decent Episcopalian, the other half of her drive home she spent examining her recent conduct. She hadn't been exactly above board with Richard, who was her best friend. She'd manipulated a starving, homeless boy with food. She'd certainly played the entitlement card when she'd telephoned Tick in the middle of the night. But her uncooperative behavior in regard to the police was the worse. Pauley McCrary needed her. She actually felt bad about holding out, and had he and Tick given her any encouragement when she'd asked if she could help, things may have been different. Like she'd told Kate, there were consequences with one's actions. She could get herself in a world of trouble.

Despite this quasi case of guilt, if she told Pauley what she knew about the diary he would take it away from her. She couldn't even hearten him with what she hoped would be helpful until after she'd broken all its codes. She would dearly love to walk into his office tomorrow and drop the damn little thing and its secrets into his lap, including the information she was going after tonight. "Soon. I'll be good soon." Inspirited, Rhys didn't go out to the farm but drove straight to the Searcy and in minutes she was banging on Hummer's door.

Hummer's room reeked of sardines. Her new friend, happily, had finished eating them. The tin was in his sink leaking a golden pool of oil. Rhys rolled up her sleeves and ran water into the basin, squirting a drop of detergent into water before she asked, "Hummer, where does Beckett live?"

Hummer frowned. "B...Beck...Becker."

"Becker, Beckett. Where does he live?"

Hummer pointed to his ceiling.

"There's another floor above this one?" Rhys was surprised.

"Attic. He's g...gone. Not here every d...day. M...M...Mister R...R...Runsick doesn't know he stays here; doesn't know he has a pallet up there."

"No kiddin."

"I don't like to k...kid," Hummer said, but he had on his funny Hummer smile, which was a very serious smile. He was not a bad-looking fellow. Not handsome, but nice looking, and tonight, sitting under a bright hundred-watt light, Rhys saw perfect teeth.

"Orthodontist," she said reflexively.

"T...th...three years." He held up the appropriate number of fingers.

"Who are you, Hummer?"

Hummer turned away.

"Sorry. It's none of my business. I'll stick to business. Can we get into Becker's attic?"

The attic was not approached by way of a staircase but by a disappearing ladder that folded into the ceiling above a narrow alcove. Hummer led the way to the alcove and pointed to the horizontal door over their heads. He tugged on a short rope and the ladder appeared. First up, Hummer disappeared into darkness. Rhys followed.

She heard the distinctive staccato of a pulled ball chain from a bare lightbulb in the ceiling, before she saw shadowy illuminations bouncing around the attic space. Old wood, open rafters, a low ceiling—it all combined to create a smell familiar to Rhys, who had spent hours of her youth in her grandmother's attic, pillaging trunks that contained the artifacts of other lives.

The quartet of round windows, reminiscent of an age when the Searcy was a queen, were now circles of night sky. There was the sheetless pallet Hummer had mentioned, a tumble of quilts, a child's pillow.

A cardboard card table with a gimpy leg and an accompanying folding chair were scooted under the one light. A hot plate, on the floor, was unplugged from the heavy extension cord that hung from a socket on the lightbulb. There was a gooseneck lamp on the floor by the pallet and a galvanized five-gallon bucket nearby that Rhys refrained from peering into. Connie Becker was not there, but her synesthetic self could taste him. He was surprisingly green and tart, like sheepshire. Her salivary glands working overtime, she swallowed reluctantly.

Before they entered his sanctuary, she'd known Connie wasn't there, Hummer had seen him leave, but she didn't know what she would have said had they found him.

Other than the sheepshire taste, there was nothing. No sense of the man, what he was like, or of his space. There was nothing that pulled her to explore. No books, no backpacks or suitcases to investigate. No extra clothes hanging from a nail, nor arsenal of weapons. And yet she was afraid.

Raggedy—Schreiber's brother—hadn't been killed with gun or knife, she had to remind herself. To her knowledge no one knew what had killed him. And drug dealers were not necessarily murderers.

"Do you think Becker would kill someone if they were blackmailing him?" She turned to Hummer.

He waited so long to answer Rhys thought he hadn't heard her. "Hummer, is Becker capable of murder?"

Hummer nodded and might have said more except they both heard a board creak somewhere. They froze, praying the noise was nothing more than the aches and pains of an old building. Bodies tense, they strained to hear, not daring to speak, barely breathing. Again the distinctive groan of old wood, but this time it seemed to be by a rhythmical tread of someone climbing stairs but not an attic ladder in the alcove. Not yet.

Rhys, closer to the light in the center of the room, slowly pulled the chain a bead at a time until the light was extinguished. In the dark she could hear her own breath, hollow with fear. Hummer began to hum.

"Shhhh!" Rhys hissed.

The third-floor stairs jauntily ascended, the footsteps paused, again at the alcove, before they began again, this time more slowly. Whoever was out there had either entered the alcove where the ladder to Becker's attic hung extended or passed nearby. Whoever it was would either deliberately climb the ladder—or ignore it. Live and let live. Wasn't that the motto at the Searcy?

Hummer's hum was not merely audible; it was turning into a low-level howl.

"Shh!" Rhys warned him again, but her hiss had become little more than a sigh. She heard Hummer take a step. She saw his shadow move slightly toward the ladder.

"Hum...mer," she said his name softly, slowly. Motionless, listening, her spine so rigid she thought her shoulder blades would crack. "Don't," her voice was mostly air, "move."

The steps continued down the hall until all that remained was a burdened silence.

The bite of her fingernails into the skin of Rhys's arm had made a red mark. She rubbed the welt, waiting with quickened senses for the right moment to leave the attic. Tonight she didn't trust her luck.

"Let's go. You first," she whispered. Knowing it would look more natural if he were seen descending the ladder. The light through the opened trapdoor was enough to let them escape. Hummer slowly folded the ladder, letting the door ease back into the ceiling.

Back in his room, they sat quietly, letting their racing hearts return to normal.

Feeling safer but still whispering, Rhys said, "Hummer, believe it or not, I brought the diary to give to you tonight. But I realize I need it one more night. Just one more and I won't ask ever again."

Hummer closed his eyes in a gesture of dismissal.

She took it out of her purse and put it on the table between them. "Hummer, I can take you out to the Razorback for dinner, if you'll just let me keep the diary until tomorrow, or I'll pay you. Whichever you prefer," she added. Everyone loved cash. Maybe Hummer loved money more than dining out. Think of the sardines he could buy. She, for her part, could go home and wouldn't have to drive out to some pool hall in the middle of the night and watch him eat a smorgasbord of fattening, delicious food.

She tried to calculate a figure of money that would work as an incentive. He glanced at her suspiciously. She reached for her handbag and began a plowing through in search of her billfold. She took out a ten-dollar bill. "How's this?"

Hummer eyed it with interest but then glanced back at her wallet, which he could easily see contained enough greenbacks to create a breeze when riffled.

"Well, I can see we're both adepts at this game." Rhys pulled another ten to join the first and put them both on his table—and grabbed the diary. "I'll bring this to you in the morning, and together we're going to take it to the police."

She thought he would object. He didn't. He seemed to have been waiting for her to come to this obviously overdue decision.

Earlier that night, a light wind whipped around the recessed doorway across the street from the Searcy. In the shelter of the entrance, Connie Becker waited for Rhys Adler to come out.

He'd seen her Jaguar and knew she was in the building. He hadn't known why she was there, or why she kept nosing around the hotel. It made him a little anxious, but it made him a little excited too. He'd just have to find out why. He grinned.

Fast and light on his feet, Connie entered the hotel by way of the back door, and then sidling through the kitchen, he spiraled up the stairs two steps at a time. The lowered trapdoor caught him by surprise. He hadn't figured she knew about the attic, or that she would have the nerve to go snooping in his space. What else had that goofy kid or the hunchback told her? It didn't take a brain surgeon to know who had told her. He'd seen all of them together.

Connie bounced his weight on a loose board under the trapdoor. He liked playing games with them—give 'em a scare. They were stupid to mess with little Dodgy Connie. He knew where they were at the moment, so all he had to do was stay out of sight and wait.

Down the hall was a janitor's closet. He left the door ajar and waited, entertaining himself by plotting what he would do with them when he was finished playing games. There was no hurry; he had this one. Soon quick, light steps followed by a soft thump as the ladder was eased back into the ceiling brought him out of his reverie. As they went into Hummer's room, Connie scooted down the stairs, out the door, and crossed the street to station himself once again in the dark three-sided recess of Creagor's Grocery. His hands shaking, he lighted a bud. He'd taken his first toke when he saw her shadow, then the hotel door opened, and Rhys stepped out into the night. She was alone. Connie Becker took a last drag and pinching the joint put it in his pocket. The silver Jag shining under the streetlight beckoned like a gemstone.

He heard the tiny ping as her key ring signaled the doors had unlocked.

"Hey! Hey, lady!" He moved toward her, sensing she would be a chump for some poor dreg in need of a handout. He waved his cap and added an impressive limp as he crossed the street. "Merry Christmas," Connie hollered cheerfully.

Rhys recognized him instantly. She shivered. "Merry Christmas, she aped his greeting like a weakened parrot." Wanting desperately to get in her car and flee, she seemed unable to move. She waited for him to cross to her. "I'm in a hurry. I'm sorry, I just have a little," she said, reaching into her purse.

Connie laughed. All he'd have to do was grab the keys, shove her into the car, and take off. She needed to think twice about messing on his turf.

No more than a few inches from her now, he raised his hands to push her just as a car turned onto Main Street a block up from the hotel and sped toward them. Connie froze as Rhys dropped a few coins into his raised hand. All he could do was watch her long legs in the light of the oncoming car swing into the Jaguar, revealing a bit of thigh as her skirt caught up on the seat belt.

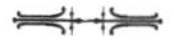

Rhys enjoyed staying home on a Saturday night, on occasion. It was peaceful; it gave her a few hours to catch up with her reading, time to kick her feet up, to put her thoughts in order, her ducks in a row, and to revisit the past week. Tonight, curled up on the sofa in the small library off her bedroom, she sipped her second glass of wine while attempting to read the evening edition of the *Riversbend Profile.*

Richard had called her to come to Cedars for a drink, and when she'd declined, he'd upped the offer to include his specialty, a light french omelet, herbs and Gruyere, JC style. (Julia Child) Beau must have asked for a night off, leaving Richard to fend for himself.

Rhys liked Beau, but he took advantage of Richard's generosity, she thought. But then, Richard let him.

She'd declined the omelet offer, explaining her desperation for a few hours of solitude in the wake of Kate's visit, but now, following their venture into Connie Becker's hideaway, she felt jitter, and the night was doing nothing to help. The wind had picked up during the last hour making the pines near the house sigh mournfully. And as the cold gusts swept through, the long branches became shadows, and every floor board creak became a step, and every thump a thud, as might a body bumping against her safety.

She reached for the newspaper. The crinkling of pages was familiar, was comforting. She scanning the front page again, trying to concentrate on the national gloom and doom headlines. She flipped through to section E. Her horoscope for the day predicted a new development in a relationship with an unsuspecting acquaintance.

Swapping the newspaper for a new still-in-its-wrapper Christmas CD, she cursed the skin-tight cellophane. Freed, she slipped the disk into the player and settled back to listen to the Cambridge Singers and the City of London Sinfonia. The rich baritone, perfectly pitched, was soon surrounded by a chorus of other voices. The music filled the room. She closed her eyes and surrendered to the music. Soon she was aloft—a new development in a relation.

Ian saw her through the window. The diner—it was Ms. Em's, and it was empty except for Rhys. Ian knuckled the window.

"Whatcha doin'?" he asked, ambling toward the counter where she smoldered alone. His slow stride was spectacular in faded, wash-soften 501s that snuggered him up just right. He threw his leg over the stool and ordered a cheeseburger.

"Running errands, visiting with Em—who seemed to have sorta disappeared. I promised Matte I'd run by Robertson's Hardware on my way home and get her some screws and a new extension cord. She's building an electric chair."

His laugh was big and open, and she imagined he looked at her with unexpected pleasure.

Rhys created Ian Languille exactly as she wanted him: handsome, a good conversationalist, soft spoken, witty, and oozing sexuality. He was smart but not pedantic, charming but not dishonest. All these characteristics worked on Rhys like champagne. And in her fantasy, she banished everyone from the diner, except Em, who in her mind Rhys couldn't get to vanish completely. Twisted, she thought.

Ian began kissing her neck. He lifted her onto the counter. His hands were warm as toast as they slid up under her clothing...

SUNDAY DECEMBER 22

Rhys passed Languille's Twenty-Four Seven Garage four times before she got up her nerve to pull in among the glut of repaired cars waiting to be picked up on Monday. She had skipped church for the second Sunday in a row. This trumped-up errand to the garage had more to do with reimaging herself in Ian Languille's eyes as a sassy, savvy, singular woman rather than as the silly, fainting goat image he currently carried from the last time he'd seen her.

The task before her was to accomplish the eradication of the fainting spell without actually using the word "faint." (Adler women don't faint.) She still blushed when she remembered him bent over her, lightly slapping her cheeks to bring her around.

That, and the other possibility for this spur of the moment errand (in her new dove-gray cashmere skirt and sweater with co-ordinating jacket that enhanced her eyes beautifully, and okay, for admittedly getting a good whiff of him) was to hand him the check he'd come to collect last Thursday before she fainted. She could have mailed it, but she wanted to thank him personally.

She glanced around hoping to see him. There were no other customers. People didn't approve of businesses being open on Sundays until after the sermons were spent, and their lunches consumed. Only then could they spend what was left of the day tending to their cars or save souls.

Rhys was pleased that her parish felt no obligation to save anything much, other than the occasional fast food coupon. She was grateful her church preferred pondering *salvation* more than hawking it. In her mind being *saved* was an odd concept. People weren't sure nowadays how to think about it. Surely no one associated it with pearly gates or streets of gold. Oh, well, she would have to leave these matters to Father Burkett. He did a fine job keeping abreast of the trendy seminarian takes on the ambiguities of modern religion.

Rhys had parked between two vehicles, one a truck and the other she didn't know what. It looked like a piece of military equipment. She turned off the engine and waited for an attendant. Several minutes later and no Mr. Goodwrench, Rhys scooted out of the car.

"Hellooo." She was not clear on garage etiquette. Should she go into the garage, which gaped wide in front of her, or into the office, which faced Lewis Street and was about the size of her closet? She opted for the office in hopes Ian Languille would be there.

He wasn't.

She wandered through the office to another door at the back that opened into the garage proper. She heard metal on concrete: the clank of a tire tool, the ring of a hubcap. Two men stood in the farthermost corner; neither was Ian. She saw a pair of legs sticking out from under a car.

"Hellooo? Anyone home?" she hollered at the legs.

"Yes, ma'am. What can I do for ya?" One of the two men in the corner started walking toward her, wiping his hands on a grime-stiffened rag.

"I'm looking for Ian Languille." She glanced at the legs.

The man smiled. "I reckon those could belong to him. Ian, there's a smart-looking lady wants to talk to you."

The legs, which were slightly bent at the knees, seemed to tilt over to the right, but they didn't move out from under the car.

She figured the way the legs ignored her meant Ian was avoiding her. He probably thought her sickly, vacuous, or insane. "Never mind," she whispered to the attendant who appeared to be one of those ever-beaming sorts. "He's busy. I'll bother him another day."

"Hang on a minute, sis, he's probably got on his headphones and can't hear thunder. He's not much of a mechanic, you know. Has to keep hisself entertained, or he won't stay under there very long. Can you tell me what your problem is? My name's Bobby Dowell, and I'm the feller who taught young Ian everything he knows about cars, which I hate to admit ain't much." Bobby Dowell grinned.

"Mr. Dowell—"

"My last name's Brooks. Bobby Dowell's what folks around here call me. Is that your Jeep I seen you drive up in?"

Rhys thought the answer rather obvious, but she avoided saying so. "Yes. Mr. Languille retuned my Jaguar a few days ago and I need to pay him."

"Are you the little lady who fainted?"

"No. I was sleepy."

"Sleepy?"

"Mr. Dowell let's get to the matter of why I'm here, shall we? The man who tends my cars mentioned the other day that we need to get my points cleaned." Her face reddened just in time for Ian Languille to walk up behind her. This morning he smelled like machine oil.

"Well, to what do we owe a visit? How are you feeling? Faint? On all fours? I was about to head out your way."

"I didn't faint…I." (Damn, she'd said the *F* word.)

"She was sleepy!"

"I stood up too fast." Her bearing incontestable she dared Bobby Dowell to utter another word. Instead, she pointed to the legs still under the car. "I thought those were yours."

"Sorry. These are mine." He patted his thighs. "Those long ones belong to Cecil. He's working on Mrs. Carmichael's something-or-other. I don't know too much about hybrids."

"You don't say."

Ian grinned. "You keep my secret, and I'll keep your little secret. You know about when you fainted." Ian winked and hurried on before Rhys could respond. "Besides not knowing much about hybrids, Bobby Dowell here says I work too slow. Cost the garage money."

"Slow as cold molasses." The mechanic shook his head. "Naw, lady, you don't want him working on ya. We'd all be better off if you'd let me clean your points, and maybe give ya a lube job."

"Oh no. My man…Mr. Schreib—"

"You don't have time to do it now, Bobby Dowell. There are several cars ahead of Miss Adler. She can leave the Jeep, and I'll run her home. I have some business out there anyway.

"Speaking of legs, I met your friend the other day."

"Kate." Rhys squawked. "Oh yes, I suppose you met her the day she brought my Jaguar to you after she wrecked it. You know I could press charges."

"The day you fainted she had on a slinky velvet robe. She had a struggle keeping it together at the knees."

"Oh, I bet she struggled! She's celibate, you know. Waiting for marriage."

Rhys almost laughed aloud at the expression on Languille's face. She wanted to punch him for looking at Kate's legs. She wanted to remind him that they—she and he—had been seeing each other for months. But, of course, they hadn't been seeing each other, had they. She had been seeing him—all but naked. Butt naked. Her eyes filled with tears. She was a fool.

"I got time." Bobby Dowell thumped Rhys on the back. "I kin do those other cars later." He turned to Ian. "But if I'm gonna, you probably outta take her indoors. Get her out of the cold." He winked at Ian. "Take her to lunch. Ain't you hungry? You got time."

"Anyway she's gone," Rhys said, feeling too stupid to live.

"Where's she gone?" The words sagged with disappointment.

"Home. Delaware. You'll have to go to Delaware if you want to see her. But if you can wait, she'd may be back in January—if she doesn't go to jail."

"You gonna bring charges against your friend for wrecking your car?"

"That's none of your business."

"Did you know when you tip your chin up like that I can see a good part of your brain up your nose?"

The chin came down. "Then don't look. You may see what I'm thinking."

"I know what you're thinking. You're wishing you'd worn a coat instead of that little sweater outfit." He twirled his hand in the direction of her chest. "You're shaking."

"Take her indoors, Ian. What's wrong with you, boy. Pretty girl like her. Don't pay no attention to him, ma'am."

Rhys wanted desperately to laugh, to leave, to never come back, but all she could do was smile like a dog at Bobby Dowell, who obviously was feeding the tension that sparked wildly and randomly like static in front of him.

"I have a check for you," she said, opening her handy, efficient, all-in-one clutch.

"You don't remember the first time we ever met, do you?

Rhys looked up, surprised at the intimacy of Ian remembering such a thing.

"My wife had laundered my driver's license in the pocket of my jeans, and I had no ID. The store wouldn't let me cash a check. You bailed me out. That was nice."

"Your wife?"

I was very nervous. "She'd sent me after a home pregnancy test. I'll never forget. I couldn't find one. When I finally did..."

"You have a child?"

"It didn't turn the right color...the test."

Rhys didn't know what to say.

Languille scratched his chin, pointing out his five-o'clock shadow, which in turn set off his lips, which were as rosy as a child's. "You're staring at my mouth," he finally said. "Would you like for me to kiss you?"

There was a sharp intake of breath. "You're married!" Rhys remembered Em's from the night before, and her face flamed. She felt like an adulteress.

Ian frowned. "I don't get you."

"I don't get you. You came out to my house last Thursday morning under the pretense of seducing my friend."

"Seducing...lady, you don't..."

"You're not a sticker type, are you? Married, but not committed."

"She left me. We're divorced."

"Divorced! Are you sure?"

Ian laughed. "I'm positive, woman. She owns half my garage. But you're still staring at my lips, and I'd like get back to you wanting to kiss me." Ian licked his lips. "I have ChapStick," he said all wide eyes and innocence. He reached into his pocket. "See?"

"You are annoying. I don't want to kiss you!"

"Your nose is growing. Wow! It's as long as a banana!"

"Hush up!" Rhys said, barely restraining herself from touching her nose. Rhys had never learned to flirt, and therefore she didn't approve of flirting. She suspected that women who did it well and men, who could only communicate through the guise of it, were shallow.

"You are embarrassing me talking this way here in front of Mr. Dowell. I don't want to kiss you, and not because of your chapped lips. You are vulgar."

"Not my chapped lips. Yours."

Bobby Dowell whistled and shook his head.

"Damn you! I wouldn't kiss you if you, if you were the last living man on earth!" She spun away from Ian toward Bobby Dowell, who, it seemed, was as helpless as a one-man Greek chorus.

"Here, Mr. Dowell, this takes care of what I owe this garage, but I believe my points would be better served at one of the other chop shops in town," she said huskily.

"Whoa!" Ian Languille laughed and turning back toward his office waved his fingers at her behind his back. "You got sweet points, sugar."

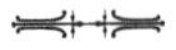

Tossing about through unsettling dreams Saturday night, plus the less-than-pleasant encounter with Ian Languille that morning, Rhys arrived at the Coffee Cupp at straight up 1:30 p.m., in a foul temper. Pauley waited in a back booth. He stood as she approached.

"You don't look happy," he said.

"You, on the other hand, look like you'd like to grow wings and fly out the window."

Spot-on, he thought, but before he could think of an appropriate wisecrack, Rhys handed him the diary. "I've been meaning to give this to you for days. If we can decipher it, the answers to Raggedy's murder are here. I'm convinced."

He wished he'd never agreed to meet with her. She was going to try and take over his investigation. He thought he just might hate her. "Have a seat," he said. "You said you wanted to talk." The café, settling down for a quiet afternoon, should have been perfect for a confidential conversation, but empty restaurants rarely are really empty.

"I've made some notes that could be helpful. Also, you need to know that the entries appear to us to be the handiwork of three diarists, not one."

Pauley's face was noncommittal, but he was sure he hated her.

Rhys slipped a paper napkin from the metal holder, and then rescuing a pen from the bottom of her purse, she began to doodle. "We've had a number of conversations with Hummer regarding Raggedy's alleged racket."

"Racket."

"Extortion."

"Extortion?"

"Blackmail."

"Ma'am, I know what extortion is. Alleged extortion, by the way. Now who is the *we* you've mentioned twice? Is Hummer a blackmailer too?" Pauley pulled a notepad out of his pocket, poised to jot his own notes.

"Oh no. Raggedy"

"You're sure?"

"Positive."

"Are you one of those sometimes wrong, but-never-in-doubt people?" Pauley cocked his head.

Rhys chuckled, bringing a tiny ray of sunshine into the room. "Touché. Perhaps you're right. I may be one of those except I'm often in doubt. I'm right about Hummer not being in Raggedy's game, though. Let me tell you about Richard's and my dinner date with Hummer."

She told Pauley about Raggedy's blackmailing business, about her ducks—her sitting ducks—and how they were identified in the diary as cartoon characters. She told him about the single letters and random numbers that peppered the diary.

"At first, we thought *H* was 'Hummer,' but after 'Louie' and 'Dewey' led us to the cartoons, *H* has to be 'Huey,' wouldn't you agree, or 'Hooie.' Raggedy can't spell worth a hoot. Of course, *H* can be anybody, I guess."

Larry Halliger popped into her mind, but she was not going to mention him.

"You say all this stuff as if it's a fact, but you don't even know if the diary belongs to Raggedy Ann," Pauley said.

"Well there's that. You've got a point. I'll hush and give you time to look the diary over and draw your own conclusions. You'll see. Would you like a cup of coffee?" She said, always the hostess.

"Milk and sugar, thanks."

"Do you want coffee with your milk and sugar?" She teased but in a friendly way.

"Yes, please, barely black, lots of sugar, mostly cream."

With that Pauley plunged into the diary. He read at it, skipping around, flipping back and forth from one section to another, occasionally making a note. He didn't ask her a single question, not one. This went on through a full cup of coffee.

"I'm gonna need some time with this," he said. Dithering the book in front of her, it fell open as if guided by an unseen hand. "Well, whatdya know!" The first thing he saw was the ragged edge where a page had been torn out. Pauley wanted to jump up and hug her. He remembered Mrs. Roach's note the cleaners had found in a pocket. Hers could have been torn from this very diary. Pauley dropped back down into their booth and began thumbing through the small book again. There was another ragged edge, and then, as luck was on his side today, he saw a number twenty with a smiley face in the zero.

"Tick's gonna kick my ass for giving this little book away."

"You think that the diary is important, then?"

"I do indeed!"

Buoyed with these possibilities, and Rhys's early assertion that the book did hold other information, Pauley aborted his desire to escape. Maybe she, irritating as a rash no doubt, also might prove to be his good luck. He'd have another cup of coffee so he could probe her blond brain a little further. "Why do you say that Hummer was not in her game, or one of her ducks. It seems logical to me that he could have been. He seems to know too much for someone on the outside. He was her heir, so to speak."

"Hummer didn't know *who* they were, Pauley—the ducks. He just told us the Donald Duck people were her sitting ducks, her victims, but he didn't know the real names. If Hummer were one of her ducks, he'd be Huey, right? *H* for 'Hummer'; *H* for 'Huey'? But why use the letter *H* at all? Raggedy Ann never referred to 'Louie' as *L*, or 'Dewey' as *D*. I'm not saying 'Hummer' is not *H*. *H* could stand for 'Halli...'" She sputtered behind a cough to camouflage the name, which had been poised on the tip of her tongue. "Pardon, I got choked on my own words trying to convince you that *H* could be anyone with the appropriate initial, but whoever he is, Hummer or someone else, nothing points to *H* as being in cahoots with Raggedy." Rhys ended on a puff of air similar to a phew.

"You sure can talk."

"By the way"—Rhys laughed lightly—"did I tell you the first time I saw 'Goofy' it was spelled with a little *g*, and I thought it was an adjective?" She laughed rushing on.

"Really?" The grammarly humor was lost on Pauley, but he smiled as if he gave a flying duck.

"By the way, do the police know that that sleazy Connie person has a hideaway in the attic at the Searcy?" Rhys asked.

"Becker? Sure," Pauley said, but he wasn't sure at all if the police knew or not. Until this moment he hadn't known it.

"Just wondered. Mr. Runsick doesn't know."

Pauley looked up. "Runsick doesn't know Becker lives in his attic, but you do?" Pauley said this with a look that could have been form of approbation but probably was far from it. "You're an interesting woman."

"That's Hummer. He's full of news when you finally get him going." Besides not mentioning Larry Halliger as possibly *H*, the second thing she had no intention of mentioning this afternoon was about her dragging Hummer to Becker's attic room.

"You ought to ask Mr. Runsick if he'd mind you snooping around up there."

"Not me. You trying to get me to tattle on Connie Becker?"

"Runsick should know he's harboring a criminal. I don't know—a trained eye, you know, might see something..."

Pulling a fresh napkin from the dispenser, Rhys doodled an eye, a large oval one with a dark, round pupil that seemed to stare off the edge of the napkin.

"What else has Hummer told you?"

"I've told you most of what I know."

"If anything comes to you...you know, like what you heard might be in the attic...or what you might have seen had you gone up there, but, I know you'd never be so stupid as to go into a drug dealer's hole...I know you know how dangerous that would be...but if Hummer has, or knows something the police...you'd tell me, right?"

"Absolutely," she lied.

"What may seem insignificant to you could be the real deal to...to a real cop."

"Of course."

"Okay going back, can I ask you a few questions to help me get things straight as you see them?"

"Shoot."

"Stuff in the diary you haven't mentioned yet, and that you didn't mention in your notes. Like Green Ink leading you to believe there was an affair going on."

"Yes."

"But did you note that Green Ink was not in the penciled section of the book, the section we think was Raggedy Ann's? Green Ink, affair or no affair, might have nothing to do with Raggedy's death."

Rhys hadn't noticed that, but it didn't dissuade her from her belief that Green Ink was involved in the whole sad mess.

"You are assuming that Green Ink is female, aren't you? That's a mistake. You're jumping to conclusions."

"Pure conjecture, I agree. But odds are with clues like Clip and Cut, which I admit is a unisex shop, but blue sweaters, and sales, and red wool dresses..."

"And you think Goofy is Connie Becker?"

"Did I say that?"

"You talked about Goofy with a little *g* and Connie almost in the same breath a few minutes ago."

Rhys was surprised at Pauley's aptitude for association. As an English major, she was aware that what was a natural talent for some people, not everyone could claim. Association was unteachable; it was an ability to which one was born. She was glad to see Pauley was associative. This would help them in their police work.

"Goofy is one of her ducks, I think, and I just wondered if it could be Connie Becker. There is something goofy about him."

"One, Goofy is not a duck. Goofy is a dog. Daffy is a duck. Have you found a 'Daffy' in the diary?"

Rhys looked nonplussed.

There was a jingle of bells. Pauley glanced up, and then sliding down in his seat, he bent over the diary as if in deep study. "Coach Wagner," Pauley whispered, nodding toward the door.

"Oh my." Rhys scooted out from the booth and walked toward the man. Pauley watched. He could hear them talking, but not their words. He hoped she didn't bring him over to the booth. He wouldn't know what to say.

"Poor man. Can you imagine? I feel so sad for him; he was a good friend once." Rhys slid back into her corner.

"Coach Wagner was a volunteer at the Boy's Ranch, when I was there as a kid."

"You were at the Boy's Ranch?"

"For a short time. Let's just say I wasn't born a cop."

"Unlike Mr. Tick, who probably came into the world with flat feet. What was Logan's job at the ranch?" Rhys smiled.

"We pitched a few baseballs back and forth. It wasn't his game, but he taught me something about practice and patience."

"Do the police have any leads on who killed his wife?"

Pauley shrugged. "That's not my case."

"The last time I saw Addie she was on the Christmas float. Like everyone, I thought the angel was the Berry girl and that she was schnockered. Is it true Addie aspirated on her own vomit?"

"That, and loss of blood."

"No one believes her death was an accident, do they?"

"Like I said it's not my case." Pauley frowned.

The couple revisited that gruesome night in their minds: the float, the wings, the death, the how, the why, and the who of it all.

There were a lot of unanswered questions in Riversbend these days. Things no one, and everyone, wanted to talk about. Things like Raggedy Ann's gender. Had everyone in Riversbend known that Raggedy was a man except her? Did it matter? Did it matter if the diary belonged to a man or to a woman? Did it have any bearing on Raggedy's death? Rhys wondered if the two crimes were connected? She knew she should say something to Pauley yet she was afraid to betray Schreiber's secret. Surely Pauley knew; surely he'd seen the autopsy.

"Pauley, I have a question for *you*."

Rhys put her hands behind her head, stretching her shoulders. Then, unfolding her long frame from the corner of the booth, she stood up. "Are you going to arrest me?

"There could be any number of charges," she said quickly to dispel any notion that she was plum crazy. "I ducked under crime tape, which contaminated the crime scene. I kept the diary longer than I should even after knowing it was important to the case," she explained. "I always knew I would. I'm just not always on someone else's clock." She sat back down. "Look at me. Don't forget you *gave* the diary to Richard, Pauley. I didn't have to bring it to you. If I hadn't read it, then I couldn't be guilty of obstructing justice. But, I did read it, so..." She shrugged.

He opened his mouth, but she raised her hand.

"I'm not quite finished with my misdemeanors: Raggedy was found in our Dumpster, and I lied about the grocery cart. I *had* put it in the stock room. I can't believe you didn't make me take you inside. You knew I was lying. So, you may arrest me, if you'd like."

"Good grief," was all he could manage.

"My intentions are good, Pauley. My interests in the diary are personal. And I do care about who killed Raggedy Ann for reasons of my own." Her voice trailed away momentarily. "Do you really know who she was? It's a rhetorical question? We never really know anyone, do we?"

Pauley was learning fast. He'd learned from his failure with Mrs. Roach that Rhys was anxious about something. The woman drew little pictures when she was distraught. That was good to know. It was also good to know that this tall, lanky, know-it-all, white woman sitting before him could be anxious. He had also observed her chin action. A mannerism reserved for a woman who knew little of defeat. There was power in her chin. He wondered what it would be like to live in a world such as hers.

Could she be an asset, open doors? Could she, like Dockers and Dr. Petitjean, become one of his people? She could be a real pain in the ass: bossy, arrogant, weird, difficult. Spoiled. But she was powerful too. Without Tick, he needed someone in his camp from this predominantly white town.

"Do you know Tick's real name? He called your Mr. Schreiber Sammy! That was strange. It caught my ear. Did Sam Schreiber grow up in Riversbend?"

"Off and on, I think. Nearer Pearl. I believe his father farmed a small acreage, mostly food crops for his family. He also farmed mussels on the river. I think I've heard Schreiber say his dad mined the mussels for a button factory that used to be down there."

Pauley remembered Willa Quinn saying something about a button factory close to where Tick grew up. "They were neighbors, then? Tick Quinn and Sammy Schreiber."

Rhys picked up the ballpoint. "Could have been. Maybe for a while." She wanted and didn't want this conversation to happen. "Schreiber's brother got hurt." His family moved."

"How so hurt?"

"I don't know. Schreiber said that Tick's father saved his brother's life."

Here it was, whatever she was trying to tell him. Pauley sensed it. He put his elbows on the table and leaned into them. "The name 'Tilman' didn't register with me much until yesterday, when I saw it on his personnel file." Pauley hesitated. He didn't want to go down this dark alley toward his unidentified blood-on-Adler's-stone-wall problem. But he had to draw her out. He was convinced she was holding back.

"What was Raggedy's her real name?" This question was innocent, but unknown to him, it also was a fluke, but so immediate to Schreiber's secret that Rhys giggled nervously to stifle a gasp. Pauley laughed too. He definitely was beginning to know this woman and her quirks.

"Butter, I think. Francie Butter." So cautiously did Rhys move this chess piece around that their tenuous partnership could gain no footing. Both withholding information, yet mentally accusing the other of the same.

The afternoon was slipping away. Rhys, in an effort to revive the confidence they had begun to establish, said, "So what have we got. Two deaths in a week, you gotta wonder." On this they both could comfortably agree. "What's next, boss?"

By 3:00 p.m., a few after-Sunday-lunch-nappers began drifting into the café for a late coffee, or piece of pie. Pauley glanced at his watch. Now or never had come, he guessed. He eased out of their booth. "Miss Adler, let's be clear. It will be up to you to prove your worth. That's not my job." That said the elephant stepped into the room. "And just so you'll know where you stand, I'm not inclined to have to second-guess people. I don't have time, and I'm not very good at it. I'm working solo on this case since Tick has disappeared. I have no team, and I have little patience if I'm forced to spend what time I do have, mollycoddling people I'm supposed to be partnering with—"

"You won't be sorry."

"Miss Adler, I…we have…hurdles—"

"You must call me Rhys?"

"Police work is not a game. It's serious. I'm not sure you're what I need. Physically you're…" Pauley rotated his hand in the universal language that indicates the speaker is floundering.

"Whoa. Are you about to suggest I'm too weak, too skinny, too tall? Too old?"

"I'm just saying…"

"But of course I am. Gee whiz, Pauley. All I want to do is be in charge of refreshments. A little tray of tea sandwiches around four every afternoon." If Rhys was amused, her face didn't show it.

Pauley wanted to slap himself. Was he crazy? What was he thinking she would do, break down doors, go on drug busts, shoot outs?

"Pauley, would you quit acting like an ass. Are you going to let me work with you on this case or not?"

He didn't do or say anything for minutes, enough minutes to make Rhys wish she hadn't pushed him quite so hard. But then his face began to relax, and then it became comically serious. "Listen, sweetheart," he was talking through the side of his mouth like an old-time movie gangster. "You must never act like you know me, see. You must never call me sir. You understand?"

When her laugh tumbled forth, it was filled with delight, and if anyone had known to listen, they could have heard the wall between them come tumbling down.

"So, I'm in?"

"Don't bug me."

He walked over to the jukebox and with a quarter bought a couple of minutes to think. He only had a vague sense of how she could be an asset. A secret weapon. *Craa-zy* Patsy Cline's mellow voice floated out into the silent spaces of the small café.

Back at their booth, Pauley picked up the diary. "It's important that we keep you under wraps," he said. "I'll contact you when I need you to do something."

"Like a secret agent!"

"More like...a fund raiser. A party planner," he grinned. "Like doing what you do every day. Don't draw attention to yourself, but keep a nose for the news. Don't run in and out of headquarters. If you have something I need to know, text me. If you hear anything you even suspect might be important, call me. I may ask you to do specific snooping if I need you to. For the moment you've done enough giving me the diary. We'll play it one day at a time."

Rhys opened her mouth, wanting more.

Pauley pointed at her. "I was serious about not acknowledging me in public other than distantly. You know like, 'how ya doin'.' If you say a word to anyone, even to Mr. Fordyce, I'll get laughed off the force or fired. And you must agree to my conditions without question. You must do no more than what I ask you to do, and no less. Is that clear?"

"I'll instruct Richard. We're in this together."

"Absolutely not!"

"Okay, okay. I'll not tell anyone. But I've never been able to keep anything from Richard."

"Your cousin is one of my prime suspects."

"That's ridiculous. Richard knows more about people in Riversbend than anyone else I know. He'll give you entrance."

"Anyone could be our killer."

"Not Richard. That is absurd."

"This arrangement isn't going to work."

"But it is. I'm just going to tell Richard."

Pauley stood up. "You're fired."

"You can't fire me."

He stared down at her. "The hell I can't," he said with just a hint of doubt.

"Relax, Pauley, I'm in your corner. Who else is in your corner?"

"Dammit!"

"Where's Tick?"

"And you're going to tell Fordyce despite my orders?"

"I would prefer not to lie unless it's important that I do."

Pauley, muttering a string of words probably best left in a clutter, walked away.

Rhys refused to turn around. She listened for the bells to jingle. In a minute she heard him at the cash register. She assumed he was paying their tab and would leave. But he didn't. He leaned over the back edge of their booth.

"Bring your cousin, and the three of us will have a discussion. If I'm not satisfied with the conclusion at the end of it, then it's over. You neither one be on this case."

Pauley started toward the back of the café. "While I'm in the men's, you be thinking. *Could* your Mr. Schreiber know where

Detective Quinn is hiding out, or why? I've got a hunch. I'll be right back, and when I get back, have your jacket on. We need to get started."

"Where are we going?"

"To the county jail. I have to lock you up for obstructing justice. While you're doing your time, I've got to go find a friend of mine who I hope can install a new windshield in my office."

Later that afternoon, after Rhys's stint at community service, which involved cleaning the kitchen, scrubbing the sink, and washing a week's worth of dirty cups, the two of them got into their respective cars.

Rhys was unusually silent. She didn't like being the butt of anyone's jokes. The policemen in the department had taken turns standing in the door way watching her work. When asked what she was doing, she'd simply say working on a Girl Scout badge. She'd kept a cool facade, smiling at the men, determined to show humor in what was surely a case of police harassment. *Just you wait, Pauley McCrary*, she thought, as she mulled her revenge in silent and partial sentences, savoring each one, as might a cow chewing her cud. At the moment, she envisioned doing something accidentally with honey and cornflakes—on his head—maybe adding ants. Maybe at the Coffee Cupp, some morning soon. Definitely in public.

Pauley was still grinning. He'd wisely kept away from the kitchen while Rhys cleaned, although he wasn't quite wise enough not to tease her now as he pulled his car alongside hers. "You're a good sport, Adler. You've repaid your debt to society, and I have to say, it was most gratifying." He thumped his chest with his fist. "Did my heart good."

Rhys's smile seemed benign. *Matte's chocolate cake with habanera chilies.*

"But"—Pauley tilted his head in a flirty way—"as the matron down at the jail says to her overnight guests, 'all good cells must come to a close,' so I'll say this, it's been an interesting day."

"Yes, very."

"Call me after you've talked to Schreiber, okay? By the way, always call on my cell phone, not at headquarters."

"Headquarters."

"See what you can learn from your Sam Schreiber. Remember you can't act like you're seeking information for any reason other than for your own curiosity."

"Why would I be curious about where Tick is when I'm not even supposed to know he's missing?"

"You'll think of something. Police work can be creative. This is your assignment. I think we've got a workable agreement." Pauley pulled his phone off his belt. "What's *your* number?

"Aww man!" Pauley hit the dash with his fist. His face collapsed into a mask of anger before he exploded expelling a string of unholy syllables. "Uh oh. Ggdamitsonabitch." He slammed the phone against the dash this time.

"Something wrong?"

Pauley glared at her, at what he considered to be the world's stupidest question.

"Pauley, your language needs a little refresher course. You're not keeping up. I can help you. I'm an adept. Learned to cuss and smoke at summer camp many years ago, and I work to stay current."

Pauley rolled his eyes.

"I give most of it up for Lent every year. What's your favorite word?"

"I didn't go to summer camp."

"My word changes with whatever it is that has provoked it. Right now, it's 'scut.' I take it you let your battery run down. Would you like to borrow my phone until you can recharge?" She thrust her high-dollar purchase into the open air between their windows.

"Won't help. Tick wouldn't know. He wouldn't know your number, wouldn't know you were helping me, wouldn't know I was so stupid that I let my battery go flat."

Pauley started his engine and then reached in the glove compartment for the charger. "I'm gonna give you my number." He reeled out a series of numbers while Rhys pegged them into her contacts. "Give me an hour before you call. I should be up to speed by then."

"It will be longer than an hour, my friend, before I'll see Schreiber for our casual chat about where his friend might be hiding. The friend who neither he, nor I, supposedly know is missing."

"When you talk to him, listen to what he doesn't say as well as to what he says."

"I can do that; I'm good at negative listening. By the way, I liked it when you call me Adler. It came out of your mouth easy."

"Yeah?"

"By the way, will I be paid?"

"Are you nuts?" Pauley laughed.

Rhys was laughing when she drove off the parking lot.

"Phew," Pauley said, exhaling. He pushed the seat back and rolled down the window a crack to let the December chill refresh his brain. Rhys Adler was sharp, energetic, and a friend of Tick's. Pauley had to admit he'd enjoyed the afternoon, but he was glad to be rid of her. Whatever else you might say about Rhys Adler, she was a strain. He put the Seville in gear and headed to Adler's Antiques. Scut? He'd be damned if he asked her what it meant.

Whatever buoyancy of spirit had carried him all afternoon had evaporated by the time he pulled into Adler's Antiques parking lot. He hated what he was about to do. He didn't have to do anything. He could tell Latimer he was leaving law enforcement. Or he could simply disappear. Why not? Tick had. He could lie.

> I will never betray my badge, my integrity, my character, or the public trust.

There were too many dead fish floating in Pauley's tank that smelled like Tick. This afternoon while he and Rhys were talking there was something just out of his reach. Something almost palatable about Tick and Sam Schreiber. He'd felt it the Sunday he and Tick were out at the farmhouse checking on the lachrymatory bottle. And he felt it again today. There were pieces between these two old men he couldn't connect.

He hadn't forgotten Latimer grilling him last Sunday after he and Tick had found Raggedy Ann's body on Saturday. At the time Latimer's questions had just seemed petty, spiteful.

> I will always have the courage to hold myself and others accountable for our actions. I will always uphold the constitution, my community, and the agency I serve.

Pauley lay his head on the steering wheel. The oath he'd sworn the day he got his badge came unbidden and unwanted. How could he justify the actions of his mentor? How could he understand this man who had taken time to teach him, to guide him, to care what happened to him when Pauley had no one else.

There was no doubt the route they took that night *had been* off their beat. Which of them *had* seen the body in the Dumpster first? How many knew about the lachrymatory bottle, and where it was kept? Who could have taken it out of the evidence room? Was the missing page in Tick's file really missing, not simply misfiled? And then there's the blood. O positive? He remembered Tick's hurt hand stuck in the half sock the last time he'd seen him.

Pauley stretched across the car seat to retrieve an evidence bag. He could stop now. Right now. If *he* never knew Tick's blood type, he could let his gut feeling about the blood drop go. He could forget it. He just wouldn't mention it to anyone. But Pauley knew Tick would kill him. It wasn't just his sense of what was right that propelled him. It was Tick's too, his determination to turn Pauley into a good cop.

Okay, maybe your gut's wrong. Discovering Tick's blood type could be a good thing. It could free him of suspicion as well as condemn him. Maybe it would be enough just to satisfy your own curiosity. No one is supervising you. Your reputation at headquarters is already in the toilet. At present you don't even have a partner. But then Pauley thought of Sagacious and Rhys. He didn't want to disappoint either of them.

Pauley knew about watching out for your friends. That's what black kids did growing up. They had to. So here was his dilemma: If he was going to do something Tick would insist that he *not* do, how could he *not* do it and still be watching out for Tick, when if he didn't Tick would probably go to jail? That was a tough one.

He couldn't do too much snooping at headquarters? He wondered if Miss Willa—Miss Willa—Pauley bopped his forehead. Tick's police record was not the only source with the blood information. Tick had served in Vietnam.

Pauley found the dark stains on Adler's stone wall easy enough. Maybe they were blood, maybe not. The building was old; it could be anything. He took his penknife and made several scrapings, dropping them carefully into an evidence bag. One thing at a time, sweet Jesus.

Back from the Coffee Cupp Logan Wagner paced from room to room, staying to the margins. He was afraid to step on the rugs; all the colors were faded. He wondered if he was going blind. Besides the rugs, he'd noticed the terracotta and blue Mexican vase on the entry table in the foyer had washed out. The earthy pigments of ocher and rust were now the color of dried mud, and the sleek, cerulean jaguar that encircled the belly of the vase had become little more than imprecise markings much like erasures from the butt end of a pencil.

Leaving his lunch forgotten by the vase, he began roaming from room to room, knowing every color and hue would leach away as soon as he entered it. His measured treads echoed as though he walked on hollow boards. It was Sunday. The fourth day after his Addie's death, and he was still alive. This surprised him.

Addie had made a perfect angel, ethereal, beautiful. She shimmered in the twinkling of lights and iridescent wings. He'd clapped along with the crowd as the float passed, whistling and waving, cheering the loudest, laughing, because only he knew of the hoax, the prank that had made Addie understudy to Jennifer Berry. It was daring and ridiculous, but he needed to be a kid again. They were all kids again, he and Addie, Jennifer and young Todd.

But there was always a moment in the inexhaustible reel of images when his happiness would slide off track. Logan sank onto the chaise lounge pressing his fists into his eyes. Dark shadows mocked his beloved, changing her face from angelic to anguished, sometimes her face morphed into her sister's face. At her funeral Addie had watched through Marilyn's eyes. And that was not all, in the ever-spinning reel he sometimes saw an impeccably dressed gentleman emerge from the crowd. But even when the gentleman wasn't there, Logan knew he lingered in the wings, waiting. Monsieur.

He made himself rewind his film and go back to their last day together, the happy part. It had started a perfect day. The youngsters were going to elope. It was a day for lovers.

A late afternoon flush from the west sent streams of rose-gold light onto the chaise lending it color and warmth. He felt Addie was beside him. Rising, he entered her closet where the scent of her climbed out on him, and it was in the midst of her, here in her closet that he understood he was as dead as she, and that there was no heaven.

He opened the drawer in her vanity and removed an envelope.

Tick was wary. Pauley should have been more resourceful. He'd hoped Pauley would trace him to a locale, if not to an exact address. It could have been done. Tick punched in Pauley's number.

He didn't know what to make of the boy's silence. Pauley'd left one short message. He had to assume Pauley was exercising caution, waiting for his moment. But as minutes drifted into hours, and there still was no response, Tick had to consider other possibilities.

How well could one man really know another? He cared for the boy, but Pauley was a different kind of man—young, inexperienced, eager to please, but also eager to stand on his own. Not to mention defiant. Tick had to consider the racial grudge that he suspected lingered in all black men. This combination could be dangerous in the wrong man. *And a murder case so early in his career*—Tick tried to shake the thought away, but it kept bobbing like a cork. Rag's murder could be the ticket out Pauley was always talking about.

And Willa. He'd heard the desperation in her messages. If he could talk to her, he could ease her mind. But it was important that she be protected for as long as possible.

He shifted the small phone to his left ear. *Two more rings, and I'll hang up.* He counted, "Two…three…he snapped the cover down. He'd try later, he had to. He had to know where they were on the investigation before he could plan his next move. When he took the fingerprint evidence he'd been lucky. He'd come in the back, slipped into the evidence room, and left. No one had seen him. But he couldn't depend on luck, and he didn't have time for mistakes.

If Willa figured out he was hiding and not just on a mission, it eventually would occur to her where he was. At first she would have been waiting for him to call, when he didn't, she would have come up with some very Willa-like rationale, as to why he hadn't. He didn't know how long she could hold out before telling someone where they should go look for him.

Pauley walked into Latimer's office midafternoon and dropped Tick's personnel file on the man's desk. "I need to speak to you, sir."

"Speak."

"Tick is missing."

Latimer's head, which had been bent over a *Gun World* magazine, popped up.

Pauley continued, "He isn't sick, and he isn't at home, and he hasn't been for days."

"Why are you just now telling me this? How long have you known this?" Latimer grabbed Tick's file, rounded the corner of his desk, and shoved it into Pauley's chest. "Where the hell is he? What is this?" He waved the file in Pauley's face.

"It's his personnel file."

Latimer looked at it like it might mutate into a rattlesnake. "What are you doing with it?"

"I borrowed it."

"What business is it of yours?

"The first page is missing." Pauley put his hand on Latimer's shoulder to keep the man from crowding him. "I want Tick's blood type, and the page in his file that would have this information is missing. Do you know anything about that?"

Latimer blinked. "Keeping up with the friggin' files is not my job. Where's Gladys? And just why do you want his blood type?"

"I want the blood type of every policeman who was at Adler's the night we found Raggedy Ann. It's called method of elimination. Gladys doesn't work on Sundays. Tomorrow I'll ask her to go back in records to see if it's been misfiled. But, to save time, if you know where it is, I need it because I don't have time to wait. I have an appointment."

"You'll ask her to go into records! *You'll* ask her?"

Pauley jerked his head much as one would at an annoying fly, which succeeded in bringing an end to Latimer's looming protest. "And while we're at it," he said, "Tick and the missing page are not our only problems. The lachrymatory bottle is gone too. And there are two types of blood on the army blanket that was in Raggedy Ann's cart. One is Raggedy Ann's. Was I wrong to assume you read the autopsy? You never read it, did you? How important could it be, huh? Old beggar woman. Old nobody."

"Watch your tone, you little sonofabitch? Of course I read the autopsy!"

"Tell you what. I'll get back with you when I have more information. If you know where Tick's first page is, put it on my desk."

The arteries in Latimer's neck were so distended that Pauley wondered if the man's head was about to explode. Spit had gathered in the corners of his mouth, and he was sputtering. But Pauley was out the door before Latimer could regain enough composure to yell at him.

Pauley had no trouble getting Tick's military papers. Willa handed them over to him with such confidence that he was doing something Tick would want that it was all Pauley could do to look her in the eye. The unbearable irony was that, in her urgency to help her husband, she might be the one to bring him down. Before they married Willa had been a nurse. She told Pauley that hospitals had labs where blood could be typed. He didn't have to wait until Monday for the lab in Little Rock to tell him what he needed to know.

"I have a friend who works at the hospital on Sunday evenings. I'll call and tell her you're coming." Pauley felt like Judas Jr. carrying the evidence bag with the chips from the bloodied sandstone.

Pauley had to locate Tick. He had to satisfy a couple of questions before he would know what he was going to do. Too many roads found Tick at the end of them. It was odd, for instance, that Tick hadn't asked Pauley to go with him to the morgue that second time when Petitjean called him back. And how could he account for Tick's peculiar behavior. Too much was missing: the man, the blood-type info, the lachrymatory bottle, and just as frustrating was the indecisive information on the fingerprint report. The only *good* thing missing was motive. It was that alone that moved Pauley toward the hospital. Lack of motive was in Tick's favor even if the sample turned out against him.

The Quick County Regional Hospital was five minutes from Willa Quinn's house. Buoyed by the thought regarding motive, when Pauley pulled onto the parking lot he was inwardly smiled. If the blood was not O, his investigation would make a 180-degree U-turn. He'd start over, start thinking different thoughts, asking different questions. He'd see if anyone had seen Raggedy Ann on Saturday afternoon late, or Saturday evening, if she was alone or with someone. The easiest people to start with would be Hummer and Toad and the other residents at the Searcy. He needed to go locate Becker's rat hole, anyway. He would talk to Richard Fordyce again too.

The cell phone plugged into Pauley's adapter began ringing. "Not now, not now," he hollered at the phone.

Pauley should have gone home, packed a bag, and skipped town. He didn't care about the law that much anymore anyway. If Boula Banjo had finished with his windshield, he would be outta here.

It had taken the lab *minutes* to type the blood samples. The technician had said she'd found three types in the mix on the sandstone, not two. Two agreed with forensics, Raggedy's and the unidentified O. The surprise was the appearance of B positive. Pauley thanked Willa's nurse friend and left.

Superstitious and possibly spineless, Pauley hadn't wanted to look at Tick's military papers before the tests. He hadn't wanted to clutter positive energy with negative thoughts. He waited until he was back in the patrol car to take the military papers out of the yellowing envelope. Tick was O.

Leaving the hospital, Pauley had worried the information from the lab in every conceivable direction. It could be someone else's. Tick wasn't the only type O in the world.

Pauley put his head down on the steering wheel. What was it Tick warned about coincidence? Coincidence was either wishful thinking or the truth dressed in camouflage. The night they found Raggedy, Tick was the one who sent Pauley up on the catwalk to investigate. The lieutenant had opted for checking the loading dock. "Get outta my light." Tick'd said. "Go see if you can find any killers." Pauley scrubbed his forehead with his knuckles.

Rather than go home, or to the Searcy where he should have gone to sniff out Becker's hideaway, Pauley drove out to the Razorback for a few beers. He was still in uniform. He knew it could get him busted, wearing his uniform in a bar where he intended to have a beer or two. Nevertheless, he was on his fourth or fifth when who should turn up but Adam McCrary.

If Pauley had seen his uncle before Adam had spun the barstool next to him, he would have decamped. But the empty stool was there, and Adam was on it before Pauley even smelled stale bourbon and cigarettes.

"Hey, nephew. What you doing out with the drunks tonight? Are you gonna bust us? 'Cause if you are, I'm leaving early. Hey, Charlie. Give me a shot of that Wild Turkey and another one for my nephew here."

"Good-bye, Adam. I'm not interested in having a drink with you."

"Now that ain't nice. That's no way to talk to your favorite uncle. Hey, Charlie, did you know this boy here is my own kin? He's my brother Adrian's son. Legitimate too. He married that pretty little colored girl. Where is your mother, Pauley? Do you ever see her? I'll say this, you shore got yourself saddled with some poor-ass parents."

Adam had two sides; he was either tolerable or mean. Tonight, he seemed tolerable. But Pauley still stood up and threw some money on the bar.

"Hey, pal, sit down a few minutes. We haven't had a good talk in a long time."

"We've never had a good talk, and I'm not interested in having one now."

"You might regret that, 'cause, as you know, in our little burg word gets around. I hear you've been driving all over the county looking for someone, and I just might know where he's at."

Pauley pretended disinterest, but his heart was pounding. "I don't know what you're talking about."

"Sure you do. And guess what? I saw him last week."

"We all saw him last week."

"But I saw him sitting on the steps behind Adler's with that skanky old bag lady. I guess she's a lady. You know the one, the dipper. Who knows, huh?"

"Shut up, Adam."

"Aw, now, call me Uncle Adam." He flashed perfect teeth when he grinned at Pauley. "Anyway, Tick and the bag queen were back behind Adler's. They didn't see me, I was walking down Bayou Street, but I definitely saw them, and I wasn't drunk, yet."

Pauley didn't say anything.

"They were kind of arguing, I guess you could say, scuffling. I figured he was trying to arrest her. And guess who else I saw going through that cart she drags around with her everywhere. Did y'all ever find it?"

"Adam. I was with Tick that night. Did you see me? No, I don't imagine you did. We found the old woman together, and when we found her she was dead."

"What time would that be?"

Here it was, and Pauley didn't know what to do to stop the information from coming out of his no-good uncle's drunken mouth.

"That's police business."

"It was somewhere around seven o'clock," Adam plowed on, "when I saw them. A regular circus it was that night. Bright moon but dark as pitch when the moon disappeared behind the clouds. I was on my way to AA. Was that when you were with him? It was after dark…"

"So how can you say you saw Tick if it was pitch black before then? How did you know it was Tick? Leave me alone, you sorry drunk. I'm not interested in what you have to say."

"His truck lights were on. I figure he saw her going for the trash, or just loitering. How do I know—maybe she was soliciting? Cops don't let you get by with much these days." Adam threw back his shot and wiped his mouth on his sleeve. "Speaking of cops, I heard the sheriff called you nigger baby. That right?"

Pauley clinched his teeth. "You said you might know where he was."

"Did I?"

"Do you?"

"I might. You interested in what else I saw?"

"That's what I thought. So leave me alone."

"I do know the sheriff's been running all over town, offering a reward to anyone who can shed any light on that bag woman's murder or on that Wagner woman's. Who was the last person to see them alive, that sorta thing? And I guess I was, you know. So how's about you buying me another little shot, and I won't tell 'im what I saw. The way I see it, you're trying to hide something. Are you protecting Tick? What's he ever done for you?"

And with that, Pauley knocked his uncle Adam off the bar stool.

"You saw him, Charlie. Police brutality. Call the police," Adam squawked seconds before passing out.

No one at the Razorback moved. It was late, most all the regulars had gone for the night and the others were too drunk or didn't care. Certainly Charlie saw no need in calling the cops, since they already had one out there.

"Are you gonna arrest yourself, Pauley?"

"There's not sufficient evidence."

"Want another beer? On the house?"

"If you're gonna field dress a deer, you gotta have a strong-bladed knife, as sharp as you can git it. Then, startin' between the legs, you cut all the way to the pelvic bone. This here large-handled knife is the one I use to cut through the breastbone to get to the heart."

"Don't cut your thumb, Dad. Mightn't you cut your thumb running it along the blade like that?"

Tick sat up with a start. It was the same dream he'd had for three nights in a row. It was so real. Tick rubbed his eyes and looked around the room as if he expected to see his father.

The house smelled of mice as did the mattress he lay on.

Wednesday night, his first night in the house, Tick had covered the bedticking with layers of newspaper to have a thickness between his body and the dank. His coat served as an extra blanket over the thin one he'd brought, but in the early hours before dawn, he was always chilled. He tugged at his coat, pulling it up around his ears, uncovering his feet in the process. He'd started sleeping in his shoes. Through the chinks, the winds played an eerie chorale about the house.

On Thursday morning he dumped the contents from his duffel bag onto his bed, gazing at it as he tried to assess his needs. Tick couldn't remember the last time he'd been out at the old house for longer than a day. A year, two, the weather was warmer for sure. Between then and now debris had blown in through an open door had crept into the corners of the rooms, the leaves disintegrating into veins and dust.

A large box of matches, a dozen cans, he counted, of things he could eat, beans, dried beef. There were some smokes, a canteen, some coffee, a hatchet, and a small shovel. He hadn't been a Boy Scout for nothing.

After the second day and night chill became an obsession. Except for the warmth of the sun, which he sought like an animal sunning on a rock, all that the house could offer was a slightly leaning wood stove his mother had cooked on. Having brushed away spider webs and small dead creatures from the warming oven when he first arrived, Tick would fill it sparingly with twigs, then small pieces of wood and let them burn long enough to take the night chill out of the house. He would use only the residual heat to warm his food. Without the stove, he wouldn't have fared as well for the four days he'd spent here; with the stove he ran a risk. It was a toss-up. It was deer season, the property wasn't posted, and wood smoke was a dead giveaway.

Lying still to keep from jockeying the coat off his rump, he eased his arm out from under the weight of it. He squinted at his watch in the dim first light of morning. It was Sunday, the Lord's Day, the day Willa made them pancakes before church.

He waited for the cordiality of a bright winter sun, knowing that when it came the rays would creep slowly, not through the small windows that he'd partially boarded up with pieces of linoleum, but through a chink in the wall large enough for a small child's arm to go through. The light would skitter on its journey to fill the room until it became strong enough to reveal fragments of old wallpaper. Scraps that clung tenaciously from another life, a scattered repetition of faded flowers and trellises that allowed his mind to slip back. Several times he'd had a glimpse of his mother in an apron he had long forgotten, standing by this same woodstove, talking to someone. He saw his dad at the supper table, reared back, snapping his suspenders, laughing. These memories were gifts. Tick had invited them as would any older man on the edge of retirement, returning briefly to his boyhood, to simpler times.

But recently the dreams, like the one this morning, filled him with alarm. A recurring dream he'd had for years when he was troubled now came every night. There was a blur of trees as they might appear to someone running through the woods. This dark fragment left him breathless. He reasoned that he was the runner, but he couldn't remember why he ran, or from what. He could hear the runner gasping for air, a sob caught in the throat, and when the picture had played itself out Tick's heart had been pounding.

This morning, waking from his dream about knives and field dressing a deer, he could have mastered his uneasiness by stepping out onto the narrow stoop to smoke. Or he could have walked down the road a piece to stretch his legs. Or he could have gone to the back of the house on another treasure hunt. Like yesterday, poking around under the house, he'd spied a shard of broken blue and white pottery. Dislodging it with a stick, he dragged it toward him. *Flow blue* his mother would have called it. She prized it. That he could remember *flow blue* astonished him. He'd found the wheel off a child's truck too and wondered if it had been his truck.

Tick couldn't grasp the meaning of all these latest dreams—glimpses, random, patchy as they were—but in the fuzzy space between asleep and awake he recognized there was a sequential ordering to them. With the running through the woods dream, and the most recent memory of field dressing the deer, the flashes had begun to piece together.

Tick clinched his teeth to keep from shaking. Was it only yesterday morning on his way to the river that he'd run upon the mangled, bloody remains of the yearling left on the side of the road? At first, he'd been disgusted at the waste, but then he'd become distraught at the desecration. He'd grown up hunting. He'd seen deer cut and dressed, even done it himself, but this was different. The animal was little more than a fawn, a useless killing left in a shallow ditch on the side of the road.

The experience had been so momentarily disabling that it aborted his trip to get fresh water, and he'd hurried back to the cabin and busied himself until the experience was pushed away, and almost forgotten, until now. Prompted by his most recent dream, he was convinced yesterday's carnage came back with such clarity that he could still smell the young deer's warm blood. The smell exploded into another scene. A different time. A boy running terrified through the woods. He remembered all of it.

Jimmy Quinn was no hero. Tick's dad hadn't saved Frankie Schreiber's life; he had ruined it. Conviction came in a flash, and Tick knew it was true.

MONDAY
DECEMBER 23
TIPSY EVE

Rhys had only three major Christmas gifts to buy, something nice for Richard, who had everything, and the special gifts, bought weeks ago, for the Schreibers. She'd found a new Stetson for him and a beautiful black cashmere coat for Matte. Good old Matte needed a special gift this year to soothe her hurt feelings following Schreiber's long kept secret.

At any rate, it was Tipsy Eve, and the real Matte apparently this morning was back. She had been her old self at breakfast. Christmas was in the air, and with the Schreibers' gifts wrapped and hiding in a summer garment bag in her closet. Rhys was in high spirits.

Richard's present she carried toward the dining room where a card table had been set up for gift wrapping. His was an ink sketch with delicate splashes of watercolor: a garden overgrown, a falling fence, minimal lines quickly drawn. Richard would instantly know why she'd bought it for him. Simple nostalgia. It would remind him as it had her of their grandmother's summer flower garden when they were small children, before the space had been converted to something much flashier. Rhys had framed the sketch in cherry with a thin gilt inlay.

A basket of lesser gifts dangled from Rhys's other arm. These were for friends, and other special people in her life, such as Mr. Neumann the postman, and Miss Fleet at the public library, who appeared so bookish in her owlish spectacles and lacy collars that she could have materialized right out of a Jane Austen. Even Mr. Tick. Rhys had heard he was about to retire. She wanted to give him a fishing hat with a Minnow Shiner Twitch Bait stuck in the band that had belonged to her father.

Waiting for Matte to join her, Rhys arranged her booty on the sideboard. She heard the telephone ring.

"Hallo. Yes, what is it?" Matte's tone was curt, as if she were being pulled away from the table at a G8 summit.

Rhys propped Richard's sketch on the sideboard and stepped back to admire it. Matte's gifts were already arranged, from most to least important, on the sideboard to be wrapped. Like Rhys, Matte and Schreiber had a small family, a niece here or there, a stray cousin out in Oregon, and with Frankie Schreiber so recently gone, the family had diminished exponentially. The thought saddened Rhys. It would be like if she lost Richard. In fact, this was a sad Christmas for Riversbend. She should take food to Logan. Something sweet, a figgy pudding, maybe? What was a figgy pudding, anyway? It reminded her of carolers in stove-pipe hats and warm, woolly mufflers. Wonder if Matte knows how to make a figgy pudding? Figgy or not, Rhys felt she ought to do something nice for Logan. She ought to invite him for Christmas dinner, but Rhys was not very good with ought-tos. She decided it might make Schreiber sadder. She wondered how long Raggedy—Frankie—had been in Riversbend. Did the brothers visit secretly?

The door to the dining room bumped open, and Matte backed through hoisting a tray.

"Oh yum! Matte, promise me we'll wrap at least two each before we start on those beignets."

Matte harrumphed. "Maybe we'll wait; maybe we won't. I've got bread rising in the kitchen. Clear me a place so I can put this here tray down."

"How's here?" Rhys shoved Richard's drawing and her other gifts, clearing a corner. Spools of red, green, and gold ribbon, cellophane tape, and two pairs of scissors, which hadn't quite made it to the wrapping table, she dropped into her emptied gift basket. "Do you know anything about figgy puddings? I would like to take one to Logan Wagner this afternoon?

"You're kidding me, right? I could make him some dilly bread. I've been meaning to make some for us, and I kin whip up some pimento cheese to go with it."

"That's not too Christmassy."

"He don't need something Christmassy. He needs something easy for sandwiches, and it keeps if he's over loaded with women dropping by and bringing food. You think the widders haven't figured out yet they got a fresh fish out in the pond?"

Rhys smiled. "He's kind of young for the casserole widows."

"What about the gay divorce-sees? He's prime for that lot?"

"Could be. Who was on the phone?" Rhys changed the subject.

"Somebody calling for Schreiber. I told him he was out with Richard's cows."

"Was it Pauley McCrary?"

"Older sounding."

"Where do you want me to start?" Rhys asked.

The system established a few years back for their gift-wrapping session went into operation. There were a few rules: the finished product could have no underwear showing, as Matte called the back side of the decorative paper. Paper cut too short could not be patched, and no paper overlong could be wadded and taped into submission. There could be no wrinkles in what should be a tight surface, and an extravagance of ribbon was a must.

The telephone rang again. This time Rhys ran into the kitchen. "Hello." Rhys could hear someone breathing. "This is Rhys Adler. Who is this?"

"Is Sam back?"

"Is that you, Mr. Tick? Where are you?" The phone went dead.

Rhys ran to her bedroom and grabbed her cell phone, but Pauley's line was busy.

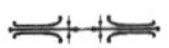

Richard's three favorite holidays were Christmas day, his birthday, and Tipsy Eve, the twenty-third of December, the day he hosted his annual Christmas dinner for his twelve favorite people. This morning he had awakened before daylight, his mind in a work with all the last-minute chores to be finished before his first guests were to arrive at eight-thirty that evening. He loved the hustle and bustle of a day like this. He should have been in theater. He would have thrived in the do-or-die of Broadway.

As usual, there would be twelve guests. He and Rhys, naturally, which left ten chairs to fill. This year seating was a breeze; his guest list was identical to last year's. But not every year was so breezy. Occasionally, if friends took leave of Riversbend or life, which to Richard were one and the same, he would spend days trying to decide with whom he should replace the dearly departed. It could get complicated.

As everyone knew, in most couples there was the one who people enjoyed enormously, and the other who was mostly tolerated as one would tolerate a hang nail.

Richard's parties were coveted, his reputation as a host was exemplary, and here it was again, Tipsy Eve. The spirit of Christmas embracing him even in the predawn darkness, he clasped his hands together in anticipation. And why Hummer popped to mind precise at this moment Richard had no idea, but he had. Wouldn't it be something if one year he could invite Hummer to a Tipsy Eve dinner! After all, Hummer had already met some of their friends at the country club. With that thought Richard laughed out loud.

The began turning on a few lamps. The house glowed in readiness, wood gleamed, windows and all things glass or crystal sparkled. A ten-foot-tall Christmas tree reigned like a queen at the far end of the living room. Richard flipped the switch, and a shower of glory filled the room.

He stepped back to admire the effect for a moment, knowing he still had game hens to rescue from the butcher, and crawfish from the fish market for bisque before he could approach Beau, whom he could hear in the kitchen shouting obscenities at Chamois, Richard's beloved golden, ancient and arthritic retriever. His overcoat he grabbed from the coat closet and passing a vase of holly stuck a leaf or two with berries in his lapel.

The stationer's shop was Richard's last stop. He held up three sheets of cardstock, one a bright green that would look nice with the gold ink he'd purchased, one berry red, and an ecru to be on the safe side. He was thinking name cards for his table in his silver holders. His guests kept their name cards from year to year, he understood. It apparently had become quite a competition to see who could boast the most.

Richard was smiling as he turned to the diminutive man in the gray cardigan and paisley bow tie who had been so close on Richard's heels for the past several minutes that Richard could hear him breathing.

"Oh, well, Mr. Bingley. I can't seem to make up my mind. I guess I'll take all these colors, two sheets of each, and also a small bottle of dark green ink, more a forest than an emerald. I'll have to see which one sets off my centerpiece best. I'll need gold ink too. My table linens are candlelight." He stopped talking to study the cardstock again. "Three of each, in case I mess up." He pulled the extra sheets from the bin and handed them to Mr. Bingley, who was hard of hearing and could only surmise and smile on his way to the cash register.

His package tucked under his arm, he walked out the door with the jingle of bells and down Main Street. The sky had cleared after a dowdy beginning, which meant he wouldn't have to manage dripping umbrellas and raincoats as his guests arrived. Always a blessing.

As he neared his car, he noticed a young man in a red truck parked in front of him. His face was vaguely familiar. Richard nodded and began fumbling in his trouser pocket for the car keys.

"Looks like you might need another hand." The young man hopped out of his truck, but rather than assist Richard, he propped a foot where in an earlier age there would have been a running board.

"Now, wouldn't you be Mr. Adler?" he said in an effort to detain Richard who was arranging his packages in the back seat.

"No. Fordyce."

The young man looked mildly surprised. "You ain't the husband of that woman who drives that silver Jaguar?"

"No. She's my cousin. And what's your name?" Richard asked, straightening up.

"You need to give her a message for me. Tell her if she don't quit sending the police over to my pad I'm gonna haf'ta give her a spankin'." The man grinned, but it wasn't boyish or pleasant.

"I didn't get your name." Richard had straightened up and was eyeing the young man from the top of his head to his feet.

"You tell her that. She'll know who I am."

Richard, knowing Rhys's penchant for prying, wasn't too concerned. "It's Christmas, my man. Here, I have bought a bunch of silly favors to give to my dinner guests tonight. Let me offer you one as a consolation for my cousin's interference." He reached back into his car and into one of several sacks and pulled out the first thing he touched, a toy pair of handcuffs and a sheriff's badge that he had intended to give to the son of his next-door neighbor who, from time to time, took Chamois, his dog, for a labored walk.

"No, I don't guess you want these unless you have children. How about this Razorback tiepin?"

"No, let me have the cuffs. I've got a girlfriend who likes that sorta thing." The man grinned again, leaving Richard feeling uncomfortable.

"Now see here; I see your license plate. If my cousin has any trouble from you, I can find out easily enough who you are. And I never forget a face."

Pauley—busily penciling the semblance of a case sheet at Tick's desk of things he thought he knew and of things he needed to know—heard the sheriff in the hall. "Oh, sir." Pauley hopped up and, walking rapidly toward the sheriff, edged the two of them back into Latimer's office. "I have a question. Why did you take the top sheet from Tick's personnel file?"

"For review." Flummoxed at the suddenness of Pauley's aggression, the sheriff spoke reasonably, until he realized that Pauley was staring at the file folder on his desk, attempting to read upside down the tab that clearly established the folder as Tilman O'Connor Quinn's.

"Have you been snooping in my office?"

"Me, sir? You've been in your office all morning, sir, except when you went for coffee."

Latimer stared at the young policeman, trying to determine if Pauley had said yes or no to snooping. "I'm telling you this, McCrary, but don't get the big idea I have to explain to you anything I do or don't do," he added.

"No, sir. And thank you for telling me."

"Have Gladys file it under Retired Personnel."

"I don't guess you want to tell me why you had to review it?" Pauley said, sensing rightly that Latimer wanted to.

"No, by God, I don't."

"Gotcha." Pauley stood up to take the folder to Gladys.

"I'm the master of ceremonies at his retirement dinner."

Pauley's cell phone saved him from laughing. "Officer McCrary," Pauley said into his mobile. "Hey!" He lowered his voice and turned to leave with Latimer fast on his heels.

"If you weren't snooping how did you know the first page was missing?"

Even when Pauley trotted down the back steps onto the parking lot, Latimer was within earshot.

"Not completely," he said to Tick's asking if he was alone. "I'll call you back in five minutes, Gran—where are you? I'll call you right back." Pauley glanced at Latimer.

"Don't you dare leave this parking lot you sonofabitch."

Pauley jumped in the patrol car and shoved it into gear as Latimer grabbed at but missed the passenger handle. Gravel flying, Pauley was off the lot in seconds.

Ten minutes later, when Pauley returned to leave the cruiser and pick up his Seville, Latimer was still standing at the back door.

"Don't you ever do that again. I'm not a fool. That was not your grandmother; where is Quinn?"

"She asked if I wanted brown gravy or cream gravy with my chicken."

"Don't you mess with me; where is the sonofabitch? I want a blood sample. I'm going with you. I've got to have a killer."

"Back off. You don't know what you're talking about."

"You get a sample of his blood with or without a warrant, because I'm telling you to. Do you understand? This is a direct order. Cut him if he resists and wipe it on your shirt. Sentiment don't get the job done, McCrary. If you don't come back with Quinn's blood, don't come back at all, because you won't have what it takes to be a cop, and you won't have a job."

"Go thuck an egg, thir. This is my case, remember."

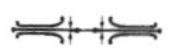

Time's moving on, Isabella Radley thought as she left the college library. She was bad to get caught up in some article on Riversbend history and let the afternoon slip away. Every now and again, she would think about purchasing a car, but she'd have to learn to drive. "Too many parts to break down," her father would have warned had he been alive. She was thankful for her bicycle. It was faster than her old legs, and kept them active to boot, but she looked forward to the arrival of spring and the balmy air to warm her bones. According to the almanac, spring would be early. Climate change, some would say, but she'd seen early spring many times.

"Ohhh!" Miss Radley dropped her feet to the ground. "Now where are you going, puss?" She watched the gray cat dart in front of her, stop, and doing as cats do, turn its head to study her. "Aren't you a pretty pet."

With typical feline arrogance, the cat ignored the compliment and continued toward the darkened house that sat in the curve of the loop.

Isabella knew exactly to whom the cat belonged. She saw the cat stop to manicure its paw, to tease her along. "No one's thinking about you, are they, dear? Are you hungry? Well, show me where your food is, and I'll feed you."

Following the tabby, Isabella pedaled up the drive in time to see it disappear around the corner of the garage. A double garage, both doors down and the animal nowhere to be seen. Isabella dismounted to look around. The house's darkness assured her that Mr. Wagner was either asleep or gone. She propped her bicycle against the garage and headed toward the same corner the cat had taken.

Not wanting to be mistaken for a trespasser, she stepped confidently, if a bit stiffly. She wanted to appear to be a neighbor attempting to be helpful, to be just an ordinary acquaintance wandering tentatively around a yard that was clearly not her own, but who felt called to help poor Mr. Logan by feed his poor forgotten cat. This is how she wanted to be viewed should someone notice her slipping out of sight around the garage.

She had to stand on tiptoe to peer through a series of narrow windows as they availed themselves. Through the second, her eyes squinted for clarity, she thought she saw a glow. Dim, still she was able to make out a side door on the wall opposite, and if her eyes were not teasing her, it stood slightly ajar, and this undoubtedly would be the crack through which the cat had entered.

An honorable woman, Isabella debated fleetingly if she ought-to go into the garage or not, even as every bone, nerve, and fiber in her being urged her to enter. That she *ought-to* won by a goodly margin, even at twilight. She knew it was an odd hour for casual callers. Mr. Wagner might think she'd come for cocktails. But even that didn't stop her. Despite her wiser self, Miss Radley was already mincing toward the door that was, in truth, slightly ajar—just enough. After all, she *should* feed the cat, poor dear. And maybe a kind word would lift the poor man's spirits should she be discovered. Her rap was light, but it enough to nudge the door open a bit more.

"Hellooo. Anyone home?" She stepped inside.

The cat was waiting. It sat on a counter by a small plastic bowl, which was as empty as Isabella had suspected it would be.

"Mr. Wagner? Hellooo! Are you in here? I'm going to feed your cat if I can find its food. It must be here somewhere near its bowl," she sang out as she pulled opened a pair of doors to the shelves below. "Ah, here we are." She found the scoop inside the large bag of cat food. She filled it and poured a measure into the cat's bowl. "Where is your water bowl, kitty? Is there a faucet in here somewhere?"

Once inside, naturally Isabella felt compelled to look about. She had a small flashlight in the basket on her bicycle, and she considered fetching it, but as her eyes adjusted to the interior, she realized there was still plenty of natural light coming in through the windows.

It was more than a garage. It was a workshop too, and a well-kept one. A long wall to the back held tools hung on stout pegs. There was an equally long countertop, above which were open shelves. There was a chainsaw and labeled plastic containers with odds and ends, duct tape, fertilizers, gardening chemicals, empty flower pots neatly nested. "Very nice, I must say—*a disorderly mind is the devil's workshop.*" Despite the proverbial misquote, Isabella Radley believed the inherent sentiment. "And this must be your bed. I see you have your own pillow for these cold nights."

Isabella wandered toward the light source, much as a phototactic moth moves toward its fascination.

"Oh, and what do we have here?" Miss Radley squinted. The soft glow she'd see through the window illuminated a shadowy corner that until her business with the cat was in order she hadn't investigated. Savoring the moment, she moved toward it. A large tea towel had been thrown over the light. "Well, well. What have we here?"

Minutes later, just as she had replaced the towel, she heard the door scrape against the floor behind her.

"Oh! Hello, hello!" Isabella turned around casually. "Well, my goodness."

The cloisonné clock dinged 6:00 p.m., awaking Rhys from her pre-party nap with a start. Groggy, she stared off into space, feeling slightly miffed for wasting time she'd planned to spend on her nails. Richard had wanted her to come early to help greet his guests.

Preferring her hair, which had a bend or two of its own, to dry naturally, Rhys had showered soon after returning from town. Touching it with her fingers, she was sure it had dried all wrong with errant tufts and cowlicks. She sat up, listened for voices, and hearing none assumed the Schreibers were still at their church social. The couple had stopped by her room to show off their Santa and Mrs. Claus costumes. Matte beamed in her large white apron, its two red pockets stuffed full of candy canes.

Tipsy Eve heralded the official beginning of the Christmas holidays. Rhys's dress for the evening was a cocktail-length, sea-blue silk shantung with a plunging décolletage. Richard had talked her into buying it. Rhys, who tended to think of her chest as bony, had bought it only under the condition that Richard let her wear the sapphire-and-pearl bib, which Rachael Fordyce had inherited from their grandmother, and which Richard kept in the lockbox at the bank to give to his bride or daughter or grand-daughter, none of whom so far had made an appearance.

Rhys's dress hung on her closet door. Her shoes, silvery, strappy, had a comfortable but well-shaped heel. The lid laid to one side on the chaise, but the shoes were in their box, still wrapped in tissue after the last fancy dress party.

In her dressing gown and having moved to her dressing table, she studied her hands. If her hair would cooperate and go up quickly, she would take time for her nails.

The telephone rang. "Tipsy Eve gift!" She sang into the receiver.

"Miss Rhys?"

"Mr. Tick! Please don't hang up!"

"No'm. I'm not. I'm down here at headquarters, wondering if you know where that little book of Raggedy Ann's that Pauley told me about is?"

"The diary? It's down there."

"You read it? It names names, Pauley said. Zat right?"

Rhys frowned uncertainly. Was that a question or statement? Rhys heard a nervousness in Tick's voice, which made her question him. She began to wonder if he was at headquarters, or had talked to Pauley about the diary at all.

"Not really names, more like Looney Tunes than proper names. Is Pauley with you, Tick? Let me talk to him. Have you just now talked to him? The diary's is at headquarters. I gave it to him." Then, pushing her luck, she added, "Or, if you need me too, I'll call him. I'll tell him to call you."

The telephone was silent except for Tick's breathing.

"Mr. Tick?"

"Go on. I'm listening."

"Yes. Well good!" Rhys hesitated. Her last tactic had spooked him. If he was not at headquarters, she had to coax him into telling her where he was or to convince him to call Pauley. Where were those skills she thought she possessed when she'd so confidently convinced Pauley she'd be an asset?

"Raggedy had been blackmailing people." Rhys dropped a crumb.

Tick response was guttural, a grunt more than groan.

"I hope the diary is not lost." She continued tentatively, "If Pauley doesn't have it, we probably can't get a conviction." Rhys thought she heard Tick laugh.

"We?"

Tick Quinn wasn't stupid. She'd overplayed her hand again.

"Don't worry, Miss Rhys, I see Pauley coming back in. Thanks for your help." As soon as she heard the dial tone, she called Pauley.

"McCrary speaking."

"Pauley, this is Rhys." She quickly told him of Tick's call, his search for the diary, and his verbal inventions regarding headquarters and Pauley. "He isn't there, is he?"

"I don't know. I'm not at headquarters. I'm on my way. I've been driving around, waiting for him to call. I gotta keep my line open. Don't call me back."

"I do have something important, I think. I came to see you this afternoon. I have something to tell you about Logan Wagner."

Tick's instructions had been firm. He'd said that when he called back, Pauley was to use his own car, come alone, and be dressed in civilian clothes. Tick would direct him to his location as Pauley drove. Pauley had been cruising for an hour and a half when Rhys called.

"If Tick calls back, tell him to call me pronto. I shouldn't have brought you into this. I'm hanging up."

When she heard the dial tone, she cradled the telephone.

"Who you talking to?" a soft voice asked from behind her.

Rhys's head jerked. In her mirror, a man stood in her doorway.

"Logan?" She yelped as her hand flew to her mouth. "What are you doing here?" She spun around on her dresser stool. "Good gracious," her voice cracked. "I'm not sure who frightened whom the most. You look like you've seen a ghost."

Facing squarely the man who strolled into her bedroom, she rushed on. "The Schreibers must be home—I didn't hear you come in."

"What were you saying about me? Just now? On the phone?"

Rhys rose from her dresser, pulling her dressing gown closer around her. "I was telling Richard that I had brought you some dilly bread this afternoon. Did you find it? I put it in a chair on your porch. I was going to call you—"

"You're lying. I know whom you were talking to. He was one of our athletes. Larry Halliger coached him."

The alarm system in Rhys's scheme of survival went on red alert.

"I knew his dad too, and his uncle. Pauley's a smart boy. He's a policeman now, isn't he?" Logan walked to her window, and pulling back the curtains, he looked out into quiet side of the house. No driveway, no stables or barns, or gardens, just an expanse of fading light and fallow fields. "Smart girls, like you, should keep their doors locked, particularly when they're alone out in the country."

Rhys reached toward an array of perfume bottles adjacent to her dressing table. She selected a heavy Baccarat cut-glass one, removing the stopper she sniffed lightly, as a woman might do before applying scent or throwing it as a weapon.

"Logan, why are you here?"

"I've been here for a while."

"Really? In my house? Why?" A tendency toward morbid curiosity commandeered the fear rushing through Rhys.

Logan shrugged, more a twitch of his shoulder as if her questions were mere annoyances like gnats.

"You look very nice in your tux." She cleared her throat lightly to camouflage the tremble. "You must be going out tonight?"

Logan nodded, and then in what appeared to be a flash of confusion as to why he was wearing a tux, he touched the front of it, rubbing the shiny satin lapels. "Sunday at the Coffee Cupp you were talking to him too? Was it about my wife?"

"Addie?"

"Addie, Addie Wagner, my wife." His voice rose, pinched, tight.

"Logan, I don't know what you want. I hardly knew Addie."

"But you were talking about her on Sunday."

"We mentioned her when you came in." Rhys tried to smile her reassurance. "That was only natural, Logan. Addie's death has shaken the town."

"That's good. I wouldn't want you talking about her behind her back"—he laughed—"which brings me to why I came out here. We want you and Richard to come for dinner one night soon."

The small hairs on the nape of Rhys's neck prickled.

"Don't look so surprised. It's Addie's idea. My wife's a very forgiving person. I think she thinks if you can't bring the mountain to Mohammed, you bring Mohammed to the mountain. Is that how it goes? Something like that." He laughed. "I do anything she wants, you know. She's an angel. You saw her on the float, I guess? That was her dream when she was a girl, wanting to ride on the Christmas Bell float."

His brow furrowed as he shook away spidery webs of memory.

"Hey, I know you're tied up tonight it's Tipsy Eve, but we couldn't have had you tonight anyway." He laughed again as if to assure her of something. "It's Tipsy Eve. I see your dress hanging on the closet door." He walked over and fingered the fabric, almost caressing it, but then, clutching a handful of the skirt, he pulled it toward him and buried his face in it for a moment.

Rhys barely breathing watched him closely. When he released it, she watched as the shantung fell, not a wrinkle in it.

"It's lovely. You'll look very pretty." He turned back to her. "We know not to ask you to dinner on the spur of the moment, like this. You and Richard are popular people. But soon—after Christmas, like we used to do. It wasn't such a long time ago, was it, Rhys?"

Rhys sighed sadly. "Let me walk you to the door, Logan." She touched his arm to direct him. "You're tired, not quite yourself tonight. The Schreibers will be back any minute."

"You loved her once, Rhys. I just think it would be nice if we could start over again."

"Oh, Logan." Tears filled Rhys's eyes. "I never really knew Addie. I haven't been to your house since—well, since Marybeth. When you two divorced, it got complicated. Longtime friends to both of you. You know that, Logan. But none of us knew exactly how to negotiate the minefield."

"Well, we'll remedy that, won't we? Give everyone at Richard's tonight my regards. Tell them to not forget me." Logan smiled, but this time it was more as if his lips had pulled back from his teeth. "Tell Richard what I said about coming to dinner, and tell him that I think of him often. All the time, really." Logan turned to leave. "You'll look smashing in that shiny blue dress, Rhys. Addie has a new dress. Red. My favorite color." He held up his hands to stop Rhys, who was about to say something that, perhaps, he didn't want to hear. "No, no. I'll let myself out. Lock up behind me."

"Don't forget the dilly bread, Logan. Matte made it from scratch. You know maybe after Christmas, Logan, you could come one night. Richard could come. Would you like that? Drinks and one of Matte's good dinners like old times?" His face was sweet; Logan was sweet. Rhys felt so guilty.

She watched his car lights refract into splinters in the beveled glass of the door and then dapple between the shadows of the pine trees before disappearing over the Blue Creek hill. How strange, she thought as she started back to her bedroom. "New red dress," he'd said. She wondered what Richard would say when she told him. She clearly saw Green Ink's spidery script in the diar...*men like me in red.* Rhys shivered. Where were all these unimaginable threads leading them? Where would it all end? Pulling her robe around her, she started for the telephone to call Richard to prepare him that she'd be a bit late, but before she could quick dial him, she heard the back doorbell. Her first thought was the Schreibers were home, but then why the doorbell? Matte was a key fanatic. Before she could be seen through the half window, she cautiously peered into semidarkness, praying Logan had not come back.

"Thank you, Jesus!"

The round face that stared back was neither Matte nor Schreiber, but Tick Quinn. Her unaccountable friend, on the lam for days, now, all smiles and teeth, beamed as Rhys turned the lock.

"What a blessing. Come in, come in. You won't believe everything what's been going on around here. Where have you been, Tick Quinn, worrying all of us?" Tick, hat in hand, stepped into the kitchen.

She patted him affectionately and would have pulled him to her in a big bear hug had she been fully dressed. "Let me pour you a cup of coffee, dear man, and I'll go slip on some clothes!"

As her words gushed out, she began to wonder if she was going to make it to Richard's party at all this year.

"Would you rather have a drink? I know I would." Rhys maneuvered Tick toward the living room. "G and T? Beer? Whisky?" She paused at the liquor cabinet. "I guess you passed Logan Wagner as you drove in? Poor man, I'm afraid Addie's death has undone him. He talks as if she's still alive." Uncomfortably aware that Tick hadn't said anything, Rhys turned to him. "Mr. Tick, are you all right? You've had Pauley on pins and needles."

"I'm fine. I've been sitting out there in your garage, making friends with your dogs, trying to decide what I need to do."

"Old Bay and Jolly? Usually they set up a howl the minute they think someone has come to play."

"No'm, not for a while—they won't. I put them to sleep."

Rhys's mouth dropped. "Dammit, Tick. I wish people would quit putting my dogs to sleep. It can't be good for them. They wouldn't have bitten you. They weren't even barking. Why did you do that?"

"I didn't like having to, but I saw how friendly they were the other day, and I have this other business on my mind tonight."

Rhys felt her throat tighten. "Is it the diary?"

"It's a police matter. I don't want to be hard about this."

"Pauley has the diary. Remember, I told you on the telephone." Rhys tried to smile. Tick Quinn was an old friend. "We've been through a lot together, Tick, and I don't know what's on your mind, but I want to help you. Let's talk. My mother always said a person can think better sitting rather than standing and letting all the blood run to their feet." Rhys laughed lightly.

Tick sat on the arm of one of the wingbacks but said nothing.

"You've been very elusive lately," Rhys prompted gently, "you're behind at work, maybe." Still he said nothing. "On the phone a while ago, you were fibbing to me. Why, Mr. Tick? You haven't seen Pauley, and you never were at headquarters, because you were here the whole time."

"You think you're pretty smart, don't you."

Rhys's smile was uneven. She wasn't sure what she should say, what she should do. At the moment she wished she'd never heard of Raggedy Ann. "Let's go down to headquarters together. The diary should be in the evidence room. I gave it to Pauley on Sunday. Have you talked to him? He's been expecting you to call him all day."

"No." Tick was on his feet. His fists clinched.

Rhys stood. "I'm going to put on some jeans. If you would like a drink, help yourself. The whiskey's in the bottom of the cabinet there, glasses too. Pour one for both of us. I'll be back in a minute." Rhys started to leave, but Tick, more agile than one would think for a man his age and size, jumped in front of her.

A flush of anger swept over Rhys. People had no right to burst into her house. No right to burst into her house, or her life, and to treat her as if she had done something wrong. "Please move from in front of me this instant." Her instincts told her to remain calm, even if she didn't feel it. "If you don't trust me, I can't help you. I'm cold. I'm going to get dressed and you're in my way."

"I'm starving." The declaration was not a request but said like a man who was desperate. "I need something to eat. So you come back in here, and while you fix me something to eat, you can study on what you've done with the diary. It isn't in the evidence room. You can tell me exactly what names are mentioned."

Rhys looked at him closely. "I can't give you names. It's cryptic, written in ciphers mostly."

"You're lying. Remember you told me it had names when we was talking on the telephone."

Rhys remembered. She'd been trying to keep him on the line. "I'm telling you the truth, Tick. The diary is nonsensical. It's numbers and initials, and Disney characters. I don't know who they represent. No one does. What do you think they mean? What are you afraid of?"

"The fact that you keep lying tells me most of what I need to know." Tick took Rhys's elbow and began moving her back toward the kitchen as if the two of them were crossing a highly dangerous intersection.

The kitchen was cold. Rhys didn't know if it was nervousness or her lack of warm clothes that made her shiver. She pulled a carton of eggs, butter, and a pound of bacon from the refrigerator. She was not afraid of Tick Quinn, but she was angry with him. She didn't know how to relate to him in ways that would be beneficial to both of them…to Pauley too. Remembering their jiggly, gelatinous partnership at least gave her a position from which to play. She set the eggs on the table and crossed the room to get a bowl and a whisk. Tick, seated at the kitchen table, watched her every move.

"Eggs and bacon? Some toast?" She asked, holding up a loaf of bread and hoping to create a more comfortable atmosphere. "I'm not much of a cook."

"Cook all of it. All you've got." His eyes followed every egg on its way from the cracked shell into the bowl.

"How long has it been since you've eaten?" Rhys tone was artificial, and suddenly weary of trying to placate this man who did not want to be pacified, she added, "Are you hiding from someone, Tick?"

He took his eyes off the bowl of eggs to look at her. "I've been working on this case. I'm trying to figure out how she died, what killed her, how she got in that Dumpster."

"Raggedy Ann's case?"

"Yes, Raggedy Ann's case. Who else?"

"Frankie Schreiber's?" Rhys continued whisking the eggs, but with her words she turned to Tick, who, until now, had seemed agitated, maybe even angry, but when she mentioned Frankie Schreiber, Tick Quinn had become something more. He had become dangerous.

"You knew they were brothers?"

Tick's face was chalky. "Frankie."

"You knew them, the Schreibers. All you boys grew up together. You tried to telephone Schreiber the other day, didn't you? Did you know Raggedy Ann was Frankie? Did you know about Frankie's terrible accident when he was a youngster?"

It might have been a mistake to push him, but Rhys knew it was a mistake she could use. She put the bowl down and, walking over to him, touched his arm lightly. "Tick…" her voice was compelling. But almost as if by design the telephone rang.

"Don't touch it." Tick leaped up from the table.

"It's Richard. He'll know something is wrong if I don't answer."

"Not for a while—he won't." He jerked the telephone cord from the jack. "Get the diary."

He picked up the bowl of uncooked eggs and threw them into the sink. He was shaking, holding on to the edge of the counter for support. He seemed to be choked. Finally, getting his breath, he began to order her in a voice broken and demanding. "She was a liar. The diary might...should be in the evidence room, but it ain't, sister, because you have it. Now get it, before I hurt you. I don't want to, but I can, and if I have to, I will. Don't doubt it."

His eyes were wild as he grabbed Rhys's arm, twisting it behind her back, he made her move forward.

"You're hurting me."

"Do like I say. I'll ransack this house if you don't tell me where it's at. Don't work me like I don't know what's going on. The diary is trash, a pack of lies. It needs to be destroyed. She wrote them for anyone to see. It shouldn't be lying around accusing people of terrible things." As he talked, he propelled her down the back hall toward her bedroom, shoving her through the door; Rhys stumbled, landing against her dressing table. A cascade of jars and glass bottles slid to the floor. The noise, the crashing, and breakage seemed to shock him. He rubbed his temples as if his own head was breaking.

"He knows; of course he knows—you all do. Well, it's a lie." Tick stood over Rhys, who by now was leaning, sitting on the edge of the bed.

"Who knows? What do they know?"

He grabbed her shoulders, pulling her up close to his face. "My dad killed Frankie Schreiber the first time." Rhys was so close to him, so repulsed by the sweet, sour sickness of his breath that she barely understood what he had said. Then, just as quickly, he let her go, and she dropped back onto the bed. Tick began massaging his forehead. "Don't listen to that. That's a damn lie. He didn't kill him. He helped him." He reached for her again, this time shaking her so hard she thought her neck would snap. "Do you understand what I'm saying? Raggedy said my dad brutalized him that day with the barrel of his gun, but it was my gun...my new gun...not Dad's." Tears began to course down Tick's cheeks.

He released his grip on her shoulders and jerked the single, top drawer out the nearest bedside table, shook it, upending it onto the bedspread and all the detritus of a bedside table drawer tumbled out. Not finding the diary, feeling his way, he lumbered around the footboard to the matching table on the opposite side.

Deep, airless gulps escaped from his throat. Rhys's cloisonné clock, tipping from the sudden motion, fell onto the rug, breaking the crown off a decorative gilt spiral. Seeing the shelf of books, he traversed the length of it, opening each one, dropping each one onto her floor.

"Get the di'ry, or I'll burn this house down with you in it." Then seeming to be astonished at his words, he bolted out of the room.

"Tick!"

"I ain't thinking right. I should've burned it down while you were at your party, and you wouldn't 've had to know, and you'd a been safe."

"Mr. Tick. You don't mean that."

Saliva stood in the corners of his mouth. "If Pauley'd had it, he'd a said so. I've got a can of gasoline in my truck."

"Let's call Pauley. Here." Rhys handed him the phone from the cradle. "He's waiting on your call. Pauley will help you."

He ripped the phone from the jack, took out a pocketknife, cut off the connector, and headed out the door for his truck.

Rhys grabbed her shoulder bag, searching for her mobile, for Pauley's number.

The phone wasn't there. She saw her evening bag and remembered she'd transferred it earlier. Her hands were shaking. She punched what she thought she remembered. A phone rang half a dozen or more times before a voice thick with sleep said, "Hello, who's this?"

"Could you help me? Please, would you please call the police and tell them to send someone out to the McGuire farm on Blue."

"Who'd you say this is?"

Rhys heard Tick's truck door slam.

"No, no, please, would you call the police, the police..." The phone flatlined. She threw it on the bed and, grabbing her shoulder bag, ran through the house and out the kitchen door. "Tick! Stop! You don't want to do this. You're breaking the law. Please... you don't want to do this."

Tick splashed gasoline along the north wall by the french doors. Pacing back and forth, he emptied the five-gallon can, and then, grabbing a border stone, he began systematically breaking windows. The fuel, once ignited, would devour the old house in minutes.

"Stop! No! Please." They were shouting at each other in the driveway under a cold winter moon, their voices carrying across the crisp air with no one to hear them.

"You're a liar."

"No. I've seen the diary. There is nothing in it about you or your father."

He pulled a cigarette lighter from his pocket. He was no longer screaming. The lighter's blue flame flashed like a tiny nova into the night sky.

"Stop it! Tick...you're not a bad man. Stop it!" Rhys lunged at him, grabbing his arm roughly and sending the silver lighter flying into a bed of gasoline-soaked leaves. She continued to hold his arm. "Please. Please...the farm, my home." Her voice broke.

For a moment Tick Quinn seemed to comprehend what she was saying—her loss, her pain. Rhys saw clarity in his eyes, but whatever synapses brought compassion was quickly gone. He shook her off and dropped to his knees in the leaves. Searching for the lighter, he frantically patted the ground all around him.

In the light of the white moon, the silvery glint of her Jaguar caught Rhys's eye. She ran toward it, grabbing the handle and jumping in all the while fully aware of how strangely one's mind works in times of stress. Like how was she going to tell Schreiber that his dire warnings about leaving her car keys in the ignition were not sound advice for every situation.

The Jaguar was already rolling when Tick lunged into its path. Rhys twisted the wheel sharply to the left, swerving across a shallow trench and along a fencerow of tall grasses. She missed hitting him, but she scraped along barbed wire for several feet. Sharply to the left again, she drove between two trees, narrowly missing one, before the Jaguar bumped back onto the driveway. Spewing gravel along the white-pine drive, she sped out onto Blue Creek Road. All she could do was pray that Tick would follow her.

She couldn't have gone more than a couple of miles when she saw headlights coming up behind her. She was the bait; she pressed the pedal, looking in the rearview mirror to see if he'd torched the house. She saw no flames licking the night sky; there was no unnatural glow. Or was there? She began to cry. Well, if he was chasing her, then he wasn't hanging around the farm. "Dear God, please don't let our house burn down."

She let him gain on her, to let him think he was catching up with her, to keep him moving farther away from her home.

Turner Road Curve loomed ahead. If she could make it around that curve before he caught her, she would be fine. She had seen enough cop movies to know that should he catch her, he would bump her off the road. But after Turner's Curve, the Jag would have more than enough power to outrun him. Her plan was to stay far enough ahead to feel safe, but near enough to tease him. If she could get to the fire department maybe.

"Now, you're quite the little driver, ain'tcha, sugar. I been wondering when you'd come take me on a little drive in your fine ride. You owe me a ride, don'tcha think?"

Rhys screamed, jerking around to see a strange man grinning at her from the back seat.

"Just a little ride. You'll like it." The voice, immediately behind her, was high pitched and syrupy. "And look what I brought for you, most girls like these too." Rhys slung her arm back in an attempt to strike him. She caught a whiff of sweet smoke.

"Who are you? What are you doing in my car? Get out!"

"I've come to collect my due." Something shiny touched her neck, and she screamed again, swinging her arm again, hitting him this time, but in doing so she lost control of the car. The silver Jaguar, like a shooting star, flew over the narrow, crumbling shoulder of the Turner Road Curve and rolled over and down the steep sides of the ravine.

After dark during the Christmas holidays, there was a tradition in Riversbend that discharged the people from their usual indifference and encouraged them to drive up and down the streets, viewing one another's decorations. Praising some, criticizing others, and always enjoying the greater reward, which was to see who was entertaining. The guests' cars, queued up in driveways and along curbs, would be identified, and soon discussions would follow as to who *had* been invited, and who *had not*.

Cocktail in hand, Richard stepped out the front door for a refreshing breath before his guests began to arrive. The air was chilly, redolent with the green scent of boxwood. Lambent light from the city shouldered against the sky's low ceiling created a sense of peace. Richard strolled to the far camber of the circular drive to look back. Cedars, a grand old queen, stately and demanding as old things are, seemed to glow with invitation. A Christmas tree ornament caught unawares in lamplight and having splintered into a thousand prisms beckoned through the beveled fanlights on either side of his front door. Richard sighed. It was time.

Inside, the dining-room table was the prettiest ever, he thought, but he thought this every Tipsy Eve. Greenhouse gardenias shipped fresh, arriving this morning from New Orleans, lent the room a sweet perfume. The candlelight damask cloth set off the dark green leaves and snowy blossoms. He was sure this was the year he should have contacted *Southern Living*.

A flash from car lights as his first guests turned onto the drive signaled Richard to lower the chandelier over the table and light the candles. Dinner would be served at nine o'clock.

A whiff of rosemary from the roasting game birds slipped through the kitchen door as the host stuck his head in to alert Beau. "How's it going? The guests are beginning to arrive."

"Thank God."

Beau, apron off and in a white dinner jacket, was at his post in the living room when the doorbell rang. Richard chug-a-lugged his drink, straightened his bow tie, and strolled toward the door.

"Christmas Eve-Eve gift," he sang out as he swung the door widely in welcome. "Tick, my man! What a surprise! Come in, Officer. I'll pour you a glass of cheer. What are you doing here? Found another body in my Dumpster, have you?"

"There's been a terrible accident." The old policeman, hat in hand, informed him.

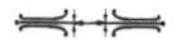

Pauley pulled into a line of traffic, which forced him to drive more slowly than he would have liked even though he didn't know where he was going. He'd wasted the best part of a day waiting for Tick to call. He was bored. He was hungry, or boreder than he thought. He scooted into the turn lane and found an open slot at the Sonic Drive In. He pulled his cell phone off his belt. It had a strong charge, and he hadn't had a voice mail sneak past unnoticed. He was holding his phone, as he ordered a third round of Cheddar Peppers, when it rang.

Tick gave Pauley a brief instruction, repeated it once, and hung up. Pauley was to begin the first leg of what would in successive calls become a circuitous route to Tick's whereabouts. When he arrived at this first destination, he was to park and wait for the next piece of the man's plan.

"I cain't stay on my phone too long," Tick had said.

"Are you cold? It sounds like your teeth are chattering—are you drunk?"

"Don't bug me! Ya wanna help me, ya gotta do es'ackly what I say! I'm not drunk; I'm freezing."

In twenty minutes the next set of directions had sent Pauley backtracking to Riversbend, and then he was instructed to head out toward Liberty, turn left on county road 235 just pass the Mabrey place, and drive on over to Powhattan. The final installment, in the third and last call, gave the location of a house out past Powhattan. The route was precise. Take the Ballard-Broadband exit, drive east for 2.3 miles, turn right on the old river road, and go four hundred feet and pull up into the yard. He was to turn off his lights and his motor as soon as he got there. "And sit tight till I come to you."

Finding what he guessed was the right house, Pauley parked at an angle that would afford him partial views in the side and rear mirrors as well as through his newly replaced windshield.

If houses were human, this one would have claimed exhaustion. Gray in the light of a full moon, the house reflected the tolerant patina of unpainted wood, but that was it. No grass or shrubbery tempered the stark poverty of the place. There was no porch, only several irregularly stacked rocks, formed rough steps to a stoop. Built on low ground, the house was slightly elevated on one side. Over time, the alluvial soil had eroded, shifted, unsettling the foundation, causing the house to tilt to one side.

There was a crooked man, he went a crooked mile, he found a crooked sixpence, against a crooked stile. The rhyme cantered through Pauley's memory. From where he couldn't remember, but this crooked house was where Tick grew up.

It was late, after ten o'clock. He stretched across the car seat to unlock the glove compartment, where he'd stuck the blood-sample kit. What kind of world forced a man to make choices between being a good friend or a bad cop, or a bad friend and good cop?

All he felt sure of was that Tick had a connection to Raggedy's death. He also knew the blood sample Latimer had ordered him to get could potentially send Tick to prison. Disgrace would ruin the life of this man who had saved Pauley when he was close to throwing his life away. Tick was more than his mentor. He was the closest thing to a father he'd ever known. Pauley shoved the blood-sample kit into his jacket pocket.

Out of the car, Pauley stepped into a sparse, moonlight-dappled wood and began moving cautiously toward the cabin that loomed before him. He wished for Sagacious. He walked slowly, lightly to quiet his step—still twigs snapped, and leaves, dead leaves, crunched under his foot. He stopped to let the earth and his heart settle. He paused to listen, straining to hear if someone was hidden among the trees, coming toward him. But the night was oddly quiet. He didn't want to be taken unawares, nor did he want to be surprised, which Tick would do just to teach him a lesson. "Aaahk!" he yelped. A frisson of terror crawled up Pauley's neck as some nearby creature scurried under the blanket of winter-dried leaves.

Pull it together McCrary. You a cop or some sissy-assed queer thang, huh? So, what you all jumpy 'bout? he wheedled his taut nerves. *Go wait in your car like the man told you to do.* But before Pauley could obey his inner voice, something happened. It was subtle. It began with a slight whoosh of wind in the trees. Then the scrap of earth, on which he seemed to be rooted, suddenly awakened, and the unnatural quiet that had spooked him moments before receded back into wherever creepiness was kept. Pauley felt he'd passed a test not of man's making. The commotion, in the undergrowth near his feet, the almost imperceptible sounds of a flying squirrel leaping from one branch to another, the rustle of crisp leaves as a foraging raccoon moved to a more promising location, grounded him. The clamor calmly melded into a cadence, and Pauley began to understand that the night was not his enemy.

The bright moon brushed past a cloud, opening the sky long enough for Pauley to see the cabin clearly. Again he began walking.

Growing up without a father, Pauley had little experience with the forest, any forest, day or night, so even with his newly found backbone, he was guarded. He realized, mixed in with his tendencies to be a fraidy cat, that some of his fears were about his friend and what he'd find inside the house, and what response he'd be called upon to make.

He thought he'd understood Tick to say he would not be in the house and Pauley should wait until he arrived. Pauley dropped onto the top rock of the irregular stack that served the house as steps to wait. He liked having the house at his back.

What would Tick do if the situation was reversed? *If I's in a mess?* Pauley snorted, remembering exactly what Tick'd do. "He'd flip his two-headed silver dollar. Heads you win; heads you lose."

In their brief communications, Tick had never said the word "confess," but this was why he'd finally called Pauley. That was what he was going to do. All the pieces except motive were in place. Pauley shivered. He was sure tonight, like it or not, he would discover Tick's motive. He felt the darkness swallow him as the moon retreated behind clouds.

Where was the man? Pauley stood up to stretch. He jiggled his legs and flexed his arms. It wasn't like Tick to play games. Unless—Pauley shook his head. *Don't go letting your imagination run away with you.*

With the whimsy of the bashful moon, the small stoop suddenly seemed to shrink. Pauley couldn't determine its edges. He couldn't even see the steps where he'd been minutes before. Easing back against the door to keep from falling, he felt it move slightly and then opened a bit. He gave it a nudge.

"Tick?"

He pushed harder and stepped inside. Suddenly he felt the hair on his neck stand up. A man sat in the dark. Pauley could see the white of his eyes. He first thought the man was dead.

"Tick?" His voice was hollow.

"Wha'cha doing?" a husky voice asked.

"Waiting on you. Why didn't you come get me?" Relief poured over Pauley.

"It took you long enough." Tick was short of breath. Between huffs he said, "Stick your head in like that again, and you're liable to get it blown off."

Pauley took the advice with a smile. "Man, it's good to see you. You been out here the whole time?"

"Build us a fire in the stove. I'm shaking. There's wood in the corner and a box of matches on the stove."

By the time the fire was going, providing a little light and a bit of warmth, Pauley's anxiety had almost dissipated. Tick was not dead, nor was the old man drunk. And as for confessions? Well, seeing his old mentor in the flesh seemed to erase Pauley's feelings of Tick's involvement in Raggedy's death. In fact, he wished he'd been a little more professional and hadn't been quite so to assume the worse.

"This a hunting shack?"

"I grew up here."

"No kiddin'. Out here in the woods?" Glancing about, Pauley could see how Tick had been living this last week. There was the wood stove, the mattress, and the boarded-up windows he'd noticed from the door.

He'd smelled the acrid odor of cold, burned wood when he stepped into the front room. Now that he was focused, he could even distinguish the scent of wood smoke from Tick's cigarette smoke. In the flickering light of the fire, he saw half a loaf of bread and the empty wrapper of another on a table. He walked over. There was a jar of peanut butter, a small piece of cheese wrapped in paper, still-damp coffee grounds. There was a tin can on a window ledge filled with cigarette butts.

"Is this what they call a shotgun house?"

"I reckon."

Starting with a front room, Pauley started walking straight back, single file, each room directly behind the one before it.

"Where's your truck?" he hollered back at Tick.

"You passed it coming in. Guess you didn't see it."

The voice that carried from the front room to Pauley in the back was tired, airy, and free floating. A voice without a body, Pauley would later describe it. There would be no wasted effort in useless talk, it implied.

"I've been watching you—through that crack"—Tick nodded toward the sagging front door—"ever since you drove up." Tick paused to catch his breath. "If I'd a wanted to—I could have shot you several times."

"You told me that already." Pauley grunted.

"There's a lantern over"—Tick flicked his wrist limply toward a corner by the stove—"and matches." Again the wrist.

"You don't have many left in the box."

Tick nodded. "Enough. Light the lantern."

The pool of light led Pauley toward Tick. "What are you doing here, man?" Pauley dropped down on the couch beside him. "Are you okay? Are you working the case? Are you hiding out from some reason? Why don't you go home?"

"What do you mean 'hidin''? Why do people keep thinkin' that?"

"What people?" Pauley wanted to touch Tick's shoulder, but he knew any gesture of affection would be rejected. This close, the old man's breath did not smell like whiskey, but it was sour, and there was a faint odor of something he couldn't identify.

"Quit hovering." Tick straightened himself up. "Did you bring a gun?"

"Nope."

"Should anyone come, tell them we're hunters."

Pauley grinned.

"You could see better if you'd take off those damn sunglasses," Tick said, even managing a smile, and for a split second, everything seemed almost normal. This Tick was the same half-teasing, half-brusque, bossy old fart he'd been from the time Pauley first knew him. Pauley felt his heart swell with an emotion almost foreign to him. Maybe with his grandmother.

"No wonder I couldn't see a damn thing out there." Pauley shoved the glasses to the top of his head. "Now tell me, how're you doing, Lieutenant? I can't tell you how glad I am to see you."

"Sit down there, McCrary." Tick pointed to a collapsing chair across from him. "I'm not much interested in tea-party talk right now." Tick pushed himself up from the sofa and moved to a metal folding chair, talking as he walked. "I've got some things to tell you," and he was into whatever it was he'd summoned Pauley out there for, before Pauley could seat himself. The young cop's raised spirits sagged.

"Wait a minute. I've got a few things too, Tick."

"I'm telling you something."

Pauley perched on the edge of the chair and pulled a small recorder from his pocket. "Hang on a minute." He pushed a button. "This is DS Pauley McCrary."

"DS, huh?"

"Not really. Implied more than official."

"This is DS Pauley McCrary. I am interviewing Detective Lieutenant Tick Quinn on Monday, December twenty-third, at"—Pauley glanced at his wrist—"about ten thirty-eight p.m." His voice wavered.

"Shut that damn thing off; I'm telling you a story."

Pauley tucked the recorder back into his jacket pocket. "Sorry."

Rarely self-conscious with one another, now the two men stared at their feet, into an empty corner, to avoid looking at each other. Tick was wondering how to start his story; Pauley was praying he wouldn't start it at all.

"What I'm gonna tell you is about two things that happened a long time ago that shouldn't have. The first one is the easiest. It's on me. I'm a phony, you see; Raggedy told me that night that when Miss Rhys Adler's mother disappeared twenty years ago, she, Raggedy, had seen what could have happened. She said she saw Miss Dora at the Stop and Shop in Oyster. She was in her car, and a young boy was pumping her gasoline for her. Then another boy showed up, and they got in the car with Miss Dora with one of them under the wheel and drove off. That might have been the last time anyone saw her. Raggedy told me this; I ignored her. Not once but several times."

Tick's head dropped.

"Do you remember when we were out at the farm, asking about the *lachrymatory* bottle? Do you remember what Miss Rhys said to me? Accused me of doing? She was right. I thought Raggedy was a crazy old woman. I didn't have time with this very important investigation to listen to some bag woman's off the wall ravings. Raggedy Ann was a gossip. She'd get our trash and then make up stories about what she got and then believing them start spreading lies. Pauley, had I listened, we would have had a serious piece of information about what happened to Dora Adler. What Raggedy told me that night convinced me that I was no better than my dad. My time as the fine law enforcer who thought he should have been elected sheriff was a joke."

"Don't be so hard on yourself, man. Lawmen make mistakes like anyone else. We're all human."

"Maybe not. Maybe not all of us. Let me tell you the second story Raggedy dropped on me that night, the worse one, and you'll see why I had to be the best cop on Riversbend's force. It starts with people who pretend to be something they're not."

Tick still breathy spoke unevenly, pausing now and again to grab air.

"You remember hearing me talk about my dad? How I always wanted to be like him. I'se so proud having a dad who helped out at the police station when they needed an extra hand. I bragged, even after I became a cop. All the long years of my career, I rattled on about my dad—how fine he was. I bragged to Willa, and pert' near anybody who'd listen."

Pauley nodded. He'd heard Tick brag about Jimmy Quinn. It'd always made him a little jealous.

"I was a fool. Everybody knew my dad was no 'count, 'cept me." Tick shook his head. "I told people he was a hero." Tick's laugh was bitter. "Scum's what he was." He looked at Pauley. "I've never said those words to a living soul."

Tick stopped and took a cigarette out of his pocket. He lighted it, inhaling deeply.

"The night Raggedy Ann died, she told me about my bungle with Dora Adler's disappearance just as a warm-up. The next story was more than I could bear, and that's why I killed her."

Pauley swallowed what felt like a stone. "But you said yourself that she made up stories. Why do you believe this one?"

"Because, I was there."

Pauley listened as Tick returned to another time, to a time the old cop could see more clearly than the present moment.

"We'd been deer hunting. We were hunting off the river road close to where it forks into the deer track out there." Tick raised his head. His eyebrows arched in sudden animation. "You probably didn't know, but it was and is today a deer path, crosses what once was a natural salt lick and then runs on down to the river. Anyway, we'd been hunting. One thing you got to understand, Dad and me were close—his best pal, he'd say. 'Hey, pal,' he'd holler whenever he'd come in the house. 'Hey, buddy,' he'd say, 'you want this chewing gum'"—Tick's voice crack—"'this chewing gum I found under the bench at the courthouse?' he'd always add." Tick looked up at Pauley. The old man's face was grievously sad; his lips moved silently as his eyes visited a scene from another time. "Daddy was always teasin' me. He'd tease, and then he'd laugh big and reach in his overalls and hand me one of those shiny round gumballs out of one of them machine they had out in the hall of the courthouse. 'Hey, pal.'" Tick clucked at the sweetness of the memory. "He was proud of me—Dad was. I was a big kid, see, and his only kid.

"This deer hunt was my first with my own gun..." Tick's voice trailed again into memory's cadence. "We'd had a good morning, got us a deer, a young deer little more than a yearling, and my dad was teaching me how to field dress it.

"Later, Dad wanted to go back to the house for something—probably to get him another pint—anyway, I was s'pose to watch over our deer so's no one would steal her. Well, I did for a while, and then I got bored and thought it'd be okay if I walked down to the river. It was just right there, don't you see? That's when I saw Frankie.

"Hand me that tin can there in the window, Pauley."

Tick reached for his ashtray to knock off the long ash growing on his cigarette, to buy himself time to build his story. When he started again, he had leaped forward to the night they'd found Raggedy in the Dumpster.

"What Raggedy Ann told me that night was true. I'd known it all along. But honest to God, it was like I never did. I've heard of it, forgetting things you don't have the stomach to remember. It's got a name. You know what I'm saying, Pauley? Dad tried to kill him. She said he should have shot him instead of what he done."

Pauley frowned. "I'm not following. Raggedy was telling you this?"

Tick nodded. "She said after Dad slapped me—sent me home—he shoved the barrel of his gun into his nuts so hard he..."

"Whoa! Wait! Your dad shot himself, crushed his nuts?"

"No! Frankie's nuts! Listen to me!"

"Who is Frankie? Who is this *she*? Are we talking about Frankie somebody or Raggedy Ann?"

Tick's laugh was hard. "Both."

Pauley had seen the autopsy. Who could ignore the section that talked about Raggedy's damaged genitalia? He thought he knew where Tick's story was heading. The elusive motive was somewhere in all this jumble of words and emotions. But Tick was gonna have to spell it out, himself. Pauley wasn't going to help.

"So, you're saying Raggedy Ann was Francie Butter, right? Frank, Frankie, Francie, right?"

Tick sounded like he laughed again, but he hadn't. He looked strange, crooked, Pauley thought. His mouth didn't look exactly right. Pauley jumped up.

"You want some water, Tick?"

"Sit down. I don't have all night." Pauley sat, and Tick began reconstructing his story.

"I hones'ly din't know till...Saturday night. I hadn't seen Frankie in fifty years. How could I have known she was the boy who'd lived so long ago. They'd been gone for years."

Tick tipped forward to get a handkerchief out of his back pocket.

"I don't remember about putting her in the Dumpster. I musta done it and forgot it like the other things. I've got something wrong with my head, Pauley." Tick leaned against the sofa and dabbed at the corners of his mouth.

Pauley struggled to keep up as Tick's memories kept coming.

"I should have told you, but I couldn't. Tha's why that girl... you know"—Tick shook his head like he was trying to shake a name loose—" that doc at the morgue..."

"Doctor Petitjean."

"Yeah, Petitjean, called me to come back. I didn't want to, but if I was going to go, I had to go alone. When I saw the scars…I knew wha' Raggedy had said was true. I couldn't tell you. How could I tell you or Willer, my wife, that Raggedy Ann had been my old friend and that I had killed her? Finished what my dad had commenced."

"Now who's ignoring facts? You can't be held accountable for what your Dad did." Pauley shook his head. "I already knew about Raggedy's…problem, anyway. It was in the autopsy."

Pauley didn't elaborate, but at this point, he was too far in to quit. Who knew? Wherever it meandered, Tick's story would either condemn or acquit him in Pauley's mind, and to Pauley's mind, it was the safest place it could be. Pauley had to hear the truth, which meant Tick had to get his memory of the night Raggedy died, and his memory of the deer hunt to merge into one whole, complex story. Pauley tried to think exactly what the autopsy had said. Raggedy had bruises on her neck. There was blood in her ear. He knew there was blood on the sandstone. He began pacing around the room. "When Raggedy was telling you about your dad…"

"I pushed her. I'se getting' there. I grabbed a pillow she'd been hugging and shoved her into the wall. She hit her head. Slipped down." Irritated by the intrusion, Tick waved his arms at Pauley. "Let me tell my ga'dam story my own way." He leaned back, his face a mass of pain. "Where was I?"

"You had gone down to the river to wait for your dad."

"He was happiest during deer season. He was usually a little drunk." Tick shrugged slightly. "He was a happy drunk, didn't take it out on Ma or me like some men."

With effort, Tick pulled himself into a more upright posture and looked straight at Pauley, making it clear how important it was for Pauley to remember what he was about to say.

"Dad had a dark side, though. Sometimes he wouldn't speak to me or Ma for days on end, and it wasn't like he was angry. He just wouldn't talk, s'all. He couldn't hold a reg'lar job 'cause there were days when he couldn't get out of bed. I always thought it was 'cause he was drunk, but it wasn't. He didn't drink all that much except during deer season. I've been thinking about that. During deer season he could put meat on the table. We weren't quite so poor during deer season." Tick nodded. "That was it, don't you see? He was proud. Pride, the fourth deadly sin.

"That morning after we'd bagged and dressed the deer, Dad was happy. It'd been a good hunt. He had his boy carrying his very own gun for the first time. He was about to finish the last little bit of bourbon, and I'll ne'er forget this"—Tick looked up at Pauley with eyes as wide and innocent as a child's—"Dad offered me the last swallow of the whiskey in his bottle. That was his way of tellin' me I was a man, I reckon. 'Don't go tellin' your mother,' he said. 'Your mother's a fine lady. She shouldn't have married a bum like me.'"

Tick could nail Pauley's attention as easily as tacking a moth to a pinning board.

"It was my fault what happened to Frankie, don't you see? Frankie was down at the river when I went down there after Dad had gone back to the house. It was just me and Frankie then. I was excited over the deer. You know how it was when you were a boy, when you were fourteen.

"Frank asked me, 'What's it like killing something as purdy as that deer?' I told him it was fun, but he said it made him sad, those big, frightened deer eyes begging with you not to kill it.

"'They don't beg; deers ain't people.'

"'So why do you do it? Does it make you get a hard-on? Because you got one.'

"'I do not; I have to pee.'

"'I know about a hard cock.'

"We'd been skipping flat rocks across the water. After he said that, we didn't say much for several minutes. Then Frankie started telling about some of the boys in gym class, and in no time, we were back on dicks, theirs or his or mine. Like I say we were both teenagers. He's a year behind me.

"'Mine's pert' near as big as my dad's,' I said.

"'Is that so?' Frank was impressed with the information. 'I ain't never seen my dad's. How old are you, Tilman?' I remember him saying that. 'How old are you Tilman?'

"'Fourteen. Call me Tick. Nobody calls me Tilman but Grandma. You thirteen or twelve? Not even growed any hair yet, I bet.'"

Tick laughed at the memory.

"I remember parts of it so clear, Pauley. Frankie rubbed his cheeks and his jaw searching for whiskers.

"'Not your face, stupid. Your man hair.' Frankie was not much younger than me, but was a still a boy, but not a little boy.

"'Man hair. Like this.' I dropped down my hunting pants so he could see the patch of hair I had sprouted. I'm no queer, Pauley, but Frank was right about one thing. I did have the start of a hard-on.

"'We just never called it that, man hair.'

"'What do you call it?'

"'We don't. We don't talk about things like that. Besides, if your pa's weenie ain't any bigger than that one there, I don't think neither one of you has much room to brag.'"

Tick laughed.

"'It's resting,' I said. 'For it to get big, you either have to pee real bad or play with it. You know, jerk off.'

"'Not me,' Frank said. 'I ain't playing with it.'

"'Did I ask you to?'

"Frank didn't say anything.

"'It won't bite ya.'"

Tick rose unsteadily from his chair and walked to the one cracked-open window to stare out into the dark.

In the low glow from the kerosene lantern, Pauley watched him. The old man looked gray in the flickering light.

"Well, neither one of us heard Dad come back."

Tick turned around. He had a lopsided smile on his face. "My dad went crazy. Have you ever seen a grown man go crazy!" Tobacco juice had gathered in the corner of Tick's mouth. "'You goddamn little queer...you butt-fuckin kraut.' It was a double hate, you see. The Schreibers were German, and it wasn't too long after the war. Dad—he jerked Frank up and commenced hittin' him, kicking at him. He slapped me and shoved me so hard I fell. 'Git outta my sight. Git away from me; I'll deal with you later.' He was screaming. I'd never seen him like that. He was foaming at the mouth like a mad dog. I remember running through the woods. I was crying.

"Raggedy said after I ran off is when my dad raped him with his gun. 'You'll never molest my boy again,' Raggedy said he screamed. He would have shot him, except, 'cording to Raggedy, I came back."

Pauley felt sick to his stomach. "Why? Why did you come back?"

Tick shrugged.

"Had you seen him do anything? Do you remember seeing Frank after your dad...raped him with the gun barrel?"

The shake of Tick's head could mean anything: he hadn't seen Frank, or he couldn't remember, or he was wondering why he'd never asked himself why he came back.

"Raggedy never told anyone until the Saturday when she told you?" Pauley asked.

"They moved away. I never saw any of them again until Sam Schreiber and his wife came back eight or ten years ago. Even then I never thought of Frankie Schreiber. He disappeared as if he'd never existed. Funny thing, though, even if I didn't remember Frankie, or what my dad did to him, whenever I'd see Sam Schreiber in town, I'd try to avoid him. I thought I didn't like him. The other day out at the farm was the first time we'd exchanged greetings in a long time."

"So when she started talking, you tried to stop her."

Tick stared out the window, rocking on his heels. The only sound in the house was the occasional crackle of the fire.

"Dad must've left Frankie down by the river." Pauley listened to the end. "You know the worst part was we never talked about it. Never. When he came home that day, I was terrified, but he never said a word. He's worked it around so as he became a hero. Maybe we worked it out together. It was easier. He said Frankie had had an accident, and I desperately wanted to believe him. Then the next thing was he saved Frank's life, took him to the hospital." Tick's face was a mixture of revulsion and bitterness.

"Is this why you called me to come out here, Tick? To tell me about your father?"

"No. To tell you that I killed her."

Pauley swung around toward Tick. "It's not that cut and dried. You pushed her; she fell. But did you put her in the Dumpster?" Pauley knew the answer to this question stood between Tick's guilt or innocence.

"Listen to me."

"The autopsy said she died of asphyxiation," Pauley said.

"I don't care what the ga'damned autopsy said. I was there; I know what happened! I want you to charge me. Promise me!" Tick struggled to stand. His face was infused with blood, dark like bluish.

"Tick?" Pauley's hands were shaking. He could see Tick gasping for air.

The old man threw his arms in front of him.

"Tick! Sit down. I'm calling EMT."

"It's…only way…forgiven." Tick's words were like stones. "I cain't live with the lies no longer…and my dad…"

The voice at EMT was calm. There were questions of location that Pauley, having Tick's earlier directions, could give quickly and easily. Tick was still trying to talk.

"Promise me...Paul..."

"I've got to get you to a doctor, Tick."

"Pauley!"

"Be calm. Let me get you some water?" Pauley started toward the bucket that Tick had hung a dipper on.

"Pauley, I'm depending on you."

Pauley knew what Tick wanted. He slipped his recorder out of his pocket for the second time. "This is DS Pauley McCrary. I'm interviewing Detective Lieutenant Tick Quinn on Monday, December twenty-third, at eleven four p.m."

"You are not interviewing me."

"On the charges relating to the death of..." He couldn't say "arresting," "killing," "murder," "manslaughter." "I'm charging him with assaulting Frank Schreiber on Saturday December fifteenth."

"She died, Pauley! Let me hear you say it. I killed her!"

"Why are you doing this to me?" When Pauley looked up, Tick was cradling his head, his face twisted with pain.

"You're a cop, ain't ya! I killed her!" These were Tick's last words before he crashed to the floor.

TUESDAY DECEMBER 24

It went without saying that Opal Robinette would fry chicken for Pauley McCrary at midnight on any night if he was hungry, especially if he teased her in that cute way he had of teasing when real conversation escaped him. Chicken was Pauley's favorite food and had been since he'd had teeth enough to eat it. But tonight, when he came through her front door, looking lower than a snake's belly, she didn't have to ask if he'd like a piece of fried chicken. Tonight, it was easy. She'd already fried a chicken for her own supper, and without even thinking, she'd saved her grandson the pulley bone.

When the 10:00 a.m. news came on and he hadn't dropped by to check on her, she'd decided he wasn't going to. She'd started turning out the lights when she heard his special whistle, their whistle, their private signal that meant, "I'm here—if you're awake."

In minutes she had set him a place, put a plate of chicken in front of him, toasted cold biscuits in the oven, and hot-potatoed them into a bread basket. Now, in her robe and slippers, she sat at the table, waiting for whatever he could tell her about why he was so upset. She watched him devour all the pieces that remained from her own supper. He didn't say anything for a long while. Then knife in one hand aimed for the butter, he began telling her about Tick Quinn, about his stroke, and about taking him to the hospital.

"I stayed with him most of last night, Gran," he said, shaking his head at the memory. "Then I spent today popping in and out of either headquarters or the hospital, back and forth. That's why I'm slow getting here."

He was young, but Opal could see her good-hearted grandson was exhausted from all his caring.

"Thank you, Lord," she whispered, looking through her ceiling all the way to heaven.

Pauley favored Lucien Robinette, Opal thought. Like his grandfather, Pauley too was tall, and a little too skinny. Lighter complexion than either she or Lucien, of course. The mix. His white, no-good daddy, and her own pretty Bonnie. Except for the birth of this boy sitting with her now, Opal would still be grieving over that union.

Opal prayed every night for Pauley's mama. She asked the Lord to take care of her daughter. To be sure, her girl had enough food and enough happiness that at some time she might feel she could come home for a visit. From week to month, Opal didn't even know if Bonnie was alive. She hadn't heard from her since summer. Last time she called, it had been from Phoenix, Arizona.

"You want some strawberry jam with your biscuits, son?"

"That'd be fine. Or sorghum? You got any more of these in the oven?"

Opal snorted. "Plenty. Enough for you to take some home." Then she said, "You got any fresh eggs at your house? I gathered four this morning and four yesterday. I'll fix you a basket. Eggs and biscuits to go, just like at McDonald's." She smiled.

"I'd rather come here. I don't have much time to fix something to eat." Pauley scooted his chair back and picked up the *Riversbend Profile.* "Besides, I don't have much time."

"Well, I guess after what all you just ate." Opal laughed. "You just don't feel right because you're fretting too much about Mr. Tick, Pauley, and I don't say don't worry, we're human, but I do say don't go borrowing trouble. You got him to the hospital, and I was reading the other day if you can start some medicine they got now, quick enough, strokes won't leave you with so many bad side effects like they used to."

"He looks like he's a hundred years old." Pauley lowered the newspaper. "Have you ever wondered if sometimes it might not be better to just go on and die instead of living?"

"Look at me, Pauley, Mr. Tick might look bad 'cause he's sick, but he's not a hundred. And for what it's worth, he's not as old to me as he is to you"—she chuckled lightly—"and he's strong. And when they let him come home, he's got a nice wife to nurse him."

"You really think he might...can come home? Do people get over bad strokes?"

Opal shrugged. "All I know is his time to live and die is not our business. And right along with a number of other things, I thank heavens for that. These days lots of folks get over worse things than what's happened to Tick Quinn."

Opal stood up and began clearing the table.

"Tick Quinn was a friend to your granddaddy, and he's been a good friend to you." Part of her body disappeared behind a curtain hanging over a door-less pantry. When she emerged, she held a Mason jar of sorghum and nestled it with the biscuits in what she called her Red Riding Hood basket. "I don't know what Riversbend will do if something happens to Tick Quinn. Uhnn uhn. That won't be a happy day. But I will tell you what *is* our business and what we can do tonight, and every night. We can pray. The good Lord takes care of these things in his own way. Trust him, Pauley."

"You pray for us both, Gran."

"God knows what's in your heart, Pauley."

"Christmas Eve gift, Gran?"

"Christmas Eve gift! It's already Christmas Day, darling."

On the drive home, Pauley wished his grandmother's good Lord would take care of his dilemma. He had a man's confession that was full of holes and a blood sample he didn't want, but accidentally had, so now he had to decide what he was going to do with it. When Tick had fallen, he'd cut his hand on the jagged-edged tin he'd been using as an ashtray. Pauley had stanched the blood with his bandana until the ambulance could get there.

Tick had said he pushed Raggedy. Okay, but pushing wasn't killing. He might have caused her death, but it wasn't intentional. Even with Raggedy pushing him to relive the tragedy Tick had so deeply buried, it wasn't intentional. There's pushing, and there's pushing.

Pauley wished he could remember Ticks confession exactly. Word for word. Everything had come so fast. He clearly remembered the old policeman had exacted a promise from him. *"You're a cop, ain't ya?"* Did it hold. Had he promised Tick something more that, in the clear light of day, he couldn't bring himself to do, but something he must do if Tick was guilty? Guilt in the eyes of the law, or guilt in Tick's eyes, or in Pauley's? Did it matter? Before he decided if he had the gumption it took to be a real cop, he had to know where he stood on guilt. Could it ever be a matter of choice? Tick believed in him. No one had ever believed in Pauley like Tick.

Blood was on the sandstone. Tick had shoved her against the wall. It would be easy to scratch his own hand. But...And the Dumpster problem was still unanswered. There was still a shadow of a third person in Raggedy's death. And with Tick's blood on his bandana, if it didn't match the blood on the wall, then there had to be someone else. But if…if it did…

Pauley was home when the thought hit him. Before he was fully aware of what he was doing, he gunned out of his driveway, made a 180 and headed back to Rock Street. It was just a thought. A bad one, probably, a silly idea, a crime probably, maybe, but brilliant nonetheless. It was just as if Gran's good Lord had put it there.

He whistled, this time at her bedroom window. "Gran, how would you like for me to cook you a big pot of chicken and dumplings for your Christmas dinner at the church. For you and all your church friends?"

"Are you crazy?"

"I'll come early, first thing in the morning, before daylight. I'll do everything, you won't have to do nothing except tell me how to make chicken and dumplings."

"Uh-huh," she grumbled just before there was a knock at the door.

"Now, who's that? It's too early for Santa Claus," Pauley said.

"Whoever it is, it's gonna be trouble," Opal said.

Opal heard the door open and Pauley say, "My goodness, what are you doing here this time of night?"

"I saw the light was on."

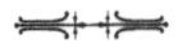

It's never totally quiet in a hospital. There are always the voices, and the rumble of wheels, meal carts, IV poles rolling up or down the corridor past your door, the hum and beeps over your head. It's never totally dark. Light seeps under the door—the palest of lights as the monitors flick like fireflies.

Tick would not open his eyes until he was sure everyone was out of his room. What had Pauley meant when he whispered, "Get well, Lieutenant. Everything's under control."

It will never be over, never under control.

"Aphasia," the doctor perched on the edge of Tick's bed had said to Willa.

Pauley had been there, Latimer too, maybe. Tick was fuzzy. He didn't remember being admitted to the hospital. He vaguely remembered being moved from ICU to a private room. He did remember the word "aphasia."

"He can't talk, and he may or may not be able to understand the simplest sentences for a while. However"—the doctor had patted Tick on the leg like a mother consoling a bewildered child—"in time and with conscientious therapy on all your parts," he had smiled at Willa, "who knows? I see miracles every day."

The doctor was wrong. Tick could understand everything he heard. But he was partially paralyzed on the dominant side of his body, leaving him essentially bedridden. He wasn't alarmed; he didn't intend to live that long. He was very tired.

He remembered that after the scrub-faced doctor left the room, Willa had soothed and fretted, plumped his pillow, and kissed him good night, promising to return first thing in the morning with an Egg McMuffin. Pauley wished him a good night and, guiding Latimer by the arm, closed the door softly behind them.

Their exit was soon followed by the arrival of a series of night nurses hurriedly finishing their bedtime rounds.

Now, enclosed in the white noise humming from the light fixture above and behind his head, Tick was alone, for the first time, in this room. He squinted at the monitor. All the squiggles and flashing numbers didn't make sense to him. The green flashing heart must mean he was still alive. His head still ached, but not as much as it had earlier. He wondered again what Pauley meant.

Tick tried to concentrate on what he had to do. He lay still. He needed an uninterrupted span of time before he could begin what would take herculean effort on his part. When no nurse had popped into his room for half an hour, he began. Slowly he began working his good hand, on slant like a ghost crab, across the pale-green coverlet to the cool metal of the bed tray.

His arm was heavy as he lifted it and felt for the micro-tape-recorder. One of the men—Latimer, he thought—had left it. By mistake or deliberately, Tick didn't know. It was a recorder from headquarters. He recognized it.

He pulled the recorder, no larger than the palm of his hand, to the edge of his tray and let it tumble onto the bed. He lifted it with his good hand high enough to locate the record button, which he pressed down with his thumb. The familiar whirr of tape began its slow advance.

"This is Detective Lieutenant Tick Quinn," he said. "It's Tuesday, December twenty-fourth." He looked at the large digital clock on the wall opposite. It is eleven fourteen p.m. I killed Frank Schreiber—a.k.a. Francie Butter, also known as Raggedy Ann—on December fourteenth. We was fightin', and I pushed her, making her fall against Adler's building. She hit her head, causing her to concuss, which led to her death. I don't remember much after her falling. I have had a memory problem most of my life. I don't know how I got her in the Dumpster behind Adler's." There was a long silence as the tape continued to whirr. Tick had said these things into the record, but Tick was aphasic, and on replay, all that interrupted the imperfect quiet of his room was a nonsensical garble.

If tears were words, Tick had made his confession.

WEDNESDAY DECEMBER 25

"Hey! Hey!" Rhys called out as loudly as she dared with two fractured ribs, a broken arm, a black eye, a thin cut above her eyebrow (enough of a disfigurement that she would need to consider bangs for a while), plus a huge chest bruise from the seat belt. The doctors had said she was lucky to be alive given the way the Jaguar had rolled. The nurses had assured her the dark bruises would go away.

As for nurses, the door opened, and a whitish nurse, who appeared to be considering a residency in Rhys's doorway, or was coming to the hard-found conclusion that she was on the wrong floor, in the wrong room, or on the wrong career track, stood gazing blankly at the bandaged-and-grouchy patient. Then like a ghostly vapor she vanished, and the room's wide door closed with the hydraulic *fusshhh* of a vacuum seal.

"Hey, you! Come back here!" Rhys hollered. How can I hear the soap opera of hospital life with my door shut?"

Rhys buzzed the nurses' station for the fifth time since the ridiculously early morning bathing event that ended with some single-minded orderly rushing from Rhys's room, carrying her soaked soft-soled wedgies.

"Yes, Miss Adler. What can we do for you, now?" The canned voice reeked attitude.

"Would someone please open my door? I'm lonesome."

"Yes, ma'am. It'll be a minute, though. The lunch trays are being delivered, and I'm the only one at the nurses' station."

"Then I won't hold my breath."

"Oh, but you should consider it."

Rhys stuck her tongue out at the smart-alecky intercom.

She was seated upright in bed, one arm in a cast, a serious-looking bandage over her left eyebrow where her head had hit the side window despite the seat belt. Unfortunately, her passenger, Connie Becker, who had slipped into her car and caused the wreck, hadn't fared as well. She hadn't been told much about him beyond his name and that he was in ICU.

There was a rumble of cartwheels that ceased grumbling right outside Rhys's door. Then, who should appear in the frame but the large black nurse responsible for waking her before daylight.

"Lunchtime," the woman sang out like an Ethel Merman understudy.

"Whoopee!" Rhys responded on a shallow teaspoon of air. She ooched up on her pillows. She loved mealtime. It gave her fodder for complaint.

"Did they bring me a grape Popsicle?"

She lifted the plastic cover to see a pile of peas and carrots, a chunk of meat loaf covered in red, a cold roll, a tub of pale-green gelatin, and a piece of white cake with chocolate icing.

"Would you, please?" She waved a carton of milk toward the nurse. "Thank you." Reclaiming the milk, she put a straw in the lip of the carton and took a sip. "This could be colder."

"Uhm. You sure are spoiled."

"Am I?" With her teeth, Rhys ripped the sterilized packet of plastic eating utensils, dumping the contents on her tray. "Don't mean to be. I come from a long line of spoiled women. What about you?"

The nurse laughed. "Me. I come from a long line of large women who folks generally don't want to get on the wrong side of. Know what I'm saying?"

"I do." Rhys claimed the fork from the tray and cut into the cake. "I'm not very hungry."

"Who would be after that basket of cinnamon rolls your mother brought you this morning."

"That was Matte. She's not my mother; she's my cook. Homemade cinnamon rolls—did you get one?" Rhys asked through a mouthful of cake. "Or were you too busy strolling up and down the halls and waking everyone before daylight? We're sick. We should be allowed to sleep late."

"No way. Uhn-uh. As soon as we can get all you layabouts up and fed and bathed, we get to give you shots. That's why we start early. We love giving shots."

"Ouch." When Rhys laughed it hurt. "Were you on the intercom at the nurses' station a few minutes ago? Or do all of you have sassy mouths?"

"Just me. I'm special." The nurse wagged a forefinger at the cinnamon rolls' basket. "You eat 'em all?"

"Have one, and hand me one."

The nurse peered into the basket, lifted the last two rolls out, and started toward Rhys but then stopped short of the bed just out of reach. "I'm gonna take both of these; you need to eat your vegetables. I don't want you coming down with diabetes on my shift." She licked the icing off the top of one of the rolls as she strolled about the room, eyeing the plants and cut flowers. "You send all these pretty things to yourself?" she asked, biting into the second roll before Rhys could protest. "You're a mess. What happened to you?"

The EMTs had told ER that an anonymous caller had reported the wreck, but Rhys was sure it had been Tick who called the ambulance. She probably owed him her life. What everyone initially thought was a serious concussion turned out to be a mild one, but she had bled a lot from the cut above her eye.

"I rolled my car," Rhys said as she licked cake icing off her fingers.

"Uh-uh."

"Are you familiar with Turner's Curve?"

"Nope."

"Well, you'd have had to be there, I guess, to understand how close I came to dying."

"Uhmm-uh. Your mama bring you anything else?"

Rhys rolled her good eye. "Do you take me for a fool? If she did, I wouldn't tell you." Cake consumed and cinnamon rolls stolen, she was poking holes in the gummy luncheon roll with her milk straw when she heard voices in the hall.

"W...where'd y...y...you p...put it? You h...have it. You stole it."

"It's safe."

"I...I w...w...w...want it."

"Hush up naggin' me, or I'm gonna keep it."

There was what sounded like a shuffle of feet and a bump against the door, and in seconds Rhys's door banged opened, and Toad walked in with Hummer glaring at him but in tow. Unlike most hospital visitors, neither had knocked, nor peered in cautiously should the patient be in a delicate situation—they just blammed in. Toad removed his fedora, and Hummer reached into his pocket and handed Rhys a cup of uneaten fruit cocktail someone had left on a hospital tray in the hall. "It's s...s... sealed," Hummer said, shrugging encouragement.

"Hey, guys, thanks. This is Nurse Ratched."

Cinnamon-roll cheeks pooching out like a chipmunk with an acorn, the nurse pointed to the metallic name tag that clearly identified her as "Nancy Hatfield, LPN."

About that time, Hummer, whose coloring was returning to normal, spied the plate of abused but mostly uneaten food on Rhys's bedside tray.

"A…a…are you g…gonna?"

"Would you like it?" Nancy Hatfield said, brushing crumbs off her uniform. "She ain't gonna eat it." She patted Rhys's foot on her way toward the door. "If that cook of yours brings you something else, let me know, and I'll see what I can do to get you out of this hellhole sooner."

Nurse Nancy bumped into Richard right outside the door. His entrance was much more conventional. Rhys saw first his hand waving his hat and then his face. "Are you decent?"

"No, I'm an ogre. I'm ready to go home. I'm waiting on the doctor. Will you come after me the minute the doctor gives me the go-ahead?"

"Hi, Hummer, Mr. Toad." The three bobbed heads at each other like a mechanical monkey band.

"How are you feeling?" Richard sat on the edge of Rhys's bed and would have held her hand, but she had only one, and it was busy helping her talk. He patted her leg affectionately. "You scared the hell out of me, you know."

"That's good."

"You look much better than you did yesterday. You don't look good with things up your nose and needles in your arms."

"My headache's mostly gone. It's just sorta sitting on the edge of my brain, waiting for me to move, but that cake helped it. I think I was hungry. Would you bring me a double-cheese burger and onion rings if the doc doesn't let me go home in time for dinner?"

The next face to appear was Pauley's. He carried a covered basket, which contained something that smelled delicious and so hot he had to lift it out with a pot holder. "I hope you like chicken and dumplings."

"Wow!" Rhys's countenance brightened. Pauley removed the top from a glass jar and began pouring a buttery potage into a real bowl, a company's-coming soup bowl, sneaked from Opal Robinette's china cabinet. With the extravagant flourish of a beaming French chef, he set the fragrant dish on Rhys's hospital tray. Then locating a spoon and a white damask napkin, he placed both beside the bowl.

"I...I l...love c...chi...chick..."

"Back off, Hummer. This is mine, and I'm eating all of it."

Accepting this unfamiliar side of Rhys, Hummer sat down on one of the two chairs in the room. He hoped once she was out of the hospital, she would go back to feeding him.

Richard on the bed and Hummer in one chair left Pauley and Toad trying to decide who one would take the empty chair. Pauley, the younger of the two, and in consideration of Toad's disfigurement, chose to sit, or half sit, on the broad windowsill. All the men watched Rhys, propped up on her pillows, consume her dumplings, and with varying degrees of fascination, they eyed the rich broth that occasionally dribbled down her chin. Each of her visitors seemed content to be there. Each drifted comfortably into his own thoughts.

Before dawn, and before going to his grandmother's house to wring a chicken's neck, Pauley, in the gray haze between sleep and wakefulness, lay in bed, revisiting the past twenty-four-plus hours. He recalled the joy of seeing Tick, and the underlying dread, but he recognized that this emotional sweep didn't compare to the sickening horror he felt when Tick had toppled to the floor. He thought the man was dead.

With the sunrise compromising his sleep, Pauley buried his head more deeply into his pillow. His problems hadn't vanished with his plan. He could still hear Tick's voice: *"I killed her."* Had he? Had Raggedy died from the injuries Tick had caused, but someone else had slung her in the Dumpster?

And then Miss Isabella's stopping by so late to say that Rhys Adler had been in an accident! *What kind of accident? Was she hurt?*

It had been hard for Pauley to concentrate on what else the old lady was saying after that. What had she been so upset about? It was important, he knew that, but this morning her words were a jumble in his mind. He'd have to track her down today, because he remembered enough to know that if she was on track, the information was important. But today was Christmas! Shit.

A man can't just go chasing around, hoping to arrest people on Christmas Day. That ain't right. Another cop to go with me would require Latimer's involvement.

Pauley had managed to avoid the blood-sample conversation when he and Latimer had bumped into each other in Tick's room. But the sheriff was chomping. No doubt about it. For protection at the hospital last night, Pauley had stuck to Willa Quinn like a pest strip on a kitten's paw until Latimer left the hospital.

Pauley chuckled at the memory, and the soft burble lifted his spirits enough to propel him toward the bathroom. The satisfaction that comes when a man faces his problems in the same mirror he uses to shave took the gloom off the holiday momentarily.

"Look at it this way, Sagacious, I may not have answers, but I at least know the questions. That's a start." Pauley stretched his mouth sideways. His razor poised below his ear, he moved the blade down in a smooth sweep to his jaw. Not for the first time he wondered how he would look with a beard.

Sagacious watched it all. As her human lifted his jacket from the back of the chair, the hound wagged her tail so vigorously her whole torso wagged. She waited at the front door. *We ready? Let's go! Where we going?* Sagacious loved going. She also loved this human who took her, fed her regularly, talked to her, and gave her baths and a warm bed next to his. This morning, she sighed happily as she settled herself full stretch in the long back seat of the Cadillac.

It was 6:30 a.m. by the time dog and man cruised down the street toward Opal Robinette's. Pauley whipped onto the dirt-patch parking space in Opal's front yard, and jerked the emergency brake. "You know what Sagacious? This case is about to make a U-turn."

The dog might or might not have caught every word, but she nodded like she had. She'd never mastered idioms.

"Merry Christmas, Gran!" He stepped through the door into the wonderful fragrance of minced-meat pies. She was waiting for him.

"Let's get started, Pauley. I got things to do today. It's Christmas."

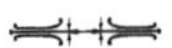

Rhys's immodest slurping brought Pauley back to the present. He eyed the second jar of dumplings he'd intended for Tick, but eyeing Hummer, who was eyeing his basket, he wished he'd brought a third jar.

"Well, can't get anything done standing around here, can I?" Slapping his knee, he pushed himself off the windowsill. "I've got lunch for the Tick and Miss Willa too." He grinned, mildly embarrassed at his domesticity. But his charm was lost to a battery of voices just outside Rhys's room. In seconds Latimer swung through the door. "I guess you've heard? Quinn's back in ICU."

Rhys winced. "Why? What's happened?" She hadn't forgotten their last encounter.

"Where's Miss Willa?" Pauley moved toward the door.

"Where's the blood sample? I gotta act fast. Can't prosecute a dead man."

"Prosecute? You don't have any evidence."

"Evidence?" Rhys was confused.

"Who are you wanting to prosecute?" Richard asked.

"This is police business."

"I saw Tick Tipsy Eve," Rhys said. She pinched the bridge of her nose, trying to foil the pain that threatened to return whenever she thought of that night. "He was ill. No one knew it, of course."

"No," Pauley said. "How could we have known?"

"He called the ambulance," she said.

Pauley shook his head. "I called the ambulance. I was with him when he had the stroke. We were together. We were in his cabin on the river."

Rhys frowned. She brushed the bandage on her forehead. Tick had tried to burn down her house. He was largely responsible for her being in the hospital; he had threatened her. Yet she had told no one except the Schreibers about the fire, and the damaged farmhouse, not even Richard.

Disregarding Pauley's account, she turned to Latimer. "Tick *was* at the farm, Price. He'd come to see Schreiber." Speaking softly, she sounded much calmer than she felt. It was as though she were being led by some force that she couldn't identify as benevolent or insane, but launched, she told about that night, some of it, about the fire, but not about who started it, and she told about finding Connie Becker in the back seat and the spinning off Turner's Corner. But by the time she'd finished, she'd reinvented the role Tick played in all of it.

"I don't know. Sometimes I have to think he didn't know what he was doing. He was...not himself." She might protect him from being a killer, but an arsonist? She was not going to let him off the hook so easily.

"What was he doing?"

"Remember the diary, Pauley? Remember I called you?" The Tick she created by the third addition was like a one-dimensional figure scissored from construction paper by a five-year-old with mitten fingers and an oversized head. A minihero who might or might not have seen a fire or quenched one or saved her home or called an ambulance. All she knew for certain was he had seen her car swerve off Turner's Curve and roll down the precipice. It was Tick who called the ambulance.

"Tick must have called the ambulance," Richard said. "He came to my house just before my guests arrived.

She saw concern in Pauley's eyes and confusion in Latimer's.

"What fire are we talking about?" the sheriff asked.

"I'm sorry. I have a headache. Go out there. See for yourself. Charred french doors. Smells like smoke." If her construct was shaky, the men would just have to put the pieces together. She thought Pauley had figured out she was telling him something. Even she wasn't too sure what. She wasn't too concerned what Latimer thought, just so long as he didn't think too much. She really didn't want Tick to go to jail. How would Tick's going to jail for arson change anything? She would be fine, her farm would be repainted, but he, poor man, was probably going to be an invalid for the rest of his life, or die.

Pauley saw a rim of tears—from pain, frustration, weariness? He didn't know, but Pauley had been blessed with a nickel's worth of Lucien Robinette's intuition, and he did know that, jumbled inside her strange behavior, she was up to something. She wasn't telling the whole truth, but she wasn't exactly lying either.

"When you called me from the farm on Tipsy Eve," Pauley began, "you said you'd talked to Tick. That he was at headquarters, looking for something. That was early...earlier than when I saw him."

Rhys nodded but didn't say anything.

"He couldn't have been. I was at headquarters. I would have seen him," Latimer said simply.

Rhys didn't challenge Latimer, but she did glance up at Pauley with one of those ubiquitous looks that seemed to speak gibberish.

Pauley desperately needed to talk to her alone. He prayed to the gods of the misbegotten that she could sense the enclosed questions he couldn't allow himself to ask and the conversation he couldn't begin now.

She was trying her damnedest for Tick. He could sense it, and it would have to be enough for now. Pauley might have thought he was the only one with Tick that night at the cabin, but maybe he was wrong. But if he'd seen Rhys, been at the farm, why had the old man not said one word about the fire or about Rhys spinning off Turner Curve?

"I'm going to find Miss Willa."

"Where's my sample, McCrary?"

"Rhys curled down among her covers and turned her back. "I'd like to take a nap now, if you'll see yourselves out."

Her sigh of satisfaction was deep. She was back on her own court.

By the time Pauley left her room, his cheeks were the color of rose gold. The lady had outmaneuvered him. The two of them were gonna play ball, and for now the lady was pitching. He was gonna have to trust her.

"Of course, he saw the Jaguar go off the curve." Pauley a few paces behind the others came back from his ruminations. Richard was talking. "He came by, I thought it was one of my guests arriving. He was upset."

"Hang on here just a damned old minute!" Latimer threw up his arms. "Let's put a clock to this man who comes and goes like a reg'lar Santa Claus. I'm not the dumb jackass y'all seem to think I am. You people are ganging up on me, you and McCrary back there, and maybe all of you, and Tick Quinn too. It's a conspiracy, and let me remind you, aiding and abetting is a criminal offense. It can send you to prison right along with the criminal. You're not above the law, Mr. Fordyce. Not in my town and not by a long shot."

By the time Pauley caught up with them, he was laughing. He was sorry Latimer had used the word "conspiracy," he'd hoped it hadn't been quite so obvious.

"McCrary, meet me at my car with the blood sample. Like I said, I'm in a hurry."

"First, I've got to find out about Tick." Pauley knew he was treading on thin ice, but like Rhys, he'd chosen his path. "I'll get the sample to you as soon as I know how my partner's doing. On second thought, would you like for me to drop it by the lab, or do you want to do that?"

"Do not tell me what you will and what you will not do! I gave you orders, and unless you're willing to face insubordination charges, I want it in my hands before one p.m. I'll meet you in front of the prosecutor's office. You are on thin ice, Sergeant. And as for the rest of 'em—"

"Shhh! You hush up. You way too loud. This is a hospital." Latimer would have expounded further about the rest of them except for Nancy Hatfield's appearance.

"I am Price Latimer; I am the sheriff of this county, and this is a county hospital."

"Well, lah-di-dah. You aren't hollering out in this hospital, sheriff or no sheriff, because I'm boss of this here floor today." She looked over at Pauley. "What kind of business you trying to run here in this hospital, Goodlookin'." She winked at Pauley.

The nurse snapped her head back toward Latimer and winked at the sheriff too.

"Now that's better.

"Nurse." A loud voice barked a few doors back. Room 210.

"Oh, Lord, there she goes bossing me. That one's rotten to the core."

"Hey, Ratched."

"Hold on to your breeches."

"I want to go home. When can I?"

"No tellin', sister. It's Christmas, and let me tell you it's awful when the doctors make rounds on Christmas afternoon. Most of them are falling-down drunk."

After the LPN disappeared into Rhys's room, Latimer, a good peeve glued to his face, glared at Pauley. "One o'clock."

"Sir, no disrespect intended, but you don't have all the information you need, and I don't either. If Tick Quinn is guilty, I'll see that he is prosecuted but not on skimpy evidence."

"He's guilty, McCrary! Blood evidence is evidence. Suddenly Latimer relaxed, and a smile bared his teeth. "Here are the facts, McCrary: the woman's dead, she was in a Dumpster too tall for her to have crawled into by herself, and she didn't die of natural causes. Those are the facts. Oh, and there's one more. We have a witness."

Pauley reached down into the bottom of his chicken and dumpling basket and handed Latimer a plastic bag. "If I were you, I'd consider letting this case go unsolved rather than condemning the reputation of a good man and one of your best officers?"

"Is that the sample?" Latimer looked surprise.

"My bloodied shirt. I had it on last night."

"I thought you didn't have it with you."

"If I'se you, sir, I'd direct my attention to finding Mrs. Wagner's murderer and let me finish the Raggedy Ann case."

Latimer shook the blood-evidence package at Pauley. "I'll wrap up this case and the Wagner one too. You're fired."

"Come on, Mr. Sheriff." Richard had turned back and was now taking Latimer's arm. "I've had enough hospital for a while, and your appointment with our fine lady prosecutor is in twenty minutes."

Latimer glanced at his watch.

"So Riversbend is your town, is it? Now how long you been here?"

A snooze between midafternoon television and supper seemed the only option for Rhys, until she heard three light raps, followed by a large face peeking around the edge of the door.

Schreiber, ever awkward finding himself in the room with Rhys when she was in bed, stood back several paces. A small case in hand, he took in Rhys's bandages, shaking his head that she had been hurt on his watch, even if he and Matte had been at church.

"I'm doing fine, Schreiber. I'm hoping they'll let me come home this afternoon. I'm waiting for the doctor to make his afternoon rounds."

"Matte packed you some clean clothes."

"Great, put the case in the closet there." She reached out for his hand. "Come over here. I'm not contagious, you know."

He did as instructed and then pulled up a chair that seemed too small for him.

"Are you and Matte doing fine without me being home to drive you crazy? You probably love the peace and quiet."

"We were just saying it's a little too quiet for our likin'."

"How are Ole Bay and Jolly?"

"Just the same. Missing you I 'spect."

"That's good. I miss them." She studied her friend's face. "I guess you've heard that Tick Quinn had another stroke early this morning. I know you have known him for a long time."

"Aw shucks, I'm sorry to hear that."

"I hope he makes it. I know you've know him longer than anyone. I haven't told you exactly the whole story about the night of the fire." It was an awkward beginning, but she sensed that if anyone could make sense of Tick Quinn, it might be Schreiber.

"He and my brother were closer than me and Tick."

"Speaking of Frankie, I hope after the investigation is over and the judicial system does whatever it is they are going to do, and your brother's body is released, we can have a small private service. And I hope this will free you to remember Frankie the way you would like to remember your brother: as boys growing up. There must be some good memories."

"Yes. I'll have to think on them. Maybe one evening this next summer, we can sit out on the back veranda and watch the lightning bugs, and I'll tell you and Matte about the time we found a cottonmouth in our fishing bucket." Schreiber's face was soft with memory.

"Yes." Rhys squeezed his hand and would love to have kissed it, but knew better. "That's good. I bet you can tell us a lot of tale about growing up down there on the river. I'd love to hear them. I'll make us some homemade ice cream."

"Better get Matte to do that for us."

It was full dark by the time Richard was wheeling Rhys out the door of the Riversbend Regional Hospital. He was regaling her with a Richard-styled, long-drawn-out tale. Something about Beau and a fourteen-pound turkey.

The Schreibers, having brought Rhys fresh clothes earlier, were in her entourage for the move home. All three were laughing as they loaded the patient and her flowers into Richard's car. None of them noticed the EMT crew rushing a gurney from an ambulance and running it through the double doors into the emergency room. There was no need to rush; there was no need for the ER—Logan Wagner was DOA.

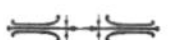

It was so still, Rhys could only marvel at the wonder of it. Snow had been falling for an hour. Still wrapped in the downy comforter Matte had tucked all round her, she watched a billion tiny flakes drift quietly down in the mellow light of the night watchers as if snow had no other purpose than to decorate the parched winter grass and red-berried bushes outside her windows. She was home. The aromas of cooking, and of Christmas, the familiar voices rising and falling from other rooms, the dachshunds sleeping on the foot of her bed filled her with joy and tears. She was alive.

Her thoughts, never far from him the past few days, flickered back to Tick—the old Tick, the good Tick—to the young cop who had escorted her across the street as school patrol, to the kind man who had worked so diligently to find her mother so many years ago.

She had begun the process of erasing the memory of bad Tick while she was in the hospital. In time, the fateful night of December 23 would fade to little more than an occasional twinge. She would attribute his behavior to lack of oxygen. He was ill, she would say to herself and to others. But to whom she would say it, or when? She wasn't sure. She didn't even know if she could talk to Richard honestly, with full disclosure. Maybe, in time, this nebulous attempt at forgetting, and her inexplicable need to protect the good Tick, would coalesce into forgiveness.

But tonight, recognizing her own part in the all of it, she wasn't sure who should forgive whom. If she hadn't kept the diary for so long, if Tick had found the small book when he first started seeking it, the terrifying incident on Tipsy Eve would never have happened. At least the frightening minutes that had involved him. And he might never have had a stroke.

Regardless of intentions, one's actions, no matter how innocent, were not without incident. The nightmare of Turner Curve was not over. Tick and Connie Becker were both in critical condition, both consequences of her conscious or unconscious behavior. Rhys would have to accept this. Acknowledging her sense of privilege, her arrogance in this whole mess was distressing. And at this hour, she wasn't sure where justice stood.

She took a sip of sherry and followed the warmth from the back of her throat down to the middle of her being. She saw the fine-limbed river birches clustered in the corner of the garden, weeping; their rough, black branches delineated in white frosting made a dramatic silhouette against the pearlescent sky.

"Forgiveness," she whispered to the vastness that filled her with such peculiar joy and sadness. Had she ever felt a need for it before?

Laughter rippled from somewhere. Richard was visiting. She wished she had said please, when Schreiber had suggested he make her a cozy nest on the sofa so she could be with them. But she was very tired. She hadn't been alone since the accident. She needed time to think without some nurse with a pill, or a tray, or doctor with a chart, or friend with flowers or food, or even her family, one of the Schreibers, or Richard popping into her hospital room. Rhys sighed. Until the past couple of days, had she ever honestly thought about what her life would be without these people?

She eased down off the stack of pillows to rest her back.

Kate had said she would come back after Christmas and stay until New Year's. Kate was part of Rhys's family too, wasn't she? What would become of Kate? She had changed very little, after all, but Riversbend had. Besides Delaware was home to her now. She had friends there. Would any of them give her counsel? Rhys wondered.

That afternoon Kate had called to relate her return to the museum. She had stolen the lachrymatory bottle twice, apparently. First taking it from the museum under the ruse of dropping it by accident into the Adler's shipping crate. But then, and this was the stunner, she had stolen it again right out from under the sheriff's nose. Kate had laughed in the telling, and Rhys had admonished her but had to admit to herself that the woman's nerve and sense of self-preservation were laudable.

Beautiful, red-haired Kate had ensnared Leonard Lockhart, with false promises and a mouthful of lies, into sneaking her into the evidence room to rescue the Brindlewick Museum's treasure and to restore it to its rightful place. She had lured him with the suggestion of a large reward. A little pocket money now (Kate had fished in her purse for a twenty) and the promise of more to come from the museum for recovering the lachrymatory bottle. This was all the incentive Lockhart needed. This and, Rhys suspected, a sweet: "And maybe the two of us could go out for drinks next time I'm in Riversbend."

What was equally unnerving was that Kate had plotted this during the very moments she and Rhys were reaching reconciliation over chili—the afternoon she slipped out of the dining room and borrowed Rhys's Jeep.

"You're incorrigible," Rhys had groaned on hearing the full account.

"I never told the museum authorities I had taken the lachrymatory bottle in the first place. When I got back to work, I simply slipped it in the case with the others. They'll never know."

"Don't count on it. The one who'll never know is you, Katy. You'll never rest as comfortably in your job again."

"Aw, pshaw! That's you, buttercup, not me."

Rhys shook her head. Maybe a day would come when she could quit judging Kate on Adler standards. Until then, Kate was Kate, and it was Christmas. No one's family is perfect. Rhys smiled, realizing, maybe for the first time, how much she loved Richard. Richard was perfect.

Rhys's hearth fire blazed in a fresh flurry of sparks. "More snow's coming," her mother would have said. "When snow falls on Riversbend at Christmastime, it is always something of a miracle." Then, one by one, she remembered all the faces of all the people who had—at one time or other—filled this house with happiness especially at Christmas. And it would end when she and Richard were gone.

She glanced at the red rose in the florist vase on her bedside table. The wispy, white nurse had brought it in before they left the hospital. The nurse had said the fellow who'd brought had parked in a tow-away zone. Said he'd move his car and come back. But he never did.

She wondered if it had been Ian Languille. Sounded like him. She removed a drop of sherry from the corner of her mouth with the tip of her tongue.

FRIDAY
JANUARY 3

Ramped-up tension radiated from the crowd in Judge James Van Wilkie's courtroom. A small courtroom, even by small-town standards—this morning it was packed for the preliminary hearing regarding Tilman O'Connor Quinn and the death of Raggedy Ann.

It was an eclectic gathering. Some were there by invitation attributable to their official involvement. Others, like Willa Quinn and Sam Schreiber, were there because of family connections, but the majority came out of curiosity. The lucky ones with no personal investment were grateful for a new diversion following Christmas and the dreary remainder of a dull winter.

Less nervous than the officials or family, the curiosity seekers tended toward rowdiness as they moved in and out of the double doors at the back of the room, giving last-minute attention to their bladders or grabbing a final smoke before the doors were closed. Even as they squeezed into the few remaining seats, they exchanged stories across the aisles or over the backs of the gallery pews. They whispered their opinions as to guilt or innocence with negligible information concerning the facts of the case, or the law, yet with a conviction that suggested little room for reexamination.

Those bent toward Tick's innocence rested on the potential of some nebulous, but newly found, evidence reported on the front page and above the fold in the previous week's *Profile.* Those preferring the titillation of Tick's guilt stood upon Sheriff Latimer's trumped-up press conference delivered from the courthouse steps the afternoon before when he promised an arrest on the basis of *unspecified evidence.*

"Oyez! Oyez!" the bailiff sang out as the double doors began closing. Pauley McCrary managed to slip through just before the unflappable court officer shouted, "This hearing is now in session." Pauley pressed himself into the narrow wall space next to the radiator. "All rise."

Conversations ceased, leaving frissons of static energy as Judge James Wilkie entered through a paneled doorway behind the bench. Seated with a modest flurry, he took a reading of his spectators before fingering the sheaf of papers on the desk. Reassured by their content that today was the right day, and that he was in the right place with the right case, he tapped his gavel.

"The prosecutor has filed a motion to bring charges against Tilman O'Connor Quinn concerning the death of"—he glanced at the papers again—"of Francie Butter." Judge Wilkie, a town boy having the usual knowledge of people peculiar to one's hometown, frowned. He glanced from his papers to the spectators several times before clearing his throat. "For clarity, Ms. Butter, or Francie Butter, is more familiar to most of us as Raggedy Ann—Butter."

There was a titter of laughter. A jarring note as Jimmy Wilkie sniffed starchily before continuing his instruction.

"Our responsibility today is to hear all the evidence and to come to some decision regarding its significance in the charges brought against Tilman O'Connor Quinn in the death of Francie Butter on December fourteenth, of last year."

Back on firmer ground, Wilkie scanned the courtroom a third time.

"Glad to see the press is present this morning." He nodded his approval. "Are we ready to begin, Madam Prosecutor?"

"We are, Your Honor." Mildred Mosby, all business in navy flannel and a creamy-colored silk blouse, stood. A pretty woman, but one not to be enfeebled by claiming the graces of the gentler sex, she moved confidently to a spot in the room where she could be seen and heard by both judge and bystanders. "We'll be brief this morning. I believe we can finally bring this case to a just conclusion before dotage descends upon us all." She flashed her wittiness with a quick smile, one of her trademarks, before firing her first shot. "Sergeant Pauley McCrary, would you come forward, please."

Mr. Jones, the bailiff, bible in tow, administered the oath of office. "Do you solemnly swear to tell the truth, the whole truth, and nothing but the truth, so help you God?"

"I do."

"Officer McCrary, would you please review the events of Saturday night, December fourteenth of last year," Mosby began the hearing.

Which Pauley did do, succinctly and without aid of notes.

"Thank you. That was very helpful."

Flushed with affirmation, Pauley squared his shoulders as he readied himself to defend Tick, if necessary, against whatever the prosecutor could bring up next.

"That being clarified, Sergeant, would you please inform the court of all the complications and peculiarities that arose with the case from the night of the murder until now? For example, the multiple disappearances, especially the disappearance of the primary investigative officer, Detective Lieutenant Tick Quinn. Also if you'd explain how key pieces of this case's material evidence, which, I understand, had been in protective police custody, went missing."

Pauley expected this, but he'd hoped it would come later after he'd established his position. How could he explain Tick's fishy disappearance, and his own ridiculous runaround to find him? Or the pinched fingerprint documents? He couldn't tell them that Tick admitted he'd taken the documents for fear his prints were on them.

"Your Honor..." Pauley's voice cracked. He whipped out a handkerchief and faked a cough. *The truth, the whole truth, and nothing but?*

He could almost hear the people in the room waiting. The unrest, the slight stir.

"Your Honor, I received a call from Tick Quinn the night of December twenty-third. He asked me to come out to his cabin, where he'd been recovering from flu for a few days. He wanted to talk about the case—what we'd been doing and how things were going. You know, those kinds of questions."

Pauley spoke quickly, running fragments of truth in between whole cloths of insignificant detail that held little content. Rhys had taught him a thing or two in the hospital about camouflage—disguise.

He described Tick's old homeplace, the shotgun cabin. He made a joke about waiting in the dark, the hoot owl, of how he, a city boy, had spooked himself. Holding his handkerchief, as a prop, Pauley would cough periodically, clear his throat, giving himself time to think. He muddied the lachrymatory question by saying he and Tick thought the little bottle was a vase Raggedy had found or stolen but that belonged to Adler's Antiques. He told them that he and Tick'd made a special trip out to McGuire farm to discuss its ownership on Sunday after Raggedy's murder on Saturday night.

Pauley's most convincing moment came when he admitted, *in all honesty*, that he couldn't explain, *exactly*, the how or the why of the disappearing evidence. "I'm new to the force, and I just figured one of the other officers misplaced the fingerprint documents, and other stuff, you know, not meaning to. My grandmother says men never put anything back. Well, I figured she was right. She usually is." Pauley laughed, and the courtroom laughed with him. Opal Robinette, from her seat in the audience murmured an audible "Amen to that," which brought another laugh.

So far, so good. He hadn't lied, and he had them in the palm of his hand. Would it matter that he hadn't told the judge exactly what had happened? He swallowed to stop remembering the whole truth.

"Tick had a fever," Pauley continued. "He'd been at home but later moved out to his cabin. A case of self-diagnosed flu, knowing Tick. He shied away from doctors. I'm fairly certain his move to the cabin was to keep his wife from catching it. Flu's tough on old people. When I saw him that night at the cabin, he was still weak, shaky. In fact, he was sicker than I knew, sicker than any of us knew. That night, my boss, my partner, my teacher, and I gotta say, about my best friend, had a stroke. I called an ambulance, and he was rushed to the hospital, or he'd have died. I'm just thankful I was there." When Pauley's voice broke this time, he didn't try to hide it. This time his handkerchief remained crumpled in his fist.

The courtroom was touched as it absorbed the scene.

"Well done, Officer McCrary." Mildred Mosby, bothered by Pauley's emerging skills as an actor, stepped forward and lightly applauded. "Well done." The words were right, but she didn't look pleased. "I appreciate your experience that night in the cabin with your friend. I know it was difficult. And I know that you would do anything to save this man if it's in your power to do so. And I think it was in your power to do so that night."

She faced the bystanders.

"Most of us would do anything for a friend, wouldn't we? A best friend, you called him." When she turned back to Pauley, she was smiling. "Your teacher, your partner, your boss. That's very tender. Men may be deficient in putting things back where they belong, as your grandmother says"—Mildred swept the room to find Opal Robinette—"but I'll bet you'll agree with me, Mrs. Robinette, men do understand loyalty. Especially loyalty to a close friend. Is it a man thing, do you think? Honor, duty, and all that."

Mildred Mosby paused as she turned to address the people.

"Have any of you ever broken the law for a friend? Now, now, I'm not asking you to confess. You can save that for your preacher." She laughed. "But I've heard stories of people breaking the law for a friend, a buddy. Maybe not always as dramatically overt as stealing or shooting someone who might be viewed as dangerous to one's friend. Those things do happen, unfortunately. We're a strange animal, we humans. Sometimes we find ourselves conflicted about what is right and what is not. I'm talking about breaking the law just a little bit for a friend. Subtler, like hiding a criminal, or taking the blame for something you didn't do, or lying. Lying under oath, even. Holding back a piece of information. As innocent as these acts seem, still they are punishable by law. Aren't they?" She swung around to face the judge. "But we're lucky this morning. Detective Sergeant McCrary, just like you and me, is an officer of the court, and like us he's been sworn to the truth? That's one thing we don't have to worry about."

Pauley couldn't breathe. *What is Mosby doing?* His grandmother had always said she could tell when he was lying, or hiding something, keeping something from her.

He struggled to regain his composure. Mosby continued talking, sermonizing.

Why's she doing...

"I beg your pardon." Mosby looked as if she'd forgotten Pauley was in the room. "Did you say something?"

"Did I?"

"Maybe not. I did rather go off, didn't I? Let's move forward, shall we? I have just one more question that needs explaining. Would you tell us about the strange escapades of Raggedy Ann's grocery cart, and presumably, a diary that I have yet to see?"

Mosby stepped back.

Am I nuts? What the fuck am I doing? This morning I was hopeful Pauley McCrary would be my way out of the mess I find myself in, but something unsettling is going on. That business with his handkerchief. Was she being made a fool? She'd let Latimer rush her into bringing charges against Quinn. She should have gone along with her instincts, but she hadn't. It was at this hearing that she'd hoped to be exonerated from her poor judgment. She'd depended on Pauley's supposed new evidence, but now she didn't know. He was hiding something. She was sure of it. She had been in trials and hearings long enough to know when someone was uncomfortable with her questions or the proceedings. It usually meant someone was lying.

"You're introducing a grocery cart and a diary as evidence then, Madam Prosecutor?" Wilkie asked.

"No, sir. Well sort of, but not yet, maybe."

"Madam! It's a simple question. Yes or no should suffice."

"Absolutely. It's just that we don't know how significant they are to this hearing. This has been a very poorly run investigation. We hear about things, but they either disappear or we simply hear no more about them. The grocery cart and diary—should they become important, then we will introduce them as evidence, but they will not appear as surprises."

"McCrary, are you content with this evasion?"

"Yessir." Pauley could have kissed the judge. He was happy to share the onus of evasiveness with Mildred Mosby. "The grocery basket and the diary were my mistakes," he began. As I said earlier, I'm new to..."

"Yes, yes, yes, yes, yes, we know. You're new to law enforcement. Move on, Sergeant."

"Yessir. Well, I didn't find Raggedy's grocery cart as soon as I should have done. Tick kept pushing me to look for any and everything, but the basket had rolled across the street and down the hill, almost landing in the bayou." There was a hum of exhilaration from the courtroom. "I didn't find it until Sunday. The morning after we'd found Raggedy Ann in the Dumpster on Saturday night. And as for the diary, it was in a storage room over the parking lot at Adler's Antiques. I thought it belonged to the Adler family, so I gave it to them."

"So the police thought the lachrymatory bottle and the diary belonged to the Adlers? Anything else? The fingerprint report, the autopsy? Did the Adler family have ownership of those too?"

Pauley looked confused. "Beg your pardon? No! Of course not."

"What's this rookie shenanigan, my young friend? You strike me as being quite capable."

Pauley looked awkward and angry.

"Is there anything more you should tell us that would help us find the truth about this murdered woman?"

At that moment, Pauley hated her.

"Truth is, ma'am, the diary may have started as an Adler possession, but it may have finished as Raggedy's."

She raised an eyebrow. "How so?"

"I've told you about everything I know, about the cart rolling. I barely saw what was in it. Nothing significant as far as I could tell." He thought about the feathers in the blanket and swallowed his lie. "Same with the diary. The initial entries were like a young girl's, but there were things in it that didn't fit an Adler, or a young girl. Different handwriting, also."

Mosby studied him closely but then chose to let it go. "The fingerprint documents then—when did you know they were missing? Speaking of missing, how long had Officer Quinn been missing before you found him at his fishing cabin? Had you known all along where he was?"

"I don't remember exactly."

"How about vaguely, if not exactly? Surely there were reasons you needed to talk to your lieutenant about the case you were working together. Could you locate him? Talk on your phones?"

"Missing? I never said he was missing."

"You did know where he was hiding, even though Sheriff Latimer suggested he did not. That neither of you knew."

"Ma'am, am I on trial here?" Pauley tried to sound calm, but antagonism edged his voice.

"No, Sergeant. You are not on trial. In fact…"

"I never said he was hiding? You're coloring my account."

"Not my intention. In fact, I would love to conclude in this hearing that the charges brought against Lieutenant Quinn are dismissible." The room of onlookers audibly reacted. "Riversbend loves Tick Quinn. Are you shocked to hear me admit this? Not the normal position for a prosecutor, huh? But as a prosecutor, I too want justice, Sergeant. And I'm trying to establish an order of events and to understand a series of happenings that led to this hearing. I trust it will take us to the truth."

"I'll try to answer your questions. First, I don't know an exact date and time when the fingerprints disappeared. We had them at headquarters, and then we did not. Okay? As to Tick's moving out to his cabin, all I can say is that, on Monday morning, after we found Raggedy Ann in the Dumpster, we were both at headquarters. I think Tick was coming down with a fever then. He was grouchier than usual, and the next day, he stayed home. I didn't call. I didn't want to bother him. When he decided to move out to his cabin, I truly do not know. Later, Miss Willa told me where he might be."

Mildred Mosby didn't challenge this giveaway answer. The judge's face was unreadable.

"Nothing more, Sergeant?" The prosecutor prompted.

He could tell them that he'd tried for days to locate Tick. He could tell them he'd phoned repeatedly, and that Tick wouldn't answer, and that for days, he didn't have a clue where Tick was, or why he was gone.

"No. Nothing."

"You said Miss Willa told you where he might be. Was Willa Quinn as much in the dark as you were regarding her husband's whereabouts?"

Pauley frowned. "I don't understand what you're gettin' at, ma'am." He said, but he did know exactly what she was gettin' at. He'd misstepped. His tongue had gotten balled up in his own words, and he just gave away what he was trying so hard to keep—that Tick was in hiding.

"Lady, it's been a long time since Tick left work on that Monday morning. All I know is Miss Willa told me where the cabin was."

Pauley straightened his back.

"I came here today to introduce new evidence. And the new evidence I have may not answer the questions about my poor memory, but it will answer the question of Tilman Quinn's innocence in the death of Raggedy Ann. You do remember that's why we're here today."

"Your Honor, may we take a small break?" Mildred Mosby asked, smiling in spite of being the target of Pauley's simple chastisement.

"Ten minutes." The gavel tapped like an exclamation point as Wilkie rose from his chair and disappeared through the paneling.

Rhys had noted Pauley's cough. She'd lived with Richard long enough to recognize that little coughs were precursors of little discomforts, and in some instances, little lies. She tried to think back to what had been said. And what was the deal with Mildred Mosby? Whatever, Rhys was pleased Mildred had finished the questions about the diary. Damn diary.

Ever since her epiphany on Christmas night, Rhys had lamented her decisions that had obviously complicated the case. She had been an obstructionist, hiding Raggedy's cart in the stock room, and her unwillingness to handover the diary except on her own terms, not to mention her silence regarding Kate's theft of the lachrymatory bottle, or Tick's attempt as an arsonist.

Would her cooperation have made a difference? She'd never know. Truth be told, she had enjoyed her little adventure. For a guilt-free minute, she exchanged her nervousness for a goofy smile. She nudged Richard's arm, sending her enthusiasm for Pauley and for her own detective work in this mystifying adventure down the row of spectators.

Richard's arm was loosely draped across the back of the chair next to him where sweet, talced, wizened Isabella Radley teetered on the edge with anticipation. Despite the squeak in her walking stick, the old lady rocked it like a throttle in front of her until the judge, ten minutes later, reentered chambers.

"If we've established that the diary and grocery cart are possibly no more than a pair of rabbits to be pursued, Madam Prosecutor, then are we are ready to hear this new evidence?"

Mildred Mosby, who had revised her tactics along with her lipstick during the break, pulled at a mock forelock. "*Mea culpa*, Your Honor. Officer McCrary, we are all ears as is said in the rabbit's warren."

Pauley began talking about a letter that he'd found in Addie Wagner's vanity. "Pink stationery. Sweet smelling. Obviously from an admirer, a lover. It was hidden in her vanity under a bunch of makeup kinds of stuff."

When the prosecution asked if he might be speculating on the nature of the relationship, Pauley admitted he had no proof. "But it couldn't have been from her husband. It didn't sound like a husband. If you read it, Judge, ma'am—the words had love letter all over it. Yearning to...wanting to...hungry for...sexy words. Not words a husband uses with his wife."

The courtroom laughed.

"Do you have this letter?" the judge asked.

"With me?"

"Young man, I'm sure you've heard about the smoking gun."

"I know where the letter is," Pauley answered. "It's still in her dresser drawer."

The judge looked at Pauley as if he were a dunce. "In her dresser drawer, Officer McCrary? You better hope it's still in the lady's dresser drawer."

"Yessir, I'll get it as soon as we break."

"If you recall, we've just had our break. We will never ever break again."

"But..." Pauley arms rose in frustration.

"I want this hearing to be over before it's time for my supper."

"Sup...sir, but..."

"McCrary, quit your monosyllabic babbling before I terminate this hearing and have you incarcerated for incompetence."

"But..."

"Ach!" Wilkie drew his finger across his throat.

Pauley pressed his lips together. He scanned the courtroom anxiously in search of someone who could go to the Wagner's house and find the letter for him. Or a friend. He saw Rhys but instantly vetoed her in fear of her uncanny talent for whipping up trouble even when there was none. Latimer was staring out the window, more interested in a family of wasps attempting to enter into the warmth of the courtroom through a loose pane than in Pauley's need of a runner. Pauley was about to give up when the god of desperation set Tom Drake on his feet. Drake gave him a wink and slipped out of the room.

"We'll have it soon. One of our men is going for it," Pauley said.

Latimer whirled around to see who was leaving only to catch a flash of blue as the door closed.

Pauley had survived a convoluted maze of challenges this morning, but uplifted as Drake swung out the doors, he gained determination. Right or wrong, he was not going to buckle now. "Sir"—he pulled the blackmail note torn from the diary—"this note was found in the Wagner's garage. It was torn from the diary." He handed it to the bailiff. "Exhibit one, sir."

"Might this be the aforementioned diary that has yet to be submitted as an exhibit?"

"Almost positive, sir."

"Then which one of you lucky people wants to admit this diary as evidence?"

"I will, sir. If that's okay with the prosecutor."

"By all means," Mildred Mosby was encouraged.

Pauley then spoke of traces of angel hair found in a garage. He reinforced this seeming bit of fluff by telling of the surplus of angel hair found in a charcoal sack under the lid of the barbeque grill.

"Hidden, sir, like the love letter. Angel hair in a sack of charcoal. Inside a barbeque grill. Doesn't that seem weird to you? All this found in a garage that did not belong to Detective Quinn. It clearly points to a third person, a person other than Tick Quinn. It strongly suggests someone other than Tick Quinn was involved in the death of Raggedy Ann." Pauley swallowed. "Should I bring the charcoal grill, sir? I can get it."

The judge didn't look as if he were being swept up in Pauley's argument.

"And...and that isn't all." Extracting a quarter sheet of paper from his other shirt pocket, Pauley spread it open. "This is a report from forensics in Little Rock. It clearly states that Addie Wagner died from asphyxiation brought on by overdoses of barbiturates and alcohol that were found in her stomach. And by spun-glass fibers. That's angel hair, sir. I submit this as exhibit number two, or three, depending on if the grocery cart is to be submitted, and if so, who would do that, the prosecutor or me, sir." It was then that James Van Wilkie's gavel hit his desk suddenly and loudly enough to make Pauley jump.

"Excuse me just a moment, McCrary. Have I missed something? Have I come to another hearing, or does Addie Wagner death have something to do with Officer Quinn and the charge brought against him regarding the death of Francie Butter, also known as Raggedy Ann?"

"Indirectly, sir."

"Indirectly." The judge scrubbed his forehead with his knuckles. "Am I being foolish to assume then that the garage, and horsehair, which apparently was not in the possession of Tick Quinn's, possibly does have something to do with Raggedy Ann?"

"Angel hair, sir. It was in Logan Wagner's garage, sir. The angel hairs, which are really spun-glass fibers, were in her throat."

"Raggedy Ann's?"

"Mrs. Wagner's."

The room groaned in appreciation of the drama Pauley was laying before them.

"Angel hair, found in her mouth and down her throat, had diminished her ability to breathe," Pauley continued. She was in an acute state of"—Pauley glanced at another scrap of paper—"of hyperemesis. The fibers from the angel hair denied Mrs. Wagner her ability to expel her own vomit, which the drugs and alcohol had induced."

"Drugs and alcohol?"

Pauley looked up. "Smashed, sir, or whatever you people call it. The drugs and the angel hair assured Adelaide Wagner's asphyxiation. This is premeditated; this is first-degree murder."

"Let me get this straight. The woman was on a Christmas float. And, to my knowledge, it is not a rarity for angel hair to be used on Christmas floats, right? You know to create the illusion of snow, or clouds, something ethereal. You with me so far? Good. But here's the problem. Addie Wagner might have been inebriated to the point to of vomiting, and she might have become strangled causing asphyxiation and death, but drunkenness and regurgitation, to my knowledge, do not indicate foul play. Without something more, Mr. McCrary, they may indicate many things, carelessness, foolishness, addiction, but not murder," Mosby said.

In an ongoing battle between frustration at Pauley for dangling hope with holes in it, and her desire to be vindicated in her unfortunate decisions regarding this hearing, Mildred Mosby squinted at Pauley. A fine sheen of perspiration like beads of dew popped out on her flushed face. When she spoke, her voice was tinged with disappointment.

"And more than that, please, Sergeant, why are we talking about the Wagner's case? If there is a connection, if you have any evidence relating to the charge against Tick, please state it for the court now."

"Other than the scrap of paper from your pocket, we have questionable material evidence," the judge said, joining the conversation. "We have no witnesses, only hearsay. Can you prove this letter, which you have yet to produce, or that the note you handed the bailiff is not bogus? Is there proof that the angel hair found in Wagner's barbeque grill was not intended for anything more than a Christmas float—or, perhaps even planted there by someone seeking some unknown agenda?"

Pauley wasn't prepared for this. His evidence was so strong in his own mind, and this shock wave of accusations so evident that he couldn't speak.

"Can any of this new information be validated?"

"I have a witness who knows that Raggedy Ann was blackmailing Logan Wagner. And another who could state under oath that a blackmail note was found in his garage."

"Witnesses? Two of them?" The judge motioned for the prosecutor and the young police officer to approach the bench. No one saw Hummer slip out of the courtroom. Like those pesky no-see-ums that hide in the underspaces, people rarely see nobodies, or what they're up to, unless they are wandering around in the wrong neighborhoods.

Pauley glanced at Mildred Mosby. He wasn't sure why they'd been summoned to the bench. He'd been about to call Hummer up to witness to Raggedy's blackmail business. Hummer who rarely spoke. Hummer who hummed. Hummer who was questionably reliable to say what needed to be said.

"McCrary." The judge leaned toward them. "You have spent the past few minutes talking about the Wagner's garage and blackmail and angel hair. For some reason, you want this to add up as a testament to Tick Quinn's innocence, but unless you are prepared to verify your documents, and to produce these witnesses, you are failing. We have no information suggesting Raggedy Ann, who is a subject of this hearing, had ingested barbiturates or alcohol before her death. And certainly, no angel hair was found on her. If these items contributed to Mrs. Wagner death, that is another issue. It doesn't belong here."

"But Tick Quinn did not kill Raggedy Ann." Pauley's voice was hollow with concern. Pauley didn't really know who for god-certain had killed Raggedy Ann. He was fairly sure he did know who had killed Addie Wagner.

"How do you know that?"

Pauley'd heard Tick confess to killing her. He'd spent every waking hour since that night trying to deny Tick's words, trying to turn them into something other than a confession.

"I know it in my heart, sir."

Mildred Mosby flinched. "Your Honor, I'm sorry, but I have questions. I know that this officer is telling us something important. I would like to ask for a short adjournment, and if you concur, I would like for Price Latimer to join us, sir, in your study." Mosby's demeanor crackled. Pauley's *heart* was exactly where she wanted it to be. But she was going to have to help him come up with something more convincing than the assurances that his heart spoke!

The judge, rising from his chair, said something to the bailiff, and then he motioned with a hitchhiker's thumb to Latimer. He tapped his gavel. "Stretch your legs, ladies and gentlemen. Have a bite of lunch. Be back at twelve-thirty. If you're late, I've instructed the bailiff to lock the doors at precisely one minute after twelve o'clock."

Some of the people were already moving toward the doors. Others remained in their seats, unwilling to relinquish their choice spots or unwilling to test the judge's instruction to lock them out.

Wilkie's chambers were spacious but not plush. This morning the room smelled of stale coffee, cigar smoke, and the need for a good dusting. A primitive painting of a dirt road, a chicken, and a water pump hung on the wall behind his desk. Other than this rather nice crumb thrown to art, his walls were bare except for a small signed photograph of a younger James Van Wilkie, fresh out of law school, standing next to Orville Faubus.

He was already seated behind his desk when Latimer entered.

"Have a seat, Price. I imagine the prosecutor is powdering her nose."

Seconds later Mildred Mosby entered on a brisk stride, slamming the door behind her.

"What is going on here, Price?" she challenged.

"McCrary's way out in left field. Inventing things. You know how they are." Latimer, confident in his charges against Tick, slumped back in his chair. He smirked, giving Wilkie a boys-together wink.

"How *they* are!" The judge's complexion flushed. "How *who* is, Sheriff?"

Latimer sat up straighter. "Ah new guys. Young cops wantin' to make a name for themselves. That's all I meant, Jim."

Wilkie sat still for several minutes, letting this soak in. "I am not your buddy, Latimer. Be mindful with your biases around me. I won't tolerate them. You are a lawman. There is no room for intolerance. Do you understand me?"

Price Latimer nodded. "I do, Judge." But Latimer wasn't happy.

"Mildred, you called for this break."

"If you recall, Jimmy, we agreed to call this hearing because the day after Christmas we learned Logan Wagner had killed himself. Three people dead in two weeks. Then Pauley McCrary told us, he had notes and witnesses that offered us a clearer view of what was happening in Riversbend, what had happened to Raggedy Ann. It seemed right to schedule a hearing. What has changed?" Mosby raised an insubordinate eyebrow at Wilkie.

"You were doing a nice job earlier, Mildred, keeping young McCrary on his p's and q's regarding the admission of new evidence," Wilkie countered. "What changed?"

"Does it stand repeating? I think Pauley's right. He's new to law enforcement, he's new to being interrogated by the courts, but here's where something changed. Something more revealing than words. Pauley McCrary was shocked when you accused him of falsifying evidence. You could see it on his face. This man is no actor; he is incapable of lying without giving it away. He honestly believes he has new evidence. I do *not* feel good about the way this hearing is going. I want to hear something to help me reconsider the charges I brought against Tick Quinn."

"You can't alter your decision to charge Tick until you have a rational reason to do so. You made your decision a week ago."

"Judge Wilkie, we"—she glanced at Price—"have allowed ourselves to slide on a slippery slope. Until Addie Wagner's death, Raggedy Ann's death was relegated to slush file. After Tick disappeared, her case was left with a good man, but an inexperienced man on a complicated murder investigation. I don't know where it's going to go from here, but the truth of this story is out there, and it's crucial to find it.

"When the sheriff came to see me on Christmas," she continued, "I had no idea Raggedy's death had not been investigated thoroughly. I don't want to point the finger, but somewhere along the line, our system judged Raggedy's death as unimportant. It was easy to do, considering her age and occupation. A death by natural causes. An easily explained death that needed to be quickly disposed of. And as for Pauley's new evidence…"

"That is not true," Price balked.

"If Pauley hadn't come to me with new evidence, would you have? I don't know who I should listen to, a green-as-a-gourd young rookie or a sheriff with uncertain motives."

"What do you mean? I have no motive."

"This information about items found in Wagner's garage should have been brought to my attention the day after Christmas, Price, not this morning. Why wasn't it?"

"I didn't know about them either," Latimer said.

"Bullshit." Mildred Mosby looked at the sheriff as if she might ignite and rise sizzling into the air like a bottle rocket.

"Calm down, Mildred."

"If this is about those scraps of paper, or the barbeque grill"—the sheriff's face was fuchsia—"this morning is the first time I've heard this crap, or that hair business.

"After Logan Wagner's wife died, I went over to their place. I didn't see no scrap of paper, or anything else.

"It's his fault." Latimer pointed at Pauley. "Maybe even a frame-up. Him lettin' a bunch of busybodies run around pretending to be cops. Isn't that against the law? Imitating an officer? Giving him their ideas, telling him what to do, winding up a young cop with no experience, and poor judgment."

"Pauley McCrary may be wrong, but he believes he's doing right. If this case has been a royal snafu, the fuckup falls back on you, Mr. Sheriff."

"Mildred, please watch your language."

"Tick disappears. Pauley, as you clearly said, has almost no experience, and you put him in charge? Were you hoping for a failure?"

"Of course, I put him in charge. He was Tick's partner. They found the body together."

"When Tick got sick—"

"Disappeared."

"We don't know that. Who did you assign to assist Pauley? Who had the experience that you signed on with him after... Tick...after Tick...went to his cabin?" Mildred Mosby was not relinquishing her ire just yet.

Latimer rubbed the back of his neck. "We were shorthanded."

"So, no one. You're saying you let Pauley go it alone? Why not? What did it matter? She was a homeless bag lady. But something happened. What? Suddenly you got interested in Raggedy's case. Why? Who or what rattled your cage, Sheriff? Addie Wagner's death?"

"I gave that one to Tom Drake about the time this new bit of poppycock popped up."

"What poppycock is that? The poppycock about the blackmail note found in Wagner's garage?" Judge Wilkie asked.

"I didn't think it was important. I just thought it was the goings-on of that Rhys Adler woman and her prissy cousin."

"Okay." Wilkie raised his arms. "Let's start over. Would someone please tell me why we're having this hearing? We know Raggedy Ann was murdered, don't we? We know certainly that she is dead. Is there probable cause to believe that Tilman O'Connor Quinn committed the crime?"

With that Mildred Mosby extracted a small datebook from somewhere, a pocket or purse, and began enumerating dates and notes:

> December 24, 10:35 a.m.: Price Latimer called late morning, insisting on seeing me.
>
> December 25, 2:00 p.m.: Price still determined to make an appointment—says he has evidence to bring charges against Tick Quinn for the murder of Raggedy Ann.
>
> December 25, 2:20 p.m.: Appt. Latimer in my office at 4:00 p.m.

"I should have questioned his urgency then, Your Honor, but I didn't. We met Christmas afternoon, and I let him convince me he had sufficient evidence against Tick, so charges were made.

"There was no mention of Wagner, or of his apparent suicide?

"No, and there was no mention of blackmail, nor that Tick had suffered a stroke."

"Hmm," the judge sighed. "Okay, one more question. Just for old times' sake, remind me why we keep talking about the Wagner woman?" the judge asked.

Their twenty minutes in Wilkie's study evaporated as all three silently rehearsed their positions on the judge's question.

James Van Wilkie, patted down an unruly cowlick in a small mirror before exiting his office. He knew why Latimer hadn't mentioned Tick's stroke to the prosecutor. He thought he was running against a clock. You can't prosecute a dead man. He caught up with Mildred outside his office. "Walk me back down the hall, Mildred?"

"It was only after learning of Logan Wagner's death that you decided to hear new evidence?"

Mosby was quiet for a few seconds, considering her answer. "Because, I was not convinced of Tick's guilt or innocence. Allowing new evidence to be admitted had nothing to do with Logan Wagner, but everything to do with Tick Quinn. Tick Quinn is a good man, a fine policeman, a man with an upright reputation who had been charged, after a long and honorable career, with a major crime. I hoped Pauley's new evidence would allow me a chance to overturn a judgment that I knew had been made prematurely, and probably in error."

"You didn't answer my question exactly. Was it after Logan Wagner's death that you began having doubts? Do you think his death was suicide, or…another murder?"

"Another murder? That's a scary thought. I certainly have not heard anything suggesting that."

The judge nodded in agreement. "Nor I."

"I never associated Raggedy's and Addie Wagner's deaths, and we have yet to prove that they are associated. But I did agree with Price that with two murders, law enforcement needed to score. Personally"—Mosby paused—"personally, I don't need bad press. I don't want my indecisiveness to appear as weakness. It's tough being a prosecuting attorney, particularly if you're a woman. It's an elected office. Often you make unpopular decisions. What has happened is exactly what I did not want to happen. I did not want my decision to prosecute or not to prosecute Tick Quinn up for public debate. If new evidence gives us an opportunity to review…" Mildred's shrug was barely perceptible. "You know how Riversbend is."

On the way up the hall, she told the judge about Latimer's concerns, legitimate concerns beginning with what he considered inappropriate procedure. He questioned why Tick drove by Adler's Antiques that particular night. It was off his route.

Latimer felt it was because Tick already knew the body was there, in the Dumpster.

"Late Christmas afternoon when he came to my office," Mosby continued, "he said that Tick had disappeared. Run away. But the convincing factor was when he insisted he had blood evidence. The stacks of circumstances against Quinn had grown so high I could no longer ignore them. Coincidences? There were too many of them. I felt I had no recourse."

"I would have done the same." The couple paused at the corner that would lead them back into the courtroom. She touched his sleeve. "Jimmy, I can't ignore the nagging voice that has awakened me every night for the past week, telling me I was wrong."

"Oh, is it your heart? You and McCrary appear to have the same heart condition." Wilkie chuckled as he stepped through the disappearing door in the paneled wall behind his bench. Voices hushed, spectators stood, and the judge's hammer came down. The session began with Price Latimer coming forward to be sworn in.

"Did you and Tick Quinn have personal problems working together?"

"We worked together okay."

"Did you consider him to be a good policeman?"

"Good enough until I had a hunch he was involved in the old woman's death. There was something strange about his behavior."

"Hunch? Such as?"

"Such as his strange appearances at places he shouldn't be, like behind Adler's the night Raggedy Ann died and then his stranger disappearance when no one knew where he was."

"Any facts over and above hunches available here?"

"I was not privy to all the facts."

"How is that?"

"I was told basically nothing of the stuff piling up around Logan Wagner. Besides, this hearing is about the old bag woman, not Mrs. Wagner."

Wilkie's trademark frown deepened into a more formidable one.

He leaned forward, focusing on Latimer, although he was addressing all his principals. "I suggest, through the remainder of this hearing, we use the name Francie Butter or Ms. Butter, as best we can, when referring to the deceased. Let us bridle our natural appetites for the vulgar, the unprofessional, or unprincipled expressions such as 'old woman,' or 'bag whomever.' This is an informal hearing, but maybe I should add a word concerning our overuse of childish nicknames regarding Raggedy Ann...er...Butter...Francie." Losing his point, he gave up.

The spectators enjoying the judge's blunder laughed guardedly, except for Miss Willa, who brayed loudly. This, in turn, set the room into a full-on roar, not only relieving tension but also creating a perfect stage entrance for Drake and Hummer.

"So where are we, Madam Prosecutor?"

"Thanks to the recent activities and return of a couple of our own Baker's Street irregulars." She smiled in the general direction of Drake and Hummer. "Have we the letter found in Addie Wagner's dressing table?"

The letter was brought forward.

"This letter, and a blackmail note—allegedly in Francie Butter's handwriting—found in Logan Wagner's garage, certainly offers a motive for killing Addie Wagner..."

"But not Raggedy Ann!" The judge thundered and banged his gavel.

Mildred Mosby drew a deep breath and a modicum of patience and continued, "The letter drawn from the pink envelop that Officer McCrary told us about suggests that Addie Wagner was either involved with a man other than her husband or was entertaining thoughts of an assignation of some sort, or at the very least a flirtation. And Logan Wagner, according to the note found in his garage, was being blackmailed. Therefore, we can offer, for the first time, the suggestion that Logan Wagner would have had a motive for murdering Francie Butter—our own Raggedy Ann for blackmailing him. And though this hearing is not about this, it also supposes a motive for killing his wife for... for betraying her marriage vows." Mildred Mosby handed the pink envelop and letter to Wilkie, who quickly read it.

"I suppose a psychiatrist or a good lawyer might put forward overwhelming guilt or grief as an explanation for Logan's suicide."

There was a buzz of agreement around the courtroom.

"McCrary, can you explain why Raggedy Ann blackmailed Wagner rather than his wife? Addie Wagner was the guilty party, or the alleged guilty party?" the prosecutor asked.

"No. I don't know why. I wondered a little about that too."

"I can suggest why she blackmailed Logan rather than Addie," a man's voice said from the back of the room, as Richard Fordyce rose from his seat.

He buttoned his sports coat before stepping into the aisle.

"Logan Wagner was a surer target than Addie, Your Honor. I've known Logan Wagner since we were grade-school boys together. Logan Wagner was complicated. He was extraordinarily egocentric, and yet he was humble to a fault, sometimes. He was famously proud, but with his pride, he carried a chip on his shoulder. Logan Wagner would have died before he would let the world know Addie had betrayed, cuckolded him. He may have killed himself"—Richard paused at the gravity of his assertion—"but it's hard for me to imagine that he killed Addie. He worshipped her."

"Are you suggesting Raggedy Ann would have known Logan Wagner this well? Could she have known he would be the better target for blackmail?" The judge had slipped unconsciously back to the dead woman's comfortable nickname.

"Raggedy Ann was shrewd. She had an uncanny understanding of people. An outgrowth of her line of work, I suppose."

Richard smiled softly at the memories he and Riversbend shared of their favorite bag lady.

"Do you believe Raggedy Ann was capable of blackmail?" Mosby interjected.

"I wouldn't have thought so three weeks ago. However, the material evidence suggests she was not only capable but also quite good at it."

"Or Tick Quinn. You know Riversbend very well, Mr. Fordyce. Do you think Tick Quinn could murder someone?"

"Madam, I believe any man is capable of murder in the right circumstances."

Lightly drumming a pencil on his desk, Wilkie seemed to consider Richard's accounting of his friends. He wasn't surprised at the man's assessment of Wagner, he'd always thought the fellow odd, but he was surprised at Richard's knowledge of Raggedy Ann.

"Thank you for your insight, Mr. Fordyce, but it's a moot point regarding Logan Wagner. A dead man cannot be tried. Logan Wagner goes to his heaven or hell according to a higher authority than mine.

"This leaves us the task of reaching a decision as to the innocence or guilt of Tick Quinn"—the judge paused—"Tick, good Lord," he muttered under his breath. "We do admire nicknames down here, don't we?"

He seemed to be addressing some invisible specter, a mentor perhaps from his past.

"Truth is often elusive and rarely whole. But we must get on, once and for all, trying to determine if there is enough evidence to bring Tilman O'Connor Quinn to trial for the death of Francie Butter. If there has been an error in filing these charges, we must acknowledge it and correct it. If not, we must get on with it." Judge Wilkie gazed toward the back of the room, pleased to see that several reporters were writing furiously on their small pads of paper. "I'm not sure we have clear proof of guilt or innocence."

Pauley sprang to his feet. "Oh, but we have, sir. Francie Butter isn't her real name, Your Honor. We don't know her real name, but we do know that Raggedy Ann was a man."

The courtroom burst into a riot of excitement, which sent Wilkie into a frenzy with his gavel.

"Silence, please!" He hammered his desk repeatedly. "Ladies and gentlemen, will you be seated; please be seated at once." The gavel came down harder followed with a threat to close the hearing to the public if order was not restored immediately. "Sit down."

Wilkie stood.

"Ladies and gentlemen, take a ten-minute breather. I would like for Ms. Mosby, and young McCrary to approach the bench. Sheriff, you too.

"Explain yourself, Officer McCrary. What do you mean Francie Butter was a man?"

"I believe that possibly Francie Butter's first name was actually Frank."

"Frank Butter?"

"Not sure about the Butter, sir. The...the sex information was in the autopsy report. His...his..." Pauley rolled his wrist to indicate the others were to understand he was talking about Raggedy's genitals. "She...he had been injured."

"She? He? Mildred, do you know what's going on here?"

"I'm flabbergasted."

"Latimer?

Price Latimer shrugged. "I might have seen it. Being a newcomer to Riversbend, I assumed everyone knew it. That it was common knowledge."

"Does this injury, or this gender confusion, have anything to do with the case, McCrary? Was it common knowledge? Did Tick know this? Why Tick contacted you the night he had the stroke."

Pauley shivered. *Yes, Tick knew.* "No, I don't think it was common knowledge," Pauley said. *Did it have anything to do with the case? It had everything to do with the case. It was the motive behind the action that killed her.* "Tick would have known if he saw the autopsy. Tick was sick."

"Look at me, young man. You have a fascinating relationship with the truth. I am confident that sometimes you speak it, but I am also suspicious that on occasion you don't. Must I remind you, McCrary, that you are an officer of the law, and under oath."

Pauley swallowed. "I haven't forgotten, sir."

I, Pauley McCrary, do swear that I will well and truly serve our country and state as a police officer without favor or affection, malice or ill will, until I am legally discharged, and that I...

It hadn't been so long ago. Pauley had memorized it at his induction, and he could still recite it, in part...*and that while I continue to be a police officer, I will, to the best of my skill and knowledge, discharge all the duties faithfully and according to law, so help me God.*

Without "favor or affection." There it was. Pauley didn't recall any wording in his oath about truth, but it was clear at this moment that he was placing favor and affection for Tick Quinn above the law. When this hearing was ended, whichever way it turned out, he would turn in his badge. He was not cut out to be a cop.

He looked Judge Wilkie in the eye, defying him to call him a liar.

"Tick Quinn is in the hospital as we speak, Your Honor. The night he contacted me he was a very sick man. He is my mentor, but we also are friends. I don't know why me, but he wanted me, probably because he's my boss and he can boss me around." Pauley smiled. "That night Tick reminisced mostly, as old men do." Pauley stuck his hand in his pants pocket and jiggled the loose silver. "Tick told me stories about when he was a boy—"

"Was he in hiding?" the judge pushed.

"Hiding? More like camouflage, I'd say." Pauley laughed, but no one else did.

"McCrary, I hope you understand that you are doing your friend no favors with your attempt to be clever and evasive. And if you have any more surprises, let us have them now. Or I shall serve you with contempt of court."

"Pauley?" Mildred Mosby turned to him.

"Hold your questions, madam. Our ten-minutes are up."

"Officer McCrary, did Tick Quinn tell you why he disappeared? Did it have anything to do with Raggedy Ann's death? Was there a reason why he took the route to the Morrissey's Place by way of Bayou Street and Adler's, which was miles off route, but a route that did have you driving by Adler's on the very night you found Raggedy in the Dumpster?"

"Tick was staying out past Powhattan," Pauley said, sliding over the prosecutor's barrage of questions. "Easy walk to the river. January first he officially retired, you know; maybe he was thinking about fishin'."

"Is that your answer, Sergeant?"

Pauley heard the displeasure in her voice, but continued, "The night at the cabin, Tick was still puzzling about the Dumpster. It's always the Dumpster that tripped us up. Seeing her body, her legs hanging there…wondering how she got in it. There's always been something so vulnerable about seeing her half in, half out, her clothes all bunched, her feet, her white shoes…her white shoes. Tick thought she might have fallen from the catwalk, or those weird steps back of Adler's." Pauley stepped back from the bench. "But…I…uh…" He seemed to look from the judge, to the prosecutor, to the sheriff, but he wasn't seeing them. He began to pace in a small space, seemingly unaware of those around him. "I know how she got in the Dumpster. They were new, and we joked about them." Now washed with a flurry of memories, Pauley started laughing. "We didn't know what we were looking for. She was a bag lady. Most of her stuff was outta someone's trash bin. Trash. Throwaways. But ladies and gentlemen"—Pauley made a sweeping bow—"the clue was right there from the start. Her shoes were almost new. And I know who killed her."

Pauley could feel the bewilderment that surrounded him, the excitement, the intense quiet.

"Late Christmas Eve I was given some information affecting Raggedy's death that needed checking. I had heard an interesting account. I wanted to believe it, but it was so bizarre, and I didn't know if what I'd been told was important to my case, or even true. I did believe it was the truth as someone understood it to be.

"I discovered the love letter and the angel hair the next day, Christmas Day, at the Wagner house. You see, I had seen Mrs. Wagner's autopsy report, and with the discovery of the angel hair in the grill and the other things, I'd thought this would be strong enough to clear Tick. That the love letter, the blackmail scrap, and the angel hair would clear Tick of all suspicions.

"But something else happened that afternoon that I am just now putting together. As I said, I had to check out this new bit of information. My investigation took me to the Wagners'. I had to park several doors down from their house. Their place is in the curve of a cul-de-sac, and there were cars and people everywhere, in the driveway, parked out front, people milling about the yard. I knew something had happened, so I started running toward the house."

The courtroom was mesmerized with Pauley's story, and no one saw Toad leave. He skirted around the courthouse and struck out for Wagner's garage. As soon as Pauley began talking about going to Logan Wagner's the day he shot himself, Toad had an idea what it was that Pauley had finally put together. Only problem was Pauley didn't know where it was. Toad did. It was

Toad who'd detailed Wagner's truck for the police. Everything he'd found he's carefully put in a plastic bag and stored in a safe.

"By the time I got close enough to work my way through the crowd to the truck," Pauley continued, "I remember seeing, for no longer than a second, a flick of something white caught in the hinge of the tailgate. I saw it, I knew what it was, but once I saw the blood, and the dead man inside the truck with his head blown off, I must have erased from my mind what would turn out to be the most important piece of evidence we have: a square of rubber about the size of a postage stamp trapped in the tailgate of Coach Wagner's truck. It was the label from one Raggedy Ann's new sneakers."

Pauley didn't think it was necessary to go into details to explain to the judge, or to the prosecutor, the impact of the still-wet blood spattered on the back window of Wagner's truck. He could still remember catching a whiff of the blood-soaked interior and throwing up. He still was sick when he heard the police car and the ambulance arrive. He could only hope the sneaker label had not become unhinged and fallen off or been thrown away when the truck was impounded.

"Funny thing is I noticed the torn place on her shoe the night we found her in the Dumpster. I mentioned the shoe to Tick.

"It had rained, remember, and there were no tracks on the dock at Adler's, and if you recall, no one thought it was murder. This was no crime. We all thought she had died of natural causes.

"We talked heart attack or stroke, over and over. Tick sent me circling the parking lot, the catwalk, all around the Dumpster for clues—looking for any evidence that would have help solve the mystery of how she'd gotten in the Dumpster," Pauley said aloud. *Or any evidence that may have condemned Tick,* he thought.

"So you thought from the beginning that Francie Butter's death was from natural causes?"

"Both of us did," he said softly. "I didn't want it to be natural causes," Pauley said quickly now, redirecting their attention. "I'd never worked a murder case. The woman was dead. I'm not saying I wanted her to be dead. I just wanted it to be a real case, a big case that needed solving.

"I know our investigation was slipshod, Your Honor. Tick was not himself. I was inexperienced. The department was shorthanded." He nodded to Latimer. "It was not until after the autopsy that I knew she'd been smothered. But hey, here's the important part. Now, I can put all the pieces together. Calling this hearing may have the cart before the horse, but I know without a doubt that Raggedy Ann was dragged across the loading dock behind Adler's and dumped into the back of Wagner's truck, and from the bed of his truck, he half tossed her into the Dumpster."

"You know this because of the brand tag you found in the hinge?"

"There were faint drag marks. I saw them the next day in the pictures. You could barely see them. You had to know what you were looking for. The crime-scene people took pictures that night. They had the big lights. Standard procedure, right. The police have impounded Wagner's truck. It's been gone over, and I'll go over it again with a magnifying glass if I must. I'll prove that they match the heel width and so forth of Raggedy's shoes. Dried dirt had been in that truck, once upon a time, but it had turned to plain old mud the night Raggedy died. Moving her before the rain could account for Raggedy's backside being dry. I figure the white tag must have got caught in the tailgate mechanism when he dragged her into the truck from the dock."

"Are there tire photographs? Molds?" Wilkie sighed, ever fearful that a clever lawyer could wreck Pauley's new evidence.

"No tire tracks or molds. Rain got 'em. But Rag's sneakers were new, silver and white. New, but the heels were scuffed, not the toes. The morgue has her shoes. And like I said, the brand logo was missing on one of her shoes."

"And we have this important white tag?" Mildred Mosby asked.

"When the truck was impounded, it is thoroughly searched, and every item or bit of dirt is cataloged. Also, it's in my notes about her shoes. Tick kept after me to record everything."

"And that's a yes? You have the shoe label with you?

"Yes, ma'am, almost he does." The heavy double doors at the back squawked as they admitted Toad into the courtroom. The little man, out of breath, hobbled as quickly as he could to offer a plastic bag to Pauley, who in turned handed it to the judge, who peered inside before handing it to the bailiff.

"It shall be admitted."

"Now that's the ticket," Mildred Mosby said with renewed enthusiasm.

Pauley grinned. Mildred Mosby returned a flashing one of her own. "It appears, Your Honor, there is evidence that Raggedy Ann may have been in Wagner's truck, prior to the Dumpster."

"Horse feathers!" Latimer stood up. "Those shoes could have belonged to his wife. She may have thrown them away. Like McCrary said, they were torn. Raggedy could have pinched them right out of the back of the truck on their way to the dump!"

A hubbub of ahas and groans rose from the audience.

"Speaking of feathers." Pauley turned to Latimer. "Duck feathers—they turned out to be just as I thought they would. I'm sure the sheriff told you about the feathers in Raggedy's throat, but I should have mentioned them this morning in my first accounting. There were feathers in Wagner's truck, not many, but there were two or three stuck in some blood when we seized the truck. I'm sure the lab will confirm they were the same kind as were in her throat."

"Feathers?" Mildred Mosby's voice rose. "In her throat?"

"They must be from a pillow, Raggedy's pillow, but I've never found it," Pauley said. "It wasn't in the grocery basket. We do have an old army blanket, though, that had feathers stuck all through it."

Isabella Radley, in the back of the room, rattled her cane as she stood. "Her pillow is in the cat's bed," Isabella Radley said in a papery voice but loudly enough to elicit a whirr of excitement.

"Cat's bed," Mildred Mosby echoed.

"Oh, my dear, yes, absolutely. If it hadn't been for the cat, we might never have found the shrine...

"The poor thing was starving, don't you see?" Isabella Radley, poised like a tripod with her walking stick, began talking as she walked. "I went into the garage to feed the cat. It was growing dark, twilight, but after my eyes adjusted, I could see very well, well enough. I noticed the pillow, a small one like a child's, in the cat's bed. I remember mentioning it to her."

"To whom did you mention it?"

"To Miss Adler, my dear; we were together in our little adventure. The pillow—it had been a child's pillow at one time, I'm sure—was in cat's bed, very near the shrine. Poor dear must have loved the cat."

"Miss Adler?"

"Mrs. Wagner."

"Shrine?"

"A Madonna presided over everything. It was a shrine to her, don't you see? Even the cat's bed. Very peculiar. But we would have to know exactly what was in his mind to understand all the symbolism, wouldn't we? But, of course, we will never know that now, bless him?"

"Madonna?"

"Oh yes, I'm sure Mr. Wagner erected it in memory of his wife."

Mildred Mosby grabbed an empty chair. "Sit here, Miss Radley, and give us an accounting of where you were and how you came to see these things."

"Well, you see, I had followed the tabby into the garage to feed him, and Miss Adler had brought a loaf of bread, dilly bread I believe with homemade pimento cheese."

"To feed the cat?"

"Oh no." Isabella chuckled. "Mr. Wagner. Rhys Adler had seen my bicycle, and having aroused no one in the house to whom she could offer her dilly bread and pimento cheese, she'd come to the garage, looking for him.

"'Come in, come in, my dear. I want to show you something very peculiar.'" And Miss Radley was launched.

"I led her toward a light that was bubbling green. 'Do you know what this is? I've never seen anything like it.'

"'It's a lava lamp. I haven't seen one in years.'

"'And is that a storybook doll?' I asked. The doll was beautifully dressed. I remember touching the white of the bride doll's gown. It felt like silk. 'She looks like a Madonna, don't you think?'

"'Very virginal,' Miss Adler said. I thought that was...well, I'm not sure what I thought. But it was true, and you know what they say about the Madonna."

Mildred Mosby had to put a hand to her mouth to keep from giggling. She was loving this little old lady.

"And then I saw a bowl that had surely been the cat's water bowl. Only the bowl was on the shelf, not the floor where one would expect a cat's water bowl to be, and it was dry. And inside the bowl there was a piece of paper, and tiny gold cross like for an infant."

In the back of the courtroom, Rhys shivered with recall. She had seen the square of paper at the same moment as had Miss Radley. Before she unfolded it, she knew it was a page that had been torn from the diary.

"'What do you make of all this, all these things, Miss Adler?' I asked her. She wasn't sure, but we both wondered if it was a memorial to Addie Wagner. An altar, a kind of shrine, if you will.

"'Should we tell someone?' I asked.

"'We'll think about it,' Miss Adler said. 'We'll talk tomorrow. I have a friend who can help us.' Miss Adler is very self-assured in whatever decision she comes to, and frankly I like that in a person. It relieves my mind.

"'May I give you a ride home, Miss Radley?' she asked me.

"'Oh no, very thoughtful,' I said, 'but the exercise keeps me moving, you see.'

"'Tomorrow then. We'll visit.' she'd said.

"But that didn't happen, Your Honor. That very night Miss Adler had her car accident."

"Let's get back to the shrine. How do you know the shrine was erected by Wagner for his wife?" Mildred Mosby asked. "She could have built it for herself. It could have been a household altar, a spiritual center. I've heard of such things."

"Don't think so, dear. I remember propped against Madonna's body was a small photograph of Mrs. Wagner when she was younger. Although"—Miss Radley hummed a second thought—"you could have a point."

"Logan Wagner killed both of them, his wife and Frankie… Francie Butter," a voice came from the back of the room. Rhys was standing when the faces turned to see who had spoken.

"Silence!" Judge Wilkie rapped his gavel. "Ladies! Miss Radley! Miss Adler!" The judge rose on the slippery peel of authority. "Perhaps, you would allow me to conduct this hearing." He flashed a stern eye toward Mildred Mosby. "Miss Adler, please be seated."

"But I know…Your Honor…"

"I'm sure you have something very important to say. But at a formal hearing, one can't pop up like a Jack-in-the-box," Wilkie said. "Is she part of your team of investigators that the sheriff mentioned, McCrary?"

"I have no team of investigators, Judge. But I did ask Ms. Adler and Mr. Fordyce to help me—with the diary after I realized it could have bearing on the case."

"Does it?" Mosby asked.

"Yes," Rhys piped up. "It does. The note was torn from it."

Wilkie sighed. "I can't seem to remember. Has this diary been submitted?" There was a note of resignation in Wilkie's question.

"It has, sir." Pauley looked over at the bailiff who nodded.

"I had a conversation with Logan Wagner the night I had my car accident. He was delusional, he—"

"Ms. Adler!" The gavel came down hard. "You have made a strong accusation against a man who has recently died. If I allow you to be heard, you had better have pertinent information regarding Tick Quinn. Not Logan Wagner."

"I do, sir. I was about to tell you about Mr. Wagner inviting us—"

"Hold your horses. Bailiff…the Bible, please. Miss Adler."

All eyes watched Rhys negotiate the aisle and reach the front without giving rise to a scattering of loose papers on Mildred Mosby's desk, or bumping into the bar, the rail, or even the folding chairs that protruded dangerously on her runway.

Properly sworn in, Rhys began her story. She told them about Logan Wagner coming to the farm and into their house, and on into her bedroom without so much as a by-your-leave. "Your Honor, he said they wanted to invited us to dinner. *They*. He and Addie wanted to invite Richard and me to dinner. That they'd been discussing it, he and Addie. Addie is dead, Your Honor. He spoke of her as if she were standing beside him.

"'Don't look so strangely,' he said. It's Addie's idea. And that's not all, Judge, Logan intimated things that made me believe he'd been with her on the float the night of the parade."

"How does Tick Quinn fitting into this, Ms. Adler?"

"Your Honor, let me jump in here." Mildred Mosby came forward. "Bits and pieces, bits and pieces. Don't you see? I'm beginning to understand that these two cases from the very beginning, other than the two dead women themselves, have been based on hearsay more than on fact. But saying that, I must say that's how it is, and it's from here we must start. If we do, if we'll trust it, and then for the first time, we may find some solid evidence that seems to have been missing and that connects these two murders together. Evidence from two cases that seem to converge at last. For instance, if we can get the cat's pillow and we can test for matching feathers?" She turned to Latimer, whose smugness had evaporated. "And we can discern if the tiny piece of white rubber found in Logan Wagner's truck did come from Raggedy's shoes. You see there is a connection."

"Sheriff Latimer, as soon as we break, you should dispatch one of your officers to Logan Wagner's garage to find the pillow," the judge ordered. "Is it still in the cat's bed, Miss Radley?" The old woman straightened her back that had started to swag.

"Unless someone has taken it, it should be there." Miss Radley rested her hands on the top of her cane.

"Would you be more comfortable if you were back in your seat? We can continue from there should we need to."

"Oh no, dear, I'm quite strong. Just need a bit of starch."

"Once we have it, the pillow will have to be examined by forensics before it's admitted as evidence," the judge said.

Pauley stood. "Yessir, if I can get my hands on it, I'll drive it down myself, and it will be a match, I promise you."

The judge seemed to reassess Pauley for several studied minutes. "Right. I hope you're right," he amended. "Because I will not sign off on this case until you present me with that report, McCrary. Is that clear? And I'll give you twenty-four hours. You may have to pull some strings. Do you have strings that can be pulled in Little Rock, young man? Because if you don't, you better be cultivating some."

"Yessir. Strings."

Good fortune has a way of finding its destination. And today good fortune came through the double doors with a bang. Lockhart, spotting Price Latimer, tapped over to him and handed him a manila envelope.

Price Latimer sprang to his feet. "What about the blood on the wall on the loading dock at the antique store, Madam Prosecutor. It was this, as I recall, that had you bringing charges against Tick Quinn Christmas afternoon. Convincing argument you said. Have you forgotten that the blood stain did not test as Raggedy Ann's? I submit that blood belonged to Tick Quinn," Price Latimer was shouting as he walked to the front of the room. "I believe that Tick Quinn met Raggedy Ann behind Adler's at ten o'clock the night of December fourteenth, and he killed her."

"What is his motive, Sheriff? What is it with you two?" Pauley was on his feet. "Tick hired you, man. Have you no sense of loyalty?"

"No! He tried to keep me from being hired."

"That is not true. He thought you'd been given a raw deal in wherever you'd come from, and that you should have a second chance."

"No. That's not right."

"Quiet!" Wilkie's gavel hit the desk. "Sit down both of you." He cleared his throat. "The blood on the sandstone behind Adler's—has it been identified?"

"Your Honor," Mildred Mosby said coolly. "The sheriff told me on Christmas Eve that he didn't have but soon would have proof that the blood was Tick's blood. Do you have it now, Sheriff?" She gestured to the envelop that Lockhart had given him moments before. "Something to support your claim that the blood is Tick's?"

Latimer was giddy with intention. "I've just received this report as you have all witnessed. I've been waiting since Christmas Eve for it. That's the reason you haven't had your proof, Madam Prosecutor." Latimer slapped the report down on the judge's desk. The judge slapped his palm down on it but didn't open it immediately.

"I haven't see this previously, nor you Madam Prosecutor; does it have the necessary foundation to be submitted as evidence, Sheriff Latimer? McCrary, are you aware of the contents of this envelop?"

"I am, sir." I was ordered to get a blood sample. I had tried early, on my own, to have gravelly pieces from the stain one the sandstone typed. I didn't get a match to my satisfaction. Tick's military records indicated he was a universal donor, type O. It's true the blood on the sandstone was O, but"—Pauley felt the thin ice beneath him crack—"O is the universal donor, like I said. Tick can't be the only O in Riversbend. So I won't swear the bloodstain *was* Tick's, nor can't swear it was not. However, I can offer a reasonable explanation if it is Tick's.

"The night Raggedy Ann died, Tick had been smoking a cigarette on the loading dock." Pauley paused, remembering. "It was a breezy night. He had trouble lighting his cigarette. But finally, the flare from his match caught my eye. It's possible he could've scratched his hand on the sandstone when he was trying to strike a match."

Pauley watched Wilkie's face.

"Another thing, Judge Wilkie"—it was the first time Pauley had used the judge's name—"someone tampered with Tick's personal police records recently." Pauley handed the judge a file folder. "See for yourself, sir, it's unclear from these records what his blood type is, right? The numbers have been written and rewritten, and you have to ask why, don'tcha? And who? Who would do this?"

Pauley's agitation grew in direct proportion to his fears.

"In my mind, sir, this makes using this blood report"—he indicated the envelop still under the judge's hand—"as evidence a problem." He turned his attention from the judge to Latimer. "I think any good defense lawyer could easily undo whatever proof you think you have in that envelope, Sheriff. But maybe it's time. Let's see what's in there." Pauley was excited, too excited, bristling with energy. Everyone in the courtroom sensed it. Latimer sensed it. "Go on; open it."

Latimer slid the manila envelope from under Wilkie's palm. He wished he had looked at it before he'd put it on the desk. Pauley's insistence made him uneasy. He could make another mistake like he had in Bayou Bleu. Naïve. He'd thought he knew how things stood in Bayou Bleu with his wife, with the police force. He hadn't known. Suddenly he had no taste for tangling himself in the tricky business of blood. All the new rules: warrants and consents. Had he followed the procedures to the letter? But at this moment, he was sure as hell he did not trust Pauley McCrary.

"I want the court to understand there are numerous subsections in the criminal code. Without the manual right in front of me, McCrary may not have had the authority to ask for blood information from the hospital. There's something about a two-hour limit on some…something," Latimer was saying. Pauley was grinning like an alligator picking bones out of his teeth.

"Take a look at your report, Sheriff, and decide if you're submitting it as evidence or not," Wilkie invited.

Price fingered the manila envelope, turning it over and around. He had to open it or look the fool. He stuck his thumb under the flap and lifted. Extracting the report, he read it for several minutes. His ears changed from a faint flush to flame.

Pauley expected an explosion. And when it didn't come, there was at least one man in the room who for a moment felt compassion. Pauley couldn't help but admire the sheriff in the face of what could only be humiliating. Rather than following his usual behavior, the man nodded slowly as if he was in agreement with the words that jumped from the document that he'd requested. There was only a slight signal of his discomfort when he said, "Dat's what I feared." Latimer flicked the sheets of paper with his fingers. "No need to read anymore." He glared at Pauley. "Da sample's contaminated."

Pauley didn't know whether to shout or cry. He hadn't forgotten the desperation he'd felt early Christmas morning in his grandmother's backyard, grabbing at the chicken that flounced at his feet, the hen whose neck he'd wrung solely to soil his shirt in its blood, the shirt he would give to Latimer as blood evidence. The same hen that would end his career in law enforcement.

Latimer faced the judge. "Maybe I'm wrong, but I still believe Lieutenant Quinn had a hand in Raggedy Ann's death. Cain't prove it. Don't have no hard evidence I can offer you. It's just a gut feeling a good law man knows to listen to."

Pauley glanced toward the back of the room, for Rhys's reaction and for Miss Willa's. They all three had won the first round, but Latimer's gut was right. Tick Quinn's hand had been an instrument in Raggedy's death. The sheriff might have been defeated today, but in truth, he'd won. Pauley shook his head. Sadly, Price Latimer would never know he'd won, not even partially. Tick, neither innocent nor guilty, yet as Latimer had said very earnestly, had been involved in Raggedy's dying. Pauley shuddered.

Staring vacantly toward the back the courtroom where a small concentration of concerned people waited anxiously for the judge's final word, Latimer understood, for the first time, that he would never be a Riversbendian.

Most of the people sure of an overturn on the charges against Tick Quinn were beginning to stir, to think about dinner or their plans for the evening. Latimer's nod of acceptance to Mildred Mosby was almost imperceptible. He'd understood in his short tenure in Riversbend that they stuck up for each other. If they'd heard about his Louisiana debacle, they didn't care. Louisiana, as far as Riversbend was concerned, might as well have been on another planet. He shook his head in amazement at the turn the hearing had taken. But there was envy too if he could have named the emotion. With a shrug to the prosecutor, he acknowledged his defeat—and at the same moment recognized his longing for a place called Bayou Bleu.

"Your Honor, if there is nothing more," Mildred Mosby said quietly, "I ask that the charge of second-degree murder against Tilman "Tick" O'Connor Quinn be expunged from the records." There was a small cheer from the back rows.

"Patience, madam, gentlemen. Let's us never be relieved of our embarrassment." He looked straight at Price Latimer and at Mildred Mosby. "A man's reputation has been tarnished regardless of what the court decides in the next few days. There will always be those people who refuse to change their views of guilt or innocence, however firm or faulty the ground upon which their opinions were formed."

He paused for his words to be measured.

"Our mission today was to review a second-degree murder charge brought against Tilman O'Connor Quinn. Due to the testimony we've heard, and in anticipation of positive results of the reports from the state's crime lab regarding the duck-feather issue, which will be on my desk in twenty-four hours"—the judge looked pointedly at Pauley—"if that report confirms a match between the feather found in the deceased's throat and ones plucked from the cat's pillow in the Wagner's garage...and...and if, on further scrutiny, the note torn from the diary confirms that blackmail was likely an acceptable motive, I shall be inclined to recommend that the charges brought against Tilman "Tick" Quinn be dropped."

Wilkie tapped his hammer to halt the people who had begun to stir. "Sit down; I am not finished. I must remind you that our state's law prohibits the system from investigating or bringing criminal charges against a person posthumously, regardless of sound evidence or implication—there can be and will be *no* actions taken or charges issued against Logan Wagner in the deaths of Francie Butter or Addie Wagner."

Wilkie's glance veered to a cluster of journalists in the back of the room, scribbling on small pads.

"Despite the press's valiant attempts to correct our mistakes. Thank you, ladies and gentlemen, for your interest and attention."

Did the judge wink? Pauley thought he saw him. The judge was rising to leave just as Rhys, working upstream through the departing crowd, hurried toward him. "My Lord!" Pauley couldn't hear the rest of whatever it was she was whispering enthusiastically, but the judge looked confounded. Whatever it was, he nodded and waved her away and then glanced over the few stragglers until he saw Pauley. "I want a word with you in my office, young man."

The folding chairs in the press corner scooted, discharging their inhabitants in a stampede toward the doors. "Yessir." In his peripheral vision, Pauley saw the hem of the judge's robe as he disappeared through the paneling into his safe haven.

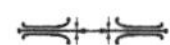

"I told you she was having an affair with Larry Halliger." Rhys, who was caught up in the last remnants of the crowd, tucked her arm through Richard's as they practically skipped toward his car. She was talking as fast as she could.

"You did? I don't remember it that way. But you should probably know; it wasn't Larry. It was his nephew. Remember him. Gym shorts, tight ass. Maybe that was why Raggedy came up with the Donald Duck motif. He still reads comic books, I imagine."

"Bronson Halliger! Bronco Halliger! You're lying."

"Heard it at the country club. The police found another love letter at the Wagner's house. Speaking of the police, what's with you and McCrary. You two were licking your paws like alley cats back there?"

"Tick was exonerated!"

"Almost. Probably will be."

"This may be the piece of good news Tick needs to completely recover."

Richard smiled. "Ever our heroine."

"*F*-ing *A*!"

The cousins walked on quietly lost in their own thoughts. "Wilkie was right, you know. If poor Logan can't be brought to account for the murders, there are people who will always believe Tick is guilty," Richard said.

The faraway look in Rhys's lovely gray eyes was inscrutable.

"What?" Richard demanded.

"Perhaps, but even if the law forbids the prosecution of a dead man, or regardless of how the judge presented his message to all of us, I believe justice will be served when the press writes its stories. As you say, it's a small town."

"I hope you're right."

Rhys stopped walking and put her hands on her hips. "Bronson Halliger? He's little more than a teenager. In case you think you're home free, Richard Fordyce, I want you to know I'm not speaking to you. When did you find out? I didn't even know Bronson was back home."

"Oh, hello, hello." Isabella Radley hurried up the sidewalk after them. "Young Miss Adler, Mr. Fordyce. Wasn't that interesting? In all my years, I've never had the pleasure of participating in a hearing before. Quite fun. It reminded me, listening to all that about blood. Now you're too young to remember Mr. Quinn's parents, but there's an interesting story that I remember my father telling me once. It was during the war," Miss Radley rattled on, but as Richard and Rhys were struggling with which war, they missed the most interesting part of what she was telling them.

In fact, they had missed some small bit of truth, and now they would never know.

"I am almost positive the Schreibers were of German extraction," Miss Radley was concluding. "So you see, it just goes on and on. Justice may be slow, but it has a way of working itself out."

"You were saying something about the Schreibers? Sorry, Miss Radley? I missed what you said," Rhys queried.

"Oh, I must go. I have been invited for coffee at the Cupp, as you young folks call it, with our good sheriff. But don't you worry; I won't tell him a thing. He's going back to Louisiana, you know. He said something about his bête noire. Speaks French, you know, coming from Louisiana.

"Oh, Mr. McCrary." Isabella Radley flapped her hands toward Pauley, who had come out of the courthouse with Willa Quinn on his arm. The woman, who had been dabbing her eyes with a handkerchief, embraced Pauley awkwardly and then waved him off. All smiles now, Pauley trotted toward the old woman, meeting her halfway.

"Your mother was a pretty thing," the tiny woman with fine hair like a dandelion was saying, "but what I remember most about your family was your grandfather Lucien. He had second sight. Do you?"

"No'm, wish I did. I could use it in my line of work. Or could have." He tipped his hat. "Nice work, Miss R. I'd like to have coffee with you to talk about my grandfather sometime, if you've got a minute."

"My pleasure, dear boy."

"Rhys, wait up." Pauley fell in step with the cousins, who had moved ahead. "Speaking of second sight, you knew Raggedy Ann was male, didn't you? I had seen the autopsy, of course. Had I known that Sunday we met at the Cupp that you already knew I wouldn't have had to work so hard to keep from letting it slip."

"How'd we do, do you think?" Rhys asked. "Did we solve all the ends and outs of Raggedy Ann, or did we just sort of fall into something that felt like answers to who she was and to what happened?"

"Miss Radley was the real sleuth. Without her we had nothing."

"Really, I'm the one who put the clues from the garage together."

"Still she was the one who wandered into Wagner's garage."

"Perhaps we should become a real team next time. A packaged deal. We'll become formidable, the next A Team."

"There'll be no next time."

"You know you enjoyed it."

"I did not enjoy it. I enjoyed how it turned out, but I feel a little bad for Latimer."

"For Latimer. He makes me see cabbage."

"Cabbage?"

"Synesthesia, don't worry. Next case I don't want to work with the sheriff. Who needs him? You were the main one, the one with the blackmail note. Next time we'll know to confide in each other, to trust each other."

"Speaking of slipping, aren't there a couple of things we need to hash out, Rhys Adler. Like the true story of why Tick was out at your house the night of your wreck?"

"What true story is that? Richard chimed in.

"Oh, and Rhys, something Tick recently learned about your mother's disappearance."

Rhys blanched.

"You'll want to wait until tomorrow to see him. He's been in therapy this afternoon, so he'll be worn out. It's working, though; he's getting stronger and beginning to get his speech back." Pauley saw hope and dread comingle cross Rhys's face. "Nothing has changed, Rhys. It's been twenty years. We still don't know much. We shouldn't try to talk about it now."

"What shouldn't we talk about?" Richard piped up.

"Matte was making homemade hot tamales when I left the house this morning. Want to come for supper?" Trying to recover from the shock, Rhys added, "We can talk about Tick and the real conversation the two of you had that night at the cabin?"

"Hot tamales!" Pauley dodged. "Wish I could. I'd love a rain check. But I'm heading to Little Rock with the all-important feather. Gotta do good on this one."

"I…I l…l…love tamales." Hummer had caught up with them. He could hear if food was mentioned a block away. He began shaking the last crumbs from a bag of potato chips into his mouth. Peering over the top of the bag, he began waving a handful of twenty-dollar bills at Pauley. "The j…judge told the s…s…sheriff I could go get my grocery b…basket. This afternoon as soon as you release it."

"Where'd that fistful of money come from, Hummer?" A foolish look, rather like suspicion, crossed the policeman's face, just as excitement, a rare animation for Hummer, crossed his.

He crumpled the greasy, salty bag and tossed it to Pauley. "In here. Raggedy kept money tucked everywhere. Th…these were underneath the chips." He scooted off only to glance back once.

"What was that all about? I'm still your silent partner, right?" Rhys, who'd been listening to the exchange, said.

"You see this silver dollar?" Pauley pulled the coin out of his pocket. "I'm gonna flip it. If it's tails, then yes, we're silent partners. If it's heads, you'll just have to wait and see."

"Those aren't very good odds."

"May I come for tamales?" Richard had been straining to hear their conversation.

Pauley and Rhys exchanged looks that Richard was bound to think were up-the-sleeve looks; in fact, they were merely the closing chapter in a complicated conspiracy.

"Richard, you don't even like hot tamales." Rhys laughed.

"I love hot tamales." Richard tucked his arm enthusiastically through his cousin's.

"Ouch! My ribs."

"Oh, suck it up, darling. Call us, Pauley, when you get back from the city." Richard waved good-bye to the policeman. "We gotta go, or Matte will make hot tamales out of us if we let her supper get cold.

ABOUT THE AUTHOR

Sandy Slaughter earned her bachelor's degree in literature and philosophy at Hendrix College. She later earned her master's degree in English with an emphasis in creative writing from the University of Memphis. She went on to teach creative writing at Lyon College and manage the campus bookstore.

Slaughter's poems and short stories have appeared in several literary journals, including the *Memphis State Review* (now called *River City*), *Oberon*, and *Passenger*. Her short story "Reflections in a Cool Case" received first place in a contest by Words, a literary group in Little Rock, Arkansas.

Slaughter, her husband, and their grown daughters live in Batesville, Arkansas.

Made in the USA
Lexington, KY
28 February 2018